RUSSIAN NIGHTS

RUSSIAN NIGHTS

by V. F. ODOEVSKY

TRANSLATED BY OLGA KOSHANSKY-OLIENIKOV
AND RALPH E. MATLAW

Introduction by Ralph E. Matlaw
Afterword by Neil Cornwell

NORTHWESTERN UNIVERSITY PRESS

EVANSTON, ILLINOIS

Northwestern University Press
Evanston, Illinois 60208-4210

Printed in the United States of America

ISBN 0-8101-1520-4

Library of Congress Cataloging-in-Publication Data

Odoevskiĭ, V. F. (Vladimir Fedorovich), kníaz', 1803–1869.
        [Russkie nochi. English]
        Russian nights / by V. F. Odoevsky ; translated by Olga
Koshansky-Olienikov and Ralph E. Matlaw ; introduction by
Dr. Matlaw ; afterword by Neil Cornwell.
        p.   cm. — (European classics)
        English translation originally published: New York : E. P.
Dutton, 1965.
        ISBN 0-8101-1520-4 (alk. paper)
        I. Koshansky-Olienikov, Olga. II. Matlaw, Ralph E. III. Title.
IV. Series: European classics (Evanston, Ill.)
PG3337.O3R813 1997
891.73'3—dc21   96-52851
                                                     CIP

CONTENTS

TRANSLATORS' NOTE

The translation has been made from the edition published in Moscow in 1913, edited by S. A. Tsvetkov. A few minor changes were made in paragraphing. All the haphazard footnotes are Odoevsky's own.

> Nel mezzo del cammin di nostra vita
> Mi ritrovai per una selva oscura
> Che la diritta via era smarrita.
> —DANTE, *Inferno*

> Lassen sie mich nun zuvörderst gleichnissweise reden! Bei schwer begreiflichen Dingen thut man wohl sich auf diese Weise zu helfen.
> —GOETHE, *Wilhelm Meisters Wanderjahre*

INTRODUCTION

Prince Vladimir Fedorovich Odoevsky (1804-1869) was one of the most versatile men on the Russian scene in the nineteenth century, and one of the most gifted. His creative career spanned a half-century, beginning with a piano quintet he wrote at the age of fifteen, and continuing uninterruptedly in music, literature, philosophy, education, science, bibliography, and library administration to the end of his life. In the early 1830's he was among Russia's most popular writers, ranked in stature not very far below the two literary giants, Pushkin and Gogol', a position which posterity rightfully has not sanctioned. He was the first man to decipher the notation of Russian liturgical music and helped shape the course of Russia's rich musical development in the nineteenth century. For many years, the leading representatives of Russia's cultural life were present at his weekly *soirées*. His eager quest for encyclopedic knowledge earned him the cognomen the "Russian Faust," after the leading character of his *Russian Nights*. Indeed, in the breadth of his pursuits he might almost have been likened to the ideal of the Renaissance Man, as exemplified most strikingly in Gianbattista Alberti, or more accurately, to the last latter-day version of this phenomenon, Goethe. Yet he was also called a "great man engaged on minor affairs," for his posts, occupations, and avocations led him to devote his energies to unglamorous and sometimes unrecognized causes like the education of children and peasants, the establishment of public libraries and adequate public schools, and the development of musical culture and facilities. His voluminous production, only a small portion of which has been published, is contained in no less than eleven different archives in Moscow and Leningrad, reflecting to some extent the multiplicity of his interests and achievements.

Odoevsky was born in Moscow on August 1, 1804. Like several other families, Odoevsky's was of the most ancient and respected lineage, although not sufficiently wealthy to live without some employment. Odoevsky's father, the director of the Moscow State Bank, had married a serf of unusual mental capacities. Odoevsky was deeply attached to his mother, and was under her guardianship when his father died in 1808. He attended the Noblemen's School of Moscow University, one of the two best preparatory schools in Russia at that time, distinguishing himself for the breadth of his knowledge. Upon graduation in 1822 he became an official in the Ministry of Justice, published reviews and articles on music and other subjects in newspapers and journals, and was active in the formation of the "Society of Philosophy" (*Obschestvo ljubomudrija*—translating the Greek word "philosophy" into its Russian equivalent), whose president he was until, in 1825, the society was disbanded and its papers burned for fear that the regime would look askance upon any private organization after the catastrophe of the Decembrist Revolt. Despite Soviet critics' attempts to prove the contrary, the society's pursuits were purely philosophical and not political. A group of brilliant young men who were later to be influential in more or less conservative slavophile circles—I. V. Kireevsky, A. I. Koshelev, Mel'gunov, Shevyrev, Pogodin (the last two later professors at Moscow University), and the young poet Venevitinov, as well as lesser names and occasional visitors—met periodically to discuss philosophy, primarily that of Spinoza and the current German Idealistic School, with Schelling as the main focus. Together with the poet W. Kuechelbecker, Odoevsky founded, co-edited, and contributed much of the material for the periodical "Mnemosyne," one of the most important miscellanies of 1824, unfortunately stopped after four issues. "Mnemosyne," graced by Pushkin's verse, had among its aims the championing of native Russian literature and of German philosophy against the Gallomania prevailing in Russia at the time.

In 1826 Odoevsky moved to St. Petersburg, serving in various capacities in the Office of the Censor, the Ministry of the Interior, the Ministry of Agriculture, the Office of Children's Homes, and the Public Library. In 1846 he became the Assistant to the Librarian of the St. Petersburg Public Library, and the director of the Rumyantsev Museum. When the latter was moved to Moscow in 1862 (it was the core of what is now Russia's largest library, the Lenin State Library), he went with it, serving also as Senator in the Ministry of Justice, where he worked until his death in 1869.

After he moved to St. Petersburg in 1826, he published nothing for several years. Then he resumed his activities in musical spheres and began to issue his stories and tales, with striking success. A collection entitled *Motley Stories* appeared in 1833, with an appropriate six-color title page executed by a process Odoevsky devised, and punctuation that attempted to improve the arbitrary rules of Russian, unfortunately without success. That same year, and again in 1835, he published collections of children's stories told by "Grampa Iriney." Together with the tales he published from time to time in various children's magazines these may be the most lasting of his work. They are still a staple of Russians' earliest reading, and at least two, "Johnny Frost" and "The Town in a Snuff-Box," rank among the best in children's fare.

Writing for children is an exacting task and a rare gift. Russia has such noteworthy verse practitioners of the art as Samuel Marshak and Korney Chukovsky. But Odoevsky's ability to write both for children and for uneducated adults is exceeded perhaps only by Tolstoy's. The problems are essentially similar: to present comprehensibly and attractively matter that is strange or unpalatable to the undeveloped but shrewd mind and to ill-formed or unformed habit. Odoevsky constantly sought new ways to transmit knowledge, and his works for children and adults place him among Russia's foremost and most interesting educators. From 1843 to 1847 he issued several fascicules entitled *Rural Reading*, whose purpose was to acquaint the uneducated with the necessity for work and cleanliness, the dangers of alcohol, the need and comfort of religion, and more practical informative articles on the nature, importance, and uses of the various sciences. Numerous handbooks on chemistry and the like, published in thousands of copies for the same audience, have unfortunately disappeared without a trace. Primers, other works, educational theories, and projects for the development of educational facilities occupied him even after the 1840's, but have for the most part remained unpublished.

It is as a writer of short stories, however, that Odoevsky gained his greatest popularity, and ultimately, perhaps his most significant contribution lies in *Russian Nights*, where the best of his stories serve as illustrations and extensions of the philosophical arguments that lie at the base of that book.

II

Odoevsky's fiction from the beginning reflects two broad tendencies: the first, an attempt to express his philosophical convictions imaginatively and frequently fantastically, in stories that move easily from a recognizable setting to a mystical and sometimes abberational realm; the second, to comment on the shortcomings of social life in Russia, primarily in a satiric mode. Each of these had an established and identifiable tradition. The provenance of the first is clearly German Romanticism, predicated upon a dualistic view of life and dedicated, more in literature than in life, to the search for the ideal realm where man could confront the higher and richer life of which earthly existence is an imperfect and unsatisfactory reflection. Its most influential practitioner abroad was E. T. A. Hoffmann, who, like Odoevsky, also distinguished himself as a musicologist and minor composer, and explored the nature and effect of art and the personality of the creative genius in numerous stories. The second strain, also continental in origin, established itself in Russia in the 1830's with Odoevsky as one of its leading practitioners as a favorite form of letters. It was known as the "social tale" (*svetskaja povest'*), whose function it was to depict life in polite society and the dissatisfaction of the best members of that society with the vapidness of their existence.

Odoevsky began by publishing two pieces in the first issue of the literary review "Mnemosyne," a thinly veiled allegory of the vanity of worldly pursuits, entitled "The Oldsters or the Isle Pankhay," and an elaborate story of social intrigue entitled "Elladij." Almost nothing in these commonplace trifles suggests the range and skill Odoevsky was to attain only a few years later. In 1825 he began a novel on Giordano Bruno and worked at it for some time. What little remains of this abandoned project shows that Odoevsky wanted to project this "martyr of the new thought" against the rich background of the Renaissance and its leading figures—Pope Leo X, Michelangelo, Raphael, Luther and others—in short, a novel perhaps less historical than philosophical, with immediate relevance and reference to Odoevsky's own theories and the cultural climate of the nineteenth century, a plan he was finally to realize in *Russian Nights*.

At the same time he conceived the character Iriney Modestovich Gomozeyko, an alter ego who was to write a chronicle of his life. Gomozeyko is a kind of Russian Faust who knows or seeks to know everything, who likes to discuss first causes and who, like his creator, is an idealistic philosopher on the one hand and a functionary and champion of enlightenment on the other. Odoevsky's notes elaborate the character and his history, but his ultimate disposition was to serve as the nar-

rator of *Motley Stories* and other tales of the same period and
to be transformed into Grampa Iriney in the tales for children. In so doing, Odoevsky followed a practice widespread
in Russia at the beginning of the thirties, when prose was
only beginning to be formed into a literary medium. It is
strange to reflect that thirty or forty years before Russians
produced the enormous tomes Henry James called "loose and
baggy monsters," significant original prose was limited to the
short form. The attempt to create more substantial works
(when these were not merely adaptations of Walter Scott,
Fenimore Cooper, and French novelists) met success only
when shorter works were grouped thematically and provided
with a "narrator," whose function, for that matter, was frequently minimal. Thus Pushkin's cycle of 1830 is called *The
Tales of Belkin* after their narrator who ostensibly commits to
paper stories he has from others; Gogol's first collection in
1831, *Evenings on a Farm near Dikanka*, is related by the bee-
keeper Red Panko; Lermontov's so-called "novel," *A Hero of
Our Time* (1841), unites five stories related by two characters by interweaving them with the travel-notes of a profes-
sional literary man who is Lermontov's own "narrator." The
form persisted more mechanically in the 1840's in such works
as Turgenev's *Hunter's Sketches* and the stories of the great
lexicographer Vladimir Dal'. Odoevsky's Gomozeyko is more
elaborately conceived and depicted. Yet in the published
works he appears as little more than a pleasant eccentric and
raconteur, with an occasional concluding remark emphasizing
the "message" of the story: "Isn't our notion of the world perhaps as distorted as his?" he asks at the end of a story depicting a spider who thought the entire universe was contained
within the jar in which he had been placed.

The publication of disparate stories in a volume whose aura
of unity is created through a central narrator clearly affects
the reader's acceptance of the material presented. Improbable
satires like the "Fairy Tale of a Corpse Whose Owner Was
Unknown," animadverting upon bureaucratic red-tape and
provincial ignorance, loses some of its pungency since it is no
stronger than some of the stories surrounding it, wherein society is literally placed in a stuffy retort (the Devil applies
heat to its nethers), or young ladies strolling along the Nev-
sky are transformed into lifeless dolls as they gleefully sur-
render their individuality in order to ape French fads and
fashions.

Among the score of stories Odoevsky published at the be-

ginning of the 1830's there are no doubt others that were
conceived in cycles and collections. Of these, the most important are the stories of musicians and artists, originally destined for a volume entitled *The Madhouse*, which never
materialized. They were later incorporated into *Russian
Nights.* Odoevsky displayed the seamier side of Petersburg
fuctionaries and rural sluggards that Gogol', his admirer and
in some respects disciple, was shortly to immortalize. In such
works as "A Story of a Rooster, Cat and Toad," where a
brilliant attempt to cure an official's imaginary disease by an
imaginary operation misfires, or the tale of officials so en-
grossed in cards that they neglect to pay their respects to
their superiors on New Year's Day, the characters' crudeness
and stolidness gives Odoevsky ample opportunity for humorous portraiture. A bizarre ending to another tale of functionary life finds the aspirant to a position who is given an
impossible trial rummaging through endless documents,
perched on top of a filing cabinet, with a red ribbon tied on
him, all the while maintaining that he is a "concluded piece
of litigation." The stories are entertaining in their portrayal of
relatively new literary subject matter, in their close approxi-
mation of functionary jargon and mentality, exaggeration of
torpor and stupidity, and they can rank with the best produced at the time. An attempt has been made by P. N.
Sakulin, the foremost authority on Odoevsky, and author, in
1913, of an authoritative but unterminated study of him, to
explain some of the grotesqueries in these works. He inter-
prets them as the intrusion of the irrational into even the lives
of the stolid citizens depicted by Odoevsky. It is a dubious
and unnecessary conjecture in the literary context of the individual stories, but not unwarranted if one considers
Odoevsky's total production at the time.

Several stories concern the direct apprehension of a higher
spiritual and mystical realm. In the best of these, "The Sylph"
the protagonist comes across occult and alchemical books
while recuperating in the country. Ultimately he succumbs to
their spell and spends his time contemplating the marvels of
another world and the sylph that appears in a filled vase he
concentrates upon. The attractions are so superior to those of
the ordinary world that he is in danger of wasting away completely. A friend arrives just in time to nurse him back to
sanity and health. He readjusts to his surroundings, marries,
and becomes a successful estate owner, but always regrets
that he was rescued from his visions, and drinks rather more

heavily than he should. As in similar works of that time—German prototypes by Hoffmann, Jean-Paul, and Novalis are some examples—the vision is the more effective for its ambiguity: the viewer's derangement increases in direct proportion to his penetration into and contact with the beautiful and meaningful world he sees, a world far more attractive than the dreary reality from which he starts and to which he reluctantly returns. The story is masterful in its portrayal of reality and evocation of the realm that contains man's highest strivings, in its psychological acuity, and its balanced, inevitable progression. Odoevsky's Gomozeyko elsewhere indicates the fascination of such stories: "Intimations and visions elicit general interest. Our minds, exhausted by the prose of life, are involuntarily attracted by these mysterious events which compose the current poetry of our society and serve to prove that in this life no one can dissociate himself from poetry any more than from original sin." In the tales incorporated in *Russian Nights* that realm appears more tangibly, since artistic strivings have a closer referent in existing works of art that we do know, albeit not in verbal terms.

A lower order of achievement, and the clearest example of Odoevsky's limitations as a writer, is seen in the social stories, particularly "Princess Mimi," "Katya, the Story of a Ward," and "Princess Zizi." Contemporaries were impressed by the detail of Odoevsky's scenes, the verisimilitude of their rich cast—dowagers, debutantes, men of the world, schemers, hangers on, and so forth, and the hopeless struggle to lead a life based on sincerity, understanding, interest in subjects more elevated than careers, marriages, and love affairs, a life where the rigid structure of society would accommodate genuine responses. The stories were thus appreciated for their artistic superiority to works by Pavlov, Narezhny, and others on comparable themes, but perhaps even more for their forthright criticism of spiritual and intellectual stagnation, prejudice, the limitations imposed on women, flaws in education, and so forth. Since such an approach to literature was to become increasingly important in nineteenth-century literature at the expense of the esthetic, there is good reason for singling out the reflection of contemporary social and cultural problems in Odoevsky's fiction. The impulse always comes from a problem or a topical theme rather than a situation or a character, and Odoevsky does not hesitate to point it out and draw the logical conclusion. But a more important flaw is Odoevsky's failure in these stories, which hinge much more than his satires and fantasies on the reader's interest in the characters before him, to endow their characters with real life. He is content to describe them and their actions rather than have action emerge from his characters. Moreover, the style is undistinguished, even commonplace. It lacks the incisiveness and humor of his satires and pictures of lesser Petersburg inhabitants, or the pathos and inflated eloquence of his visionary and mystical works. It may also be added that almost all of Odoevsky's works have an interior setting, and nature plays no role in them. In part, of course, this was conditioned by their urban setting and by Odoevsky's philosophical conviction that nature, when not subservient to man, is reflected in him in any case. But he seems really not to have had very much interest in nature or feeling for it, devoting himself, so to speak, to its scientific rather than poetic manifestations. For all that, the stories rank among the best of the period and in time would have assured him a respectable place in the literary Pantheon.

III

It may well be that Odoevsky's realization that his works were being neglected and his reputation as a writer was diminishing compelled him to rescue the best he had produced and give it more lasting form in a book of greater magnitude. Upon the appearance of *Russian Nights* in 1844 several critics, chiefly Belinsky, questioned the propriety of resurrecting stories published in the preceding dozen years and providing them with explanations and commentaries. But research has shown that the work was, in various forms, constantly in Odoevsky's mind, and that many of its philosophical, artistic, and scientific questions stem from his preoccupations during the middle 1820's. The political questions, the superiority of Russia over the West (the idea of Russian messianism that was to play so large a role in later thinkers and in Dostoevsky, had its earliest programmatic statement in the "Society of Philosophy" in the 1820's), the criticism of Malthus, Bentham and the Utilitarians, anti-slavery, and anti-Americanism, all these were important themes in Odoevsky in the 1830's. *Russian Nights* thus represents an amalgam of the most creative part of his life, the summation of his views in many fields, an approach to that all-embracing system he constantly sought. The work's rejected sub-title, *Russian Nights, or the Indispensability of a New Science and a New Art*, discloses the author's aspirations. The range of problems and questions raised by the discussants and the illustrative stories is enormous: the boundaries of knowledge, the meaning of science and art, the sense of human existence, atheism and belief, education, government rule, the function of individual sciences, madness and sanity, poetic creation, logic, Slavophilism, Europe and Russia, mercantilism, to name some of the important issues. Clearly, this is not merely a collection of stories, or a novel, but an imaginative exposition of human achievement and limitation at a specific time.

The book thus differs from collections like Hoffmann's *Serapionsbrüder* and others that intersperse commentary between stories. The primary argument rests in the speeches of the four leading characters, to which the stories are subordinate. Odoevsky bases his work on Plato's dialogues, and in his introduction attempts to justify his new, hybrid form. The verbal response no longer suffices. Only the artist can create symbols and symbolic lives that extend and amplify historic and rational knowledge, that disclose the inner meaning of an epoch. The scheme that might serve to embody his conception he designates as "dramatic novel," wherein the "entire life of one person would act as a question or an answer to the life of another person." The lives, or the stories, are placed in a particular progression, corresponding to the development of the argument, and culminate in "Sebastian Bach," Odoevsky's apotheosis of art. However, the epilogue, the longest section of the work, reduces it to verbal argumentation about specific issues. While it is a rich mine of thought, it undermines the unity that Odoevsky had established.

The shortcomings of *Russian Nights* as a work of art lie precisely in Odoevsky's inability to dramatize his dialogues sufficiently. Originally he had conceived five interlocutors, noting the function of each: "Faust—Science, Victor—Art, Vecheslav—Love, Vladimir—Faith, Me—Russian Skepticism." But in working over his plans, in setting the action back in time he saw the conflict taking place essentially between three types—a follower of Condillac (a rationalist), a follower of Schelling (an idealistic romantic philosopher), and a mystic (Faust). The fifth character (Odoevsky) was eliminated, and two others combined. The result, although there are four characters, is a conflict between two principles. Faust, Odoevsky's alter-ego, now combines scientific empiricism with a view that may best be called idealistic or even mystical. Trained in the Schellingian school, he now realizes some of its limitations. Victor is the spokesman for rationalism and utilitarianism. The other two are mere appendages: Vecheslav (later in the book given the more usual form of the name— Vyacheslav) sides with Victor. We know almost nothing about him and he adds nothing significant to the discussion. Rostislav, apparently now the spokesman for Love and Faith, supports Faust, and he too adds little to the discussion after launching it with his parable on the First Night. Faust dominates the scene, voicing Odoevsky's cherished notions, overcoming all objections, and at the appropriate time doling out the stories of "previous questors for knowledge" that happens to be in his possession. It may be argued that Socrates similarly dominates Plato's dialogues, but the differences in dramatic tension and philosophical depth between Plato's works and Odoevsky's hardly require comment. Yet Faust emerges as a memorable phenomenon, perhaps even as a character. His eccentric habits, irony, enthusiasm, and range of knowledge, reflecting Odoevsky's own, are a constant source of intellectual stimulation and literary enjoyment.

Odoevsky's prefatory remarks on his aims properly stop short of explaining the structure he has imposed on his material, for this must be conveyed by the work of art itself. The nine unequal periods that compose *Russian Nights* form a logical and a dialectic progression. The First Night launches the discussion through Rostislav's parable of the rise and threatened fall of civilization, and the questions it must raise about the meaning of life in the minds of the young participants introduced here. The questions that are asked in florid form, or are merely adumbrated, are stated more concretely and far more fully in Faust's monologue during the Second Night. The thirst for knowledge is now given as a constant and fundamental trait of the human personality. The search for it in the previous generation has been expressed in the "Manuscript" that will be the main part of *Russian Nights*. Odoevsky has managed by this device to state the philosophical beliefs and reprint the artistic works representing the cultural climate of the 1820's, while indicating that they no longer provide a satisfactory solution. Faust's introductory remarks about the manuscript explicitly indicate the historical context, but the questions in the manuscript amplify those Rostislav had asked the previous night. The achievements and limitations of various sciences are not catalogued. Recent philosophical thought is shown to be incapable of providing satisfactory answers. The manuscript itself begins with a statement of the generative power of madness, and this will lead to the core of the book both in tracing the mechanics of thought and, more significantly, examining poetic creation. Madness and art thus offer one possible solution to the epistemological questions raised, not so much in the analysis of madness now introduced (an earlier essay by Odoevsky) as in the stories that deal with it. This elaborate exposition significantly ends with Faust's lyric invocation to the beauties of morning and the "symbol of eternal light," just as the Epilogue, the second, contemporary statement of the various issues will end with a paean to Russia and its future.

The Third Night begins to test the propositions of the Second through the story *Opere del Cavaliere Giambattista Piranesi.* As in the other manuscript stories of artists the starting point is factual. Piranesi's splendid drawing of Italian edifices and ruins are exaggerated into impossible and quite insane architectural projects. The madman who claims to be Piranesi expresses two important notions: the desire to create beautiful structures that have no utilitarian value, and the mental torture the creator undergoes when his conceptions cannot be realized in life.

The opposing view, in the Fourth Night, is that of the rationalists and utilitarians. It is presented in six stories where there can be no question of madness or of art as subject. Instead, the disillusioned economist realizes that calculation, mathematical exactitude, and absence of the poetic element, lead—if not to madness—to something far worse, to a living death. "The Brigadier" portrays a successful man who discovers as he dies the senselessness of his life, a life he spent in obedience to propriety and decorum—without thinking, without loving, without any spiritual satisfaction. The theme, later developed so profoundly in Tolstoy's "Death of Ivan Ilych," is varied in the other stories of the Fourth Night and is applied to specific situations, rising to a sardonic climax in "The Last Suicide." Malthus' theory of overpopulation and its prevention destroys all the social and moral attitudes deemed to underlie civilization as we know it. Logic is always ready to provide an answer, but that answer may not be satisfactory in terms of other values. The economist who has occupied the Fourth Night is forced to seek a more satisfactory solution than logic offers. But he can only dimly approximate the harmony and beauty of a higher life (in the fragment "Cecilia") before his life ends, possibly by suicide.

The Fifth Night completes the condemnation of English social and political theory with the story "A City Without Name," a bitter and somewhat stilted picture of civilization predicated on Bentham's ideas of individual advantage and social utility. On a higher plane it is a condemnation of the mercantile spirit of the age, an even greater danger to moral and spiritual bankruptcy than the theories of Malthus.

The three nights devoted to inadequate, pernicious, and materialistic views of life are now balanced by three nights devoted to higher, but still not entirely adequate, approaches through the realm of art. To mark the transition, the Sixth Night begins with a discussion of the deeper life man seems to feel at night and the fears that prey upon him then. Night is opposed to the clarity and logic of day. It is no longer the inspiring contact with primordial forces, the deeper penetration into the essentials of life, the heightened creativity that Romantics, particularly Schelling, found it. It points, however, to something not entirely amenable to reason, something that, like art itself, cannot be clearly defined, something that carries within itself unknowable, disturbing, and not immediately discernible elements.

The three stories about artists examine differing aspects of art, but they share at least two traits—the sacrifice of worldly happiness to creative achievement and the inability of others to understand and truly appreciate the discoveries of artistic genius. "Beethoven's Last Quartet" appears first because it raises fundamental questions of art. In the first place, art, particularly music, is not merely a reflection of nature but a higher organization of the materials nature provides, or a creation of something quite different. In the second place, the medium—whether words, notes, or colors—never adequately embodies the artist's original vision. Finally, the interpretation of music, or the understanding of art, discloses a greater gulf between the work of art and the audience than the gulf between the creator's vision and his product. The story, then, deals with the question of artistic genius, the problems of communication, and the relationship of the artist to the public. Beethoven's dissatisfaction with his work, with the limitations of musical instruments, his search for new harmonics and combinations, and his contempt for those who misunderstand him are attributed, for all Odoevsky's obvious admiration, to Beethoven's lack of Faith. Beethoven's life in *Russian Nights* serves as a response to that of Piranesi. His apparent madness to those who do not understand his daring innovations, differs little from that of the mad architect. Yet we know that it is not madness at all.

"The Improvvisatore" of the Seventh Night acquires all the powers of creative genius through the black magic of Segeliel, without having the inspiration that gives them true meaning. He is merely a virtuoso, delighting the crowd by his showmanship, and is himself interested only in the financial gain his performance provides. Such gifts of penetration and form without the meaning only inspiration, love, and faith can give to art become a curse worse than that suffered by Beethoven, whose vision, at least, will sustain him. Cypriano is driven mad by the microscopic clarity that deprives everything of meaningful existence, as, indeed, the modern era of specialization has deprived scientists of the overall view.

The supreme example of the artist is Bach. To music he brings his astounding genius and the inner peace that only Faith and Love can give. The glorious vision that Bach has in Eisenach appropriately takes place in a church, at night, in sight of the richest of musical instruments, the organ, and this vision sustains him throughout his life. Unlike Beethoven's restless seeking and turbulent life, Bach calmly and methodically expreses in traditional forms the inspiration within him. Yet this highest manifestation of art lacks human passion; Bach's life is dedicated to music at the expense of everything, including family happiness. Even the highest artistic achievement is not an adequate answer to the ideal of human life that Odoevsky has tried to find. Therefore, in the Ninth Night, the characters are arraigned and found wanting. The great figures that have been paraded before the reader only offer a more appealing and substantial solution than those in the fourth and fifth nights, but they do not offer final solutions. The quest must begin anew. In the epilogue, the possibilities for a new art, a new science, a new life, that will achieve more satisfactorily all the desiderata of those responsible for the manuscript are examined and then raised to the communal and national level in the concluding exaltation of Russia.

Odoevsky's stories do not pretend to be accurate biographically. We are told nothing of Bach's second wife and his twenty children, for these might indicate a family life and less peaceful daily routine than those necessary for Odoevsky's picture of total dedication to art. The episodes of Beethoven's life are also carefully selected. His preference for the bombastic celebration of Waterloo emphasizes his search for more expressive forms but does not correspond to fact. Each of the stories has its own independent narrative scheme and unity, but it is precisely the subordination of the stories to the larger scheme of *Russian Nights* that shows them to best advantage. This may be tested by reading two stories of Odoevsky's on the same themes, "The Painter" and the utopian fantasy "The Year 4338 A.D." which would have added nothing to the argument of *Russian Nights* and would have derived little from it in turn.

Russian Nights thus emerges as a work of grandiose intentions and formal innovation. Had these goals been more fully realized, it would have presented a picture of the ideal human and social life Odoevsky sought in a combination of art, science, faith, and love. He was perhaps more of a thinker than an artist, and even his thinking on such broad issues is derivative and synthetic. But the book remains a significant philosophical contribution and work of art, summarizing intellectual and political currents during two turbulent decades and expressing imaginatively, in fiction of high caliber, the quest for ultimate knowledge and perfect communication.

RALPH E. MATLAW

University of Chicago

Note:

Ralph Matlaw's 1965 introduction still stands scrutiny, other than for a small number of minor points. Odoevsky's date of birth is now thought to have been July 31, 1804; new information on his mother reveals that she was of lower landowning stock, but not a serf (although Prince Fedor Odoevsky certainly married beneath him); Vladimir Odoevsky did not enter government service upon his graduation in 1822, but upon his marriage and removal to St. Petersburg in 1826; he did not then publish "nothing for several years," but it would be true to say that he published little; his *Pestrye skazki* (*Motley Stories*) are now perhaps more frequently referred to in English as *Variegated Tales*.

N. Cornwell, 1996

FOREWORD[1]

by Prince V. F. Odoevsky

The most difficult thing for a writer is to speak of himself. Every explanation and every possible rhetorical precaution is futile here. He will inevitably be accused either of vanity or, what is even worse, of false humility. One cannot draw a definite line between one and the other, or at least it is difficult to find it. One can only follow the example set by Cervantes, who began one of his books as follows: "I know, dear reader, that there is no need for you to read my foreword, but it is essential for me that you read it." Such a frank explanation seems to reconcile all contradictions.

My works were first collected and published in 1844. As is known, they were sold out in the course of two or three years and soon they became a bibliographical rarity. I was frequently asked why I did not undertake to reissue them, why I did not write or at any rate publish something, and so on, and so on. To ask a writer about such *domestic* circumstances is almost like inquiring of a Moslem about his wife's health. It is a good thing if the matter is limited only to questions, but it is bad when answers appear, and not by the one who should answer them. It is a good thing, too, if these answers are only absurd; but it is bad if, at times, these answers are incongruous both with your way of looking at things and with your principles.

As people used to say in olden times, once a person tries to let himself *be subjected* to pressure, from that very moment he becomes public property which anyone may *treat* as he pleases. But this *treatment* not only gives a man of public activity the right to explain himself publicly at some time; it also obliges him to do so.

The matter is quite simple: in 1845 I intended to undertake a new edition of my works, to correct them, to supplement them, and so on, as is usually done in such cases. But at

[1] The foreword was written by the author for his collected works, then in preparation, but never completed—EDITOR'S NOTE.

the beginning of the following year (1846) another task came my way. My friends know what it was (it would be too early to talk publicly about it now). They also know very well what kind of task it was and what persevering effort it required. For nine years I sacrificed everything I could to this task: work and love. These nine years swallowed up all my literary activity without leaving a trace. I confess that I do not regret it, but naturally I cannot remain indifferent if others regret it.

Then too, it is not easy, as everyone knows, to return to smoldering ruins after a long absence, and to connect the present with the remote past, one end with another. At that moment some reflection is unavoidable.

In the meantime, while I was *away*, good people took advantage of the fact that my book had become a bibliographic rarity and on the sly began pilfering out of it whatever anyone needed in his art. Some followed the literary practice, that is, they borrowed in a very refined manner under various guises; some were less ceremonious and simply replaced the names of personages in my works by those of their own choice, changed the time and place of action, and claimed it as their own; there were also some who without further ado took, say, a whole story of mine in its entirety, called it a biography, and signed their name to it. There are plenty of such curious works wandering around in the world. For a long time I did not protest against such *borrowings*, partly partly because this particular kind of new edition of my because I simply did not know about many of them, and works seemed rather amusing to me. Only in 1859 did I consider it necessary to warn certain gentlemen about the possible consequences of their unceremonious fraud.[2]

Finally, there are people who practice another trade along with that of innocent borrowing: ascribing absurdities of their own making to a certain person after naming him, even zealously providing these with quotation marks in order to avoid any doubt. Such a trick was allowed in an edition . . .

[2] In . . . of the *St. Petersburg News (Vedomosti)*. In this case I must express my gratitude to the publishers who in . . . of the *News* exposed one such fraud that I otherwise probably would not have noticed. In cases like this all honest men of letters must help one another—this is a matter of general literary security. Whatever a work may be, it belongs to one; there is nothing consoling in seeing one's work distorted. Such deeds, independently of their worldly significance, abuse artistic feeling, a writer's best asset.

about which I will not permit myself to speak since it has
now ceased. And the editor, a man with rather strange notions of worldly affairs but a man not untalented, is no longer
alive. *De mortuis seu bene, seu nihil.* Nevertheless, I consider
it a duty to expose such childish forgetfulness to the general
public, and to support my exposition by straightforward information.

Thus, the fate of my book was as follows: people pilfered
it, distorted what they took, and abused it; and the majority
of readers did not have any means of checking these frauds.

All these reasons taken together, which are of such importance to a person for whom the rights and obligations of a
literary man are sacred, have prompted me to proceed with a
new edition of my works.

I thought of improving much of it, of changing many
things, but soon I realized that it was impossible. Seventeen
years is almost half of an active life. In such a period of time
much has been reconsidered, much has been forgotten, much
arose anew, and it is impossible to hit the key in which one
had started; the tuning fork has changed; both the inner life
and the environment are different. Any change would not be
a living, organic creation but a mechanical addition. Moreover, are our thoughts really our own, even at the moment of
their conception? Are they not a living chemical recasting
within us of external and complex principles, the spirit of the
epoch in general, the medium in which we live, impressions
of childhood, conversations with our contemporaries, historical events, in a word, everything that surrounds us? It is difficult to isolate oneself from the family; it is even more difficult
to isolate oneself from the people; from mankind—it is quite
impossible. Each person, independently of his own will, is its
representative, particularly a person who writes, be he a man
of great or small talent. Between him and mankind a sort of
electric current is established—weak or strong, depending on
the representative himself—but it is incessant, implacable.
From this point of view, a human word at the time of its
appearance in a given people and at a certain moment is a
historical fact, more or less important, but no longer belonging to the so-called author. If at that time he expressed this
word unsuccessfully, if he was not conscious of his representative functions, it is his own fault, and he must bear the
responsibility. One can no longer finish saying the word later:
the hand on the world's clock has already moved; birth does
not take place twice.

This book appears now as it was published in 1844. I have allowed myself to correct only some all too obvious mistakes (not all!), to insert conscious and unconscious omissions, to introduce some articles that were forgotten during the first edition, and some new ones, and finally, to add separate notes, which, as far as I can see, may have some historical significance. *Dixi.*

P.S. The public is a being with which one can never talk enough. This involuntary loquacity makes itself noticeable particularly after a long life, in the course of which all kinds of nonsense have accumulated in one's head. Everyone has the right to justify himself in his nonsense—but a literary man has an obligation to do so. I am generally accused of some kind of encyclopedism, although I could never quite understand what sort of animal that is. This word may be understood variously. If a person takes up one thing, then another, at random, on the off chance, when his activity is disjointed, and when it lacks the living organic connection—should he be called an encyclopedist? On the other hand, if one thing grows out of another organically, as a leaf grows out of a root, a blossom out of a leaf, a fruit out of a blossom—would this also be encyclopedism? Of the first I am not guilty, no matter what people may say. I *take* up quite little, but, really, I *hold onto* everything that comes my way. Life has taught me this art. The story of this process may be of some use to the new generation. My youth passed at a time when metaphysics was just as common an atmosphere as political sciences are now. We believed in the possibility of an absolute theory by means of which it would be possible to build (we said "construct") all the manifestations of nature, just as now they believe in the possibility of a social form which would fully satisfy all man's needs. Perhaps both such a theory and such a form will really be found some day, but *ab posse ad esse consequentia non valet.* However that may be, at that time all nature, all human life seemed quite clear to us, and we used to look from above at physicists, chemists, utilitarians, who were digging in *crude matter.* Of the natural sciences, only one seemed worthy of the philosopher's attention—anatomy, as a science of man, and the anatomy of brain in particular. We took up anatomy experimentally, under the guidance of the famous Loder, whose favorite students many of us had become. We had cut many a *cadaver* to pieces, but anatomy, naturally, brought us to physiology, the science which at that time had only begun, and whose first fertile embryo, one must say, appeared in Schelling and later in Oken and Carus. But in physiology with each step we naturally encountered questions inexplicable without physics and chemistry. And many places in Schelling (in his *Weltseele* in particular) remained obscure without natural sciences. That's how the proud metaphysicists, even in order to remain true to their calling, were reduced to the necessity of acquiring flasks, retorts, and similar stuff needed for coarse matter.

Actually, it was precisely Schelling, perhaps unexpectedly for himself, who was the real creator of the positivist movement in our century, at least in Germany and in Russia. In these countries, thanks only to Schelling and Goethe, we became somewhat more condescending toward French and English science which, as coarse *empiricism*, we did not even want to consider before.

As you see, these various occupations were not an unaccountable encyclopedism; they were harmoniously joined to our previous work. I fully appreciated the importance of my versatility of knowledge when circumstances of my life brought me to deal with children. Children were my best teachers, and I have retained till now a feeling of deep attachment and gratitude to them for it. Children showed me all the paucity of my knowledge. One should talk to them for a few days in a row, prompting their questions, in order to become convinced how often we do not know at all the things that we seemed to have learned thoroughly. This observation struck me and forced me to look deeper into various branches of sciences which I seemed to know so well. This observation gave me a new insight, unexpected at that time, namely, how artificial, how arbitrary, how false a division of human knowledge into the so-called sciences was. In the vast catalogue of sicences, actually, there is not one which would give us a definite idea of a subject as a *whole*. Take, for instance, a man, an animal, a plant, the smallest particle of dust; sciences have torn them into pieces: some got their chemical, some their ideal, some their mathematical meaning, and so on, and these artificially separated members were then called special fields. They say that in olden times we used to have professors of the first volume, of the second; in order to get a complete idea of each of these subjects, it is necessary to accumulate all their separate parts, which have fallen to the lot of various sciences. For the fresh mind of a child, unspoiled by any scholasticism, there exists neither physics nor chemistry nor astronomy nor grammar nor history, and so on, individually. A child will not listen to you if you begin discussing separately, in the most systematic way, the anatomy of a horse, the mechanism of its muscles, the chemical transformation of hay into blood and flesh, a horse as a motive power, a horse as an aesthetic object—a child is an inveterate encyclopedist. Give him a whole horse as he is, without splitting the object artificially, but presenting it in its living entirety—this is the task of pedagogy, unsolved till now. To satisfy this strict, inexorable demand, fragmentary, so to say literary, or incorrectly called *general* knowledge is not enough; but it is essential, as the French say, *mettre la main à la pâte,* and only then can one speak with children in a language comprehensible to them. This, then, is the secret of my apparent encyclopedism which, perhaps involuntarily, was reflected in my works. But the fault here is not mine; it is that of the age in which we live and which seeks a reunification of all split-up parts of knowledge, if it has not found it yet. If one so selflessly descends into details, creates special sciences like entomology and ichthiology, then it should be done solely with the purpose of finding the point of connection between veins and arteries of human understanding. Until a general human science has been formed, it is necessary that each person, having thrown off scholastic swaddling clothes, create for the field of his activity, in proportion to the extent of his understanding, his own science, a nameless science that could not be put under any undivided heading. I admit—I have concerned myself with this science. Whoever reproaches me with this concern will hear from me only the answer: *"Mea culpa!"*

NOTES TO *RUSSIAN NIGHTS*[1]

Habent sua fata libelli! It is no wonder that a man who writes, or is active in general, commits offenses in various ways: for instance, he presents his own thought as someone else's, or, unfortunately, someone else's as his own. But often, as happens to Sofiya Pavlovna: "Things may be worse—and yet one gets away with them." But suddenly, God knows through what associations, people begin accusing you or justifying you in something of which you are not guilty, either in your soul or body. Some people have thought, some with praise, some with condemnation, that in my *Russian Nights* I tried to imitate Hoffmann. This accusation does not worry me too much. There has not been a writer, great or small, in this world in whom someone else's thought, word, method, and so on, is not reflected, independently of his own will. It is inevitable even because of a harmonious connection which naturally exists between people of all epochs and all nations. No idea is born without another preceding idea, one's own or someone else's, participating in its conception. Otherwise, a writer should renounce his ability of receiving impressions from what he has read or seen, that is, renounce his right to feel and, consequently, to live. Of course, I am not at all offended when I am compared with Hoffmann—on the contrary, I take this comparison as an honor, because Hoffmann will always remain a man of genius in *his own way*, like Cervantes and Sterne; and I do not exaggerate, if the word "greatness" is synonymous with ingenuity. Hoffmann, after all, invented a special kind of the wonderful. I know that in our century of analysis and doubt it is rather dangerous to speak of the wonderful, and yet, this element exists to this day in art; for instance, Wagner, undoubtedly also a man of genius,[2] is convinced that opera is almost impossible without

[1] Published from the manuscript for the first time.

[2] To the number of proofs of Wagner's greatness, I add the failure of his *Tannhäuser* in Paris, where Meyerbeer's *Ploërmel* and even the so-called operas by Verdi which occupy the same place in music that Chinese works, done in silk and tinsel, occupy in painting, now flourish.

this strange element, and a musician cannot help agreeing with such a conviction; Hoffmann found the only way by means of which this element may be brought into the literary art in our time. His element of the wonderful always has two sides: one—purely fantastic, the other—real, so that an arrogant reader of the nineteenth century is not at all invited to believe completely a wonderful event told to him. The circumstances of a story expose everything by means of which this very event may be explained quite simply—thus he runs with the hare and hunts with the hounds. The natural inclination of man for the wonderful is satisfied, and at the same time the inquiring spirit of analysis is not abused. It was the work of a true talent to reconcile these two opposite elements.

And yet, I did not imitate Hoffmann. I know that the very form of the *Russian Nights* is reminiscent of Hoffmann's *Serapien's Brüder* [*sic*]. It also has a conversation among friends, and individual stories are introduced into the conversation. But the fact is that at the time I was meditating the *Russian Nights*, that is, in the twenties, *Serapien's Brüder* was completely unknown to me. Apparently this book did not even exist in our bookstores at that time. The only work of Hoffmann's which I had read then was *Majorat*, with which, apparently, I have nothing in common anywhere.

Not only was my point of departure different, but the dialogue form came to me in another way. Partly as a logical deduction, partly owing to the natural disposition of my mind, it always seemed to me that contemporary dramatic works for theater or for reading lacked the element which in ancient times was represented by the *chorus* and which for the most part expressed the audience's own perception. Indeed, it is odd to sit for several hours facing a stage, to see people speaking, acting—and to have no right to utter one's own word; to see them cheat, slander, rob, kill—and to look upon all this silently, with one's hands folded. The reserved objectivity of the contemporary theater requires from us a particular kind of cruelty. The feeling which does not allow us to remain indifferent at the sight of such events in real life, this beautiful feeling is obviously abused, and I understand Don Quixote perfectly when he rushes with the naked sword at the Moorish puppet theater, or an eccentric of our theaters who, watching a performance from his seat, can't help cutting into the actors' conversation. A playwright should appreciate such an audience. Unquestionably, only they wholly sympathize with a play. The chorus of the ancient theater used to give at least some room to this natural inclination of man to participate personally in events taking place before his eyes. Of course, it is impossible to transfer the ancient form of chorus into our new drama completely, as attempts of this kind have proved. But there must be a way of introducing into our merciless drama some advocate of the audience, or, to put it better, an advocate of ideas prevailing at that time, in a word, what our ancient teachers of art considered an indispensable accessory of drama. One should *find* it. It is more necessary to find it in our age than it was at any other time. For example, "self-government" penetrates all movements of thought and feeling; and "self-government" in no way agrees with this Brahman immobility which contemporary drama requires from its audience. The way is thin as a hair, as the Moslem way leading into the abode of houris; on one side there is a threat of lyricism and philosophizing, on the other, cold objectivity. Perhaps someday the desired goal will be reached by conjoining two different dramas presented at the same time, both linked, so to say, morally, so that one would serve as a supplement to the other; in a word, using philosophical terminology, the *idea* would be presented not only from an *objective* but also from a *subjective* point of view, and, consequently, would be expressed *completely*, and, consequently, would fully satisfy our aesthetic feeling. This problem has not yet been solved; to solve it one way or another—to solve it successfully—is the task of a talent, but the task exists.

I am returning now to my own defense. As to the psychological fact, perhaps it will not be without interest for my readers. At the time of which I am speaking, I studied Greek and read Plato, using for difficult passages the Russian, or, to be more precise, the Slavonic-Russian translation by Pakhomov, which in our literature is like Amyot's translation of Plutarch in French. Plato made a profound impression on me, and it has remained alive until now, as any strong impression of youth does. Plato was not only of philosophical interest to me; the fate of one *idea* or another in his dialogues stimulated in me almost the same concern as the fate of one or another person in drama or an epic; even the fate of Homer's heroes interested me much less at that time. In general, neither Achilles nor Odysseus attracted my particular concern at that time.

The prolonged reading of Plato led me to the thought that

if the task of life has not yet been solved by mankind, then it is only because people do not quite understand one another, because our language is inadequate fully to express our ideas, so that a listener never hears everything he is told, but either more or less, either to the left or to the right. Hence arose the conviction in the indispensability and even in the *possibility* (!) of bringing all philosophical views to one denominator. Youthful arrogance thought it to be within its reach to investigate each philosophical system individually (in the form of a philosophical dictionary), to express it in strict formulas accepted once for all, as in mathematics, and then to reduce all these systems into a huge drama, which would be enacted by all the Philosophers of the world, from the Eleatics to Schelling, or better to say, by their teachings and their respective subjects, or even more properly, its basic anecdote would be nothing more or less than the *task of human life*.

But here occurred what Pushkin wrote about the landowner of Gorokhovo [*sic*] village, who thought of writing an epic poem, *Rurik*, but who then found it necessary to restrict himself to an ode, and finished with an inscription to the portrait of Rurik.

The dream of early youth collapsed; the work was beyond my power. Man's lifetime would not suffice for a philosophical dictionary alone, as I understood it, and yet, this work was to be only the first step toward the further main work . . . what else should I say?—fractions remained with different denominators, as they will perhaps remain forever—at least it was not for me to make this calculation.

But the union of all this preliminary work, and almost incessant thought about it, involuntarily found its reflection in everything I wrote, and particularly in the *Russian Nights* although in a different situation. Instead of Thales, Plato and others, contemporary men appeared on the stage: a disciple of Condillac, of Schelling, and finally a Mystic (Faust), all three *carried in a stream of the Russian spirit*; the latter (Faust) makes some fun of one trend and another without expressing his own judgment, perhaps because for him it is just as nonexistent as for the other two—but he finds satisfaction in symbolism. However, I shall discuss Faust later. To bring these three trends of thought to definite points, various persons were chosen whose entire life expressed what philosophers expressed in compressed formulas—so that one answered the life of the other, not only in words but with a whole life.

The subject of this new, if you wish, drama, remained the same: the task of life, and, of course, the unsolved task.

I am afraid of wearying the reader with a detailed description of these domestic circumstances of my writing. However, I have tried to restrict myself to what actually belongs to a psychological process which took place within me, and each psychological process as a *fact*, I repeat, may be of significance anyway.

I shall also add that in the *Russian Nights* a reader will find a rather accurate picture of the intellectual activity to which the Moscow youth of the twenties and thirties gave themselves and about which almost no other information has been preserved. This epoch had its significance; doubts and conjectures were seething, thousands of questions which arose again, but with greater precision at the present time. Purely philosophical questions, economic, worldly, and national questions which occupy us now, occupied people at that time as well, and much of what is expressed now, directly and at random, even recent Slavophilism, all this was stirring at that time like a growing embryo. It will not harm the new generation to know how these questions were understood by the generation preceding it, how and with what it fought, and what made it suffer; how it made both the good and poor material with which the new men must work. The history of human work belongs to mankind.

FOREWORD TO THE
1844 EDITION

In all ages the human soul, urged by an invincible power, unconsciously turns, like a magnet to the north, to a task whose solution is hidden in the depth of mysterious elements which form and unite spiritual and material life. Nothing stops this striving, neither life's sorrows nor joys, nor turbulent activities, nor humble contemplation; this aspiration is so abiding, that sometimes it seems to arise independently of the human will, like physical functions. Centuries pass, time consumes everything: concepts, morals, customs, trends, manners of action; all of past life sinks to an inaccessible depth, and a wonderful task comes to the surface of the sunken world. After long struggle, doubts, and mockeries, a new generation, like the one before it, which it had ridiculed, experiences the depth of the same mysterious elements; the course of centuries varies their names also, changes their concepts, but it changes neither their essence nor their mode of action. Eternally young, eternally powerful, they constantly abide in their pristine virginity, and their unsolved harmony is clearly heard through the storms which so often exasperate the heart of man. In order to explain the great meaning of these great powers, a natural scientist inquires into the works of the material world, the symbols of material life; a historian, into the live symbols entered in chronicles of nations; a poet, into the live symbols of his own soul.

In each case the method of investigation, the points of view, and the devices can vary infinitely: in natural sciences some take all nature in all its entirety as the subject of their investigations; some, a harmonious structure of one individual organism. So it is in poetry, too.

In history we encounter persons who are entirely symbolic, whose life is the inner history of the given epoch of all mankind; we encounter events, the solution of which, from a certain point of view, can stand for the way mankind went in one direction or another: not everything is told by the dead

letter of a chronicle; not every thought, not every life reaches
its full development, just as not every plant reaches the stage
of blossom and fruit; but this does not exclude the possibility
of such a development. While dying in history, it comes to
life in poetry.

In the depth of his inner life a poet encounters his own
symbolic persons and events; sometimes, in the magic light of
inspiration, these symbols are supplemented by historical
symbols; sometimes the first ones coincide with the second
ones. Then people usually think that the poet places his own
insight, his hopes, his sufferings on a historical personage as
on a purifying sacrifice. In vain! The poet only obeyed the
laws and conditions of his world; such an encounter is a
chance, which could have happened or not, because a soul in
its natural, that is, inspired state, finds in itself indications
more reliable than those in the dusty charters of all the
world.

Thus, historical and poetic symbols may exist separately
and together. Both originate from one source, but live different lives: the first—an incomplete life in the narrow world of
the planet, the others—a boundless life in an infinite kingdom
of a poet. But alas! they both keep hidden within themselves,
under several layers, a secret that is perhaps inaccessible to
man in this life but that he is permitted to approach.

Do not blame an artist if under one layer he finds another
layer, just as you would not blame a chemist for not discovering at the first attempt the simplest but also the remotest elements of a substance he investigates. The ancient inscription
on the statue of Isis, "No one has seen my face yet," has not
lost its meaning in all fields of human activity.

That is the author's theory. Whether it is true or false is
not his concern.

A few words now about the form of the work called *Russian Nights*, which, probably, more than anything, will be
subjected to criticism: the author thought possible the existence of a drama the subject of which would be not the fate of
one man, but the fate of a feeling common to all mankind,
which manifests itself differently in historic-symbolic persons.
In a word, of a drama where not a speech, the subject of
momentary impressions, but the entire life of one person
would act as a question or an answer to the life of another
person.

After this already too lengthy theoretical exposition the
author finds it superfluous to enter here into any further ex-

planations. Literary works that claim aesthetic merit must speak for themselves, and it would be an unnecessary abuse of the artist's rights to defend them prematurely by a full dogmatic exposition of the theory on which they are based.

The author cannot and must not finish this foreword without thanking people whose advice he followed, as well as those who found his works, until now scattered in various journals, worthy of translation, in particular to the noted literary man in Berlin, Varnhagen von Ense, who amidst his own incessant noble activity presented his compatriots some of the works of the author of this present book in an elegant translation, far surpassing the original.

On the difficult and strange road of a man who has got into the enchanted circle called literary, out of which there is no way, it is gratifying to hear an echo to one's feelings among people whom we do not know, who are separated from us by space and circumstances of life.

THE FIRST NIGHT

The mazurka ended. Rostislav had gazed his fill at his part-
ner's white, sumptuous shoulders and had counted all the
violet little veins on them. He had breathed her air, talked
with her about everything one can talk about during a
mazurka, for example, about all the houses where they would
meet next week—and he, the ungrateful one, felt only the
heat of the place and his weariness. He went up to the window, inhaled with delight that particular fragrance created
by ringing frost, and examined his watch with extreme curiosity. It was two o'clock in the morning. Outside, everything
was white, and whirled in a dark, bottomless chasm; the
north wind howled; snowflakes blew against the windows,
decorating them in arbitrary patterns. A wonderful sight!
Wild nature had its feast outside the window, threatening
man with the cold, storm, and death, while here, only two
inches away, there were sparkling lights in chandeliers, frail
vases, spring flowers, every comfort and whim of the Eastern
sky, Italian climate, decolleté women, indifferent mockery at
the threats of nature. In the depths of his soul Rostislav involuntarily thanked the ingenious person who thought of building houses, inserting window frames and heating stoves.
   "What would have happened to us," he reasoned, "if it
were not for this intelligent person? What effort had it cost
mankind to arrive at a thing so simple that one usually pays
no attention to it, that is, to live in a house with window
frames and stoves?" These questions imperceptibly reminded
Rostislav of a fairy tale by a friend, which apparently starts
at the time fire was invented, and ends with a scene in a
drawing room where certain people find it quite praiseworthy that in educated England artisans break and burn
their masters' precious machines. A group of the earth's primordial inhabitants, wrapped in animal skins, sits on the bare
ground around the fire; they are hot in front and cold in
back; they curse the rain and wind, and laugh at one eccentric who tries to make a roof, because the wind, of course,
constantly carries it away.
   Another scene: the people now are already sitting in a hut;

a fire is set in the middle of it; the smoke burns their eyes, and sparks are carried around by the wind; the fire must be watched constantly, otherwise it will destroy the dwelling that man has barely put up; the people curse the wind and the cold, and again they laugh at one of the eccentrics who tries to surround the fire with stones, because, of course, this frequently causes the fire to die. But then comes a genius who thinks of placing the chimney in a stove! The poor devil had to endure a barrage of mockery, epigrams, and reproaches, because many people were asphyxiated by the first closed stove in the world. And what was the lot of the man who first thought of preparing a meal in an earthenware pot, of forging iron, of turning sand into a transparent surface; of expressing his thoughts in signs that were difficult to remember, finally, of subjecting a mob of people used to willfulness and to giving full vent to their passions to some legal order? What accomplishments had to be attained by physics, chemistry, mechanics, and so on, in order to turn the product of a bee into a candle, to glue this table together, to paper these walls, to decorate the ceiling, to burn oil in lamps? Our mind gets lost in countless, infinite, variegated discoveries without which a well-lighted house with window frames and stoves would not exist. "Whatever one may say," thought Rostislav, "enlightenment is a great thing."

"Enlightenment!" . . . At this word he stopped involuntarily. His thoughts ranged farther and farther and became more and more serious. . . . "Enlightenment! our nineteenth century is called enlightened; but are we really happier than the fisherman who once cast his nets, perhaps in this very spot where a gay, gossamery crowd is standing now? What is around us?

"Why are the people rushing about? Why does the whirlwind drive them around like the snow? Why does a baby cry, a youth suffer, and an old man become sorrowful? Why does one society disagree with another, and even more, with each of its own members? Why does steel cleave bonds of love and friendship? Why are crime and misfortune considered indispensable letters in the mathematical formula of society?

"In life's arena nations resplendent with fame appear; they fill pages of history with themselves, and suddenly they grow weak, give themselves to some sort of a frenzy, like builders of the Tower of Babel, and a foreign archaeologist finds their names among dusty charters only with difficulty.

"Here a society suffers for lack of a strong spirit among them who would pacify vicious passions, and direct the noble ones toward the good.

"Here a society banishes a genius who has appeared for its glory—and a faithless friend commits the memory of a great man to disgrace, just to please society.[1]

"Here all the forces of spirit and matter move; imagination, mind and will are strained—time and space are turned into nothing, man's will has its feast—and the society suffers and sadly anticipates the approach of its death.

"Here, in a stagnant swamp, forces are falling asleep; like a hitched-up horse a man diligently turns one and the same wheel of the social machine all the time, his sight weakening from day to day; the machine is falling apart. One move by a young neighbor—and the hundred-thousand-year-old kingdom will vanish.

"Everywhere there is hostility, confusion of tongues, punishment without crimes and crimes without punishment, and life ends in death and nothingness. The death of a nation—what an awful word!

" 'The law of nature!' says one.
" 'The form of government!' says another.
" 'Lack of enlightenment!' says a third.
" 'Excess of enlightenment!'
" 'Lack of religious feeling!'
" 'Fanaticism!'

"But who are you, you the arrogant interpreters of life's mystery? I don't believe you, and have the right not to believe! Your words are impure, and they hide even less pure thoughts.

"You speak to me of the law of nature, but how did you unearth it? Prophet without calling! Where is your sign?

"You speak of the usefulness of enlightenment, but your hands are bloodstained.

"You speak of the harm of enlightenment, but you are tongue-tied; your thoughts conflict with each other; nature is obscure to you; you don't understand yourself!

"You speak of the form of government, but where is the form which pleases you?

"You speak of religious feeling, but look—your black dress

---

[1] A hint at Thomas Moore who, because of family circumstances, could not resolve to publish Byron's memoirs, which had been expected with impatience.

is singed with fire which tormented your brother; his moans burst out of your throat in spite of yourself, along with your sweet words.

"You speak to me of fanaticism, but look—your soul has turned into a steam engine. I see screws and wheels in you but I don't see life!

"Away with you, possessed ones! Your words are impure: dark passions breathe through them. It is not for you to break away from life's dust; it is not for you to penetrate life's depth! Pernicious winds and the plague have their play in the desert of your soul, leaving no feeling uncontaminated!

"It is not for you, decrepit sons of decrepit fathers, to enlighten our mind. We know you as you don't know us; in silence we watched your birth, your diseases, and we foresee your death; we cried and laughed over you; we knew your past, but do we know our own future?"

The reader has probably already guessed that all these beautiful thoughts crossed Rostislav's mind a thousand times more quickly than I could relate them, and, indeed, they lasted no longer than a usual pause between two dances.

Two friends approached Rostislav.

"What have you found in this window?"

"What are you thinking about?" they asked.

"About the fate of mankind!" answered Rostislav, with an air of importance.

"Better think about the fate of our supper," objected Victor; "the martyrs of the dance are organizing still another contradance here, before supper."

"Before supper? Rascals! . . . Your obedient servant!"

"Let's go to see Faust!"

We must inform our benevolent reader that Faust was the name they gave one of their friends who had a strange habit of keeping a black cat, of not shaving for several days in a row, of examining gnats in a microscope, of blowing into a melting pipe, of latching his door and spending hours filing his nails, as people of society would say.

"To see Faust?" said Rostislav, "Excellent! He will help me to solve the problem."

"He will give us supper."

"We may smoke there."

Several other friends joined them, and all together they went to see Faust.

When stepping into the carriage, Rostislav paused on the footboard.

"Listen, gentlemen!" he said. "Do you know that a carriage is an important product of enlightenment?"

"What are you talking about enlightenment for!" cried out his impatient companions. "It's cold; it's five below zero! Take your seat!"

Rostislav obeyed, but continued: "Yes! A carriage is an important work of art. When it has sheltered you in wind, in rain and snow, you've probably never thought of what scientific achievements were needed to produce a carriage!"

At first everyone laughed, but when they began analyzing the parts of this great work, they realized that mines had to be dug for making springs, merino sheep grown and a weaving loom invented for producing cloth, properties of tanning matter discovered for making leather, almost all of chemistry was needed for dies, the existence of navigation and discovery of America by Columbus—for wood, and so on. In a word, they found that almost all the arts and sciences, and almost all the great people were needed in order that we might sit comfortably in a carriage, and now all this seems so simple, so available to every craftsman. . . . Meanwhile the high object of our analysis stopped at a doorway.

Faust, according to his habit, was still awake; he sat in his chair unshaven; before him were a black cat and all sorts of scissors, knives, files, brushes, pumice, which he recommended to everyone as the best means for filing nails, because nails don't break or split after treatment with it—in a word, they don't cause you any of the aggravations which can disturb a man's peace of mind in this life.

"What's enlightenment?"

"Can we have supper?"

"What's a carriage?"

"May I have a cigar?"

"Why do we smoke tobacco?" shouted several voices at once.

Faust, not in the least confused, set aright the cap on his head, and answered: "I won't give you any supper because I don't eat supper myself; you can make yourselves tea in the machine *à pression froide*—a wonderful machine; only, it's a pity that the tea in it is usually very bad; I'll answer the question why we smoke tobacco if you'll find out from animals why they do not smoke; a carriage is a mechanical device to be used by people arriving at four o'clock in the morning; as to enlightenment, I am getting ready to go to bed and put out lights."

THE SECOND NIGHT

The next evening around midnight, the crowd of young people burst into Faust's room again. "You drove us away last night to no purpose," said Rostislav. "We began a discussion the likes of which we never had before. Imagine, I took Vecheslav home, but he kept standing on the steps of the carriage and we all continued arguing in such a way that it alarmed the whole street."

"What excited you so?" asked Faust, idly stretching himself in his chair.

"A trifle! Every day we discuss German philosophy, English industry, European enlightenment, achievements of mind, movements of mankind, and so on, and so on, but up till now it has not occurred to us to question one thing: What kind of cog are we in this wonderful machine? What have our predecessors left for us? In a word: What are we?"

"I maintain," said Victor, "that this question cannot exist, or that the answer to it is very simple: We are, first of all, people. We came after others; the road was laid out and we must take it whether we want to or not. . . ."

Rostislav: "Excellent! It's just like a book over which a man works for forty years and in which he very sensibly tells his reader at the end: 'Gentlemen! One person has said one thing; a second, another thing; a third, something else; as for myself, I do not say anything.' "

"Even that is useful as information," remarked Faust. "Everything is of use in life. But the question is: Isn't there really anything left to say?"

"And why should it be said?" objected Vecheslav. "All this is nonsense, gentlemen. Speakers need listeners, and the age of listening is over. Who will listen to whom? And why bother? The world began without us, and it will end without us. I declare to you that I am bored with all this futile philosophizing, with all these questions about the beginning of things, about the causes of causes. Believe me, all this is nothing in comparison with a good beefsteak and a bottle of red wine. They only remind me of Khemnitser's fable *The Metaphysicist.*"

"Khemnitser," said Rostislav, "despite his talent in this fable, was only a servile echo of the impudent philosophy of his time. He himself probably didn't foresee to what extent this glorification of cold egoism would affect young heads. In this fable the person worthy of respect is precisely the metaphysicist who did not see the pit beneath his feet, and, sitting up to his neck in it, forgot about himself and thought of means to save those who were in danger, and pondered the meaning of time. Anyone who answers these questions with rude mockery reminds me of those sensible people who during the French Revolution replied to the unfortunate and famous Lavoisier's petition to be allowed to finish his experiment that the wise Republic had no need of chemical experiments. As to the beefsteak and red wine, you are quite right, as long as you are at table. Unfortunately, everything perfect is so difficult for a man to achieve that he even lacks means to become completely bestial. He seems to have given himself to sensuality; everything is forgotten, intoxication is complete, but sadness knocks at his heart, an unexpected, incomprehensible sadness. He tries to reject it, to fathom it, and his soul again comes to life in his coarsened body; his mind seeks life; his thought seeks expression; and man's confused and bashful spirit knocks again at the unattainable gates of paradise."

"That's because we are stupid!" objected Vecheslav.

"No!" exclaimed Faust, "it's because we are people; no matter how hard you try, you can't get away from your soul. See what has happened to chemistry, proud chemistry, which wanted to believe only what it could touch! . . . Its material methods disintegrated before this strange power of nature which created all forms of plant and animal life out of carbon, water, and nitrogen. 'Weigh, determine the composition of matter, and we shall discover all nature!' chemists used to say in their material madness, only to find bodies with identical composition and different properties or identical properties and different composition. . . . They had come across life! What a mockery of our senses! What a lesson for our common sense!

"You ask, why do we live? It is a difficult and an easy question. Perhaps it can be answered in one word, but you will not understand this word if it does not find expression in your own soul. . . . You want to be told the truth? Do you know the great secret? The truth can't be expressed! First examine what it means *to speak*. I, at least, am convinced that to speak means nothing else than to arouse in a listener his own inner word. If his word is not in a harmony with yours—he will not understand you. If his word is sacred—even your bad words will do him good; if his word is false—you will do him harm with your best intentions.[1] No doubt,—one word may correct another, but to do this the active word must be pure and sincere, and who will guarantee the purity of his own word? Here is a fable similar to the one by Khemnitser:

"A man, blind, deaf, and mute from birth, stood in the street. Nature had left him only two senses: smell and touch. He wanted to touch whatever his sense of smell disclosed to him, and whenever this proved impossible the deaf-mute-blind man would become awfully angry, and in his annoyance he would even hit people with his crutch. Once a kind-hearted man gave him alms. The blind man felt that it was a gold coin, and was beside himself with joy, considered himself the richest man in the world, and began to jump around . . . but his joy didn't last long: he dropped the coin! In despair he searched in vain in the corner of a wall and around himself on the ground, both with his hands and his crutch—in vain did he grumble and complain; often he felt the smell of the coin so near himself—but it was a vain hope: the coin could not be found! How could he ask passersby about it? How could he hear what they might say? In vain he implored people around him with motions of his body to help him in his distress: some did not understand him, some laughed at him, others told him something, but he could not hear them. Boys laughed and pulled at his clothing, thus aggravating him even more, and, angrily chasing after them with his crutch, he even forgot his coin. Thus he spent the whole day in a constant torment. Toward evening he came home tired, and threw himself on the stone heap which served him as bed. Suddenly he felt the coin rolling over his body and dis-

[1] Faust got this thought from the work of Pordetsch and *Philosophie inconnu*. Faust quotes these writers three or four times without referring to them, because he is afraid of being reproached with mysticism and of being under the influence of a non-German philosopher, which at that time seemed unpardonable.

The period described in *Russian Nights* is the moment of the nineteenth century when Schelling's philosophy ceased to satisfy searchers for truth and they scattered in many different directions.

appearing under the stones—this time for good: he had had it next to his breast all the time!

"Aren't we like that man, deaf, mute, and blind from birth? Whom can we ask about our coin? How will we understand if somebody should tell us where it is? Where is our word? Where is our hearing? Meanwhile, we are zealously searching around ourselves on the ground and we forget only one thing: to look in our own breast. . . . Your question is nothing new. Many people have racked their heads over it. Two friends of my youth had run across this very question. Only, to them it seemed that the question Why do we live? can be answered only after we have made sure why *other* people live. To investigate these *other* people in all, *or, at least,* in the most important phases of their earthly life, seemed to them to be worth their curiosity. It was a long time ago, when Schelling's philosophy was at its height. You can't imagine what an impression it created in its time, what an impetus it gave to people who had been lulled to sleep by the monotonous melodies of Locke's rhapsodies.

"At the beginning of the nineteenth century Schelling was what Christopher Columbus was in the fifteenth: he disclosed to man an unknown part of his world, about which only some legendary tales had existed—man's *own* soul! Like Christopher Columbus he did not find what he was looking for; like Christopher Columbus he aroused unrealizable hopes. But, like Christopher Columbus, he gave a new direction to man's activities! Everyone rushed to this wonderful, luxurious land, some excited by the example of the courageous seafarer, some for the sake of science, some driven by their curiosity, some for profit. Some brought back many treasures, some only monkeys and parrots, while many things sank into the sea.

"My young friends also participated in this general movement; they worked in the sweat of their brow. Would you like to know the result of their efforts? Their story is quite interesting: will you have patience to listen to it?"

Everyone gave his consent. Victor lighted his cigar and sank gravely into an armchair; Vecheslav jeered and bent over the table to draw caricatures; Rostislav meditatively squeezed himself into the corner of the sofa.

"You see," said Faust, "like you, they inherited from Adam's grandchildren an unfortunate passion, a kind of disease—the lust to inquire about everything. In childhood they were frequently scolded and punished when they bored their teachers with questions like Why does fire burn upward and water run downward? Why isn't a triangle a circle, and a circle a triangle? Why does a human being come out of his mother's womb with his face toward the ground and later constantly turn his eyes up to the sky? and so on. In vain they were told that there are two kinds of questions in this world: the solution of some is necessary and useful to know, while others may be put aside. Such a division seemed quite reasonable to them, quite handy for life and even quite logical; their soul, however, could not keep silent.

"The trivial phrases of the old and the new paganism seemed odd to them, phrases like: Happiness is not attainable to man! Truth is not given to man! It is impossible to comprehend the original cause of things! Doubt is man's lot! There are no rules without exceptions!

"In the worn-out pages of an old and forgotten book the youths came across an observation which struck them." At this point Faust pulled out an old briefcase a little sheet on which the following was written, and read:

" 'Not in vain does man seek the point of support at which all his desires could be reconciled, all the questions disturbing him could be answered, all his abilities could find a harmonious direction. Only one thing is needed for his happiness: a bright and extensive axiom, which would embrace everything and save him from the pain of doubt; he needs an unsetting and unquenchable light, a live center for all things —in a word, he needs truth, complete, undisputable truth. Also, it is not without purpose that man's lips have preserved the belief that one can desire only what one knows. Doesn't this desire alone indicate that a man has a concept of such a truth, although he cannot account it to himself? Otherwise how could this desire invade his soul? Doesn't this presentiment of an absolute truth indicate that there is some basis for this presentiment, no matter how dark and confusing, no matter how it may resemble dreams or that false sensation when a bead under our crossed fingers seems to be divided in two, which, however, convinces us of the fact that the bead really exists.

" 'Equal is understood by an equal; if there is an attraction, there must be an object which attracts, an object akin to man, which draws man's soul to itself, as the center of the earth attracts objects on its surface. The need for complete bliss indicates the existence of such a bliss; the need for shining truth indicates the existence of such truth, and equally the fact that darkness, delusion, and doubt go against human nature. Man's striving to understand the cause of causes, to penetrate the focus of all beings, the need for awe indicate that there is something into which a soul can immerse itself with confidence. In a word, the desire for a full life indicates the possibility of such a life; it indicates that only in it can man's soul find its peace.

" 'A coarse tree, the least blade of grass, each object of coarse, temporary nature indicates the existence of a law that leads them directly to the level of perfection they may attain. From the beginning of time, despite all the destructive influences surrounding them, natural bodies have been growing for thousands of generations in a harmonious and monotonous way, and always reached their full development.

" 'Is it possible that the sublime power endowed man alone with unanswerable desire, unsatisfiable need, aimless striving?' "[2]

Faust continued: "These questions led my friends to another and rather odd question: Weren't people mistaken in the true way to the object of their attraction? Or they knew it and then had forgotten it—and how do you then remember it? What awful, painful questions for a thinking mind!

"Once a teacher told my searchers that now that they had finished grammar, history, and poetry, they would at last take up the discipline which will solve all possible questions, and that this discipline was called philosophy.

"The youths were beside themselves with amazement and were about to ask, What is grammar? What is history? What is poetry? However, the second part of their teacher's announcement comforted them, and this time they decided to keep silent and secretly to prepare a great number of questions for their new science.

"Then, one teacher brought them Baumeister, another

[2] These lines contain almost the entire theory *du Philosophie inconnu* of the famous St. Martin, who is usually confused with the Portuguese Martínez de Pasqualis, the founder of the Martinists' sect. St. Martin was his pupil for a while but then left him, and perhaps just because he knew all the secrets of this sect he was always an antagonist of every possible sect and did not belong to any. It is rather remarkable that this circumstance remained unnoticed even by men of such knowledge as Schelling was. Once, in a conversation with him, we touched upon the subject, and he confessed with his usual frankness that he, too, confused St. Martin with Martínez.

brought Locke, a third Dugald, a fourth Kant, a fifth Fichte, a sixth Schelling, a seventh Hegel. What abundance! Ask whatever you wish and there would be an answer to everything. And what an answer! Clad in syllogistic form, speckled with quotations, showing their ancient origin, elaborated and polished.

"Indeed, while on this path our searchers had exquisite moments, divine moments, the sweetness of which cannot be appreciated by anyone who has not felt the torments of an emotional thirst, whose burning lips have not touched the fountain of thoughts and have not reveled in its magic spurts, who has depraved his mind by the lust of reckoning before reaching maturity, who from his early age has given his heart to bargaining and overturned the treasure chest of his soul in the marketplace.

"Happy, heavenly moments! During that time youth sees the sincere conviction with which his professor speaks to him; during that time he sees all nature in a harmonious system; during that time you do not want to doubt—everything is clear to you! You understand everything!

"Happy moments, heralds of paradise! Why do you fly away so soon?

"In order to pursue the subject of their investigations more conveniently, to test it in its development, to reach the goal which disturbed their sleep and aggravated their vigil, my friends divided their work. One of them took up sciences. choosing political economy as the most important of them, as a science where theory needs the most tangible application; another gave himself to the arts, and chose music as the most important of them, as an art the language of which expresses the innermost feelings of man, inexpressible in words. They hoped to be able to observe all of life from these opposite ends of human activity and to meet in the solution of the problems which Providence made the task of man.

"Our investigators came across books and people. Some assured them that mankind has reached its highest level of perfection, that everything has been explained, done, and that there was nothing left to do or to explain; others assured them that mankind has not progressed a step from the time of its fall, that it was in motion but did not move. Others still maintained that although mankind had not yet reached the level of its perfection, our time has at least solved the question of how to distinguish truth from nonsense, reasonable things from unreasonable ones, and important from non-important ones; that in our time it has become unpardonable for a so-called educated man not to know how to determine the range of his occupations and to be unaware of the goal toward which he must strive; that, finally, if mankind can approach its perfection, it can do so only by following the way which it has chosen now.

"The advocates of the present day maintained also that recognizing all the imperfection apparently connected with all human endeavor, one cannot overlook the fact that the scattered philosophical systems of ancient thinkers have now been replaced by harmonious systems; that in medicine unfinished experiments and old wives' tales have now been replaced by harmonious theories which classify all possible diseases of man, where each is given an appropriate name and a definite cure; that astrology has become astronomy; alchemy, chemistry; magical exultation, a disease curable by carefully compounded pills; that in the arts, the poet's field of activity is now free from prejudices which used to impede his flight and that only necessary limits have been set to his poetical freedom; and finally, in the structure of society has not security replaced former unrest and, in general, are not international rights and the rights of individuals determined with greater accuracy now? Didn't civilization do away with all the former absurd demands in the smallest manifestations of society, even in clothing? These demands, just like the opinions of those days, used to restrict every motion and make social intercourse difficult work. And what about book printing? What about steam engines? And railroads? Haven't they widened the circle of man's activities, have they not shown his glorious victories over nature which opposed him?

" 'That's so!' they exclaimed. 'The nineteenth century has understood the task which the Providence assigned to it!'

"All this made my young observers think again and again. Meanwhile, time was passing by; the youths grew into men, and their questions . . . the questions still remained without an answer. Involuntarily they again looked into the worn-out pages of the old forgotten book, and their questions began growing more forcefully, like seedlings in fertile soil. The emotional state of my young searchers is rather well expressed in their notebook with a rather strange epigraph:

Humani generis mater, nutrixque profecto *dementia* est

"I shall read you a few excerpts from it:

DESIDERATA

"What! Medicine is at its highest stage of perfection, but the cause of health, the cause of disease, the manner in which medicine works—all these still remain a mystery? A doctor hands his patient a health-giving phial, and he doesn't know himself what takes place in this very phial, to say nothing of what takes place within the organism. The medicine succeeds or fails to cure, and' man does not know the cause. In vain he interrogates another man's corpse: the corpse is silent, or it gives answers which only make one doubt the actions of life. Proud of his knowledge of a corpse, the doctor approaches a living sufferer. With horror he sees what his science has not foreseen, and in despair he becomes convinced that his science is only now beginning. He leaves the house and sees a pernicious pestilence killing inhabitants by the thousands, and the amazed son of Aesculapius follows its progress dumfounded, without even knowing how to name this awful new wayfarer.

"Mathematics has reached its highest level of perfection, indeed. By long, devious ways it brings us to a few formulas, some of which cannot be applied at all, while others are applied only approximately. In other words, mathematics brings us to the doors of truth, but does not open them. In every mathematical process we feel that our being is joined by another strange being which works, thinks, and calculates, while our real being seems to have stopped acting and, without participating in this process, like something external, it waits for its own food, namely, for a bond which must exist between it and this process. But this bond is precisely what we cannot find. Thus, mathematics keeps us on a leash; it allows us to calculate, to weigh, and to measure, but it does not let us take a single step out of its anticipated, passive circle. In vain we ask to be allowed into the active work, into the sphere, which cannot be embraced but which embraces. Our efforts to test the passive sphere by means of the active one would be futile—there is no kinship with mathematics in it. Its precise, singularly correct language remains only for its own use. In vain do other sciences beg a few formulas from the sumptuous feast of its expressions: it counts figures, whereas the inner number of objects remains unattainable to it.

"Physics, this triumph of the nineteenth century, has

reached the highest level of its perfection. Proudly we discuss the force of gravitation, which we have discovered. But in this force we discovered only its lifeless side—the fall. The other, active side of this force, the one which contributes to the formation of a body, is forgotten by us, and to explain the living gravitation we do not want to consider the fact that a dead mass has no reason to gravitate to another dead mass. We forget that dead masses do not seek each other, and unite without any desire; we forget that this famous gravitation should actually create not harmony which, contrary to our logic, surprises us in nature, but complete chaos. This living gravitation is hidden from physicists and there exists no phenomenon for which thousands of contrary explanations could not be found. Like craftsmen, we pick up one instrument after another, while nature taunts us, and for every step that we take forward, it pushes us back two steps.

"Chemistry is on its highest level of perfection! We have decomposed all nature's products, but which one of them have we restored? Which one did we explain? Have we understood the inner connection between substances? What is their affinity, their mysterious interrelations—and this still on the lowest level of nature, among coarse minerals? And what happens to chemistry at the sight of organic life? What has been discovered in inorganic nature only confuses concepts of live nature. Not a single thread of its cover has been lifted. We have filled nature by the products of our own laboratory, we have given the same name to various substances, various names to the same substance, have described everything accurately—and we dared to call that science!

"Astronomy is on its highest level of perfection! Having calculated the motion of stars accurately, astronomy attempts to equate their mutual gravitation to the gravitation of a magnet, and it cannot understand why the gravitational force of a magnet is incalculable when the magnet is right there! With more success it has compared nature to a lifeless clock, accurately described all its wheels, gears, and springs. Astronomy lacks only one thing—a key to wind this clock. But astronomers don't even bother about it; they watch the dial carefully, but its hand does not move, and astronomers are compelled to answer the question as to the actual time by an obvious absurdity, as once answers were given in mystical lodges.

"And the laws of society? People have spent many sleepless nights thinking about this subject! There have been many arguments which have destroyed the concord between the masters of people's opinions! Much blood was shed for the defense of ideas the existence of which was limited to two days! First, there were men who had the honor of having invented the phantom which they dared to call 'human society'—and everything was sacrificed to this phantom, while the ghost remained the ghost! Then other men came. 'No!' they said, 'happiness for everybody is an impossibility; only happiness of many is possible.' People were taken for mathematical figures; equations and computations were worked out, everything was foreseen and calculated. One thing was forgotten, one profound thought which had been miraculously preserved only in the expressions of our ancestors: happiness for *all* and *everybody*. And what happened? Outside society there are lawless wars, the most immoral of crimes fill the pages of the history of mankind; and within society there is the transformation of all the laws of Providence, cold-blooded vice, cold art, passionate hypocrisy, and shameless disbelief in everything, even in the perfection of mankind!

"The country which wallowed in the moral bookkeeping of the past century was destined to create a man who focused in himself all the crimes, all the fallacies of his epoch, and squeezed strict and mathematically formulated laws of society out of them. This man, whose name ought to be preserved for posterity, made a very important discovery: he realized that nature had made a mistake by endowing mankind with the ability to multiply, and by not knowing how to make people's lives conform to their housing. This profound man decided that nature's mistake ought to be corrected, and its laws sacrificed to the phantom of society.

" 'Rulers!' he used to exclaim in his philosophic rapture, 'my words aren't just an empty theory; my system is not just a result of intellectual speculations. It is based on two axioms. The first: man has to eat, the second: people multiply. You do not contradict? You agree with me? Then listen: you think about prosperity of your subjects; you think about their observing the laws of Providence, of how to multiply the power of your state and to increase the human power? You are making a mistake, as nature made one. You are calm; you do not see what misery it had spread around you. Look what I have discovered: if your state were to prosper, if it were to enjoy peace and happiness, its population will have doubled in twenty-five years; in the next twenty-five years it will have doubled again, then again and again. Where will you find means in nature to provide food for them? True, the increase in population should increase the number of workers, and along with it should increase the products of nature. But how? . . . Look, I have foreseen everything; I've taken everything into account: population increases in a geometrical progression, 1, 2, 4, 8; the products of nature, in an arithmetical progression, 1, 2, 3, 4, and so on.

"'Don't delude yourself with dreams about the wisdom of Providence, about virtue, love toward mankind, and charity. Try to understand my calculations: whoever comes late into this world has no place at the feast of nature; his life is a crime. Hasten to prevent marriages; let depravity destroy whole generations in their embryonic state; care not about the happiness of your people and of peace. Let wars, pestilence, the cold, and mutinies destroy the faulty decrees of nature. Only then can the two progressions fuse, and the crimes and misery of each member of society will make possible the existence of a society itself.'

"And these ideas did not surprise anyone; people opposed them, as they would any ordinary opinion . . . what am I saying? The Malthusian ideas, based on the coarse materialism of Adam Smith, on a simple arithmetical mistake in calculation, have poured into society from the heights of Parliament chairs like molten lead, burning its noblest elements and freezing its lower levels.[3] Perhaps there is one consolation in this phenomenon: Malthus is the last absurdity in mankind; one cannot go any further in that direction.

"Really, what does science mean in our day? Everything is solved in it, everything but science itself. Everything is proved, everything, both sides of a question, both the false and the true, both yes and no, both enlightenment and ignorance, both harmony of the world and chaos of creation. One thought grew and spread over a great expanse; but another thought stands facing it and contrasted to it, and is just as strong, just as proved as one power against another. And there is no battle—the battle is finished. On the battlefield pale, wearied, and dispirited warriors meet, and with a sickly voice ask one another, 'Where are the conquerors?' There are no conquerors. It's all a dream. In the ideal world, as in the coarse material world, burrs grow near roses, manchineel trees

[3] See the speech of Lord Broom in the Parliament session of Dec. 16, 1819.

near cocoanuts, without disturbing one another! Is this the perfection anticipated by humanity? Is this the perfection ordained by the wise men? Is this the perfection predicted by saints?

"And poetry? With a philosophical knife you disclosed its composition, severed mysterious bonds which united its elements, you disjoined and labeled them and placed them under glass; you raked up the ash of India and Greece; you scraped the rust off medieval chain armor and you wanted to find poetic life in the graveyard of history. You attempt to draw up a theory of painting, but you haven't yet solved the questions: Why do we involuntarily compare any degree of beauty to the beauty of man? Why may all parts of the body be covered without harming a person—except his face? Why can the whole body endure the touch of coarse matter—except the eye? Why, in a moment of sadness, are looks involuntarily cast down? Why does the eye, always the same, always unchangeable outwardly, serve to express all the innermost gradations of human feeling and give character to the whole physiognomy? In a word, what does the expression of the eye mean?

"O, great poet, were you not wrong, when you proclaimed on your deathbed, that with you the age of poetry was ended? On the contrary, didn't your impaired organs express the inspired thought, as it happens in that strange sickness of mind and imagination when man calls stone bread and snake fish? Your lips did not speak so, when, full of life, you communicated to us the future destiny of mankind in symbols. Perhaps the real age of poetry has not yet arrived. Perhaps you yourself were an incidental harmonic sound, which incidentally escaped the chaos of discordant musical instruments. Is poetry really a sickly groan? Is the destiny of perfection really in suffering? So, you think, the wisdom of the world suffers too? This is a criminal thought, prompted by hell, trembling for its fall! Only allegedly poetical paganism could chain Prometheus to the rock.

"A poet! A poet is the first judge of mankind. When in his high tribunal, illuminated by the ever-burning brush, he feels that the breath is stormily passing over his face, he reads the letter of the age in the shining book of eternal life, divines the natural path of mankind and punishes its corruption. Is the prophetic judge in a position to pronounce his incorruptible judgment now? Now, when he steps down from his throne so low that he suffers together with others, now that he shares the mournful bread of the soul's poverty with the people and forgets where his throne and his royal table are, and doubts its existence?

"Science and art both present a strange spectacle, or, to put it better, what we dare to call science and art. Whole lives pass not in studying them but in learning how to study them. Perhaps they keep man back from some errors, but they do not nourish him. They are like a bandage which a lazy governess winds around a child's head, so that his skull won't break if he falls; but this bandage does not save him from frequent falls; it does not safeguard the body from diseases and, what's more important, it does not favor his organic development.

"And what happens? In the obscure world of human knowledge those who strive for depth encounter only riddles. Those who are satisfied with the outer crust drift from one dream to another, from one fallacy to another. Those to whom even that outer crust is inaccessible, that is, the commoners, approach the condition of animals with every passing day. The wisest man can only wail and cry in the graveyard of human thoughts!

"But meanwhile our planet grows old; the indifferent pendulum of time swings incessantly, with each swing carrying ages and peoples away into the gulf. Nature grows decrepit; frightened she raises her heavy veil before man, shows him her trembling muscles, the wrinkles of her face, and entreats man; her sandy steppes become mortified at his departure; the watery element forced out of the bowels of the earth by coral islands calls for him. Ruins of nameless nations tell the terrible story of the punishment which awaits the carefree indolence of man who allowed nature to outstrip him. Loud and incessant are nature's entreaties to the power of man: without the power of man there is no life in nature.

"Moments are precious. And yet there are people who argue among themselves about their power, about daily cares, as the Byzantine courtiers argued at the time of the barbarian invasions! They gather their feeble vessels, delight in them, price things, and trade. But the raging foe is already at the gate: the fragile edifices of ancient science are already rocking; the burning fire already threatens them, and soon clouds of cold ashes will rise over its palaces. They will crumble. Nothingness will swallow all in which the might of man took pride. . . .

["Those were the sort of dreams that disturbed my friends. The jeremiad *continues* for a rather *long* time. Don't worry, I won't read all of it, but I'll try to give you some in its full form, some in extracts—only that which is necessary in order to explain the point of view of my soul-searchers."]

Faust read:

"Meanwhile there rose before us visions of the past, holy men passed before us in rows, men who had pledged their lives on the altar of disinterested knowledge, men whose sublime thoughts, like shining comets, spread over all the spheres of nature, at least for a moment illuminating them with a bright light. Could it be that the work, the vigilance, the life of these men were an empty mockery of fate over mankind? Legends remained of the time when man was truly the ruler of nature; when every creature obeyed his voice, because he could name it; when all the forces of nature, like obedient slaves, cringed at the feet of man: has mankind really been corrupted from its true path and is it now swiftly and willfully rushing toward its own destruction?

["Do you know to what this long path finally led my dreamers? Having lost their patience before this huge mass of puzzles which crowd upon a man in the process of development of any thought, they finally asked themselves:]

"Do we really understand one another? Doesn't a thought become dim while being expressed? Do we pronounce what we think? Is not our ear cheating us? Do we hear what our lips utter? Aren't the thoughts of great minds exposed to the same optical illusion which deforms objects remote from us?

"A common person understands his fellowman, but not the words of an enlightened man; enlightened people understand one another, but they don't understand a scholar; and some scholars have succeeded in writing whole books with the firm conviction that only two or three persons in the whole world would understand them. If you join both ends of this chain, confronting a common man with the thought expressed by the wisest among mortals, you will have the same language, the same words—but the lower will accuse the higher of insanity! And after all that can we still believe in our expressions? Aren't we afraid of entrusting our thoughts to them? And do we dare to think that the confusion of tongues has ceased?

"One of the observers of nature went still further: he provoked a doubt even more bitter for man's pride: examining the psychological history of men who are ordinarily considered insane, he asserted that it is impossible to draw a true and definite line between a healthy thought and a mad one. He maintained that for each craziest thought taken from a madhouse, it is possible to find an equally strong thought circulating in the world daily. He questioned what difference there was between the conviction of a certain woman who thought that her breast contained a whole city with its towers, sounds of bells, and theological debates—and the thought of Thomas Willis, the author of a famous book on madmen, that the vital spirits being in ceaseless movement, and strongly attracted to the brain, cause in it an explosion similar to that of a gunpowder? What difference between the concept of one madman that when he moves all objects around him move also—and the evidence of Ptolemy that the whole solar system revolves around the earth? What difference between a poor young girl who deemed herself sentenced to death, and Malthus's idea that in the end all the inhabitants of the earth will have to die of starvation?

"Doesn't the state of a madman resemble the state of a poet or of any inventive genius?

"Indeed, what is it we notice in madmen?

"All their concepts, all their feelings are gathered at one focal point. The particular power of one certain thought in them attracts to itself everything allied to that thought from the entire world. The madman has the ability, so to speak, of tearing off parts from objects which are tightly united for a normal person, and of concentrating them in some sort of symbol. We say that the concepts of madmen are absurd! But no healthy person is capable of gathering so many different ideas about a subject into one point. And one must admit that this phenomenon is very much like the moment when a person makes some sort of discovery, because for any discovery one must sacrifice thousands of ideas universally accepted and seemingly correct. That's why there has practically never been a new idea which didn't seem mad at the moment it appeared. There isn't a single unusual event which wouldn't provoke doubt at the first moment. There isn't a single great person who, in the hour when he conceived a new discovery, when his thought had not yet been developed and justified by tangible consequences, did not seem to be a madman.

"Wasn't Columbus considered a madman when he spoke of the fourth part of the world; Harvey, when he affirmed circulation of the blood; Franklin, when he undertook to rule thunder and lightning; Fulton, when he endeavored to oppose the stormy forces of nature with a drop of hot water? And what is even more remarkable, the state of genius at the moment of discovery is really similar to that of a madman, at least for those around him: he is so struck by his own idea that he doesn't want to hear of any other, sees it everywhere and in everything, is ready to sacrifice everything in the world to it.

"We call a person insane when we see that he finds relationships between objects that seem to us impossible. But isn't each invention, each new idea, a reconsideration of relationships between objects, unnoticed by others, or even incomprehensible to them? Thus, isn't there a thread weaving through all the actions of human soul and joining ordinary common sense with the disturbance of concepts observable in a madman? On this scale isn't the exalted state of a poet, or an inventor, closer to what is called insanity than insanity is to an ordinary animal-like stupidity? Isn't what we call common sense a highly elastic term, a term used by an ordinary person against a great man who is incomprehensible to him, and also by a man of genius to cover up his reasonings and not to frighten an ordinary person with them? In a word, isn't what we frequently call madness and delirium sometimes the highest degree of intellectual human instinct, a degree so high that it becomes completely incomprehensible, unattainable to ordinary observation? In order to embrace it, isn't it necessary to be at the same level, just as in order to understand a man one must be a man?

"But they say that insanity is a malady: the nerves become irritated, the organ is shattered—and one's mind doesn't work! Thus do medical men talk. They ask: 'Do you really think that one's soul is enhanced when it acts through the diseased organ? that a person sees better when his vision is inflamed? that he hears better when his ear is in pain?' I don't know, but in medical literature we come across people whose irritated condition of sight or hearing enabled them to penetrate where others didn't, to see in the dark, to hear a slight rustle—non-existent for others—to guess events taking place at an immeasurable distance. What if the same applies to the brain? . . . Can't the dilation of a nerve extending from the brain to the organs of sense hamper this or that part of the brain? Ask a phrenologist what a constriction of this or that part of the brain can bring about.

"Such observations—I don't know whether fair or not—raised an irresistible desire on the part of my young philosophers to investigate several people, who, living among others, are, by and large, considered either great or mad, and to find in them the solution of the problems which up to now have been hidden from people with common sense. This intention set them traveling in the world.

"I don't know how long their trip lasted or how it ended. In addition to the booklet from which I read to you in passing, my friends also left some excerpts from the notes they wrote. Here they are:

"Deeds of the days gone by,
Legends from the deep past!

"These notes give the impression of hasty, fragmentary work. Evidently my friends didn't have time either to give their manuscript more polish and uniformity, or to smooth its style. Here are thrown together in a disorderly manner their own observations, travel notes, letters addressed to them, all sorts of unfinished material supplied to them—all this put together haphazardly, and in this form the manuscript got into my hands after the death of my friends. A great deal is not finished; much has been copied and much was lost. But perhaps this manuscript will be of some interest to you, at least as a representation of one of those epochs in the history of human endeavor through which everyone passes, but each in his own way.

"But it is already morning, gentlemen. See what luxurious purple stripes have spread from the dawning sun. See how the smoke from the white roofs bends toward the ground and with what effort it drifts in the frosty air. And there . . . up there in the unattainable depths of the sky—it's light and warm, as if it were the dwelling of a soul—and the soul involuntarily feels drawn to that symbol of eternal light. . . ."

THE THIRD NIGHT

(*The Manuscript*)

"Apparently," Faust said, "my friends had intended to keep their notes very accurately, and being efficient, like natural scientists, to enter in them every detail, even the slightest, from the moment their experiment began. Here is the thick notebook the first pages of which are written very neatly, apparently in a calm state, and the following ones are still neater—they remained white. The written-up pages in this notebook of my investigators have the following title":

OPERE DEL CAVALIERE GIAMBATTISTA PIRANESI

Before our departure we went to say goodbye to a relative of ours, an elderly, sedate man, respected by everyone. All his life he was given to a single passion about which his late wife used to say: "Look, for example, Alexei Stepanych, he is a good man in every way, a kind husband, a kind father and a good provider—everything would be all right, but for this unfortunate weakness."

Here the old aunt would stop. The stranger would ask: "What, my dear, not an inveterate drinker?" and was prepared to offer some remedy. But it would turn out that this weakness was only bibliomania. True, this passion was very strong in our uncle, but it seems that it was the only little window through which his soul looked into the world of poetry. In everything else he was an uncle like any other uncle: he smoked, he played whist for days, and gave himself with enjoyment to our northern indifference. But when it came to books, the old man would seem reborn. When he learned the purpose of our trip, he smiled and said: "Youth! Youth! Romanticism, pure and simple! Why don't you look around yourselves? I assure you that you would find plenty of material here without going far away."

"We have nothing against it," one of us answered. "When we have succeeded in looking at others, then, perhaps, we shall take a look at ourselves. But it seems to be more polite and modest to begin with others. Besides, those people whom we have in mind belong to all nations alike, whereas many of our people are either alive or not quite dead yet: who knows? —their relatives may feel offended. . . . We have no business following the example of those men who worry about making themselves and their friends famous during their lifetimes, firmly convinced that no one will do it after their death."

"That's true! Quite true!" answered the old man. "Oh, these relatives! First of all you don't get anything out of them, and second, a remarkable man is nothing else for them but an uncle, a cousin, and so on. Go ahead, young men, see the world: it's good for one's soul and body. In my youth I, too, went abroad searching for rare books, which one could buy here twice as cheap. Apropos, bibliography. Do not think that it consists only of lists of books and of bindings; at times it gives you quite unexpected enjoyment. If you wish, I'll tell you about my encounter with your sort of person. See if he doesn't get into the first chapter of your travels!"

We expressed our readiness, which we recommend to our readers, too, and the old man went on: "Perhaps you have seen the caricature depicting a scene in Naples. In the open air, under a torn awning, there is a bookshop; heaps of old books and old engravings; above it a statue of the Madonna, Mount Vesuvius in the distance; in front of this little shop—a Capuchin monk and a young man in a large straw hat; a little lazzarone is skillfully pulling a handkerchief out of the latter's pocket. I don't know how all this was caught by the damned painter, only this young man—is I. I recognize my coat and my straw hat. On that day my handkerchief was stolen, and my face must have had the same stupid expression.

"It happens that at the time I had very little money, and what I had was far from adequate to satisfy my passion for old books. Besides, like all bibliophiles, I was extremely stingy. This circumstance made me avoid public auctions, where, as in a card game, a zealous bibliophile may go broke. But to make up for it, I diligently visited a little shop, where I didn't spend much but had the pleasure of rummaging from one end to another.

"Perhaps you are not familiar with the raptures of bibliomania: it is one of the strongest passions, when given its freedom; and I completely understand the German pastor who was led by his bibliomania to commit murder. Quite recently, although old age quenches passions, even that of bibliomania,

I was about to kill one of my friends, who cold-bloodedly, as
if he were in a public reading room, cut the only leaf in my
Elzevir which served as proof that this copy had full margins.[1] But he, the vandal, was even surprised at my vexation.
I still keep visiting bookdealers; I know all their superstitions,
prejudices, and tricks by heart; and even today I still consider
these moments, if not the happiest, at least the most pleasant
moments of my life. You enter: the hospitable owner takes off
his hat, and with all his merchant's generosity offers you
Genlis's novels, and last year's almanacs, and *Scot's Medical
Handbook*. But you utter only one word, and it immediately
pacifies his annoying enthusiasm; you ask him only, 'Where
are the medical books?' and the shop owner puts his hat back
on his head, shows you to the dusty corner, filled with books
in parchment bindings, and calmly takes his seat again to
read last month's *Academic News*.

"Here I should point out to you, young men, that in many
of our bookshops any book in a parchment binding with
Latin heading has the right to be called medical; thus you
can imagine what a freedom it offers a bibliophile: among
*The Science of Midwifery, divided into five Parts and pro-
vided with Illustrations*, by Nestor Maksimovich Ambodik,
and *Bonati Thesaurus medico-practicus undique collectus*,
you'll suddenly come across a small booklet—torn, soiled, and
dusty; you look at it—it's *Advis fidel aux véritables Hollandais
touchant ce qui s'est passé dans les villages de Bodegrave et
Swammerdam*, 1673—how interesting! But this is an Elzevir!
Elzevir! a name which makes the whole nervous system of a
bibliophile tremble sweetly. . . . You push aside a few yellow-
ish volumes of *Hortus sanitatis, Jardin de dévotion, les Fleurs
de bien dire, recueillies aux cabinets des plus rares esprits
pour exprimer les passions amoureuses de l'un et de l'autre
sexe par forme de dictionaire*—and you come across a Latin
booklet without a binding and without a beginning; you open
it: it seems to look like Virgil—but almost every word has a
mistake! . . . Could it really be? Aren't you deceived by a
dream? Is it really the famous edition of 1514, *Virgilius ex
recensione Naugerii*? And you aren't worthy of being called
a bibliophile if your heart doesn't jump for joy when at the
end you find four full pages of errata, a sure indication that

[1] It is well known that the width of margins plays a great role
for a bibliophile. There is even a special instrument for measuring
them, and a few lines more or less frequently increase or decrease
the price of a book by half.

this is precisely the rarest, the most precious edition of Aldes, the pearl of book treasures, most copies of which were destroyed by the publisher himself, vexed at all the misprints.

"In Naples I had very little occasion to satisfy my passion, and therefore you can imagine how amazed I was when passing through the Piazza Nova I noticed heaps of parchments. This was the very moment of bibliomaniac stupor caught by my unbidden portraitist. Anyway, with all the cunning of a bibliophile I approached the bookshop indifferently; hiding my impatience, I went through old prayer books, and at first did not notice that in the other corner a man approached a huge folio. He was dressed in an old-fashioned French coat, and wore a powdered wig, with a neatly tied bun hanging down. I don't know what made us both turn, but in this man I recognized the eccentric who, always wearing the same kind of outfit, used to walk around Naples, and smile and lift his worn boatlike hat every time, especially when meeting ladies. I had already seen this eccentric often and I was very glad to have the opportunity of making his acquaintance. I looked at the book open in front of him: it was some collection of badly done reprints of architectural engravings. The eccentric was examining them very attentively; measuring the painted columns with his fingers, occasionally putting one finger to his forehead, and sinking into profound reflection.

" 'Apparently, he is an architect,' I thought. 'To make myself liked, I'll pretend to be a lover of architecture.' At this moment my eyes fell on a collection of huge folios with the title *Opere del Cavaliere Giambattista Piranesi.* 'Excellent!' I thought. I picked up one volume, opened it—but seeing there projects of colossal builidngs, constructing which would require millions of people, millions of pieces of gold, and centuries—seeing these hewn rocks carried to mountaintops, these rivers turned into fountains, all this so attracted me that for a moment I forgot about my eccentric. Most of all I was struck by one volume, filled from one end to another with pictures of all sorts of prisons, with their endless vaults, bottomless caves, locks, chains, moss-covered walls, and for adornment, all the punishments and tortures which were ever invented by the criminal imagination of man. A chill ran through my veins, and involuntarily I closed the book. However, having noticed that the eccentric did not pay any attention to my architectural enthusiasm, I decided to approach him with a question.

" 'You are a lover of architecture, of course?' I said.

" 'Of architecture?' he repeated as if in horror. 'Yes,' he said, with a glance and a contemptuous smile at my worn coat, 'I'm a great lover of architecture!' and he became silent. 'Only that?' I thought, 'that's not enough!'

" 'If so,' I said, reopening one of Piranesi's volumes, 'better take a look at this wonderful work of fantasy, instead of those cheap prints you have in front of you.'

" 'He came to me unwillingly, as if vexed at being disturbed in his preoccupation, but as soon as he glanced at the book which lay open in front of me he jumped aside in horror, waving his hands, and shouted, 'For heaven's sake, close it, close this useless, horrible book!'

"This appeared to me to be rather intriguing. 'I cannot but wonder at your aversion to such a wonderful work; I like it so much that I'll buy it immediately.' And with these words I pulled out my wallet.

" 'Money!' uttered my eccentric with that sonorous whisper of which I was recently reminded by the incomparable Karatygin in *The Life of a Gambler*. 'You have money!' he repeated, trembling all over.

"I admit, this exclamation of the architect somewhat cooled my desire to become his friend; but my curiosity got the better of me. 'Are you in want of money?' I asked.

" 'I? I need it very badly!' utttered the architect. 'And I've been in need of it for a very long time,' he added, stressing each word.

" 'And how much do you need?' I asked with feeling. 'Perhaps I really can help you.'

" 'To begin with, I need just a trifle—a real trifle: ten million gold coins.'

" 'But why so much?' I asked in amazement.

" 'To build a vault connecting Etna with Vesuvius for the Arch of Triumph, the gate to a park and a castle which I've projected,' he answered as if unconcerned.

"I could hardly keep from laughing. 'Why, then,' I asked, 'being a man of such colossal ideas, did you show such aversion for the work of an architect whose ideas somewhat resemble yours?'

" 'Resemble?' shouted the stranger. 'Yes, resemble! But why do you pester me with this damned book, when I myself am its author?'

" 'No, that's too much!' I answered. Saying this, I opened the *Historical Dictionary* which lay at hand, and showed him the page on which it was written: 'Giambattista Piranesi, the famous architect . . . died in 1778. . . .'

" 'Nonsense! Lies!' cried my architect. 'Oh, I would be happy if it were true! But I live; to my own misfortune, I live—and this damned book doesn't let me die.'

"My curiosity grew from moment to moment. 'Explain this strange phenomenon to me,' I said; 'confide your misery to me. I repeat that I may be able to help you.'

"The old man's face brightened. He took my hand. 'We can't talk about it here; we may be overheard by people who can do me harm. Oh! I know people. . . . Come with me; on our way I'll tell you my awful story.' We left.

" 'Thus, sir,' continued the old man, 'you see the famous and ill-fated Piranesi in me. I was born with a talent . . . what am I saying? It's too late to deny it now—I was born an extraordinary genius. My passion for architecture has been with me since my childhood, and the great Michelangelo, who erected the Pantheon on the so-called great church of St. Peter in Rome, was my teacher in his old age. He was delighted with my plans and building projects, and when I became twenty years of age the great master sent me away, saying: "If you remain with me longer, you'll only become my imitator; go and start a new way for yourself, and you'll make your name eternal, without my efforts." I obeyed, and that very moment was the beginning of my troubles. Money became scarce. I was unable to find work anywhere; in vain I presented my projects to the Roman emperor, to the French king, to popes and cardinals. They all listened to me, they were all delighted, they all approved of me, because passion for art, ignited by Michelangelo, was still smoldering in Europe. They protected me, as a man who had the power to link nonfamous names to famous monuments; but whenever it came to building, they would delay year after year: "Wait, our finances will improve; wait, the ships will bring gold from overseas!"—in vain! I used every possible scheme, every flattery unworthy of a genius—in vain! I was afraid myself, seeing all the humiliation that my elevated soul had to experience—all was in vain! Time passed, buildings which had been started reached their completion, my rivals attained immortality, while I was still wandering from court to court, from waiting room to waiting room, with my portfolio which uselessly was getting fuller by the hour with wonderful and unfeasible projects. Shall I tell you what I felt when entering rich palaces with new hope in my heart and leaving them with new despair? The book of my prisons depicts only the hundredth part of what took place in my soul. My genius was su fering in these caves. Forgotten by ungrateful mankind, I was gnawing these chains. . . . It was an infernal enjoyment to invent tortures conceived in my embittered heart, to make the sufferings of the spirit turn into the sufferings of the body —but this was my only enjoyment, my only repose.

" 'Feeling that I was getting old, and thinking that even if anybody did want to entrust me with some building my life would not suffice to complete it, I decided to publish my projects to the shame of my contemporaries and to show posterity what sort of man they did not know how to value. I eagerly took up this work; I engraved days and nights, and my projects appeared in the world, causing laughter or amazement. But what happened to me? Listen and wonder. . . . Now, through bitter experience I had learned that each work created by an artist conceived a tormenting spirit; each building, each painting, each line, unexpectedly drawn upon canvas or paper, serves as the dwelling place of such a spirit. These spirits are evil: they love to live, love to multiply and torture their creator for the narrow dwelling he gave them. As soon as they sensed that their abode must be limited to engravings alone, they became indignant with me. . . . I was already on my deathbed, when suddenly . . . Have you heard about the man called the Eternal Jew? Everything they tell about him is a lie: this ill-starred man is before you. . . . As soon as I began closing my eyes for ever, I was surrounded by phantoms in the shape of palaces, castles, houses, vaults, columns. All together they pressed with their mass, and with horrible laughter they implored me to be given life. From that moment on, I have not known rest; the spirits created by me pursue me: there an immense vault embraces me; here towers chase after me with their mile-long steps; here a window rattles with its huge frames. Sometimes they lock me in my own prisons, lower me into bottomless wells, forge me in my own chains, let the cold mold rain upon me from the half-ruined vaults—they make me endure all the tortures I had invented; from the fire they throw me onto a rack, from a rack onto a spit; they subject each of my nerves to unexpected suffering, while they, the cruel ones, jump around me and laugh, and do not let me die, trying to find out why I've condemned them to live an incomplete life and to suffer eternally; and, finally, they thrust me, back onto earth.

" 'In vain I go from country to country; in vain I look around to see if some magnificent building has not become damaged, the building constructed by my rivals to laugh at me. Often, in Rome, at night I approach the walls built by this lucky Michel, and strike with my weak hand upon this damned cupola which has no intention of moving, or, in Pisa, I hang with both hands onto this worthless tower which has been bending toward the earth for seven centuries and still does not fall. I've crossed all Euorpe, Asia, Africa, gone across the sea: everywhere I've been looking for a ruined building which I could reconstruct with my creative power; I applaud storms and earthquakes. Born with the bared heart of a poet, I have felt all the sufferings of ill-fated men deprived of their dwellings, struck by horrors of nature; I cry along with the unfortunate, but I can't help feeling tremors of joy at the sight of destruction. And all this in vain!

" 'The hour of creation has not yet arrived for me, or it has already passed: many things go to ruin around me, but many of them still live and prevent my ideas from living. I know that I won't be able to close my weakening eyes in peace until I find my savior, and all my colossal plans have become more than just paper work. But where is he? Where shall I find him? Even if I should find him, my projects will have become obsolete; the century has outstripped much that was in them—and I have no more strength left in me to renew them! Sometimes I deceive my tormentors, assuring them that I am working on the realization of one of my projects; and then they leave me in peace for a while. I was in just such a state when I met you; but it occurred to you to open my damned book in front of me: you didn't see it, but I . . . I saw it clearly, how one of the pillars of the church, built in the middle of the Mediterranean Sea, began nodding its shaggy head at me. . . . Now you know about my misery: help me, then, as you've promised. Only ten million gold coins, I implore you!' And with these words the wretched man fell on his knees before me.

"I looked at the poor devil with wonder and pity, took out one of the gold coins, and said, 'Here is all I can give you now.'

"The old man looked at me sadly. 'I've foreseen this,' he answered, 'but even that much will do: I'll add this money to the sum I'm collecting for the purchase of Mont Blanc to level it to the ground; otherwise it will obstruct the view of my pleasure castle.' With these words the old man disappeared in haste. . . ."

"Here the neatly written pages end," said Faust. The continuation is missing. Tomorrow I'll try to arrange the bunch of letters and papers, which seemed to me to be more interesting."

"It seems to me," remarked Victor, "that your seekers for adventure lay great claim to originality. . . ."

"That's one of the whims of this century," added Vecheslav.

"That's why there is nothing more trivial now than being original," said Victor. "What attention, what sympathy can a crank who wants to revive the past, the distant past, evoke when treasures and effort went for the satisfaction of childish vanity, for building useless edifices? . . . There is no money now for that kind of thing, simply because now they are using it for building railroads."

"Then you think," Faust answered, "that Egyptian pyramids, the Strasbourg steeple, the Dome in Cologne, the Piazza in Florence—all that is merely the creation of childish vanity; true, your assertion doesn't contradict those of many historians of our century, but, while carefully gathering the so-called *facts* they have perhaps forgotten two rather important ones: first, that the names we give human passions never express them fully, only approximately, which apparently has become the habit of mankind since the times of Babylon; and second, that under every feeling there is hidden another, deeper feeling, perhaps even a more selfless one, under that a third still more selfless, and so down to the recesses of the human soul where there is no place for any crude outward passions, because there is neither time nor space. A more or less callous person sees his own pure inner feelings as an external passion, like vanity, pride, and so on; he thinks that he satisfies this passion, but actually he obeys only his inner feeling incomprehensible to himself. I see a symbol of such a *realization of passions* in a comet. A comet never follows its normal path: it constantly deviates from it, attracted now by one celestial body, now by another, and that's why early astronomers, who didn't take into account these *perturbations,* were wrong in their predictions. But despite the fact that an elliptical or parabolical path of a comet assumes the shape of other curves, its initial path remains unchanged and still draws it to a sun of some planetary system."

VICTOR: "I agree that such an optical illusion really exists for man, but I still do not see any reason in turning back to the path already covered, and in crying, along with Piranesi, that the time has passed when money was spent for constructing gigantic and yet useless buildings. . . ."

FAUST: "It seems to me that in Piranesi human feeling cries about what it lost, what may have been the clue to all its external actions, what had made the adornment of life—about *the useless.* . . ."

VICTOR: "I admit that if the Strasbourg steeple could be extended in length—into railroad tracks, it would mean to me an even better adornment of life; because, say what you will, railroads have poetry of their own, besides their practical use. . . ."

FAUST: "Unquestionably. Because, as I have said once already, it is impossible for man to get rid of poetry; it enters every action of man as one of the necessary elements; without it the *life* of this action would be impossible. Each organism reveals to us a symbol of this psychological law. An organism is made of carbon dioxide, hydrogen, and nitrogen; the proportion of these elements varies almost from one living body to another, but the absence of one of these elements would mak the existence of such a body impossible. In the psychological world poetry is one of the elements without which the *tree of life* would have to disappear; that's why even any industrial enterprise of man contains a quantum of poetry, just as each purely poetical work contains a quantum of material usefulness; thus, for instance, we can't doubt that the Strasbourg steeple had its say in the stockholders' calculations and was one of the magnets that attracted the railroad to the city."

VICTOR: "We are quits. I prefer usefulness with the smallest proportion of poetry. . . ."

FAUST: "In that case you are like a man who wants to build a whole city of houses with identical façades. It would seem all right, but the city would oppress one with its unbearable boredom. Yes! railroads are a very important and great thing. It is one of the instruments which is given man to conquer nature. A deep meaning lies within this phenomenon, which apparently has dissipated itself in shares, debits, and credits. In this urge to conquer time and space lies the feeling of man's dignity and his superiority over nature; this feeling perhaps carries the recollection of his former power and of his former slave nature. . . . But God keep us from concentrating all our intellectual, moral, and physical strength in one material direction, no matter how useful it be: be it railroads, cotton mills, fulleries, or cotton factories. One-sidedness is the poison of present societies and the secret cause of all complaints, troubles, and bewilderment; when one branch lives at the expense of the whole tree—the tree withers away."

ROSTISLAV: "By the way, do you know what Hegel said, the man you respect! 'A fearful anxiety not to be one-sided very frequently exposes a weakness capable only of superficial versatility. . . .' "

FAUST: "Despite all my respect for Hegel, I can't help noticing that, either because of the obscurity of human language or because of our inability to understand the secret bond of reasonings of the famous German thinker, in his works one often encounters statements on the same page which are obviously in complete contradiction to one another. Thus, in that same work[2] preceding the lines you just quoted, Hegel said: 'Only that can be called the harmonious *whole* which, *having delved deeply into its own principle*, attains its perfection; *only then* does it become *something* real and acquires depth and a *strong potentiality for versatility.*' If *the whole, reality,* and *versatility* are inseparably interconnected; if the condition of the wholeness of a phenomenon means delving into its principle, this indicates a necessity of commonality and versatility rather than the importance of one-sidedness. But you can't convince Victor with such authorities; for his sake I'll refer to a positive fact.

"Michel Chevalier, one of the famous advocates of industrialization, speaks[3] ironically of difficulties which existed for ancients in undertaking a journey from poetic Sparta to poetic Athens and back, and by means of indisputable facts and numbers he tries to prove that when perfected steam engines become commonly used one will be able to complete a journey around the earth—what a horror! in *eleven* days! But the penetrating mind of this remarkable writer did not overlook

[2] The university speech of 1837. See the translation in the *Moscow Observ.* 1838, No. 1. This speech is the more remarkable for the fact that it can be taken for the last phase of Hegelian positions.

[3] See *Recherches nouvelles sur l'industrie,* par Michel Chevalier. 1843.

the question: What will the moral state of society be when man reaches this stage? He doesn't answer this question positively, but he turns to America, and here are his observations: In that country the speed of communications, the comfort of going from one place to another have done away with all the differences in customs, in the way of life, in clothing, housing, and in concepts (when they do not concern personal gain of an individual). Hence there is nothing new, interesting, and attractive for the inhabitant of that country. He is at home everywhere and crossing his land from coast to coast he encounters only what he sees every day. That's why personal gain is always the goal of a journey for an American, and never enjoyment. It may seem that nothing could be better than such a state. But our intelligent Chevalier in his laudable frankness admits that the full consequence of such a useful, comfortable, and prudent life—is an *invincible, unbearable boredom!* A highly remarkable phenomenon! Where did this boredom come from? Please, gentlemen utilitarians, explain! Isn't it to this boredom and irritability which it creates that we should also ascribe daily duels in America, which now have become customary and the details of which make even European journalists shudder? What do you think? Well, gentlemen, there are the consequences of one-sidedness and specialization, which is now considered the purpose of life; that's what complete immersion in material gain and complete oblivion of other, the so-called useless, transports of the soul, means. Man thought of burying them in the ground, of caulking them up with paper, and covering them with tar and fat—but they keep appearing to him in the shape of a ghost: *incomprehensible boredom!"*

THE FOURTH NIGHT

The dusty sheaf lying on the table was entitled:

THE ECONOMIST

Faust read:

"Gentlemen, I am sending you fragments found among the papers of a young man who died recently, because he seems to have been the kind of man you made the object of your observations.

"There was nothing remarkable in the life of this young man; he was born with a positive, even a dry mind, a mind which expected actions to follow causes. In discussions he liked to attack idealism, dreams of the imagination, unaccountable feelings—and used to prove that they alone were to blame for all the calamities of mankind. As a result of his way of thinking, he directed his entire intellectual activity to positive sciences, entered the service of the Ministry of Finances, read only economists, from Galiani to Say, worshipped Malthus, and constantly filled sheets of paper with statistical calculations.

"The jump he made from cold numbers to the fragments which I am sending to you seems surprising to many people. They cannot understand how these strange, often absurd dreams could enter the head of a man who was so obviously reasonable, so indifferent, and so far removed from transports of the imagination.

"Reading these fragments and noting the deep pensiveness to which our economist was given during his last days made his relatives suspect attacks of madness in him, the more so since the last day of his life he was perfectly well, and since sudden death interrupted his life without any obvious reason. Considering all these circumstances, along with a few unfinished words the youth uttered at the moment of his last sufferings, the doctors at first thought that the poor fellow had taken his own life. But careful examination revealed no signs of any internal or external wound on him. The autopsy showed no signs of poisoning: all his inner organs were intact, and the doctors had to admit that the physical cause of poor B's death was inexplicable.

"Contrary to medical opinion, I am convinced that poor B should not have been buried in hallowed ground. He was in fact a suicide; only, he killed his body by a poison the doctors did not suspect, the honor of discovering which belongs to our nineteenth century, the poison which has personified in itself all the effects of the legendary aqua tofana, and which, according to alchemists, does not kill at once, but affects one in a year, or two, or sometimes even ten years. This poison has not been given an exact and definite name. This fact, however, does not prevent it from existing and the present fragments prove it.

"I don't know if I am correct, but to me these fragments explain a great deal. It seems to me they show that poor B's logical mind, enthusiastically following its own conclusions, found something at the end of his syllogisms that escaped numbers and equations and that could not be communicated to others, that could be understood only by instinct of the heart and that could not be encompassed by the saying What is clearly understood may be clearly expressed.

"The poor youth was frightened by this discovery; it refuted all the calculations of his positive mind while remaining inexplicable itself. Looking back upon the path he had traversed, his strict dialectic saw that it was wrong, but it could not see why. The whole world seemed to the poor man to be overturned, as to a man who wants to examine small earthly bodies through a telescope intended for celestial bodies. This spectacle struck him. At this moment of despair he was suddenly overcome by the feeling of poetry—the consoler, which lives in everyone—and he committed to paper the sufferings which tormented his soul. No doubt, the fragments he wrote are a symbolical story of his own sufferings. I am convinced of this by the chronological order in which I arranged them, following certain indications as to the period during which they were written, and which also agree with the recollections of B's relatives. He hid these fragments from everyone, as he hid his sufferings; his positive mind was afraid of these sufferings, was ashamed of them, and called them a momentary weakness. This incessant struggle was slowly but surely exhausting his strength, although no one noticed that under his frigid outward appearance there lay a whole world of insufferable torments.

"I left these fragments completely uncorrected; I added only a few explanations to them to show how I thought they were connected with each other.

"The first fragment, which I called *The Brigadier* to avoid the confusion of numbers, was written by the youth soon after he graduated from school, as the handwriting shows. It has the imprint of a young mind, suddenly disturbed at the sight of the world and, in particular, of that secret, intimate hypocrisy which, under the cover of moral sententiousness, undermines all moral and social ties. It still reminds one of themes written in literature classes. But here he already reveals his secret decision: not to leave his soul in a state of inactivity. Since that time B seems to have abandoned poetry; at least, since that time, in the course of eight years there is nothing among his business papers but statistical tables and economic calculations. It is also apparent that at that time he studied physical sciences."

The Brigadier

He lived and lived, and in the papers there just
Remained "left for Rostov"
—Dmitriev

Recently I happened to be at the deathbed of one of those people whose existence seems not to be written in any stars, who die without leaving a single thought or feeling after them. I had always envied the late man: he lived in this world for more than half a century, and during all this time, while kings and kingdoms rose and fell, while one discovery was made after another, turning into ruins everything that was formerly called laws of nature and mankind, while ideas created by centuries of long efforts, expanded and carried the whole world in their wake—my late friend paid no attention to all this. He ate, he drank, he was neither kind nor evil; he was neither loved nor did he love anybody; he was neither gay nor sad. He attained the rank of Councilor of State for his long service, and set off to the other world in full dress: shaven, washed, wearing his uniform.

How unpleasant and depressing this sight is! At the solemn moment of man's death your soul involuntarily expects a strong shock, but you remain cold; you look for tears, but a scornful, almost contemptuous smile appears on your face! . . . Such a state is unnatural; your inner feeling is shamelessly deceived; it is torn; and, what is even worse, this sight makes you become aware of another sight, still less tolerable —of yourself; it incites an annoying activity in you; it compels you to part with the sweet indifference which had kept everything upon earth enclosed in a smooth icy crust for you. Farewell leaden somnolence! With the voluptuousness of a suicide you used to heed that dull pain slowly gnawing your organism; now you fear this faithful, invariable enjoyment; again you resolve to take up a new struggle with people and with yourself, to take up old and already familiar sufferings. . . .

That is how I felt. The funeral service was coldly performed, coldly they threw handfuls of dirt over him, coldly covered it with earth. Not a tear, not a sigh, not a word anywhere. Everybody left; I left along with the others. . . . I felt like laughing; I felt sad and stifled. Thoughts and feelings were crowding in my soul; they jumped from one object to another, confusing thinking with unaccountability, faith with doubt, metaphysics with an epigram; for a long time they were rising, like magic vapors over Cagliostro's tripod, until finally, little by little, they shaped the image of the dead man before me. He appeared just as if he were alive. He showed me his abdominal cavity, and stared at me with eyes that expressed nothing. My attempt to run away, or to cover my face with my hands, was futile; the corpse followed me everywhere, laughing, leaping, mocking my aversion, and showing off some sort of kinship with me. . . .

"You coldly watched me die!" said the corpse, and suddenly his face assumed quite a different expression: I was amazed to see a profound and inexhaustible sadness taking the place of insensibility in his gaze; his senseless features expressed only cold and fixed despair; the lack of inspiration turned into an expression of incessant, bitter reproach. . . .

"You even looked at my last sufferings with scorn and contempt," he continued sadly. "You were unjust! You did not understand them. People are usually sorry, and weep for a dead genius who planted a fertile thought in the soil of mankind; for an artist who left all the kingdom of his soul in sounds and colors; for a legislator who held the fate of millions in his hands; and whom do they pity? whom do they weep for?—for lucky men! Everything beautiful created by

them soars over their deathbed; their right to feel pride,
which invigorates a human soul, sweetens their parting from
the world; in their last moment, more than ever, they remember the deeds they have accomplished; in this moment both
the praises they heard and anticipated and their burdensome,
mysterious sufferings, even the very ungratefulness of people
—all this fuses for them into a loud hymn of thanksgiving, the
marvelous harmony of which resounds in their ears! But what
about me and people like me? We deserve pity and tears a
thousand times more! What, what could have sweetened my
last moment? Oblivion, that is, a continuation of the same
state in which I have been all my life? What shall I leave
after myself? *All that is mine is with me!* But if that which I
am revealing to you now occurred to me in my last moment,
if something was moving in my soul in the course of all my
life, if the last convulsive shock of nerves had suddenly
brought out my thirst for love, for self-perception and activity, suppressed during my life—would I then have deserved
pity?"

I shuddered, and uttered almost to myself, "But whose
fault was it?"

The corpse did not let me finish; he smiled bitterly and
took my hand in his.

"Look at these Chinese shadows," he said, "that is I. I am
in my father's house. My father is preoccupied with his position, cards, and the hunt. He feeds me, dresses me, scolds
and beats me, and he thinks that he is bringing me up. My
mother is busy watching the morality of the entire neighborhood, and therefore she has no time to take care either of my
morality or her own. She pampers and caresses me, and spoils
me with sweets in secret from my father; for the sake of
decency she makes me pretend—for the sake of decorum—not
to say what I think; she makes me respect our relatives, and
learn by heart words which she doesn't understand—and she
also thinks that she is bringing me up. Actually, I am brought
up by our house servants: they teach me all the inventions of
ignorance and lewdness, and—I understand their lessons! . . .

"Here I am with my teacher. He is trying to explain to me
what he does not know himself. Never having given a
thought to the fact that concepts have their own natural
course, he jumps from one thing to another, omitting the necessary transitions. Nothing remains, and cannot remain, in my
head. When I do not understand him, he accuses me of stub-
bornness; when I ask him about something, he accuses me of

playing smart. School is torture for me, and learning, instead of developing me, only kills my abilities.

"I am not quite fourteen years old, and that is the end of my learning! How happy I am! I am already squeezed into a sergeant's uniform; in the daytime I mount guard and undergo training, but most of the time I spend visiting relatives and my superiors; at night I curl my hair, powder myself, and dance till exhaustion. Time flies, and I physically lack time to think. My father teaches me to pay calls and to fawn; my mother points rich girls out to me. When I dare to make any kind of objection, they call it disobedience to parental authority; when I accidentally manage to express an idea which I didn't hear either from my father or from my mother, they call it freethinking. I am scolded and threatened for everything for which I should be praised, and praised for everything for which I should be scolded. And the natural state of my soul changes: I become frightened, confused. Besides, nature has endowed me, quite inopportunely, with weak nerves, and I became *dumfounded for the rest of my life*: some sort of numbness overcame all my spiritual abilities; there was nothing that could unfold them: while still in the bud they were crushed by everything that surrounds me; there was nothing I could think about; perhaps I could think, but I did not know where to start; neither could I imagine that there was something to think about, except my jackboots, just as a deaf-mute cannot imagine what a sound means. . . . Meanwhile I drank, I played, so as not to be called a bad sport, which would have been very deplorable for me.

"Everybody was getting married. I must get married too. Now I am married. My wife is my equal. I've remained the same: in my head I have only my father's ideas so far. If by some chance an idea dissimilar to my father's occurs to me, I wave it away as an evil obsession; I am afraid of being a bad son, because even if I do not understand what virtue is, I instinctively want to be virtuous. That's why in the mornings my wife and I go through our accounts—because my father laid it close to my heart not to squander our property, and then—then there is a time for dressing, for dinner, cards, dancing, parties. We lead a very gay life; time flies, flies very fast. Whenever my instinct tells me to change something in our way of life, my wife threatens to call me a bad husband, and I continue to obey her, because I feel like keeping the name I've already acquired, that of a true Christian and of a man of principles. The fact that I zealously keep visiting my relatives and do not forget a single name, day or a birthday helps me to preserve this reputation.

"Now I have children; I am very happy; they say that children have to be brought up—why not! I've never had time to think what an upbringing really means, and therefore I think it best to follow my father's advice and begin to bring up my children just the way I was brought up, and to say to them exactly the same words my father used to say to me. It is much better this way! True, I repeat many of his words simply by force of habit, at random, without associating any sense with them—but that does not matter! Obviously, my father could not have wished me anything bad, and therefore his words will at least be of some use to my children. Sometimes such repetition of another's words makes me blush; but I don't know what can prove my filial respect better than such incessant remembering of fatherly instructions, or what can better give me in turn the right to be respected by my children.

"My instinct tells me to send my children to a public school; but my relatives tell me that in school my children will lose the principles of morality acquired at home, and will become freethinkers. To preserve peace in the family I decide to teach them at home, and not knowing how to choose teachers, I choose them and pay them dearly; all my relatives praise me highly for that, and assure me that God's blessing is upon my children because they are so much like me in every respect. But this is not quite true: my wife hinders me a great deal.

"I have never loved my wife, and I have never known what love is. At first, I didn't notice it; while we didn't have the time or anything to talk about, we managed somehow to agree; but now, with the children around, we go out less—and my troubles have started! My wife and I cannot agree on anything: I want one thing, she wants another; we start for no reason; we both talk; we do not understand each other—and I don't know how, but every argument turns into an argument about who is the more intelligent of us, and this argument always lasts for twenty-four hours. And so, as soon as we are together, we either keep silent and feel bored, or we raise a real row! She begins to shout—I pacify her; she begins to scream—I shout back; she bursts into tears, then she becomes ill—I take care of her. Entire days pass like this; time flies, and flies very quickly.

"I really do not understand what causes our arguments—

we both seem to be of a quiet temper, and moral people (so everyone says). I am a respectful son; she is a dutiful daughter. As I've said already, I am teaching my children what my father taught me, and she is teaching them what her mother taught her—what could be better? But, unfortunately, my father and her mother were of contradictory opinions; therefore, while we faithfully fulfill our parental duties, we confuse our children: she keeps them warmly wrapped up; I take them out into the cold for a walk—our children die. Why is God punishing me?

"At times I can't stand it any longer, and, for the sake of the children, I feel like getting rid of my wife, but how would I be able to look into people's eyes after such an example of immorality? There is nothing I can do! Apparently I'll have to suffer all my life; my only consolation is that at least strange people praise us and call us an exemplary couple because, although we can't stand each other, we abide by the law.

"Meanwhile time keeps flying and my rank increases; in accordance with it I'm given a corresponding position; instinctively I feel that I can't occupy it because I'm not used to reading, and when I read I don't understand anything. But they tell me that I would be a bad father if I didn't take advantage of this position to get my children settled. I don't want to be a bad father, and therefore I accept this position. At first my conscience bothered me, and I began to read; but things turned out worse; so, I entrusted my secretary with all the papers, and began to sign them, and to think of advancing my children—thus gaining the reputation of a good superior and a loving father.

"Time keeps flying; I am past forty; the period of life during which intellectual activity reaches its highest point of development has already passed; my abdomen expands and I begin, as they say, to put on weight. If not a single thought could find its way into my head ever before, up to this period, what could I expect now? Not to think has become my habit, my second nature. When I feel too weak to go out—I am bored, very bored, but I myself don't know why. I start playing solitaire—boredom comes over me. I get into an argument with my wife—again I feel bored. I overcome myself and go to a party—still the same boredom. I start reading a book—they are all Russian words, but they might as well be written in Tartar; a friend comes and tells me about it—it seems comprehensible. I go back to reading it myself—again

I understand nothing. All this drives me into a fit of spleen, for which my wife scolds me; she keeps asking me if I need something, or if something is making me unhappy. I ascribe everything to hemorrhoids.

"Here I am ill, for the first time in my life; I'm seriously ill —they've put me to bed. How unpleasant it is to be ill! I can't sleep, I can't eat! How boring! And then comes the suffering! How can I alleviate it? When people come to see me—since all my relatives hold family bonds sacred—I seem to feel better, but boredom and fear do not leave me. Now I notice that the visits of my relatives have become more frequent; they talk with my doctor in whispers—things look bad! Ah! now they talk to me of communion, of extreme unction. Oh, they are all such good Christians—but doesn't that mean that I am near the finish? Is there no more hope? I must leave life and everything: dinners, and cards, and my uniform, and my four raven horses which I haven't had a chance to try out yet—oh, I feel so miserable! Bring in the new livery for me to see; call my children; can't I still be helped? Call for more doctors. Give me whatever medicine you want to; give half of my property, give all my property away; if I live, I'll make a fortune again—only help me, save me! . . .

"But suddenly the scene changed; and awful convulsion shook my nerves, and it seemed as if a veil fell from my eyes. Everything that makes an active man's soul worry, an insatiable thirst for knowledge, an urge to act, to astound the heart with the power of words, to leave a sharp trace in people's minds, to envelop in lofty feelings as if in a passionate embrace both nature and man—all this flamed up in my head. I became aware of the immensity of love and self-perception. The sufferings of a genius's entire life, unappeased by any gratification, cut deep into my heart, and all this happened at the moment when my activity had come to an end. I tossed around restlessly; I uttered disconnected words with which I sought to tell myself in a twinkling all that couldn't be expressed in a lifetime; my relatives thought that I was unconscious. Oh, in what language could I express my sufferings! I began to *think*! To think—it's an awful word after sixty years of an unthinking life! I understood *love*! Love—an awful word atfer sixty years of an insensible life!

"And all my life presented itself before me in all its ugly nakedness!

"I forgot all the circumstances which surrounded me from

the day of my birth; all the implacable conditions of society which kept me enslaved during all my life. I was aware of only one thing: I had disgraced the gifts of Providence. And all the moments of my existence that were trampled in sense-lessness, decorum, and nothingness fused into one horrible reproach and poured the burning cold over my heart!

"In vain did I search in my existence for a single thought, for a single feeling which could protect me from the wrath of the Almighty! A wilderness answered me, and in my children I saw the continuation of my nothingness; oh, if I could only speak, if I could only make those around me listen to reason, if I could only confide in them, share with them the feeling that enflamed my soul! In vain I extended my hands to peo-ple—cold and callous, they longed to learn a friendly hand-shake; but people shun a corpse growing numb—and I saw only myself before me—myself, lonesome and ugly! I was thirsty for a glance which might pour the joy of sympathy into my soul—and I encountered only scornful contempt in your face! I understood it, and I shared it! With an awful, inevitable, and eternal bitterness I left my earthly shell! . . . Now, if you wish, do not pity me, do not weep over me; despise me!"

Bloody tears came running down the bluish cheeks of the corpse, and he disappeared, smiling sadly. . . . I went back to his grave, fell on my knees, and prayed and wept there for a long time. I don't know if passersby understood what I was weeping about. . . .

After eight years of an isolated life devoted to dry numbers and calculations, the author of these fragments apparently began to feel the inadequacy of his theories, and in order either to distract himself or to hear the opinions of living people, or perhaps even to refresh his strength through a momentary rest, he plunged into the social whirlpool. This atmosphere was not to his liking, and he probably put these lines on paper at a moment of disdain. I called one of these fragments *The Ball*, another, *The Avenger*. Both stories re-flect a certain turgidity common to an active man who takes to poetry, and a certain statistical habit to calculate, and to-gether with these an impression which he must have carried away from reading current novels—reading so indispensable for the visitor of drawing rooms.

The Ball

Gaudium magnum nuntio vobis.[1]

Victory! Victory! Did you read the bulletin? An important victory! a historical victory! Canister shots and explosive bombs were particularly effective; ten thousand men have been killed, twice as many wounded; there were heaps of arms and legs; cannons have been brought from the battle-field, and banners bespattered with blood and brain, some of them showing the imprint of bloody hands. Why this battle took place, what it was for, for what reason it occurred only a few men know, and they keep it to themselves; but never mind! Victory! Victory! The whole city is rejoicing! The sig-nal has been given: festivals follow one another; no one wants to lag behind. Thirty thousand men are out of service! That's no trifle! Everybody rejoices, sings, and dances. . . .

The ball was reaching its high point. A delicate haze floated over numerous candles growing dim; through it, dra-peries, marble vases, golden tassels, bas-reliefs, columns, paintings seemed to quiver. Hot air was rising from the decolleté bosoms of beautiful ladies, and often, when dancing couples flashed by in a swift whirl, as if broken loose from the hands of a sorcerer, a hot, stifling breeze enveloped you, as in the waterless sands of Arabia. Fragrant curls were com-ing looser from hour to hour; crumpled airy shawls all the more carelessly rolled over burning shoulders; pulses were beating faster and faster; hands were meeting more often and flaming faces were nearing one another; looks were becoming more tender, laughter and whisper more audible. Old men were rising from their seats, stretching their feeble limbs, and their dim, dumbfounded eyes showed bitter envy mingled with bitter recollections of their past. All were whirling, twirling, raging in a voluptuous madness. . . .

On a little platform bows glided with a squeak over tightly drawn strings; the sepulchral voice of the horns quivered in the air, and the monotonous sounds of kettledrums answered it with mocking laughter. The gray-haired conductor, smiling and beside himself with excitement, kept increasing the tempo and stimulating the musicians with his eyes and the movements of his body.

---

[1] "I announce to you a great joy" is the usual formula by which the election of a Pope is announced in Rome.

"Wasn't I right?" he was saying in a jerky manner without leaving his bow, "Wasn't I right? I told you that the ball would be a success—and I've kept my word. Everything depends on the music; I composed it with the purpose of raising people from their seats . . . of not letting them think . . . such was the order. . . . In the works of famous musicians there are strange passages, and I made a good job of selecting them, that's all. Now, you hear? This is Donna Anna wailing, while Don Juan laughs at her; here the dying Commendatore is groaning; here is the moment when Othello begins to believe his jealousy; here is Desdemona's last prayer."

For a long time the conductor went on enumerating to me all the human sufferings which found their expression in the works of famous musicians, but I wasn't listening to him anymore—I noticed in this music something fascinatingly horrible: I noticed that each sound was joined by another, more piercing one, which chilled your blood and raised the hair on your head. I began to listen more attentively: at one time I seemed to be hearing the cry of a suffering child; at another, the wild shout of a youth, or a mother's piercing cry over her bloodstained son; now the trembling moan of an old man; and all these voices of various human torments seemed to me to have been arranged in an endless scale, from the first cry of a newborn baby to the last thought of the dying Byron: each sound tore itself from an irritated nerve, and each melody was a convulsive movement.

This terrible orchestra hung like a dark cloud above the dancers. With every stroke of the musicians, down from this cloud came loud words of indignation, the disconnected babble of a man struck by pain, the dim voice of despair, the sharp sadness of a groom separated from his bride, the repentance of treason, the shouts of an enraged, triumphant crowd, the scorn of disbelief, the fruitless crying of a genius, the mysterious sadness of a hypocrite, together with weeping, sobbing, and laughter. . . . All this fused into furious chords, loudly cursing nature and grumbling at Providence. At every stroke of this orchestra out of the cloud came either the blue face of a man exhausted by torture or the laughing eyes of a madman, the trembling knees of a murderer or the parched lips of a slain man. Out of this dark cloud and down onto the parquet floor came drops of blood and tears—the beautiful ladies' satin shoes glided over them . . . and all were whirling, twirling, raging in a voluptuous madness as before. . . .

The candles began to form snuff and to grow dim in the

stuffy air. When you looked through this quivering haze into
the crowd, it seemed to you sometimes that these were not
people dancing there. . . . In swift motions they were loosing
their clothing, their hair, their bodies . . . and you saw skeletons dancing and knocking with their bones against one another . . . and above them, accompanied by the same music,
there stretched another train of skeletons, broken and de-
formed. . . . But no one in the ballroom noticed it. Everyone
was dancing and whirling unconcernedly.

The ball continued till long after dawn. People risen from
their beds to attend their daily cares stopped to look at the
shadows gliding past the lighted windows.

Dazed, tired, and exhausted by its tormenting gaiety, I left
the stuffy ballroom and rushed into the street, gulping the
fresh air into my lungs; church bells summoning to matins
were lost in the noise of departing carriages; I found myself
before an open church door.

I entered. The church was empty; one candle was burning
in front of an ikon, and the quiet voice of a priest was heard
under the vaults: he was uttering the sacred words of love, of
faith, of hope; he spoke about the sacrament of redemption,
he spoke about Him who took upon Himself all the sufferings
of man; he spoke about lofty contemplation of divinity, about
peace of soul, about compassion for one's neighbor, about the
brotherly union of mankind, about forgetting a wrong and
forgiving one's enemies, about the futility of godless intentions, about the incessant perfection of man's soul, about submission to the will of the Almighty; he prayed for those
killed and for those who killed; he prayed for those who are
about to become Christians, for those who were present!

I rushed out of the church. I wanted to take hold of the
raging sufferers, to snatch their lifeless hearts away from their
lusty resting places, to wake them from their cold sleep by
the warm harmony of love and faith—but it was already too
late! Everyone had passed the church by, and no one heard
the words of the priest.

The Avenger

. . . The culprit triumphed. But at that moment I caught sight
of a man who stared intently at the lucky man. In these star-
ing eyes I saw a noble anger and an insatiable, inexorable,
but lofty vengeance. His glance penetrated the lucky man to

the marrow of his bones; they understood everything, all the depth of his baseness, counted all the lawless trepidations of his heart, guessed all the filthy calculations of his mind. . . . A horrible smile was on the stranger's lips. . . . He will not leave the lucky man; nowhere will the criminal find a refuge from the poisonous blade; the image of the monster of morality had cut deep into the memory of the avenger, and someday he will perform a purifying funeral feast over the lucky man; he will strip him of his shimmering habits and, having pushed him naked and in all his infamy onto the place of execution, he will brand his face with shame unto the third generation. . . . A youth will feel a holy fire of indignation in himself, and an old man with a trembling hand will point out the lucky man to his grandchildren; perhaps sometime in the silence of night, amidst the joys of her domestic happiness, a wife, carried away by the enchanting story of a poet, will suddenly cover up her face, and exclaim: That is my husband! Perhaps during an animated conversation a youth will listen to his friends, will share with them deep scorn aroused by the poet's words, and suddenly, coming to himself, he will say in his own heart: That is my father!

And the lucky man will wonder why, amidst all the gifts of happiness, he cannot find a friendly smile, why he can't invoke anyone's sympathy, why his wife trembles in his arms, why the color of shame spreads over his son's face when he looks at him. Lying on his sickbed, with his strength gone and his heart heavy, he will look around himself for a sweet compassion, which like a legendary elixir of life heals all wounds—but the image branded by the poet will stand between the lucky man and his friends. This image will restrain a friendly hand extended to the sufferer, will turn his groan into the despicable prattle of a poisonous insect, will turn pity into an involuntary smile, help into a burdensome duty, and the lucky man will realize all the horror of fruitless repentance. He will seek that invisible hand which struck him, but that hand will already have forgotten about him; it will be leading new victims to the altar of Nemesis, where a mysterious service of a poet takes place at the times of spiritual stench and social decay. . . .

It seems that our author had lost himself in the social whirlpool for much longer than he wanted to, and for a very simple reason: he fell in love. But apparently he did not succeed in his new undertaking, and tasted only love's bitter

fruit. The fragment which he himself entitled *The Mockery
of a Corpse* reveals the sufferings which can be experienced
only by one who is not used daily to spending of his soul and
who feels very seldom but strongly; along with this it already
reveals irony toward his former teachers—accountants, whose
calculations could not be of any use to him in his enterprise.

The Mockery of a Corpse

The autumn storm was raging; the river was bursting out of
its banks; lanterns were swaying in the wide streets, casting
long, moving shadows; dark roofs, bas-reliefs, windows
seemed sometimes to rise from the ground, sometimes to
descend to it again. Everything was still moving in the city;
people were crowding the sidewalks; tardy beauties would
first cover then uncover their faces, as though from the
storm; they would turn around, or stop; a crowd of young
men was following them, and, laughing, thanked the wind
for its impoliteness; sedate people blamed one group or the
other, and continued on their way, regretting that it was
now too late for them to set about the same thing; carriage
wheels would rattle over the pavement hastily or lazily; the
sound of street organs was in the air; and all these manifold
individual movements constituted one general agitation
which was the breath and life of this strange monster made
of heaps of people and stones called a populous city. Only
the sky was clear, formidable, and motionless, and in vain
it waited for a glance to be turned in its direction.

From the direction of the bridge came a luxurious carriage, resembling other carriages in everything but containing something that would make people stop and say to one
another, "Must be newlyweds!" and with stupid joy follow
the carriage with their eyes for a long time.

A young woman sat in the carriage; a shimmering band
interlaced with rosebuds flowed through her black curls; a
light-blue velvet cloak tightly pressed the wide blond lace
which, trying to free itself from its prison, fluttered above
the lady's face, like those airy veils painters use to set off
portraits of their beauties.

Beside her sat a middle-aged man, with one of those faces
which strike you neither with their physical ugliness nor their
spiritual beauty, and which neither attract you nor repulse
you. You would not feel offended to meet this person in a

drawing room, but you would pass him by twenty times without noticing him. You would not have a single sincere word to say to him, but in his presence you would fear the feeling which bursts out of your heart spontaneously and keeps tormenting you until you give it body and shape. In short, in a moment of intense intellectual activity you would feel uneasy and restless with this person; in a moment of inspiration you would throw him out of a window.

Frightened by the waves of the enraged river, by the fierce howling of the wind, the beautiful lady would now look out of the carriage window, now timidly draw nearer to her friend; her friend tried to comfort her with those trivial words which cold cowardice had invented and which are said without persuasion and accepted without conviction. Meanwhile the carriage was rapidly approaching a brightly lighted house, with the shadows in its windows moving to the rhythm of dance music.

Suddenly the carriage stopped; long-drawn-out singing was heard; crimson flames lighted the street; a few men carried torches; behind them a coffin was slowly moving along the street. The beautiful lady looked out; a strong gust of wind flipped the frozen cover back from the corpse, and it seemed to her that the dead man slightly raised his blue face and looked at her with that fixed smile with which the dead laugh at the living. The beautiful lady gasped and pressed herself against the inner wall of the carriage.

The beautiful lady had seen this young man before. Seen him! She knew him; she knew all the turns and twists of his soul, understood each tremor of his heart, each unfinished word, each unnoticeable line in his face; she knew, she understood all this, but at that time one of those worldly opinions called the eternal and indispensable basis of family happiness, and to which they sacrifice genius and virtue, compassion, and common sense—all this for a few months— one such opinion placed an insurmountable obstacle between the beautiful lady and the young man. And the lady yielded; she did not yield to her feeling—no, she extinguished the sacred spark which was about to begin gleaming in her soul, and having fallen, she bent her knee to the demon who distributes the happiness and glory of this world. And the demon praised her obedience and gave her a "good match" and called her prudence, virtue; her servility, wisdom; her optical illusion, an impulse of heart; and the beautiful lady was almost proud of his praise.

But the youth's love contained in itself everything that is sacred and beautiful in man's life; his life lived in its great passion like a shiny and fragrant aloe under the rays of the sun. The moments when the breath would stormily pass over thought, the moments in which centuries live, when angels preside over a mystery of the human soul, and a mysterious embryo of future generations reverently heeds the pronouncement of its fate—these moments were dear to him.

Yes! There was so much of the future in this thought, in this feeling. But could they fetter the indolent heart of a beautiful woman of the world, a heart incessantly chilled by the prospect of decorum? Could they capture a mind incessantly led astray by the judges of general opinion, who have mastered the art of judging others by themselves, measuring feeling by prudence, thought by what they happened to see in the world, poetry by pure profit, faith by politics, future by the past?

And all was disdained: both the selfless love of the youth and the powers it incited. The beautiful lady called her love an impulse of the imagination, the youth's agony, a passing sickness of the mind; and his imploring glances, a fashionable poetical whim. Everything was disdained and forgotten. The beautiful lady led him through all the sufferings of an offended love, offended hope, offended pride. . . .

What took me so many words to relate crossed the heart of the beautiful lady at the sight of the corpse in one moment; the youth's death seemed awful to her—not the death of his body, no! The features of his distorted face told her an awful story of another death. Who knows what happened to the youth when, gripped by the cold of suffering, the strings of the harmonious instrument of his soul were torn asunder; when he broke down, tormented by his unfulfilled life; when his soul became exhausted in futile fight, and, humiliated but not convinced, rejected with laughter—even doubt—the last, sacred spark of his dying soul. Perhaps it summoned all the inventions of depravity from hell; perhaps it attained the sweetness of insidiousness, the bliss of vengeance, the profit of an obvious, shameless meanness; perhaps the strong youth, inflaming his heart with prayer, had condemned all that was good in life, had become absorbed in the science of vice, and exhausted its wisdom with the same intensity with which it would once have exhausted the science of the good; perhaps that activity, which had had to reconcile the pride of knowledge with the humility of faith, fused a bitter, suffocating repentance with the very moment of crime.

The carriage stopped. The beautiful lady, pale and trembling, could hardly walk up the marble steps, although her husband's mockery aroused her failing strength. Now she has entered; she dances, but the blood rushes to her head; the wooden hand that carries her along with the dancers reminds her of the passionate hand which would tighten convulsively when touching her hand; the senseless din of the dance music recalls to her the imploring which burst out of the soul of the passionate youth.

Various people wander here among the crowds; thousands of intrigues and snares are woven and unwound to the gay melody of a contradance; crowds of servile aeronauts circle around a one-day comet; a traitor in all humility bows to his victim. Here an insignificant word attached to a profound plan of many years was heard; there a smile of contempt glided upon a beautiful face and froze an imploring glance. Here dark sins quietly crawl, and solemn meanness proudly carries the seal of rejection.

But suddenly there is a noise. The beautiful lady turns around and she sees that some are whispering among themselves and that others hastily run out of the room and come back all trembling. The shout, "Water! Water!" is heard on all sides. All rush to the door, but it is already too late. The water has flooded the entire first floor. At the other end of the ballroom music is still playing, and people are still dancing there; there they are still discussing the future, thinking of the meanness performed yesterday, of the one to be performed tomorrow; there are still people there who are not thinking about anything. But soon the horrible news is known to all; the music stops and confusion follows.

Why do all these faces grow pale? Why does this adroit and eloquent orator clench his teeth? Why has this somber hero become so talkative? Why is this proud lady running back and forth, her blond lace trailing in the dirt? What is this noble gentleman, for whom even a superfluous glance seemed to be an insult, asking about? So, honored gentlemen, is there really anything else besides your daily intrigues, plotting, and calculations in this world? It can't be true! Nonsense! Everything will pass! Tomorrow will come again! One will be able to go on with the things one began! To eliminate his enemy, to deceive his friend, to crawl up to a new post! Listen: There are several daredevils who have thought of either life or death less than anyone else and who maintain that the danger is not great and that the water may begin subsiding at any moment now. They laugh, they joke, they suggest going on with the dance, with cards; they welcome the chance to stay together till tomorrow night; during this time you won't be exposed to the slightest discomfort. Look, tables are set in the other room; luxurious wines sparkle in crystal glasses; all nature's products have been gathered for you on golden plates. What does it matter if you hear the moans of people dying around you? You are wise, for you have trained your heart not to be carried away by such weak impulses. But you do not listen; you are trembling, you break out in a cold sweat, and you are afraid. And in truth the water is rising more and more; you open the window, and you call for help; the whistling storm answers you, and whitish waves rush into the lighted windows like infuriated tigers. Yes! it is horrible, indeed. One more minute and these luxurious, airy dresses of your ladies will be water-soaked; one more minute, and everything that so happily distinguished you from the crowd will only add to your weight and will pull you down to the cold bottom. It is frightful! frightful! Where are the all-powerful means of science that laughs at the efforts of nature? Honored gentlemen, science has come to a standstill under your breath. Where are there magnanimous people, ready for any sacrifice to save their neighbors? Honored gentlemen, you have trampled them into the ground; they cannot rise anymore. Where is the power of love that moves mountains? Honored gentlemen, you have smothered it in your embraces. What is left there for you? Death, death, a horrible slow death! But cheer up: What is death? You are sensible, prudent people; true, you've disdained the purity of a dove, but you've attained the wisdom of a snake. Can it be that something you've never thought of in your fine and clever reasoning may be such an important matter? Summon your insight to your help, and try your usual means with death; see if you can't deceive it with your flattery, if you can't bribe it, finally, if you can't slander it. Won't it understand your weighty, implacable glance? But it is all futile! The walls begin to shake; one window falls in, then another; water rushes into them and fills the room. Now something huge and black appears in the gap—is it not a means of escape? No, a black coffin is carried into the ballroom—a corpse has called upon the living and is inviting them to his feast! Candles hiss

and die, waves lash over the parquet floor, lifting and turning everything upside down; paintings, mirrors, vases with
flowers—everything is jumbled, cracking and falling. A
frightened face appears from under the lashing waves, a
shrill cry is heard, and both disappear in the deep. Only the
open coffin is floating atop, now beating against the edges
of a precious statue, still intact, now starting back to the
middle of the ballroom.

The beautiful lady cries for help and calls her husband in
vain. She feels her dress clinging to her body, getting heavy
and pulling her into the deep. . . . Suddenly the walls fall
in with a roar, the ceiling gives way—and the waves carry
the coffin and everything there is in the room into the boundless sea. Everything grows silent; only the wind roars and
chases tiny smoky clouds before the moon, whose light from
time to time illuminates the formidable skies and the implacable deep like a bolt of blue lightning. The open coffin
rushes along this deep, the waves pulling the beautiful lady
after it. They are alone in the midst of the rebellious elements: she and the corpse; there is no help, no escape! Her
limbs become stiff, her teeth clench, her strength is exhausted; unconsciously she grips an edge of the coffin—the
coffin leans, the corpse's head touches the head of the lady,
cold drops from his face fall upon her face, in his dumbfounded eyes there is reproach and mockery. Struck by his
look, she lets the coffin go; then again, tormented by an unconscious love for life, she grips it tight—and again the coffin
leans and the corpse's face hangs over hers, again sprinkles
it with cold drops; and with grinning lips the corpse laughs:
"Hello, Liza! My prudent Liza!" and an invincible power
pulls the beautiful lady to the bottom. She feels salty water
in her throat, filling her ears with a whistle; her brain is
swelling in her head, her eyes are turning blind; but the
corpse is still bending over her, and she hears his laughter:
"Hello, Liza! My prudent Liza!"

When Liza came to herself, she was lying in her bed; the
sun's rays gilded the green curtains; her husband, sitting in
the long armchair and yawning, talked with a doctor.

"You see," said the doctor, "it is very clear: any strong
emotion of the soul, resulting from anger, illness, fright, or
bitter recollections, any such emotion directly affects the
heart; the heart in its turn affects the brain nerves, which
impair their harmony when they merge with external feel-

ings; as a result, a person arrives at a sort of somnolent state and perceives a peculiar world, in which one half of the objects belong to the real world and the other half to the world within this person. . . ."

The husband was not listening to him anymore. Meanwhile, two men met at the doorway.

"Well, how is the princess?" one asked the other.

"Nothing serious! Ladies' whims! She only spoiled our ball by fainting. I'm sure it was nothing else but pretense. . . . She just wanted to draw attention to herself."

"Oh, well, don't blame her!" said the first. "Poor thing! I think she has been scolded enough by her husband. Though anyone would be vexed: never before had he been in such good form; imagine, he drew the king ten times in a row, won five thousand in a quarter of an hour, and if it were not for . . ."

Thus talking they went away.

About a year after this fainting fit, at a ball given by B, an elderly gentleman said to a lady:

"Ah, how glad I am to see you! I have a favor to beg of you, Princess. Are you going to be at home tomorrow night?"

"Why must you know?"

"I have been asked to introduce to you a young man who is said to be very remarkable."

"Oh, for Heaven's sake," objected the lady indignantly, "spare me these remarkable young men, with all their dreams, feelings, thoughts! While talking with them one has to think of what to say, and thinking makes me bored and restless. I make a point of it with all my friends. Bring to me people without any pretensions, who are excellent at speaking about gossips, balls, receptions—and that's enough; I'll be delighted to see them and my doors are always open for them."

I consider it my duty to remark that this lady was the princess, and the man talking to her—her husband. . . .

The offended, tormented youth broke out of the social whirlwind and thought of forgetting his sufferings in his former occupations, in his former numbers, but his heart, aroused by the feeling of love, was no longer in harmony with his reason. Nor could it conquer it, because the instinct of his heart had hardly begun to develop. Little by little the youth lost faith in everything, even in the existence of science, even in the perfectibility of mankind. But his logical, positive mind acted with all its strength and expressed the youth's own sufferings in forms of syllogisms, and all the difficulties that formerly seemed to him easy to overcome appeared now in the shape of horrible, all-devouring dialectical doubts. He needed something else besides his reasonings to defeat this monster; he became fully aware of their futility, but, being used to this weapon, he didn't know of any other.

"From that moment on, it seems, his mind became disturbed. His offended feeling of love fused with the illness of his discontented reason, and this horrible state of his organism found its reflection in the monstrous creation of his pen which he himself named *The Last Suicide*. This story shows both his bitter scorn at the absurd reasoning of the English economist and the terrible state of his soul, which was accustomed to considering faith as something necessary only in political relations. Don't be tempted by some of the poor sufferer's strongly worded expressions, but pity him. His monstrous creation can serve as an example of what we can be led to by simple, tested knowledge with our faith in Providence and the perfection of man, and of how the strength of the mind is brought to decay, when the instinct of the heart is forgotten and unrefreshed by the life-spending dew of revelation, of how insufficient even love is to mankind, when this love does not come from a lofty source! This work is nothing else but a development of a chapter in Malthus, but a sincere development undisguised by any of the ruses of dialectics which Malthus employed as a protective weapon against mankind insulted by him.

The Last Suicide

The time predicted by the philosophers of the nineteenth century arrived: the human race had multiplied; the balance between nature's production and the needs of mankind was lost. Slowly but incessantly it had been approaching this catastrophe. Driven by destitution the city dwellers ran to the fields, the fields turned into villages, villages into towns, and the towns imperceptibly expanded their limits. In vain did man apply all the knowledge he had acquired during centuries in the sweat of his brow, in vain did he add to the contrivances of art the powerful activity stimulated by fateful necessity: The sandy steppes of Arabia had long been turned into fruitful fields; northern ice had been long covered by a layer of soil; by enormous efforts of chemistry artificial heat enlivened the kingdom of eternal cold . . . but all this was to no avail: centuries passed, and the animal world forced out the plant world; cities' limits merged, and the whole earth, from pole to pole, turned into an immense inhabited city with all the luxury, all the diseases, refinements, and depravity, all the activities of former cities. But an awful destitution weighed upon this luxurious universal city, and perfected means of communications carried news of the horrible phenomenon of starvation and diseases into all parts of the globe. Buildings still rose high; more fields, arranged in several tiers, illuminated by an artificial sun and irrigated by artificial water, brought an abundant harvest—but it would disappear before it was gathered: at every step, in canals, in rivers, and in the air, there were crowds of people, everything was bursting with life, but life was killing itself. In vain, people implored each other to find means of opposing the all-enveloping disaster: old men remembered the days gone by, and blamed luxury and depraved morals for everything; young people called the power of intellect, of will and imagination to their assistance; wise men searched for means of continuing existence without food, and no one laughed at them.

Soon man began to think of buildings as a superfluous luxury; he would set his house aflame and, wild with joy, cover the soil with the ashes of his dwelling; marvels of art, the creations of cultured life, huge libraries, hospitals—everything that might occupy some space, everything was destroyed and all the earth turned into a single fruitful field.

But hope didn't last long; it was to no avail that contagious diseases spread from one end to another, killing thousands of inhabitants; Adam's sons, struck by the fateful words of the Scriptures, kept growing and multiplying.

Long ago everything that formerly had meant the happiness and pride of man had disappeared. The divine flame of the arts burned no more, and both philosophy and religion were considered knowledge similar to alchemy. Along with this all bonds uniting people among themselves were torn apart, and the more their destitution forced them together, the more their feelings parted. Everyone saw in his fellowman an enemy ready to deprive him of the last means of his destitute life: a father would cry when learning that a son had been born; daughters would dance around their mother's deathbed; but most frequently a mother would strangle her child at birth, while the father would applaud her. Suicides ranked as heroes. Charity became an act of freethinking, scorn at life became a usual greeting, love became a crime.

All the refinements of legislation were used to prevent marriages from taking place: the slightest suspicion of relationship, age difference, any deviation from the ceremony annulled marriages and created an abyss between husband and wife. At the dawn of each day, wakened by hunger from their sleep, emaciated, pale people would gather and accuse one another of overeating, or reproach the mother of a large family of dissoluteness; everyone thought of seeing his general enemy in his fellowman, an unattainable cause of life, and with words of despair they challenged one another to fight: swords were drawn, blood was shed, and there was no one to part them, no one to help the one who fell.

Once a crowd was parted by another crowd chasing after a young man; he was accused of a horrible crime: he saved the life of a man whose despair made him jump into the sea. There were still some people who wanted to protect the poor fellow. "Why do you defend the man-hater?" shouted one of the crowd, "he is an egoist, he loves only himself!" This word alone put off the defenders, because egoism was a common feeling then; it created an unconscious contempt toward themselves in people, and they were glad to punish their own feelings in another person. "He is an egoist," continued the accuser; "he violated the general peace; he hides his wife in his hut but she is his sister in the fifth generation."

"In the fifth generation!" roared the infuriated crowd.

"Is this my friend speaking in you?" uttered the wretched fellow.

"Your friend?" interjected his fiery accuser, and then went on in a whisper, "And with whom did you refuse to share your food just a few days ago?"

"But my children were starving" said the ill-fated man in despair.

"Children! children!" resounded from all around. "He has children! His illegal children eat up our bread!"—and, with the accuser at their head, the crowd rushed toward the hut where the poor wretch was hiding everything dear to him in life from the sight of the crowd. They broke inside—on the bare ground lay two dead children, with their mother next to them; her teeth pressing the hand of her baby. The father tore himself from the crowd, and rushed toward the bodies, while the laughing crowd moved away, throwing dirt and stones at him.

A dark and horrible feeling was born in men's souls. People of former days wouldn't have known what to call this feeling; in those days only the hatred of denied love, only the fear of sure death, and a senselessly tortured man could give a faint idea of this feeling; but this feeling had no object. Now everybody saw clearly that man's life had become impossible, that all the means of supporting it were exhausted, but no one could make up his mind to say what there was left for man to do.

Soon there appeared among them men who seemed to have been keeping count of man's sufferings from ancient times—and as a result they deduced his entire existence. Their boundless insight grasped the past and pursued Life from the moment of its inception. They recalled her, thief-like, creeping first into a dark clod of earth, and there, between granite and gneiss, destroying one matter by another and slowly developing new, more perfect creations; then she made the death of one kind of plant bring about the existence of thousands of others; by destroying plants she multiplied animals. With what cunning she made the enjoyment, the very existence of one kind depend on the sufferings of the other! They recalled, finally, how ambitious Life, extending her authority from hour to hour, kept increasing the irritability of feelings, constantly adding new ways of suffering to a new perfection in each new being until she created a human being, and in his soul she unfolded with all her reckless activity, and placed the happiness of all people against the happiness of each man. The prophets of despair measured the suffering of each nerve in man's body, of each feeling in his soul with mathematical precision.

"Remember," they said, "the hypocrisy with which inexorable Life calls man out of the sweet embraces of nothingness. She covers all his feelings with a magic veil at his birth, she is afraid that man, seeing all the ugliness of life, would recoil from his cradle into a grave. No! cunning Life appears to him first in the shape of his mother's warm breast; then she flutters like a butterfly before him and entices his eyes with gay colors; she takes great care to safeguard him and the state of his soul, as Mexican priests used to take care of the sacrifices for their idol. With foresight she endows a

child with soft limbs, so that an accidental fall might not
make man less capable of suffering; she carefully covers his
head and heart to keep the instruments of future torture
within them intact; and poor man becomes accustomed to
Life, begins to love her: now she smiles at him in the guise
of a beautiful woman; now she glances at him from under
her long eyelashes, covering the ugly holes of her skull; now
she breathes passionate words; now, in poetic sounds, she
personifies all non-existent things; now she takes him to an
empty well of science, which seems to him an inexhaustible
source of enjoyment. Sometimes man tears the shroud enveloping him, and catches sight of Life's ugliness, but she
had anticipated that and implanted in him curiosity to assure
himself of her ugliness, to learn to know her; she endowed
man with the pride of seeing the infinite kingdom of his
soul, and man, enticed and intoxicated, unnoticeably reaches
the moment when all the nerves of his body, all the feelings
of his heart, all the thoughts of his mind, at the high point
of their development, begin to ask: What is the point of
their activity? Where is the fulfillment of their hopes? Where
is the purpose of their life? And Life was only waiting for
this moment—she quickly throws him upon an executioner's
block, strips off the protective veil which she gave him at
the moment of his birth, and, like a skillful anatomist, having
bared the nerves of his soul, she pours the burning cold
over him.

"Sometimes Life hides her chosen victims from the sight
of crowds: in silence and with care she nourishes them with
mysterious food of thoughts, sharpens their feelings, pours
all her endless activity into their frail breasts, and, having
elevated their spirits to heaven, scornfully throws them into
the midst of the crowd. There they are strangers; no one
understands their language; they lack their usual food, and,
tormented by inner hunger, enclosed in the fetters of social
conditions, they measure human sufferings with the loftiness
of their thinking, with all the irritability of their feelings; in
their slow languor they experience the languor of all mankind: their longing after their own imaginary land remains
futile, and they die, having lost faith in their entire existence;
and Life, satisfied, but not satiated with their sufferings,
contemptuously throws the barren incense of a long-delayed
veneration upon their graves.

"There were men who learned about Life's nature early
enough, and, despising her deceitful phantoms, turned in

the firmness of their spirits to their only true and unfailing ally against her contrivances—to nothingness. In ancient times weak-minded mankind called them cowards; we, being more experienced and less liable to deceit, have called them wise. Only they knew how to find sure means against the enemy of mankind and nature, against violent Life. Only they understood why she gave man so many means to feel and so few ways to satisfy their feelings. Only they knew how to end her malicious activity and to solve the age-old argument about the alchemic stone.

"Indeed, consider it in cold blood," continued the ill-fated men, "what has man done since the creation of the world? He tried to escape from Life, which burdened him with her reality. She drove a free and solitary man into leaden social conditions, and what happened? Man replaced his pain of loneliness by another pain, perhaps a worse kind: for the sake of his body he sold the bliss of his soul to society, as to an evil spirit. He employed all his ingenuity to adorn his life or to forget about it. He employed all nature but to no avail: to forget Life became synonymous with the expression to be happy. But this is an unattainable dream. Life keeps reminding man about itself at every moment. It didn't help him to set another man in the sweat of his brow to seek out for him even the shadows of enjoyments —Life appeared as superabundance, more horrible than hunger. In the embraces of love man sought to hide from Life, but it came to him again under the name of crimes, perfidy, and diseases.

"Outside Life's domain man found something inexpressible, some sort of cloud which he called poetry, philosophy. In these clouds he sought salvation from the sight of his persecutor, but Life turned this consoling phantom into a fearful, pernicious ghost. Where else could one hide himself from Life? We had crossed the limits of the most inexpressible. What else could we expect? We have finally fulfilled all the dreams and expectations of the wise men who preceded us. We learned through long experience that the only difference between people lies in a variety of sufferings, and, finally, we reached the state of equality our ancestors dreamed about. See how blissfully happy we are: there is no authority; there are no rich men, no machines among us; we are very tightly united with one another; we are members of one family! Oh, people! people! let us not imitate our ancestors; let us not be deceived—there is another, serene realm, and it is very near!"

The speech of the prophets of despair was quiet; it penetrated men's souls like seed into ready soil, and it grew like an idea that has long been developing in the heart's deep solitude. Everyone understood it; it was sweet to the ear, and everyone wanted to say it to the end. But, as was the case in all decisive moments of mankind, there was no man who could fully express the idea hidden in man's soul.

Then, at last he came, the Messiah of despair! His look was cold, his voice was loud, and his words dispersed the last remnants of ancient beliefs. He was swift in pronouncing the last word of the last thought of mankind—and everything was set in motion. All the efforts of ancient art, all ancient achievements of anger and vengeance, everything that could ever kill man, everything was summoned, and the vaults of the earth crumbled under the light cover of soil; and artificially refined nitrate, sulphur, and carbon filled them from one end of the equator to another. At a fixed, solemn hour, people finally fulfilled the dreams of ancient philosophers about a common family and general agreement of mankind. Wild with joy they joined their hands. Thundering reproach was in their eyes. Suddenly a young couple, recently saved by the furious crowd, appeared from under a clod of earth; pale and exhausted, like shadows of corpses, they kept pressing each other in an embrace. "We want to live and to love amidst sufferings," they shouted, and falling to their knees they implored mankind to stop the moment of its vengeance; but this vengeance had been nursed by centuries of life's generosity; terrible laughter came as an answer; it was a prearranged signal—the next moment fire flashed high, the roar of the disintegrating earth shook the solar system, torn masses of Alps and Chimborazo flew up into the air, groans were heard . . . then . . . again . . . ashes returned to ashes . . . everything became quiet . . . and eternal Life repented for the first time!

———————

"The preceding fragment was written by its author shortly before his death. Fortunately, he did not remain in this unnatural state of his soul. . . . His last fragment, *Cecilia*, shows an influence of religious feeling; it was apparently written during a strongly agitated state of his spirit and employs certain biblical expressions which the author probably read at that time; his hand is almost illegible: in many

spots words have remained unfinished, and the fragment
seems to lack an ending."

Cecilia

Give me power over hearts,
Tear the veil of secret thoughts:
Let my mighty spirit fill the entire world
With sounds of inspiration and love
—SHEVYREV: *Song to Cecilia, the*
Guardian of Harmony

. . . He did not flee people, but their happiness; not misfortunes, but life; not life, but an inquiring soul. He did
not seek peace, but heavy sleep. He did not find what he
was looking for, and what he had been avoiding melted the
cold vaults of his prison. Here sorrow made home for him;
it cast a look of despair over him, filled him with inaudible
cries, bashful tears, and mad laughter; it tore apart his mind
and heart, and immolated them on its altar; it filled his cup
of life with gall.

Where art thou, wisdom? Where are thy seven pillars?
Where is thy repast? Where the regal word? Where are thy
slaves sent to do thy lofty deeds?

Is our life so sad? Is there no cure for us, and the graves
maintain silence? Are we born by incident, live and return
into nothingness? Will man's soul disappear like smoke and
a warm word die like a spark carried away by wind? Will
our names be forgotten in time and will no one remember
our deeds? Is our life a trace of a cloud? And will it become
dispersed like fog under rays of the sun? And will the
tabernacle, the trysting place of the Lord not open, and will
no one remove the seal?

Who will pacify my groaning? Who will give reason to my
heart, word to my spirit? . . .

. . . .

And there, behind the iron bars in a temple, dedicated to
St. Cecilia, everything rejoiced; the rays of the setting sun
in flaming sparkles poured over the image of the guardian
of harmony, the golden organs sang, and sounds full of love
floated in the church in rainbow-like circles. How the desperate man longed to look deep into this shimmering, to listen

to these sounds, to pour his soul into them, to formulate what they left unexpressed—but only a dim reflection and a confused echo reached him.

That reflection, those echoes spoke of something to his soul, of something for which he couldn't find human words.

He believed that beyond that blue reflection there was light, that beyond that dim echo there was harmony, and that the time would come, he dreamed, when Cecilia's light would reach him too, when his heart would dissolve in her sounds, and his tormented mind would find its rest in the bright heaven of her eyes and he would know the joy of crying out his soul in tears of faith. . . . Meanwhile his life was pouring out of him drop by drop, and in each drop there were poison and bitterness! . . .

"What follows is really quite illegible," said Faust.

"Even what he has written *is* enough," scornfully remarked Victor.

"It's horrible, horrible!" muttered Rostislav, lowering his head. "Indeed, one need only look deep into one's soul, and everyone will find in himself an embryo of every possible crime. . . ."

"No, not deep into one's soul," said Faust, "but rather into the depths of logic. Logic is a very strange science; begin wherever you wish—from truth or from absurdity—it will give a beautiful and correct course of thought to everything, and it will lead you with your eyes closed until it stumbles. Bentham, for instance, thought nothing of switching from *individual* to *social* advantage without noticing that there was an abyss between them in his system. The good people of the nineteenth century made this switch along with him, and by his own system they proved that social advantage is nothing else but their own advantage; the absurdity became evident. However, that wouldn't be a misfortune; what was bad was only that this course may take half a century. Thus Adam Smith's logic stumbled only in Malthus. Our century lived by it up till this moment, and even now you won't convince many people that the Malthusian theory is a complete absurdity; they begin a new syllogism with it."

"I want to say only one thing," said Vecheslav, "that both your seekers and their mad economist seem to accuse Malthus of a cock-and-bull story. Actually, I don't remember his recommending indulgence in lust as a remedy for population increase."

"Don't forget," answered Faust, "that my seekers have been dead long since and that they probably read the *first* edition of Malthus, who in his first enthusiasm, thrilled by the clear logical sequence of his thoughts, made a slip and expressed frankly all the wonderful conclusions of his theory. As usually happens, the majority of well-mannered people, who paid no attention to the immorality of the very origin of his theory, were tempted by some secondary conclusions, which, however, of necessity had their source in this very principle. To reconcile these so-called moral people, and to remain true to English decency, in the following editions of his book Malthus eliminated all the conclusions that were too clear while leaving the theory itself intact. His book became less comprehensible; the absurdity remained in it as it was, but virtuous people were reconciled. Let anyone in England try to say that Malthus's absurdity surpasses that of an alchemist searching for a universal remedy! And yet, if the Malthusian theory is correct, mankind really won't have anything else left to do than to blow itself into the air with the aid of an explosive, or to find some other equally effective means to justify the Malthusian system.

"Next time I'll read to you the travel notes of my friends, which closely touch upon the same subject. There you'll see the full, or, as they say, practical application of the theory of another philosopher of logic, whose reasonings, along with those of Malthus, had the honor of forming the so-called political economy of our time."

THE FIFTH NIGHT

A CITY WITHOUT NAME

In the vast plains of Upper Canada, on the deserted shores of the Orinoko, there are remnants of buildings, bronze weapons, works of sculpture, which bear witness to the fact that in former times enlightened people inhabited those countries where today only herds of savage hunters lead a nomad life.

—HUMBOLDT, *Vues des Cordilières*, I

The road led through moss-covered rocks. The horses slipped on the steep ascent and finally stopped altogether. We were forced to step out of the carriage.

Only then did we notice at the top of an almost inaccessible rock something resembling a man. This specter, in a black cloak, sat motionless among the heaps of stones in deep silence. Coming nearer to the rock, we wondered how this being could climb the almost bare, sheer walls to the top. The coach driver replied to our inquiries that this rock had been the abode of the man in black for some time, and it was said in the neighborhood that this man in black would rarely descend from the rock, only to get his food. Then he would return to his rock again, and wander for days dejectedly among the stones, or sit motionless, like a statue.

This story aroused our curiosity. The coach driver showed us a narrow stairway which led to the top. We gave him some money to encourage him to wait for us more patiently, and in a few minutes we were already on the rock.

A strange sight appeared before our eyes. The rock was littered with fragments of stone resembling ruins. Sometimes nature's capricious hand or an ancient, long-forgotten art laid them out there in a long line like a wall; at others it heaped them into a caved-in vault. In some places our deceived imagination beheld something like peristyles. Young trees sprang out from these ruins in all directions; thyme broke through the clefts, completing the enchanting picture.

The rustling leaves made the black man turn around. He got up, leaned upon a stone which looked like a pedestal, and gazed at us with some amazement, but without annoyance. The appearance of the stranger was stern and majestic: his big black eyes burned in deep hollows; his eyebrows were tilted like those of a man accustomed to thinking incessantly; the stature of the stranger seemed even more majestic because of the black cloak which gracefully flowed from his left shoulder and down to the ground.

We tried to apologize for disturbing his solitude.

"It's true," said the stranger after a moment's silence. "I seldom see visitors here; people live, people pass by . . . striking spectacles are left aside; people go farther and farther—until they turn into sad spectacles themselves."

"No wonder you do not have many visitors here," objected one of us, in order to start a conversation. "This place is so dismal, it resembles a graveyard."

"A graveyard," interrupted the stranger, "Yes, that is true," he added bitterly. "That is true—there are graves of many thoughts, many feelings and memories here."

"You have probably lost someone very dear to your heart," continued my friend.

The stranger cast a swift glance at him; his eyes expressed amazement. "Yes, sir," he answered, "I lost the most precious thing in life—I lost my fatherland."

"Your fatherland?"

"Yes, my fatherland! You behold its ruins. Here, on this very spot, former times saw stirring passions, burning thoughts; splendid palaces rose to the sky; the power of art left nature bewildered. Now only stones covered with grass have remained here. My unfortunate fatherland! I foresaw your fall, I moaned at your crossroad: you did not hear my moaning . . . and I was destined to survive you." The stranger threw himself upon the stone, covering his face. Suddenly he started up and tried to push away from himself the stone which supported him.

"Again you appear before me!" he shouted. "You, the cause of all my country's calamities. Hence, hence, my tears will not warm you, you inanimate pillar. Tears are useless. Useless, aren't they?" The stranger burst out laughing.

Wishing to change the train of his thought, which became more and more incomprehensible to us every minute, my friend asked the stranger for the name of the country among whose ruins we found ourselves.

"This country does not have a name—it is unworthy of it; in former times it had a name, a resounding, glorious name, but it has trampled it into the ground; the years have covered it with dust; I am not allowed to remove the veil from this mystery."

"May we ask you," continued my friend, "whether the country of which you speak is really not marked on any map?"

This question apparently struck the stranger.

"Even on a map . . ." he repeated after a moment's silence. "Yes, that may be . . . it must be so. Amidst the numerous upheavals which shook Europe during the last centuries, it could easily have happened that no one paid any attention to a small colony which had settled on this inaccessible rock; it managed to form itself, to flourish, and . . . to die unnoticed by historians, although, pardon me, this is not what I wanted to say; it was not even supposed to be taken notice of. My grief confuses my thoughts, and your questions trouble me. If you wish, I shall tell you the story of this country in proper order. That will be easier for me; one thing will call to mind another . . . only do not interrupt me."

The stranger leaned on the pedestal, as on a rostrum, and with the important air of an orator began his story:

"A long, long time ago, in the eighteenth century, the minds of all people were excited by theories of social order. Everywhere they argued about the causes of the decline or prosperity of states: in city squares, in university disputes, in ladies' bedrooms, in commentaries to ancient writers, on battlefields.

"At that time a young man in Europe was struck by a new, original idea. He said: 'We are surrounded by thousands of opinions, thousands of theories; they all have one purpose—the prosperity of society, yet they all contradict one another. Let us see if all these opinions do not have something in common. They speak of human rights and obligations. But what can force a man not to exceed the limits of his right? What can force a man to regard his obligations as something sacred? Only one thing—his own benefit. Your attempts to diminish a man's rights would be futile if keeping them were to his benefit. It would be futile to prove to him that his obligations are sacred, if they contradict his benefit. Yes, *benefit* is the essential motive power of all man's actions!

Whatever is useless is harmful; whatever is of benefit is permitted. That is the only firm basis for a society! Let benefit, and benefit alone, be your first, as well as your last, law! Let all your resolutions, your occupations, your morals and manners spring from it; let benefit replace the unstable foundations of so-called conscience, of so-called inborn feeling, of all poetic nonsense, of all the inventions of philanthropists—and society will attain lasting prosperity!'

"Thus the young man spoke among his friends, and he was—I do not have to mention his name—he was Bentham.

"Brilliant conclusions built on such a firm positive basis excited many people. It was impossible to implement Bentham's vast system amidst the old society: old people, old books, and old beliefs were against it. Emigration was in fashion at that time. Wealthy people, artists, merchants, and craftsmen turned their estates into money, provided themselves with agricultural instruments, machines, mathematical instruments, boarded ships and set off in search of some unoccupied corner of the world where it would be possible to put the brilliant system into operation in peace and away from dreamers.

"At that time the mountain on which we now are was surrounded on all sides by the sea. I still remember the sails of our ships unfurled in the harbor. Our travelers delighted in the inaccessibility of this island. They cast anchor, stepped ashore, and since they did not find a single inhabitant on the island, occupied the land by settlers' rights.

"All members of this colony were more or less educated people, endowed with love for sciences and arts, notable for their fine taste and refinement in their pleasures. Soon the land was tilled; huge buildings containing all the whims and comforts of life rose above it as if on their own accord; machines, factories, libraries—all appeared with incredible speed. Bentham's best friend was chosen the ruler, and he promoted everything by his strong will and his bright intellect. If he happened to notice the slightest weakening, the slightest negligence anywhere, he would utter the sacred word *benefit*—and the established order was restored again, lazy hands began to move again, and new flame was breathed into a smoldering will. In short, the colony prospered. Full of appreciation for the source of their prosperity, the inhabitants of this fortunate island built a colossal statue of Bentham in their main city square, and on its pedestal they inscribed in gold letters: BENEFIT.

"Many long years passed. Nothing disturbed the peace and delights of the happy island. At the very beginning an argument concerning a rather important matter had almost arisen. Some of the first colonists, brought up in the faith of their fathers, found it necessary to build a church for the inhabitants. Of course, this immediately led to the question whether it was of any benefit. Many people maintained that a church was not a manufacturing enterprise and that, consequently, it could bring no tangible benefit. But its proponents objected, saying that the church was needed in order to have preachers incessantly reminding the inhabitants that benefit was the only basis of morality and the only law for all man's actions. Everybody agreed to this—and a church was established.

"The colony prospered. Common activity surpassed all belief. All classes of inhabitants were up from early morning, afraid to lose even the smallest part of their time—and everyone went about his business: one was busy building a machine, another tilled new land, a third invested money—they hardly had time to eat. Social conversation considered only the question of what one could extract benefit from. Many books on this subject appeared. What am I saying? That was the only kind of book that was published. A girl would read a treatise about a weaving factory instead of a novel; a boy of twelve would begin saving money for capital to be used for mercantile operations. Families had no knowledge of useless fun, nor of useless pastime—each minute of the day was scheduled, each step was weighed, and nothing was lost to no purpose. We did not have a moment's repose; we did not have a minute of what other people called self-enjoyment—life incessantly moved forward, whirling and crackling.

"Some of our artists suggested that a theater should be established. Others found such an institution utterly useless. The argument lasted for a long time—but, finally, it was decided that a theater could be useful if all performances in it were aimed at proving that benefit is the source of all virtue and that the useless was the main cause of all man's misfortunes. This was the condition under which a theater was founded.

"Many similar arguments arose; but since our state was ruled by people endowed wtih Bentham's irrefutable dialectics, they were usually settled in a short time to everybody's delight. The harmony was not disturbed—the colony prospered!

"Enraptured by their success, the colonists made a resolution never to change their statutes, as a well-tested ultimate stage of perfection attainable by man. The colony prospered.

"Thus many long years passed again. Not far away from us there settled another colony, likewise on an uninhabited island. It consisted of common people, farmers, who did not come here to put any system into operation but simply to provide for their existence. Whatever we created through our enthusiasm and the rules which we imbibed with our mothers' milk, our neighbors created through the necessity to live and by their unaccountable but steady work. Their fields and meadows were cultivated and the land, aided by science, rewarded man's work a hundredfold.

"This neighboring colony seemed to us a rather convenient place for the so-called *exploitation*;[1] we started trade relations with it, but guided by the word *benefit*, we didn't consider it necessary to spare our neighbors. By various guises we detained the transport of things they needed and then sold them ours at three times the price. Many of us, using all the legal forms for our protection, undertook rather successful bankruptcies against our neighbors, which caused their factories to go to ruin, to our own benefit. We made them quarrel with other colonies, helped them in such cases with money, which, of course, returned to us a hundredfold. We enticed them into stock-jobbing and by means of clever manipulations we always came out ahead. Our agents lived with our neighbors uninterruptedly: by flattery, insidiousness, money, and threats, they constantly spread our monopoly. Our people grew wealthy—the colony prospered.

"When our neighbors were completely ruined, thanks to our wise, firm policy, our rulers summoned the elective officers and proposed to discuss whether it would not be for the benefit of our colony to acquire the land of our impoverished neighbors for good. Everybody's answer was affirmative. This motion was followed by the other: how to acquire this land, by money or by force? It was suggested that money should be tried first, but if this means should not prove successful, to use force. Although some of the members of the council

---

[1] Fortunately, this word in this particular meaning does not exist in Russian yet; it can be translated as making a profit at the expense of one's neighbor.

agreed that the population of our colony required new land,
they thought it would be more just to occupy some other uninhabited island rather than to encroach upon somebody
else's property. But these people were identified as harmful
dreamers, idealists. By means of mathematical calculations it
was demonstrated to them how many times more profitable it
would be to use land already cultivated than land as yet un-
touched by human hands. A resolution was passed to propose
to our neighbors to cede their land to us for a certain amount
of money. The neighbors refused. Then, having balanced
mercantile accounts of expenditures for the war with the
profit which could be extracted from the land of our neighbors, we attacked them with our armed forces, destroying
everyone who showed resistance; the rest of them we forced
to leave for distant countries, and took possession of the
island.

"Guided by our needs, we acted similarly in other cases.
Unfortunate inhabitants of the surrounding lands seemed to
be cultivating them only in order to become our victims at
the end. Incessantly keeping only our own benefit in mind,
we considered all means permissible in dealing with our
neighbors: political shrewdness, deceit, and bribery. We
made our neighbors quarrel with one another with the purpose of weakening their strength as we had done before; we
supported the weak in order to raise the strong against them;
we attacked the strong in order to set the weak against them.
Little by little all the surrounding colonies fell under our
domination one after another, and Benthamia became a rigor-
ous and powerful state. We praised ourselves for our great
deeds and we taught our children to uphold as an example
those illustrious men who by weapons, and even more by
deceit, added to the wealth of our colony. The colony prospered.

"Many long years passed again. Shortly after we subdued
our neighbors, we met others whose subjugation was not
quite so convenient. This led to arguments. The frontier cities
of our state, enjoying sizable profit from trade with the foreigners, considered it useful to be on peaceful terms with
them. On the other hand, inhabitants of our internal cities,
limited in space, sought an expansion of the state borders and
found it rather profitable to start quarreling with neighbors if
only for the purpose of getting rid of their own surplus population. The vote was divided. Both sides had one and the
same thing, the common benefit, in mind without noticing

that each side used this word only to mean its own good. There were still others who thought of preventing this argument by starting to talk about self-sacrifice, about mutual concessions, about the necessity of sacrificing something now for the good of future generations. Both sides overwhelmed these people by irrefutable mathematical calculations. Both sides called them harmful dreamers, idealists, and the state split into two factions—one declared war against foreigners, the other signed a trade treaty with them.[2]

"This breaking up of the state affected its prosperity greatly. Need made itself felt in all classes of the population; it became necessary to deny oneself certain comforts of life which had become a habit. This seemed to be intolerable. Competition brought about new industrial activity, a new search for means to attain the former state of well-being. Despite all their efforts the Benthamites were unable to reintroduce the former luxury into their homes—and there were many reasons for that. During the time of the so-called noble competition, with the increased activity of one and all, individual cities frequently had the same relationship as the two factions of the state. Contradictory benefits conflicted with each other; one did not want to give in to the other: one city needed a canal, another needed a railroad; one needed it in one direction, another in the other. Meanwhile, banking operations continued, but, being limited to a small space, of necessity, in the *natural order of things*, had to turn upon Benthamites themselves, rather than upon their neighbors. And merchants, following our high principle—benefit—began quietly to enrich themselves on bankruptcies, to detain objects *that were in demand* in order to sell them later for high prices; to indulge steadily in stock-market speculation and to establish monopoly under the guise of the unlimited and so-called sacred freedom of trade. Some grew rich—others were ruined. Meanwhile, no one would sacrifice a part of his profits for the common good, when the latter was of no immediate benefit to him. Canals became obstructed; roads remained

[2] The American republican journal *The Tribune* (an excerpt from which is published in the *Northern Bee*, 1861, Sept. 21, No. 209, p. 859, col. 4) enumerating the consequences of the triumph of the ultra-Democratic party, says: "One state will immediately declare the tariff of the Union invalid, another will object to military taxes, a third will not permit mail to be delivered on its territory; as a result of all this the Union will collapse completely."

unfinished for lack of common cooperation; factories and plants went to ruin; libraries were sold out; theaters closed. Want increased and struck all equally, both rich and poor. It irritated the heart. Reproaches led to discord, swords were drawn, blood was shed, one country rose against another, one settlement against another, the land remained unsown; the rich harvest was destroyed by the enemy; family men, craftsmen, merchants left their peaceful occupations; along with all this, the common suffering increased.

"Many years passed in these external and internecine wars, which would now stop for a while, now flare up again with added bitterness. Common and individual sorrows led to a common feeling of general despondence. Exhausted by the long struggle people gave themselves up to idleness. No one wanted to do anything for the future. All feelings, all thoughts, all man's incentive were limited to the present moment. A father of a family would return home bored and sad. Neither his wife's tenderness nor his children's intellectual development comforted him. Upbringing seemed to be superfluous. One thing only was considered necessary—to obtain a few material benefits for oneself by hook or crook. Fathers were afraid to impart this art to their children in order not to give them weapons against their own fathers: and it would have been superfluous at that. A young Benthamite learned one thing, from his early years, through legends, through stories he heard from his mother: to avoid divine and human laws and to look at them only as means to extract some sort of profit. Nothing was left to revive man's struggle; nothing to comfort him in his sorrow. The divine, inspiring language of poetry was inaccessible to a Benthamite. Great phenomena of nature did not plunge him into lighthearted thought which diverts man from earthly sorrow. Mothers knew no songs they could sing at their babies' cradles. The natural, poetical element was long since killed by selfish calculations of profit. The death of this element contaminated all other elements of human nature; all abstract, general thoughts which unite people seemed to be madness; books, knowledge, laws of morality—useless luxury. Only one word—*benefit*—had remained from former glorious times, but it, too, acquired an indefinite meaning; everyone interpreted it in his own way.

"Soon discord arose within our main city. In its vicinity there were rich coalmines. The owners of these mines received great profit from them. But prolonged use and constant deepening caused water to accumulate in them.

Coalmining became difficult. The owners raised the price for coal. The rest of the inhabitants of the city could not afford to buy this indispensable material in sufficient quantities because of its high price. Winter came; the lack of coal made itself felt even more. Poor people resorted to the administration. The administration proposed means for drawing the water out of the mines, and thereby easing the mining of coal. The rich people objected, proving by irrefutable calculations that it was of greater profit for them to sell small quantities for high prices than to stop work in order to drain the mines. This started arguments which ended with a crowd of paupers, trembling with cold, rushing to the mines and taking possession of them, proving on their side, and also irrefutably, that it was much more profitable for them to take coal for nothing than to pay money for it.

"Similar phenomena were incessantly repeated. They occurred both in the city squares and in the homes, and created a strong feeling of unrest in all the city's inhabitants. Everybody saw common disaster—and no one knew how to avoid it. Finally, searching for the cause of their misfortune everywhere, they decided that the cause rested with the administration, because in its proclamations from time to time it reminded them of the necessity to help one another, to sacrifice their good for the common good. But all proclamations were already too late in coming; all concepts in society were confused; words had changed their meaning; the common good seemed already to be a dream; egoism was the only sacred law of life; madmen accused their administrators of the most horrible crime—of poetry.

" 'What do we need these philosophical interpretations of virtue, of self-sacrifice, of civic virtue for? What interest will they bring in? Help our real positive needs!' cried the unfortunate ones, without realizing that the real evil was in their own hearts. 'What do we need these men of learning and philosophers for?' said the merchants. 'Is it their business to govern the city? Our occupation is the real thing; we receive money, we pay, we buy products of land, we sell them, we contribute the really useful. We should be the administrators!' And everyone in whom there was the slightest spark of divine flame was driven out of the city as a harmful dreamer. Merchants became administrators and the administration turned into a company of shareholders. All big enterprises which were of no immediate profit, or the purpose of which was not clear to the limited, selfish view of the merchants, vanished. Political insight, wise foresight, attempts to improve manners and customs, everything that was not immediately directed to commerical aims—in a word, whatever could not bring in any profit—was called dreams. Financial feudalism triumphed. Sciences and arts were completely silent; no new discoveries, inventions, or improvements took place. The increased population demanded new industrial forces, but industry was dragging itself along the old beaten paths and did not meet the ever-increasing needs.

"Unexpected, destructive phenomena of nature confronted man: storms, pernicious winds, plague, and starvation. Humiliated man bent his head before them, and nature, untamed by his power, destroyed the fruit of his former efforts at one blast. Man's strength was dwindling. Ambitious plans, which could have increased trade activity in the future, but were at present dissipating the merchant-administrators' profits, were called prejudice. Deceit, forgery, intentional bankruptcies, total disdain of human dignity, idolatry of gold, satisfaction of the crudest bodily needs became an obvious, permissible, and indispensable matter. Religion became a completely foreign subject; morality was reduced to the proper balancing of accounts; intellectual occupations, to searching for means of deceit without any loss of credit; poetry, to the balancing of an account book; music, to the monotonous rattling of machines; painting, to the drawing of plans. There was nothing there to strengthen, stimulate, or comfort man; there was no place where he could forget himself for a moment. The secret sources of the spirit ran dry. People were thirsty, and they did not know what to call this thirst. The general suffering increased.

"At that time in the square of one of the cities of our state there appeared a pale man, his hair in disorder, wearing a funereal cloak. 'Woe,' he shouted covering his head with ashes. 'Woe to you, country of disgrace; you massacred your prophets, and your prophets became silent! Woe to you! Look, ominous clouds are already gathering high above in the sky. Do you not fear that heavenly flame may descend upon you and burn your settlements and fields? Do you think that your marble palaces, luxurious clothing, heaps of gold, crowds of slaves, your hypocrisy and fraud are going to save you? You have depraved your souls, you have sold your hearts and forgotten everything high and sacred; you have confused the meanings of words and named the good, gold, and gold, the good; fraud, intellect, and intellect, fraud; you have disdained love; you have disdained the science of the intellect and the science of the heart. Your palaces will collapse, your clothing will be rent, grass will cover your fields, and your name will be forgotten. I, the last of your prophets, implore you: abandon bribery and gold, lies and dishonor; bring back to life your thoughts of the mind and your feelings of the heart; bow your knees before the altar of unselfish love, not before the altars of idols. But I hear the voice of your callous heart; my words smite your ears in vain: you will not repent—I curse you!' With these words the prophet fell face down to the ground.

"Police drove off the crowd of curious people and brought the unfortunate man to an insane asylum. A few days later the inhabitants of our city were struck by a terrible thunderstorm. It seemed as if the entire sky was aflame; blue lightning tore the clouds apart; claps of thunder followed one another uninterruptedly; trees were uprooted; many buildings were ruined by thunderbolts. But there were no more accidents; only somewhat later we read in the *Price List*, the only newspaper we had, the following article:

"Soap market calm. Batch of cotton stockings at twenty per cent discount. Printed linen required.

"P.S. We hasten to inform our readers that the thunderstorm of two weeks ago caused terrible damage within a radius of a hundred miles from our city. Many cities were destroyed by lightning. To complete the disaster, a volcano developed in the neighboring mountain; its lava destroyed what was spared by the thunderstorm. Thousands of inhabitants lost their lives. Fortunately for the others the hardened lava proffered them a new source of industry. They break off the many-colored pieces of lava and use them in rings, earrings, and other jewelry. We advise our readers to take advantage of the unfortunate state of these manufacturers. Of necessity they sell their work almost for nothing, although it is well known that all articles made of lava can be resold with a great profit, etc. . . ."

Our stranger paused.

"What more can I tell you? Our artificial life, made up of mercantile operations, could not last long.

"Several centuries passed. Merchants were followed by craftsmen. 'Why,' they shouted, 'do we need these people who make use of our work and grow rich just sitting quietly at their desks? We work in the sweat of our brow; we know work; they could not exist without us. We are the ones who are of benefit to our city—we should be the administrators!' And everyone who had any general knowledge of matters within himself was driven out of the city; craftsmen became administrators, and the administration turned into a workshop. Trade activities disappeared; industrial products filled the markets, but there was no central market; means of communication came to a standstill owing to the ignorance of the administrators; the art of turning over capital became lost; money had become a rarity. Common suffering increased.

"Craftsmen were followed by farmers. 'Why,' they shouted, 'do we need people who are busy producing trifles and sitting in their warm homes, who eat up the bread which we provide in the sweat of our brows, day and night, out in the cold or heat? What would they do if we did not feed them through our work? We are contributing the essential benefit to the city; we know its first indispensable need—we should be the administrators.' And everyone whose hands were not used to the coarse work on land was driven out of the city.

"Similar events, with some variation, took place in other cities of our country as well. Those driven out of one place found a temporary abode in another; desperate want that grew worse and worse made them go and look for something new. Chased from one part of the country to another, they formed bands and provided for their livelihood by force of arms. Fields were trampled down by horses; harvests were devastated before they were ripe. Farmers, in self-protection from attacks, were forced to leave their work. Only a small part of the land was sown, and being cultivated amidst anxiety and disquiet, yielded only insignificant fruit. Left to its own resources, without any artificial aid, it became overgrown with weeds and brush, or was covered by sand. There was no one to tell them about the powerful aid of science which could have prevented the common disaster.

"Starvation, with all its horrors, spread over our country like stormy waters. Brother would kill brother with what was left of a plow, tearing the scarce food from his bloodstained hands. The magnificent buildings in our city had stood empty long since; useless ships were rotting in our harbor. It was strange and terrible to see, in front of the marble palaces which spoke of former grandeur, rude wild crowds arguing

in raging depravity about power, or about their daily suste-
nance. Earthquakes completed what was begun by people:
they overturned all the monuments of ancient times, covering
them with ashes; in time grass grew over them. Only one
square stone remained to sustain old memories, the stone on
which in olden days the statue of Bentham stood.

"Inhabitants retired into the woods where hunting beasts
enabled them to provide for their livelihood. Separated from
one another, families became savage; with every new generation part of the recollections of the past was lost. Finally, oh,
woe! I saw the last descendants of our glorious colony bending their knees in superstitious fear in front of the pedestal of
Bentham's statue, taking it for an ancient deity, and sacrificing to it prisoners they captured during their fight with other
tribes as savage as they. When I showed the ruins of their
fatherland to them and asked what people left these ruins,
they looked at me in surprise and did not understand my
question. Finally, the last men of our colony died of starvation and disease, or were killed by beasts. This lifeless stone
is all that has remained of the entire country, and I alone
weep over it and curse it. You, people of other countries, you,
worshipers of gold and flesh, tell the world the story of my
unfortunate country. . . . But now go away and let me weep."

Full of bitter grief the stranger grasped the square stone
and, seemingly with all his might, tried to throw it to the
ground. We went away.

When we came to another station we made an effort to
gather some more information about the hermit we had
talked to.

"Oh," answered the innkeeper, "we know him. Some time
ago he expressed his desire to preach during one of our meet-
ings. We were all very glad, particularly our wives, and we
went to listen to the preacher, thinking that he was a decent
person. But with his first words he began to scold us, trying
to prove that we were the most immoral people in the world,
that bankruptcy was the most dishonest thing, that a man
must not think constantly about the growth of his wealth,
that we were sure to die . . . and other similar reprehensible
things. Our pride could not tolerate such an insult to our national character, and we showed the orator the door. Apparently that stung him to the quick; he became insane, and
now he wanders from place to place, stops passersby and
preaches to them the excerpts of the sermon he had composed for us."

"Well, how did you like this story?" asked Faust, having finished the reading.

"I don't understand what these gentlemen wanted to prove by it," said Vecheslav.

"To prove? absolutely nothing! You know that during chemical experiments observers are accustomed to taking notes of everything they see during the progress of these experiments; without having anything in mind to prove as yet, they simply write down each fact, actual or delusive. . . ."

"But there is no fact here!" shouted Victor. "There never was such a fact. . . ."

FAUST: "For my seekers of the spirit the fact was a symbolic perception of the events in that epoch, which in the natural course of things must inevitably have occurred, if good Providence did not deprive people of the capacity *fully to implement* their ideas and if, for the happiness of mankind itself, each thought was stopped in the course of its development by some other thought, no matter how false or true, but one which, like a float, keeps a hook (by which someone makes fun of us) from sinking to the bottom and pulling out all the slime. However, despite all the hindrances which man encounters while developing an idea, one must admit that the bankers' feudalism in the West didn't quite follow the Benthamites' path, whereas on the other side of the globe there is a country which even seems to have gone beyond it. It is quite a usual thing for the people there to duel, not with words or swords, but simply with their *teeth*."

VECHESLAV: "Very well, but I don't see the purpose of all this. What did these gentlemen want to prove, or, if you wish, what did they observe? That material benefit alone can not be the goal of human society, nor serve as a basis for its laws. But I would like to know how they could exist without this benefit. According to their system one should not worry about firewood or cattle or clothing. . . ."

FAUST: "But who says we shouldn't? All that is very good and necessary! But that's not what matters, and the economists-materialists seek in vain to obscure this fact. I'll give you a not quite prepossessing example; but you, utilitarians, do not mind it; in your opinion every object has a right to exist because it does exist. The men who carry all sorts of rubbish and dirt out of the city do a very important

job: they save the city from unpleasant odors, from contagious diseases—without their help a city could not exist; no
doubt, they are very useful men, right?"

VICTOR: "Of course!"

FAUST: "But what if these people, proud of their stench-
filled work, were to demand the first place in a society and
were to consider it their right to decide its purpose and
activities?"

VICTOR: "That could never happen."

FAUST: "You are wrong; it obviously happens, although
in another sphere: the economists-utilitarians, preoccupied
solely with material control levers, also rummage only in the
rubbish which hides from them the real purpose and nature
of mankind, and because of their ill-smelling work, along
with bankers, tax farmers, stockjobbers, merchants, and others, they consider themselves rightly qualified to occupy the
first place among mankind, to prescribe laws for it and point
out its purpose. Land and sea, gold and ships of the entire
world are in their hands. They could apparently provide man
with everything; and yet man is not happy, his existence is
incomplete, his needs are not satisfied, and he looks for something that can't be entered in an account book.

VICTOR: "Shouldn't poets, then, be entrusted with this
matter?"

FAUST: "Poets have been banished from the city since Plato;
they are delighted with the wreaths that crown them. Sitting
on a hill and looking down at our city, they can only wonder
at the motion which sets in with the rising sun and dies with
the sunset; sometimes they reread the speeches of clever
Burke about the welfare of India under the rule of a business
company, which, as the famous speaker put it, 'coined money
from human flesh.' "[3]

VICTOR: "Then why don't you invent new laws of political
economy, gentlemen, and see if they work?"

FAUST: "Invent! Invent laws! I don't know, gentlemen, why
such a thing seems possible to you. I find it quite incomprehensible that there should be a being sent by someone to live
in this world with the mission of inventing laws for this world
and for himself, since one would have to conclude therefrom
that that world has no laws for its existence; that is, it exists
without existing. I think that each world must have its laws
quite ready; one has only to find them. Actually, this is not

[3] See Burke's speeches at the beginning of 1788.

my business. I am like the scholar mentioned by Rostislav: I note only what other people say, without saying anything myself. However, it seems to me that precisely the less tangible, or less useful, plays the greatest role in the world. Read in Carus[4] the interesting proofs of the fact that all solid matter, like muscles and bones, is the product of liquid matter; in other words, it is the remnant of an already processed organism. Apparently one can notice this gradual development even in nature. The lower we descend along its levels, the less cohesion, strength, and power we find in objects, despite their external density; if you crush a rock, it will remain crushed; if you cut a tree, it will grow over; an animal's wound is curable. The higher you move into the sphere of objects, the more power you detect in them. Water is weaker than stone, steam seems to be weaker than water, gas weaker than steam, and yet the power of these agents increases with their seeming weakness. Moving still higher, we encounter electricity, magnetism, which are intangible, incalculable, and of no immediate use, and yet they move the entire physical nature and keep it in harmony. It seems to me that this is quite a hint for economists. But it is already late, gentlemen, or, as Shakespeare put it, 'the dawn grows apace.' Tomorrow I'll show you the notes of our adventurers about the strange symbols called poets, artists, and so on, in this world."

"One more word," said Victor. "You gentlemen the ideologists, flying high up in the skies, like to order us about, who are but poor mortals digging in rubbish, as you put it. Can't you be less pronounced about it? Let Malthus be—God be with him—but Adam Smith, the great Adam Smith, the father of the entire political economy of our time, who founded the school made famous by the names of Say, Ricardo, Sismondi! Isn't it too harsh to accuse him of obvious absurdity, and with him two whole generations? Has mankind then turned so blind that for half a century no one has noticed this absurdity?"

[4] See Carus, *Grundzüge d. vergl. Anatomie.* This famous book, which caused a change in the concepts of the organism, is known to every natural scientist; we recommend it, along with another book by the same author: *System der Physiologie* (Dresden, 1839), to poets and artists, the more so since these books combine a profound positive knowledge with the poetic element owing to which Carus was able to unite within himself the qualities of a great physiologist, an experienced doctor, an orginal painter and a writer.

FAUST: "No one? No, I follow Goethe's advice:[5] when I praise, I do so without a twinge of conscience, but when I am forced to reproach someone, I always try to support my opinion by some important authority. At the beginning of our century there lived a man named Melchiorre Gioia, mentioned by English and French economists in their histories of the science, to ease their conscience, although none of them, probably, was patient enough to read the half-dozen quarto volumes written by the humble Melchiorre—this marvelous achievement of profound thought and learning. In 1816 he added to his book[6] an appendix which he ironically called 'The Present State of Science.' In this, he gathered various so-called axioms of political economy by Adam Smith and his followers. It shows clearly that these gentlemen simply didn't understand themselves, despite a deceitful clarity which they were after. Thus, for instance, the great Adam Smith is trying to prove that work is a primary and not a primary source of national wealth;[7] that the perfection of industry is completely dependent and does not depend at all on the division of labor;[8] that division of labor is and is not the main cause of national wealth;[9] that division of labor incites and does not incite a spirit of inventiveness;[10] that agricultural industry depends and does not depend on other branches of industry;[11] that agriculture is and is not of greatest profit for capital;[12] that intellectual work is and is not a productive power, that is, the power which multiplies national wealth;[13] that private interest sees the advantages of a society better and worse than someone in the government;[14] that private profits of

---

[5] *Wilhelm Meisters Wanderjahre.*

[6] See *Nuovo prospetto delle scienze economiche,* 6 vols. in quarto, Milano, 1816. Tomo V. Parte sesta, p. 223, "Stato della scienza."

[7] Adam Smith (French ed., 1802) T. I., p. 5, and T. IV, p. 507.

[8] *Ibid.,* T. I, pp. 11, 17-18; T. II, pp. 215-216; T. III, p. 543.

[9] *Ibid.,* T. I, pp. 24-25, 29, 262-264; T. II, pp. 193, 210, 326, 370; T. III, p. 323.

[10] *Ibid.,* T. I, pp. 21-22; T. IV, pp. 181-183.

[11] *Ibid.,* T. II, pp. 408, 409-410.

[12] *Ibid.,* T. I, pp. 260-261; T. II, pp. 376-378, 401-402, 407, 481, 483, 485, 486, 487, 413, 498.

[13] *Ibid.,* T. I, pp. 213-214, 223, 262-265; and T. II, pp. 204-205, 312-313.

[14] *Ibid.,* T. I, pp. 219-227; T. II, pp. 161, 248, 249, 423-424; T. III, pp. 60, 223, 492; T. V, p. 524.

merchants are closely connected and not at all connected with the profits of other members of a society.[15]

"It seems that this should do? I took examples from the appendix at random. But this concerns the most important axioms of the science. Adam Smith's success was quite understandable; his main purpose was to prove that no one should interfere with mercantile affairs, but that they should be allowed to follow the so-called *natural course* and to practice noble competition. You can imagine the delight of English merchants when they learned that from a professor's chair they were given the right to speculate, to farm, to raise and lower prices as they pleased, and, using a cunning trick without any further effort, to gain a hundredfold—that doing all this 'they are not only right, but almost holy. . . .' "[16]

"From that time on, such sonorous words as 'extension of trade,' 'importance of trade,' 'freedom of trade,' became fashionable. With the help of the last phrase, Adam Smith's theory penetrated into France and, solely owing to the harmony of words, their meaning (if there is one) became an axiom there: Adam Smith was recognized as both a profound philosopher and a benefactor of mankind; afterward few read him and none understood what he wanted to say; but despite that, out of the obscure, complicated labyrinth of his thoughts, poured many beliefs, unfounded, useless, but such as flattered the lowest passions of man, and therefore spread among the crowd unusually quickly. Thus, thanks to Adam Smith and to his followers, *soundness, business* now mean only that which can promote mercantile turnover. Only that man is called sound and able who knows how to increase his profits; while under the obscure expression *natural flow of business*, which should on no account be violated, are understood such things as banking operations, money feudalism, stockjobbery, stock gambling, and similar matters."

"Consequently," noted Victor, "in your opinion political economy does not exist?"

"No!" answered Faust. "It exists; it is the first of the sciences. In it, perhaps, all sciences will have to find their tangible support, but only—I'll say it to you in Gogol's words, it exists—*from the opposite side.*"

[15] *Ibid.*, T. II, pp. 161, 164, 165; T. III, pp. 54-55, 59, 145, 208-209, 239, 295, 435, 465.
[16] Krylov.

THE SIXTH NIGHT

"Tell me," said Rostislav, as he came to Faust at the usual time of their discussions, "Why do you and all of us like to stay up late at night? Why is it that at night our concentration is more constant, thoughts are livelier, and our souls are more talkative?"

"It's easy to answer that question," said Vyacheslav. "General silence involuntarily disposes man to meditation."

ROSTISLAV: "General silence? Here? Where the real traffic in our city begins only by ten o'clock at night? And what sort of meditation is it? People simply congregate for some reason; that's why all gatherings, discussions, balls take place at night; it is as if man instinctively puts off his joining others till night. But why so?"

VICTOR: "It seems to me that that can be explained by a physiological phenomenon: it is well known that around midnight a sort of fever takes place in an organism—and in this state all nerves are excited, and what we take for liveliness of mind, talkativeness, is nothing but a result of our sickly state, a sort of delirium."

ROSTISLAV: "But you haven't answered my question: Why does this sickly state, as you say, make people congregate?"

FAUST: "If I were a scholar I would say to you, with Schelling, that from time immemorial night has been considered the oldest of beings and that it was not for nothing that our ancestors, the Slavs, figured time by nights.[1] If I were a mystic I would explain this phenomenon to you quite simply. You see, night is the domain of a power hostile to man; people feel it, and in order to escape their enemy they unite, they look for support in one another: that's why people are more fearful at night; that's why ghost stories, stories about evil spirits produce a stronger impression on them than in the daytime."

[1] See Schelling's small yet amazing work in its depth and scholarship, *Uber die Gottheiten von Samothrace* (Stuttgart, 1815), p. 12.

"And that's why people," added Vyacheslav laughing, "try very hard to kill the hostile power by playing cards; and Carsel's lamp chases away goblins."

"You won't stop mystics with this mockery," said Faust. "They will reply to you that the hostile power has two profound and clever ideas: the first—it tries to convince man with all its might that it does not exist, and therefore it suggests to him every possible means of forgetting it; and the second—to equalize people as much as possible, to unite them so that not one head, not one heart should stand out; cards are one of the means the hostile power employs to achieve this double purpose. First, while playing cards one can't think of anything else but cards, and second, all are made equal during a card game: both the superior and his subordinate, handsome and ugly-looking man, a scholar and an ignoramus, a genius and a cipher, an intelligent man and a fool; there is no distinction betweeen them: the worst fool can win from the greatest philosopher on earth, and a minor employee from a great nobleman. Imagine to yourself the delight of some cipher when he can win from Newton, or say to Leibnitz: 'But, sir, you don't know how to play; you, Mr. Leibnitz, don't know how to hold cards!' That's Jacobinism at its height. Meanwhile, the hostile power profits also from the fact that during a card game, under the cover of an innocent entertainment, almost all vices of man are encouraged secretly: envy, anger, self-interest, vengeance, cunning, deceit —everything on a small scale; nevertheless, one's soul gets to know them, and that is of great advantage to the hostile power."

"Well, can't we do without mysticism?" Vyacheslav finally interjected, losing his patience.

"I'll spare you gladly," answered Faust.

"And yet my question has remained unanswered," Rostislav noted.

FAUST: "You know my unalterable conviction that man, even if he can answer some question, can never translate it correctly into ordinary language. In cases like that I always look for some object in external nature which, by analogy, could serve at least as an approximate expression of the thought. Have you ever noticed that long before sunset, especially in our northern skies, down at the horizon, behind distant clouds, a crimson strip unlike an evening glow appears, while the sun is still shining in all its brightness? That is part of dawn to people in the other hemisphere. Consequently, each minute there is dawn upon the earth and each minute a part of its inhabitants, like an ordinary sentry, rises to its post. Providence arranged it so purposely: perhaps this phenomenon tells us clearly that nature may not take advantage of man's sleep for a moment, since all nature's harmful influence upon man's organism really increases at night: plants do not purify the air but spoil it; dew assumes harmful properties; an experienced doctor watches over his patient predominantly at night, when any disease becomes worse. Maybe we should follow the doctor's example and observe our diseased soul, as he observes a diseased body, just at the moment when the organism undergoes harmful influences most of all. The sun is more favorable to man: it is the symbol of some sort of preference shown to him; it disperses harmful mists; it makes coarse plants process the living part of the air for man.[2] He invigorates man's heart, and perhaps that is why his sleep is so sweet at sunrise: he feels the symbol of his ally and peacefully falls asleep under his warm and light cover."

VICTOR: "Oh, you dreamer! Facts are nothing to you. Doesn't man suffer from the sun's heat, like all plants?"

FAUST: "I assure you that my facts are more reliable than yours, perhaps because they are less tangible. Yes, the sun's heat is unbearable for man! But this fact contains another, namely, that the sun does not affect us directly but through the coarse atmosphere of the earth. Aeronauts did not feel the heat when they rose into the upper layers of the air. To me this is an important proof: the higher we are from the earth, the less we are affected by its nature."

VICTOR: "That's completely true, and here is another proof: beyond a certain limit of the atmosphere, blood came out of the aeronauts' ears; it became difficult for them to breathe; and they shivered from cold."

ROSTISLAV: "This fact, it seems to me, expresses the real and difficult problem of man: to rise from the earth, without leaving it."

VYACHESLAV: "That is, in other words, one must seek for the possible—and not chase in vain after the impossible."

Faust answered nothing but changed the subject.

"We won't be able to outargue one another till dawn," he said, "but, although you are my friends, I will not let you

[2] It is known that the green parts of plants exhale oxygen, but only under the light of the sun.

deprive me of my sweet morning sleep for anything. Should we proceed with the manuscript? After all, we must finish it."

Faust began: "In the numbered order *The Economist* is followed by *Beethoven's Last Quartet*:

BEETHOVEN'S LAST QUARTET

I was convinced that Krespel had become insane. The professor maintained the contrary. "Nature and special circumstances," he said, "have removed from some people the mask behind which we indulge in all kinds of absurdities. They are like insects whose tissue an anatomist removes, thereby revealing the movement of their muscles." Krespel puts into action what we merely think.

HOFFMANN

In the spring of 1827, in one of the houses on the outskirts of Vienna, a few music lovers were practicing Beethoven's new quartet that had just been published. With amazement and annoyance they followed the formless outbursts of the enfeebled genius: his idiom had changed so much! Gone was the charm of an original melody, full of poetic concepts; the artistic touch had been replaced by the painstaking pedantry of an inept counterpointist; the fire that formerly blazed up in his fast allegros and, gradually growing, poured out like burning lava in full, great harmonies had died down amidst incomprehensible dissonances; the original, humorous themes of the gay minuet had changed into leaps and trills impossible on any instrument. Everywhere there were immature, vain attempts to create effects that do not exist in music. Yet that was the same Beethoven, the one whose name, along with the names of Haydn and Mozart, the Teuton utters full of rapture and pride! Often led to despair by the absurdity of the piece, the musicians would throw down their bows and were on the point of asking if this was not a mockery of the creations of the immortal one? Some ascribed the decline to his loss of hearing, which had afflicted him in the last years of his life; others, to his insanity, which sometimes overshadowed his creative talent; some expressed false regrets, and a scoffer remembered an incident during the concert when Beethoven's last symphony was performed, when he waved his hands completely off beat, as if he were conducting the orchestra, without even noticing that the real con-

ductor was standing behind him. But soon they would pick
up their bows again, and out of respect for the former glory
of the famous creator of symphonies, and as if against their
own will, they continued playing his incomprehensible work.

Suddenly the door opened and in came a man in a black
suit, without a tie, his hair tousled; his eyes were aflame—but
this was not the flame of a genius; only the low-hanging,
sharply cut extremities of his forehead showed an unusual
development of the musical organ, which once so delighted
Hall, when he examined Mozart's head.

"Pardon me, gentlemen," said the unexpected guest, "allow
me to have a look at your apartment . . . it is for rent. . . ."

Then, with his hands folded behind his back, he approached the musicians. He was offered a seat respectfully;
he sat there, inclining his head now to one side, now to the
other, trying to hear the music, but in vain, and tears came
streaming from his eyes. Quietly he left the performers and
took a seat in a remote corner of the room, covering his face
with his hands. But no sooner had the bow of the first violinist sounded upon touching the string near the bridge while
playing an incidental note added to the seventh, and a wild
harmony resounded in the doubled notes of the other instruments, than the poor man started and shouted: "I can hear! I
can hear!"—and wild with joy he began clapping his hands
and stamping his feet.

"Ludwig!" said the young girl, who had followed him into
the room. "Ludwig! It's time to go home. We are in the way
here!"

He glanced at the girl, understood her, and followed her
without a word, like a child.

On the outskirts of the city, on the fourth floor of an old
house, there is a little stuffy room, divided by a partition. Its
only adornments are a bed covered by a torn blanket, several
rolls of music paper, and the remnants of a piano. This was
the abode, this was the world, of the immortal Beethoven. He
did not utter a word all the way. But when they reached the
room, Ludwig sat down on his bed, took the girl's hand into
his, and said:

"My kind Louise! Only you understand me; only you are
not afraid of me; you are the only one I don't disturb. . . . Do
you think that all these gentlemen who play my music understand me? Nothing of the sort! Not one of the local conductors even knows how to conduct it; all they care for is that
the orchestra plays in time; music doesn't concern them!

They think I'm growing weak. I even noticed that some of them seemed to smile while playing my quartet; that's a true sign that they never understood me. On the contrary, I have only now become a true and great musician. On the way home, I conceived a symphony that will immortalize my name; I'll write it and burn all the former ones. In it I'll change all the laws of harmony; I'll find effects no one has suspected until now. I'll build it on a chromatic melody and use twenty kettledrums; into it I'll introduce hundreds of chimes tuned to various pitches, because," he added in a whisper, "I'll tell you a secret: when you took me to the belfry, I discovered that chimes are the most harmonious instrument, and can be used successfully in a quiet *adagio*. Into the finale I'll introduce drumbeats and gunshots—and I will hear this symphony, Louise!" he shouted, beside himself with rapture. "I hope I'll hear it," he added, smiling after a moment's reflection. "Do you remember, in Vienna, in the presence of all the crowned heads of the world, I conducted the orchestra in my "Battle of Waterloo"? Thousands of musicians, obeying the wave of my hand, twelve conductors, and all around, the gunfire and cannon shots. . . . Oh! that's my best work to date, despite that pedant Weber.[3] But what I am going to create now will overshadow even that work. I cannot refrain from giving you an idea of it."

With these words Beethoven went up to the piano, which did not have a single string intact, and with an air of dignity began playing on the dead keys. They hit the dry wood of the broken instrument monotonously, while the most elaborate fugues in five and six voices passed through all the mysteries of counterpoint, obediently, and as if on their own, taking shape under the fingers of the creator of the music to *Egmont*, and he himself tried to give his music as much expression as he could. . . . Suddenly, powerfully, he struck the keys with his whole hand, and stopped.

"Do you hear?" he asked Louise. "Here is a chord no one has dared to use until now. That's it! I shall combine all the tones of the chromatic scale in one chord and I shall prove to the pedants that this chord is correct. But I don't hear it, Louise; I don't hear it! Do you understand what it means not

[3] Gottfried Weber, the well-known contrapuntist of our time, who should not be mistaken for the composer of *Freischütz*, quite strongly and justly criticized *Wellington's Victory*, the weakest of Beethoven's compositions, in his interesting and scholarly journal *Cecilia*.

to hear one's own music? And yet, when I gather all the wild sounds into one chord, it seems to me as if they do resound in my ear. And the more depressed I feel, Louise, the more notes I want to add to a seventh, the true essence of which no one has perceived before me. . . . But enough of that! Maybe I have bored you as I have bored everybody else? Now, do you know what? For such a wonderful invention I should reward myself today with a glass of wine. How do you like the idea, Louise?"

Tears came to the eyes of the poor girl, who alone of all Beethoven's pupils did not leave him and who provided for his livelihood by the work of her hands, under the pretext of taking lessons with him. She added to the scanty income Beethoven received for his works, most of which had been spent senselessly, moving from one apartment to another, and giving money away to anyone who cared to ask for it. There was no wine! There were barely a few pennies left for bread. . . . But, turning her head away from Ludwig, so as to hide her confusion, she poured a glass of water and gave it to Beethoven.

"What an excellent Rhine wine!" he said, sipping from the glass with the air of a connoisseur, "A regal Rhine wine! Just like the one from the wine cellar of my late father Frederick, God bless his soul. I remember this wine very well. It improves from day to day, as a good wine should!" And with these words, in a hoarse but firm voice, he began to sing his music to the famous song of Goethe's Mephistopheles:

"Es war einmal ein König
Der hatt eine grosse Floh,"

but involuntarily he kept changing it to the mysterious melody by which Beethoven explained Mignon.[4]

"Listen, Louise," he said finally, returning the glass to her, "the wine has given me strength now, and I intend to tell you something which, for a very long time, I've been of two minds about telling you. You know, it seems to me that I won't live long now—and what kind of life do I lead? It is a chain of infinite torments. In the earliest days of my youth, I became aware of the abyss that separated thought from expression. Alas, I was never able to express my soul; I was never able to put on paper what my imagination told me. I wrote, people played it—it was never the same! . . . It was not only not what I had been feeling; it was not even what I had

[4] Kennst du das Land, etc. . . . (Knowest thou the land, etc.).

written. Here, a melody was lost because it had not occurred to a lowly craftsman to put in an extra valve; there, an intolerable bassoonist made me rewrite a whole symphony because his bassoon couldn't play a couple of bass notes; there, the violinist did away with a necessary sound in the chord because it was difficult for him to take double stops. And the voices, the singing, the rehearsals of oratorios, of operas? . . . Oh, that inferno! It still sounds in my ears! But I was still happy then. Sometimes I would see the insensible musicians become inspired; I would hear in their sounds something like a dark thought that had sunk in my imagination: then I would be beside myself, dissolved in the harmony I myself had created. But the time came when my sensitive ear gradually became coarse: it was still sensitive enough to hear the mistakes musicians made, but it was closed to beauty, a dark cloud enveloped it—and now I can't hear my works anymore, I can't hear them, Louise! . . . Whole series of harmonic chords float in my imagination; original melodies cross each other, fusing in a mysterious unity; I want to express it, but everything disappears: stubborn reality won't emit a single sound for me—coarse feelings destroy all my soul's activity. Oh, what can be more horrible than this strife between the soul and feelings, between soul and soul? To engender an artistic creation in your mind and to die hourly in the torments of giving birth! . . . This is the death of a soul! How terrible, how full of life is this death!

"And what's more, this insensate Gottfried involves me in these senseless musical arguments, compels me to explain why I used such and such a combination of melodies, or such and such a combination of instruments in one place or another, when I cannot explain it even to myself! As if these people knew what the soul of a musician is, what the soul of a man is! They think one can pattern it as a craftsman patterns his instruments, all according to the rules invented at his leisure by the dried-out brain of a theoretician. . . . No, when the moment of rapture overcomes me, I become convinced that art can no longer remain in such a false state; that new, fresh forms will take the place of decayed ones; that all the present instruments will be abandoned and will be replaced by others which will perform the works of talented men perfectly; that the absurd disparity between written music and the music heard will finally disappear.

"I spoke to our gentlemen the professors about it, but they did not understand me, as they did not understand the power of rapture given to the artist, as they did not understand that I am forestalling time and acting in accordance with laws of nature as yet unnoticed by ordinary men and at times incomprehensible even to myself. . . . Fools! In their cold rapture, in their moments of leisure, they choose a theme; they develop and expand it and do not even fail to repeat it in another key; or in someplace they indicate wind instruments, or some strange chord over which they ponder again and again, and they polish and refine it all so sensibly. What do they want? I can't work that way. . . . They compare me to Michelangelo—but how did the creator of 'Moses' work? In anger, in rage, with powerful strokes of his hammer he hit the motionless marble and made it impart a living idea, hidden beneath the stone. This is how I work too! I do not understand cold rapture! I understand only the kind of rapture when the whole world turns into harmony for me, when every feeling, every thought sounds within me; when all the forces of nature become my instruments; when blood boils in my veins, my body shivers, and my hair stands on end. . . . And all is in vain! And what is the sense of it all? What is the purpose? You live, you suffer, you think; you write it down— and that's the end of it: the sweet agonies of creation are chained to the sheet of paper—you can't make them come back! The thoughts of a proud creative spirit are humiliated and imprisoned, the lofty effort of the earthly creator, challenging the force of nature, becomes the work of human hands! And people! They come, they listen—as if they were judges, as if you had been creating for them! What do they care that a thought which has assumed an image understandable to them is only a link in the infinite chain of thoughts and sufferings, that the moment when the artist descends to the level of man is only a fragment of the long and painful life of immeasurable feeling; that each of his expressions, each line was born out of the bitter tears of a Seraph who is imprisoned in human flesh and who would give half of his life for a moment of the fresh air of inspiration? And then the time comes, as it did just now, when you feel that your soul has burnt out, your forces have weakened, your head is in pain; your thoughts become confused and everything is covered with a veil. . . . Oh, Louise, I wish I could reveal to you my last thoughts and feelings, which I keep and guard in the treasury of my soul. . . . But, what do I hear?"

With these words Beethoven jumped up and with a powerful blow of his hand opened the window, through which harmonious sounds were floating in from the neighboring house. . . .

"I hear!" shouted Beethoven, throwing himself on his knees, full of tender emotion, stretching his hands toward the open window. "This is Egmont's symphony—yes, I recognize it: here are the wild battlecries, here the storm of passions; they flare up, they seethe; here they are at their fullest—and everything is quiet again; only the vigil light is left gleaming, but it is dimming, dying, but not forever. . . . Trumpets sound again: they fill the entire world, and no one can silence them. . . .

Crowds of people were coming and going at a splendid ball given by one of the ministers in Vienna.

"What a pity!" someone said. "The theater conductor Beethoven has died, and they say that there is no money for his burial."

But the voice was lost in the crowd: everyone was listening attentively to the words of two diplomats discussing an argument that had taken place between some people at the court of a German prince.

"I should like to know," said Victor, "to what extent this anecdote is true."

"I cannot give you a satisfactory answer to that," said Faust, "and the owners of the manuscript would hardly have been able to answer your question because, it seems to me, they weren't acquainted with the methods of those historians who read only what is written in a biography and refuse to read what is not written in it. Apparently they reasoned thus: If this anecdote was really true, all the better; if it was invented by someone, it means that it happened in the heart of the writer; consequently, this event *was*, although it didn't *happen*. Such a view may seem strange, but in this case my friends seem to have followed the example of mathematicians, who in higher calculations do not worry whether 2 and 3 or 4 and 10 were ever united in nature, but daringly conceive the equation $a + b$ as all possible combinations of numbers. However, constant moving from place to place, deafness, a kind of madness, constant dissatisfaction—all these belonged to the so-called historical facts of Beethoven's life; except that honest writers of biographical articles, for lack of documents, didn't undertake to explain the connection be-

tween his deafness and madness, between his madness and
dissatisfaction, between his dissatisfaction and his music."

VYACHESLAV: "What need had they! Whether a fact is true
or false, for me it expresses, as Rostislav said, my constant
conviction, which I mentioned at the beginning of the evening, namely: man should limit himself to the possible, or, as
Voltaire said in his answer to a moral axiom: *Cela est bien
dit; mais il faut cultiver notre jardin.*"[5]

FAUST: "That means that Voltaire didn't even believe what
he wanted to believe."

ROSTISLAV: "One thing struck me in this anecdote—the inexpressibility of our sufferings. Indeed, the most cruel, the
clearest torments for us are those we cannot communicate.
Whoever is capable of communicating his sufferings has already halfway rid himself of them."

VICTOR: "You, my dreamer friends, have thought of a nice
trick: in order to get rid of positive questions you tried to
convince us that human language is inadequate to express our
thoughts and feelings. It seems to me that it is rather our
knowledge that is inadequate. If man were to devote himself
to pure, simple observation of coarse nature, which you try
to keep in the background—but, please note, to *pure* observation, eliminating all his own thoughts and feelings, every internal operation—then he would be able to understand both
himself and nature much more clearly and he would find
enough expressions for himself even in an ordinary language."

FAUST: "I don't know if this so-called pure observation
doesn't contain an optical illusion; I don't know if man can
completely separate from himself all *his own* thoughts and
feelings, all his own *recollections*, so that nothing of his *I*
would enter his observations; the very thought of observing
without thinking is in itself a theory *a priori.* . . . But we have
strayed from Beethoven. No one's music impresses me so
much as Beethoven's. It seems to touch every string of the
heart; it raises in it all the forgotten, most secret sufferings
and gives them shape; Beethoven's joyful themes are even
more horrible; in them someone seems to laugh—out of despair. It is a strange thing: any other music, particularly that
of Haydn, creates a pleasant, soothing impression in me. The
effect Beethoven's music has is much stronger, but it disturbs
you: through its wonderful harmony you hear some inhar-
monious cry. You listen to a symphony of his, and you are

[5] *Candide.*

enraptured—yet your soul languishes. I'm sure that Beethoven's music must have been a torment to himself.

"Once, at a time when I did not yet have any idea of the composer's life, I told a passionate admirer of Haydn about this strange effect Beethoven's music had upon me. 'I understand you,' replied the Haydnist. 'The reason for this effect is the reason why Beethoven, despite his musical genius (perhaps a higher genius than Haydn's), was never able to write spiritual music that would come close to the oratorios of the latter.' 'Why so?' I asked. 'Because,' answered the Haydnist, 'Beethoven did not believe in what Haydn believed.' "

VICTOR: "So! I expected that! Yes, tell me, gentlemen, what pleasure do you find in mixing things that have nothing in common? How can man's convictions influence music, poetry, science? It is difficult to speak about such subjects, but it seems obvious to me that if something extraneous can effect aesthetic works, then it is perhaps only the degree of knowledge. Knowledge, obviously, may extend the circle of the artist's vision; he must feel roomier within it. But how he came to this knowledge, in what way, dark or light, doesn't concern poetry. Recently someone had the happy idea of making up a new science—physical philosophy or philosophical physics—the purpose of which would be *to affect morality by means of knowledge*[6]—this, in my opinion, is one of the most useful undertakings of our time."

FAUST: "I know that this opinion is now triumphing. But, tell me, why wouldn't anyone ask a doctor who is known to be an inveterate atheist to the bedside of a sick man? What does there seem to be in common between a medical formula and a man's convictions? I agree with you in one thing: in the necessity of knowledge. Thus, for example, contrary to general opinion, I am convinced that a poet needs physical sciences; it is useful for him to descend sometimes to external nature, if only to convince himself of the superiority of his inner nature, and also to see that, to man's shame, letters in the book of nature are not as changeable and vague as in a human language. Letters there are constant, *stereotyped*. A poet can read in them much of what is important, but to do this he has to make sure he has good *glasses*. . . . However, my friends, sunrise is near. 'It's time for us to calm down, dear Eunom,' as Paracelsus says in one of his forgotten folios."

[6] In this spirit the journal *l'Educateur* by Mr. Rocour was published.

THE SEVENTH NIGHT

THE IMPROVVISATORE

Es möchte kein Hund so länger leven,
D'rum hab' ich mich der Magie ergeban. . . .
—Goethe

Loud applause resounded in the hall. The improvvisatore's success surpassed the expectations of the audience and his own expectations. No sooner was a topic suggested to him than lofty thoughts and tender feelings, decked in sonorous meters, poured from his lips, like phantasmagoric visions from a magic sacrificial vessel. The artist did not reflect even for a moment: in the same instant an idea was conceived in his mind and went through all the stages of its development and was transformed into expression. The intricate form of a piece, poetic images, elegant epithets, obedient rhymes, appeared at one stroke. Yet this was not all: two or three topics completely different in character were suggested to him at the same time. He dictated one poem, wrote another one, improvised a third, and each was exquisite in its own way: one brought about rapture, another moved you to tears, the third made you split your sides with laughter. And yet he gave the impression of being unconcerned with his work; he constantly joked and talked to his audience. All the elements of poetic creation were at his fingertips, like figures on a chessboard which he carelessly manipulated as needed.

Finally the attention and amazement of the audience was exhausted; they suffered for the improvvisatore. But the artist himself was quiet and cold—there was not a trace of fatigue in him. His face, however, did not reflect the lofty enjoyment of a poet, satisfied with his creation, but rather the simple, self-satisfied look of a juggler surprising the crowd with his skill. Full of mockery he watched the tears, the laughter he had produced; he alone of all those present neither cried nor laughed; he alone did not believe his words, and treated his inspiration as an indifferent priest, long accustomed to the mysteries of his temple.

The last of his audience had not yet left when the improvvisatore rushed to the man collecting the entrance fee, and began counting it with the greediness of Harpagon. The take was very large. The improvvisatore had not seen so much money in all his life, and was beside himself with joy.

His delight was pardonable. From his youth cruel poverty had pressed him in its icy embrace, like the statue of a Spartan tyrant. Not the songs of his mother but her painful moans lulled the child into his sleep. With the dawn of his understanding, life did not appear to him in its irridescent dress; instead, the cold skeleton of indigence greeted his developing imagination with a fixed smile. Nature was a little more generous to him than fate. True, she endowed him with a gift for creating, but condemned him to search for the expression of his poetic ideas in the sweat of his brow. Booksellers and journalists paid him some money for his verses, which would have been enough for his living if Cypriano had not been forced to spend an endless amount of time creating each poem. Back in those days, a dim thought, like a barely visible star, was rarely conceived in his imagination, but even when it was born it brightened slowly, and was lost in a mist for a long time. Only through immense effort would it assume some hazy shape. At this point a new stage of work would begin: myriad worlds separated the poet from expression; he could not find words, and those that he did find would not coalesce; the meter was not pliable; an importunate pronoun would appear; a lanky verb would spring up between nouns; a cursed rhyme would hide between dissonant words. Each verse cost the poor poet several gnawed pens, torn hair, and broken fingernails. His efforts were in vain! Often he wanted to exchange versifying for the lowest of trades; but scoffing nature, along with the gift for creating, had also endowed him with all the whims of a poet: innate passion for independence, insurmountable disgust for any kind of mechanical occupation, the habit of waiting for a moment of inspiration, the carefree inability to schedule his time. To this you may add all the irritability of a poet, his inclination toward luxury, toward easy comfort, to the petty tyranny toward all those things by means of which nature likes to distinguish its own aristocrat, in spite of society! He was unable either to translate or to work to meet a deadline. Thus, while fellow poets collected good money from the public for some works which happened to excite its curiosity, he couldn't even make up his mind to sit down to work. Booksellers stopped placing orders with him; none of the journalists wanted him as a co-worker. The money the unfortunate man received for some poem that had cost him half a year's work was usually snatched away by his creditors, and again he was in utter need.

In that city there lived a doctor by the name of Segeliel. Thirty years ago he was known to many as a man of great knowledge; but he was poor then, and his practice was so insignificant that he decided to quit medicine and go into business. He traveled much—in India, it was said—and finally returned to his native land with gold bars and a heap of precious stones. He built a huge house with an extensive garden and hired numerous servants. People were amazed to see that neither the years nor extended travels in a hot climate had brought about any change in him. On the contrary, he seemed to be younger, healthier, fresher than before. The fact that plants of all climates took root in his park, although no one tended them, seemed no less surprising. Yet there was nothing unusual in Segeliel: he was a handsome, dignified man, well behaved, with black, fashionable whiskers; he wore loose but dandyish clothing; he entertained the best society at his house, but he would almost never leave his huge park himself; he lent money to young people without asking that it be returned; he had an excellent cook, wonderful wines; he liked to spend a long time over dinner, to retire early and to rise late. In short, he lived in the most aristocratic, luxurious idleness.

Meanwhile, he did not abandon his medical art, although he would set to it unwillingly, like a person who did not like to disturb himself. But once he set to it, he performed miracles. No matter what the disease, whether it was a mortal would or the last feverish convulsion—Segeliel would not even go to look at the sick person: he would ask the relatives a question or two; as a matter of form, he would get some water from a well and order his patient to take it—and the disease would disappear the very next day. He did not charge for his services, and his unselfishness, together with his miraculous art, could have brought him all the sick people of the world if it were not for the most peculiar conditions he set as a price for healing. For example, he would demand that respect be paid to him in a manner abjectly humiliating to the other person; he would ask that some disgusting deed be performed, such as throwing a large amount of money into the sea or destroying one's own house or leaving one's native country, and so on. There were even rumors that sometimes he would ask a price so infamous that virtuous tradition has not preserved any information about it. These rumors cooled the zeal of relatives, and for some time no one sought his favor. People also noticed that when someone did not agree to the doctor's conditions, the patient would invariably die. The same fate overtook anyone who said anything against him or who was simply not to his liking. Of course, Dr. Segeliel made many enemies, and some began to seek the source of his incredible wealth. Physicians and druggists said that he had no right to cure by diabolical methods. Many accused him of the greatest immorality, and some even of poisoning persons who subsequently died. The outcry of the people finally forced the police to summon Dr. Segeliel for questioning. A thorough search was made in his house. His servants were taken away from him. Dr. Segeliel submitted to everything without resistance, and permitted the police to do whatever they wished. He interfered with nothing, hardly deigning to glance at them, and merely smiled contemptuously from time to time.

Indeed, they found nothing in his house except golden dishes, censers, costly furniture, chairs with pillows and springs, extension tables with all kinds of fancy gadgets, several beds supported by musical sounding boards and with aromatic fragrance floating around them, like the beds of Dr. Grem, for which the latter used to charge English voluptuaries hundreds of pounds per night. In a word, in Segeliel's house they found only the inventions of a wealthy man who liked sensual enjoyments, but nothing else, nothing that could give rise to the slightest suspicion. All his papers consisted of commercial correspondence with bankers and prominent merchants in all parts of the world, a few Arabic manuscripts, and heaps of papers covered with numbers from top to bottom. The latter delighted the police officers at first: in them they hoped to find a ciphered letter. But a careful examination showed that they were simply draft accounts that had accumulated, according to Segeliel, through many years' transactions, which was quite probable.

In general, Dr. Segeliel's answers to all points of accusation were quite clear and satisfactory, and he gave them without hesitation. His testimony and actions betrayed more of an annoyance at this senseless disturbance of his person and house than a fear of becoming entangled in his own answers. To explain his wealth he referred to his papers in which one could see the entire history of his business. It was true that he conducted his business with incredible success, yet there was no evidence of any criminal action. His answer to the physicians and druggists was that his doctor's diploma give him the right to treat whomever he desired and in whatever way he wanted to; that he was not imposing his services on anyone; that he was not obliged to announce the composition of the medicine he gave his patients, but that they might analyze his prescriptions as they pleased; that since he did not offer his services to anyone, he was justified in setting any price he liked for them; and that if he frequently set peculiar conditions, which anyone was free to accept or decline, it was only to get rid of tiresome crowds disturbing his peace—that was the only purpose of his desires.

Finally, as to the poisoning of people, the doctor objected that, as the whole city knew, his patients were for the most part total strangers to him; that he never asked either for the name of his patient or that of his messenger, or for his address; that patients, in case he refused to treat them, died because they had turned to him when they were about to die anyway; finally, that his enemies most probably died in the natural course of events. Moreover, he proved by means of obvious evidence and arguments that neither he nor anyone of his household had anything to do with the deceased. Segeliel's servants, interrogated individually and with all judicial ingenuity, confirmed all his depositions word for word. Meanwhile the investigation went on, but whatever was disclosed spoke in favor of Dr. Segeliel. A council of scientists analyzed Segeliel's medicines chemically, and after a long discussion announced that this renowned remedy was nothing but ordinary river water and that its supposed effect was a mere fairy tale or was attributable to the patients' imagination. Information gathered about the diseases of the persons of whose death Segeliel was accused showed that none of them had died suddenly and that the majority of them had died of chronic or inherited diseases. Finally, the autopsy of those strongly suspected of being poisoned showed not even the slightest trace of poison, and revealed only the common signs of ordinary disease.

This trial had attracted a multitude of people to the city and had lasted a long time, because almost half of the inhabitants had accused him. But in the end, no matter how much the judges were warned against Dr. Segeliel, they were forced to declare unanimously that the accusations brought against him were quite groundless, that Dr. Segeliel should be freed and cleared of any suspicion, and that his accusers should incur a penalty according to law.

Segeliel, who had maintained an air of indifference until now, seemed to come to life upon hearing the sentence. Immediately he presented to the court unquestionable proofs of the losses he had suffered in his vast business during the course of this trial, and asked that they be exacted from the accusers. Furthermore, he demanded from them satisfaction for the dishonor they had brought upon him. Never before had anyone seen him so tirelessly active. He seemed to have been born anew. His pride disappeared. He went from one judge to another himself, paid countless sums to the best attorneys, and sent messengers all over the world. In a word, he used all the means which the law, his wealth, and his connections could provide him to bring to complete ruin his accusers and every last member of their families, as well as their relatives and friends.

Finally, he achieved his goal: many of the accusers lost their positions, and thus their only means of existence; entire estates of several families were adjudged into his possession. Neither the appeals nor the tears of his victims touched his heart; he cruelly drove them out of their dwelling places, destroyed their houses and establishments to the very ground, uprooted their trees, and dumped their harvest into the sea. Both nature and fate seemed to assist him in his vengeance; all his enemies, their fathers, mothers and children died torturous deaths; a contagious fever would steal upon an entire family and devour all its members; ancient diseases, long since dormant, would rage again; the slightest injury acquired in childhood, an insignificant prick in a hand, the slightest cold became a fatal disease, and soon the very names of entire families were erased from the face of the earth. The same thing happened to those who escaped the penalty of the law. This was not enough: if there were a storm or whirlwind, the clouds would pass over Segeliel's castle and burst open above the houses and granaries of his enemies,

and many people saw Segeliel come out onto his terrace at
such a time and happily clink glasses with his friends.

The affair had at first horrified everybody, and although
Segeliel right after his trial moved to the city of B—— where
he resumed a life as luxurious as hitherto, many of his
compatriots who knew all the circumstances of the trial and
who had been irreparably injured by him did not abandon
their plan to destroy him. They turned to the old men who
still remembered the former trials dealing with sorcery, and
after discussing the matter with them, compiled a new
petition. In it they explained that although the existing laws
did not permit the prosecution of Dr. Segeliel, one could
not help seeing some supernatural power in his actions and
therefore asked that the whole affair be investigated again,
in accordance with the former laws on sorcery. Fortunately
for Segeliel, the judges who happened to get this petition
were enlightened men: one of them was known for a translation of Locke into his native tongue; another, for quite an
important work on jurisprudence, to which he had applied
Kant's system; the third had rendered invaluable services to
anatomic chemistry. They could not help laughing while
reading this strange petition, and returned it to the petitioners
as unworthy of attention. One of them good-naturedly added
to it an explanation of all the incidents that had seemed so
unnatural to the petitioners. And, thanks to European enlightenment, Dr. Segeliel continued to live in luxury, to
entertain the best society, to treat his patients according to
conditions proposed by him; and his enemies continued to
fall ill and to die as before.

To this terrible man our future improvvisatore determined
to go. As soon as he was let in, he threw himself on his
knees before the doctor and said: "Doctor! Mr. Segeliel!
You see before you the unhappiest man in the whole world.
Nature endowed me with a passion for poetry but deprived
me of all the means to follow this inclination. I have no
ability to think; I have no ability to express myself. I want
to speak—words escape me; I want to write—it's even worse.
God could not have condemned me to such an eternal suffering! I am convinced that my trouble stems from some kind
of disease, from some moral tension that you can cure."

"Look at you, sons of Adam!" said Dr. Segeliel. (This was
his favorite saying when he was in good humor). "Adam's
children! They all remember their father's privilege. They
want to get everything without any effort! There are people

more worthy than you in this world, and they work. However, be it as you wish," he added, after a moment of silence. "I'll help you, but as you know, I have my own conditions. . . ."

"Whatever you say, Doctor! I'll agree to anything you suggest; anything is better than dying every minute."

"And aren't you frightened by everything people in your city say about me?"

"No, Doctor! You could not invent a state worse than the one I am in now." The doctor laughed. "I'll be frank with you: it was not only the poetry, not only the desire of fame that brought me to you; another feeling, more delicate . . . If I had more ingenuity in writing, I could make my fortune, and then my Charlotte would be more favorably disposed toward me. . . . You understand me, Doctor?"

"I like that!" shouted Segeliel. "Just like our mother, the Inquisition, I adore frankness, and complete confidence in me. Only those who want to outsmart me will fare ill. But I see that you are a very direct and outspoken person, and you should be rewarded as you deserve. Therefore we agree to fulfill your wish and give you the ability to *create without any effort*; but our first condition will be that this ability will never leave you. Do you agree to that?"

"You are joking with me, Mr. Segeliel!"

"No, I am an outspoken person, and I don't like to hide anything from people who give themselves up to me. Listen and try to understand me well: The ability I give you will become a part of yourself; it will not leave you for a single moment during your life; it will grow with you, it will mature and die with you. Do you agree to that?"

"Can there be any doubt about it, Doctor?"

"All right. Another condition is as follows: you will *see everything, know everything, understand everything*. Do you agree to that?"

"Really, you are joking, Doctor! I don't know how to thank you. . . . Instead of one good thing, you are giving me two! How can I disagree?"

"Understand me well: you will *know everything, see everything, understand everything*."

"You are the most generous of men, Mr. Segeliel!"

"Then you agree?"

"Of course; do you need my signature?"

"No, I don't need it. It was of value at the time when acknowledgments of debt did not yet exist; now people have become clever. We shall do without your signature; the spoken word is just as impossible to undo as the written word. Nothing in this world, *nothing* is forgotten or destroyed, my friend."

With these words Segeliel put one hand on the poet's head, another on his heart, and in a most solemn voice he intoned:

"From secret magic receive thy gift: to ponder everything, to read everything in the world, to speak and to write with beauty and ease, moving to tears and bringing laughter, in verse, in prose, in warmth and in cold, awake and asleep, on desk, on sand, with knife and pen, with hand, tongue, finger, crying and laughing, in all tongues. . . ."

Segeliel placed a piece of paper in the poet's hand and led him to the door.

When Cypriano left Segeliel, the doctor shouted with laughter: "Pepe! the flannel coat!"

"Oohoo!" resounded from all the shelves of the doctor's library, as in the second act of *Der Freischütz*.

Cypriano took Segeliel's words for an order to his valet, but he was somewhat surprised that a dandyish and elegant doctor would need such odd clothing. He peeped through a chink and saw that all the books on the shelves were moving; the number 8 jumped out of one of the manuscripts, the Arabic alif out of another, then the Greek delta, then many others, until finally the entire room was filled with living numbers and letters; they twisted, they stretched feverishly, they swelled, they interlaced their clumsy legs, they jumped and fell; numerous dots whirled among them, like infusoria beneath a microscope; and all the while an old Chaldean polygraph was beating time with a force that made the window frames tremble.

The frightened Cypriano rushed away headlong.

When he had calmed down somewhat, he unrolled Segeliel's manuscript. It was a huge scroll covered from top to bottom with incomprehensible numbers. But no sooner had Cypriano glanced at them than, enlivened by supernatural power, he understood the meaning of the magic writing. All the forces of nature were calculated in them: the systematic life of crystal and the lawless imagination of a poet, the magnetic pulsation of the earth's axis and the infusorian passions, the nervous system of languages and the capricious change of speech, everything lofty and of an affecting nature was reduced to an arithmetic progression; the unforeseen was expressed in Newton's binomial theorem;

a poetic flight was determined by a cycloid; a word be-
gotten together with a thought was expressed by logarithms;
an unconscious impulse of the soul was reduced to an
equation. All nature lay before Cypriano, like the skeleton
of a beautiful woman whom an anatomist had dissected with
consummate skill.

In an instant the lofty mystery of the conception of a
thought seemed quite easy and natural to Cypriano; a
devil's bridge with Chinese rattles stretched itself before
him across the abyss that separates thought from expression,
and Cypriano began speaking in verse.

At the beginning of our story we witnessed Cypriano's
wonderful success in his new craft. In triumph, his purse
full of money, and feeling tired, he returned to his room; he
wanted to freshen his parched lips; he took a glass of water,
but what did he see in it? It was not water: he saw two
gases fighting, and myriads of infusoria floating between
them. He poured another glass—still the same; he ran to a
spring with its cool waves rippling like silver in the distance,
but when he approached it he saw the same thing he had
seen in his glass. Blood rushed to the poor improvvisatore's
head. In despair he threw himself on the grass, hoping to
forget his thirst and misery in sleep, but as soon as he lay
down he heard a noise, a knocking and squealing beneath
him, as if thousands of hammers were coming down upon an
anvil, as if rough pistons were rubbing through a heap of
stones, as if an iron rake were catching and gliding upon a
smooth surface. He got up, and saw moonlight in his garden,
the striped shadow of the fence softly gliding over the
leaves of the bushes, and ants building a hill nearby. Everything was quiet and calm. He lay down again, and again he
began to hear the noises. Cypriano could not fall asleep
anymore; he spent all night with his eyes open.

In the morning he ran to his Charlotte, hoping to find
peace of mind and to share with her his joy and his grief.
Charlotte already knew about the triumph of her Cypriano.
She was waiting for him, dressed up, with her blond hair
done up and adorned with a pink ribbon, glancing into a
mirror with an air of innocent coquetry. Cypriano rushed
toward her; she smiled, stretched out her hand to him—
suddenly Cypriano stopped and stared at her. . . .

And, indeed, it was a curious sight! Through a cellular
web, as through a veil, Cypriano saw that three-faceted
artery called the heart palpitating in his Charlotte; he saw

the red blood rush out of it and reach the hair follicles and produce the delicate pallor he had loved so much in her. Poor devil! In her beautiful, loving eyes he saw only a kind of camera obscura, a retinal membrane, a drop of hideous liquid; in her graceful walk, only the mechanism of levers. . . . Poor wretch! He saw her gallbladder, the movements of her digestive system. . . . Poor wretch! His Charlotte, this earthy ideal, to whom his inspiration used to pray, had become an anatomic specimen!

Horrified, Cypriano left her. In a nearby house there was an ikon of the Madonna. Cypriano used to turn to it in moments of despair and from its harmonious appearance receive consolation for his suffering soul. He went to it now; he fell on his knees; he implored. Alas! The image no longer existed for him: the paint moved on it, and he saw in the work of art only chemical fermentation.

Unhappy man! He suffered unbelievably; all his senses—his sight, his hearing, his sense of smell, taste, and touch, all his nerves—acquired a microscopic ability, and, in a certain focus, the smallest particle of dust, the tiniest insect, which does not even exist for us, crowded upon him, pushing him out of the world; the flickering of a butterfly's wing tore his ears; the smoothest surface tickled him; everything in nature decomposed before him, but nothing united in his soul: he *saw everything*, he *understood everything*, but there was an eternal abyss between him and people, between him and nature; nothing in this world sympathized with him.

He sought to forget himself in a lofty poetic work, or to come upon a profound thought in historical writings; he wanted to rest his mind in the harmonious edifice of philosophy—all was in vain: his tongue babbled words, but his thoughts disclosed to him something completely different.

Through the thin veil of poetic expression he saw all the mechanical devices of creation; he felt the rage of the poet, saw how many times he mangled his verses, verses that seemed to be spontaneous outbursts of the poet's heart. In the most pathetic moment, when it seemed that all the inner strength of the poet was straining and his pen could hardly follow his words and words his thoughts, Cypriano saw him reach for the *Dictionary of the Academy* and search for an effective word. In the midst of an exquisite portrayal of repose and inner peace, he saw the poet pull the ears of the capricious child who wearied him with his cries, and saw him close his ears to the powerful torrent of his wife's chatter.

While reading history, Cypriano penetrated the consoling good intentions concerning the general fate of mankind and its constant process of perfection, those profound surmises about the important deeds and the character of one nation or another, surmises that seemed to be the result of historical findings but that were actually held together by artificial combinations. He saw this combination upheld by a combination of authors writing on the same subject, and this combination upheld by an artificial combination of chronicles, and this in turn by some mistake of a copyist, on which, then, as on the point of a pole, jugglers balanced the whole edifice.

Instead of being amazed at the harmony of a philosophical system, Cypriano saw that at first a philosopher conceived a desire to say something new; then a fortunate, passionate expression occurred to him; then he attached to his expression an idea, to that idea a chapter, to the chapter a book, and to the book a system. Whenever the philosopher abandoned his strict form, as if carried away by some strong emotion, and made a brilliant digression, Cypriano saw that this digression was there only to cover up the middle term of a syllogism in which the philosopher himself felt only a play on words.

Music ceased to exist for Cypriano; in reading and listening to the ecstatic harmonies of Handel and Mozart he saw only an airy space filled with countless little spheres, each of them being sent in different directions by different sounds. In the heartbreaking wail of an oboe, in the shrill sound of a trumpet he heard only a mechanical concussion; in the singing of Stradivari and Amati he heard only horsehair gliding upon animal gut.

During an opera he felt only the suffering of the composer and conductor; he heard the instruments being tuned, parts rehearsed; in a word, he felt all the delights of rehearsals. But in the most pathetic moments of the performance he saw the rage of a producer behind the scene, his arguments with supernumeraries and with a stagehand; he saw hooks, ropes, flats, lights. . . .

Often, in the evening, the exhausted Cypriano ran out of his house into the street: luxurious carriages rolled by him; people returned to their peaceful hearths after their daily work. Through the lighted windows Cypriano looked at their quiet family happiness: he saw fathers and mothers with their children around them, but he was deprived of the enjoyment of envying their happiness: he saw only a retort of rules and manners, of rights and obligations or codes of morality, all slowly producing a social irritant, searing the nerves of each member of a family. He saw a tender and thoughtful father grow tired of his children, a respectful son waitingly impatiently for his father's death, a passionate couple holding hands and reflecting how to get rid of each other as soon as possible.

Cypriano lost his mind. He left his country, hoping to escape from himself, and fled through many countries; but, as before, everywhere and always he continued to *see everything* and *understand everything*.

Meanwhile, the insidious gift of creating poetry did not slumber in Cypriano. As soon as his microscopic insight lessened for a moment, verses began pouring from his lips like water; as soon as he restrained his cold inspiration, all nature came to life with dead life before him again, and he saw it undressed and indecent, like a naked woman with her shoes on. With what grief he remembered that sweet torment, when a rare wave of inspiration overcame him, when vague images floated before him, billowing and fusing with each other! . . . Then the images grew brighter and brighter; a host of poetic creations drew near to him from another world. Slowly, like a long kiss of love, they came quite close, breathing with unearthly warmth, and nature fused with them in harmonious sounds, and his soul felt easy and light! What a futile and oppressive recollection! In vain did Cypriano try to master the fight between Segeliel's antagonistic gifts: as soon as an unnoticed impression touched the unhappy man's irritated senses, insight would again overpower him, and an unripe thought would seek expression.

For many years Cypriano wandered from country to country. Sometimes poverty forced him to avail himself of Segeliel's pernicious gift, providing him with plenty and all the material enjoyments of life; but each of these enjoyments bore a poison within it, and each new success only increased his suffering.

Finally, he decided to make no use of his gift, to deafen it, to strangle it, to buy it off at the price of need and indigence. But it was too late! The long struggle had shattered the foundations of his soul. The delicate bonds that tied the

mysterious elements of thoughts and feelings were broken—
and they fell apart like crystals eaten through by caustic
acid. Neither thoughts nor feelings remained in his soul: it
harbored only phantoms clothed in words, incomprehensible
even to him. Destitution and hunger mutilated his body,
and he wandered aimlessly, begging alms. . . .

I met Cypriano in a village of a landowner on the steppe.
He was employed there as a jester. Dressed in a flannel coat
with a red scarf for a belt, he spoke incessantly in verse, in
a language that was a mixture of many languages. . . . He
related his story to me himself, bitterly complaining about
his poverty and even more about the fact that no one
understood him. He complained that people beat him if in a
fit of poetic rapture and for lack of paper he cut his verses
on tables, and even more that everyone laughed at the only
sweet recollection Segeliel's pernicious gift had been unable
to erase—the first verses he had ever written for Charlotte.

"Treason, gentlemen!" shouted Vyacheslav. "Faust purposely chose this excerpt from the manuscript instead of an
answer to our objections yesterday."

"Nothing of the sort!" answered Faust. "There was no
chicanery on my part; I read each number in order. I'm sure
that when the writers themselves compiled the notes that
were furnished to them, they left the establishment of their
proper sequence to the best systematizer—time."

VYACHESLAV: "And you want to convince us that it was
merely chance that brought Beethoven together with the
Improvvisatore, when both stories deal with one and the same
thought, although expressed from opposite points of view?"

ROSTISLAV: "I don't know whether it was one of Faust's
usual jokes, but I must say I have yet to see things happen
by chance in nature. For instance, in nature you can observe
the gradual development of the plant world into the animal
world. It's even difficult to determine where one ends and
the other begins. And yet one seems to be a total negation
of the other. In plants, all the important organs appear on
the surface. The inside of a plant is frequently quite empty.
The fibrils of a root are the organs of feeding; the leaves,
the organs of respiration; the wedding bed is all outside,
among the fragrant petals. Animals, however, have all these
organs carefully hidden inside, under several covers. From

outside, you can see only skin, hair, corneous substance—
the less important and almost insensitive organs. Animal life
always seemed to me to be an answer to plant life, and man
a judge between them. If Nature plays this drama with her
lower creations, could she leave her higher creations, that
is, humans, to chance? I am convinced that there must be a
reason why the creations of man, whether a great poetic
work, a frank discussion, a lighthearted traveler's note, why
all these phenomena follow one another in a particular order,
although frequently we are unable to comprehend this reason,
just as we are unable to see why such contradictory phenomena as day and night follow each other constantly."

VICTOR: "But one should first prove if the creations of man
are really on the same level as the creations of nature, or
perhaps even superior to them."

ROSTISLAV: "Of course they are superior, and for the same
reason that an animal is superior to a plant. . . ."

VICTOR: "That is a very praiseworthy conviction. It is a
pity, however, that man has never succeeded in creating, for
instance, the Alps, or the shores of the Mediterranean Sea,
or in achieving the perfection that one can see, for instance,
in the tissues of a plant. You know that the finest lace seen
through a microscope is nothing but a coarse ligament of
cords, while the epidermis of the lowest plant surprises us
with the regularity of its structure."

ROSTISLAV: "You are confusing two completely different
states of man, two completely separate levels, because man
has many of them. Some scientists tried to prove that a
pyramid was the symbol of fire (Phtasos) for the ancients.
It is quite likely, because both the flame of a fire and a
pyramid have a pointed end. But it seems that another, a
more profound symbol was contained in the symbol of fire—
and that was man. Look at a flame: it has a dark, cold part[1]—
the product of the crude fumes of a burning substance. It
has also a light part where the flame takes the life element
out of the atmosphere;[2] this part only oxidizes metals. Between these two parts is a point, one point, with a degree of
heat so intense that nothing can resist it: at this point
platinum passes into an incandescent state: and almost all

---

[1] Murray placed gunpowder for a few seconds into the dark part
of the flame in which gases are separated and which is seen
through its light cover: there was no explosion, and the gunpowder grew damp.

[2] Oxygen.

metals[3] are reduced. You compare the creations of nature with the creations of a dark, cold, and helpless sphere of man; nature triumphs over the men who have lowered themselves to it; but what creations of nature could attain the level of the bright and burning hearth of the human soul? Man's spirit, being of the same origin as nature, produces phenomena similar to phenomena in nature, but spontaneously, unconditionally; this affinity or similarity deceived the ancient theoreticians, who based on it the so-called imitation of nature. . . ."

VYACHESLAV: "You forget one important stipulation: imitation of *refined* nature. . . ."

ROSTISLAV: "This stipulation made the theory even more vague and obscure, because along with the word *refinement* something penetrated into the theory that destroyed it completely; because if we admit that man has the right to choose what is refined, that means that his soul has its own *measure* by which to evaluate both the creations of nature and his own. Why does he need nature then?"

VYACHESLAV: "In the first place, he needs it at least for the comparison of *both measures*, as you say: his own and the one provided by nature."

ROSTISLAV: "But to compare them, he needs still a *third measure*, the truth of which would convince man—and so on *ad infinitum*; but in the end, the last judge will still be man's soul. . . ."

VYACHESLAV: "But why is it, then, that the closer a human creation, a painting, let's say, is to nature, the more we like it?"

ROSTISLAV: "That's a sort of optical illusion. Closeness to nature is entirely a relative concept. Anatomical errors are found in Raphael, but who notices them? If we liked what is closest to nature, then Ruisdael's tree, for instance, would be inferior to a tree made by some flower seller. The daguerreotype appeared in our time as if purposely, to show the difference between mechanical and live creation. The appearance of the daguerreotype made materialists very happy. 'What do we need painters for now? or inspiration? The picture will be painted, and far more accurately, without inspiration, by an ordinary craftsman, with the help of a few drops of iodine and mercury.' But what happened? The

[3] It is well known that the action of a soldering pipe, or, more accurately, a blowpipe, is based on this phenomenon.

daguerreotype produced perfect imitations, yet the same objects (I won't mention a human face, but take a tree, for instance) were dead in the daguerreotype, and they come to life only under the painter's brush. On the other hand, a few thousand years ago ashes covered a whole city and buried it alive, teeming with activity, in an instant of disaster; our contemporary, by the power of his artistic spirit, resurrects this moment, and as if by magic makes us see what, in all likelihood, no human being has ever seen. And yet Karl Bryulov's painting is true; it convinces you by the sensation it creates."

VYACHESLAV: "I agree, but Bryulov, like Raphael, like Michelangelo, most likely, also copied his groups from live models, observed the eruption of volcanoes and other phenomena of nature. . . ."

ROSTISLAV: "True! But is the feeling that is aroused in us when we see a broken carriage, a knocked-off wheel, a rain of ashes, even people's faces at the moment of a similar disaster in nature, the same as that as when we see similar objects in Bryulov's painting? What has imparted beauty to objects that are devoid of any beauty in nature?"

FAUST: "I don't know what theory our great painter created on this topic, but I shall mention only that painters are given to optical illusions, if they think that they are *copying* nature in their painting. In copying from *nature*, a painter is only *nourished* by it, as the human organism is nourished by the raw products of nature, But how does this process take place? The substances on which we feed undergo a lively fermentation; only their finest particles remain in our organisms, and go through a number of lively transformations before they become our body. Food is useless to a diseased organism, and even more so to a dead one. A living organism can do without food and exist by its own power for a long time. But that does not mean that it could do without food completely. All that matters is good digestion, and its first condition is—life power."

VICTOR: "Your conversation, gentlemen, reminds me of an ancient anecdote. Once, while casting a silver statue, Benvenuto Cellini noticed that there was not enough metal; fearing that his casting would be a failure, he gathered all the household silverware—goblets, spoons, rings—and threw them into the furnace. Another artist, confronted with a similar obstacle while casting a copper statue, remembered Benvenuto's procedure, and began throwing all his copper household utensils into the furnace. But it was too late: there was no time for them to melt. When the form was broken, the artist, in despair, saw the bottom of a pan sticking out of Venus's breast, a spoon protruding over her eyes, and so forth."

FAUST: "You understand my idea perfectly. Woe to the artist if his inner furnace is unable to melt crude nature and transform it into a loftier thing! That's necessary in all of man's encounters with nature. Woe to him if he bows down to it!"

ROSTISLAV: "Oh, no doubt about that! If man were not forced to get his subsistence from nature, there would be no inducement for crime. Man's need of nature's products is precisely the cause of theft and robbery, for example."

FAUST: "One can hardly agree with that. You yourself remarked quite justly that man has not only a light side but also a dark side; in it are conceived the inclinations which lead to crime. Sometimes a crime is already committed in a man's soul before the act that is usually called crime and that is nothing else but a vicious inclination in its tangible form. There are dark passions; and therefore also the crimes that may be committed within a man—even if he were not an inhabitant of the earth, even if he were not associating with his kind—as, for instance, idleness and pride, which (and this is rather remarkable) are considered the mother of all vices by all peoples and in all traditions. I shall say more: in nature there is actually no evil."

ROSTISLAV: "You are contradicting reality. One has only to look at nature. Every plant, every animal is compelled to live by the destruction or suffering of some other plant or animal. If suffering is not an evil, then I don't know what this word really means."

VICTOR: "For the sake of posterity I want to say that the idealists argue precisely as do we, poor servants of crude nature that we are. Consequently, the ideal mystical world is not yet the kingdom of the world."

FAUST: "In the first place, I am neither an idealist nor a mystic. I am an epicurean because I am looking for the place where I could find the greatest sum of enjoyments for man. If you like, I am a scholar of nature, even an empiricist, with this difference only: I do not limit myself to observations of the material facts only; I find that spiritual facts need to be analyzed as well. Second, I'll say it also for the sake of posterity, that no matter what the argument of idealists may be, there is nevertheless a possibility that they will agree at some time in the future because they are drawn toward the center; but every one of you, the materialists, is drawn toward some point at the periphery. That is what makes your paths part constantly."

VICTOR: "Perhaps! But using your favorite expression, the constantly approaching but never merging asymptotes seem to be the symbol of ideal ways."

FAUST: "I agree with you more than you think. You are right, and you will be right until man can really square the circle—of course, not in a geometric sense.[4] But let us return to our problem. Our opposition to Rostislav is not so great as it seems, but we do not agree either. This kind of contention, despite all its outward absurdity, is the one that occurs most frequently among people. In order to determine if there is any evil in external nature, one should first determine what evil is. That would lead us too far, and would almost be superfluous. For me it is much more important and interesting to determine how man's soul is affected by the exclusive concern for material nature and how the analogy between man and his occupations works. As we can see, every phenomenon in nature is subject to constant laws: you sow a seed, provide it with all the conditions necessary for its vegetation—it grows; you disregard one of these conditions—it perishes. It is always like that—today as yesterday and tomorrow. You can't move external nature with your entreaties, you can't move it with your repentance; it does not know of forgiveness: if you make a mistake—you must pay, there is no salvation for you, no deferment. If one day you forget to water your favorite costly plant, it dries out and there is no way to bring it back to life, despite all your regrets. This law is wonderful in its own place, that is, at the lower level of nature. A man who never rose above this level, amazed at this law, wanted to apply it to other, for example, to moral phenomena. 'Look at nature, observe its laws, imitate its laws!' said the encyclopedists of the eighteenth century, and their followers in the nineteenth are still saying it."

VYACHESLAV: "But show me even a single system of morals

---

[4] One must remember that in the theories of mysticism, a circle is the symbol of the material world, and a square and triangle, of the spiritual world.

which would reject repentance and consequently the possibility of forgiveness."

FAUST: "Fortunately, men of theory through instinct frequently betray logical consistency. True, I don't remember anyone directly denying the right of repentance, but this denial stems directly from many theories, for example, say Bentham's or Malthus's. It has even become watered down. From the seventeenth century on, the fable 'The Ant and the Grasshopper' has been known all over the world; it has been translated into all languages; it is the first one that children learn by heart. It would not have been such a success in the eighteenth century if it had not expressed the prevailing theory of that time, a fact that never even occurred to our kind La Fontaine. If you turn the moral of this fable into a rule, if you follow its applications, you will arrive at the conclusion that a sick man should not receive any treatment at all: 'He is ill; consequently he is at fault, and consequently he must be punished!' Such a conclusion is as absurd and as logically correct as the famous Malthusian phrase 'You were late in coming into this world; there is no place for you at nature's feast'; in other words, 'Starve!' This worship of the laws of material nature fortunately does not always attain such logical clarity, but by analogy strongly influences human soul. Excuse me, my materialist friends, but the law of plants, when fully applied to human beings, turns into senseless pedantry and dries the human heart. Such a pedant cannot be called evil, in the true sense of that word. A dry man will not commit evil needlessly; he will do it without taking any pleasure in it. An evil man will do evil with pleasure, just because he desires evil. However, a most evil man is capable of suffering, of repentance. In our language, a dry pedant, extremely correctly and with deep insight, is called *derevyashka* (a piece of wood). According to his nickname, he doesn't love anyone, does not sympathize with anything, does not repent anything, but blindly follows the so-called laws of nature. He grows, spreads his branches and roots, overgrowing other plants not because he is angry with his neighbors but only because one side gives him more warmth and humidity."

VICTOR: "You forget that among the so-called materialists and preachers of the laws of nature there were men distinguished by great philanthropy, as, for instance, Franklin."

FAUST: "Franklin knew how to play his role with such

success that until now it is difficult to distinguish it from the essence of a cunning diplomat. Go through his writings and you'll be horrified by the false and proud humility, by that constant hypocrisy and egoism hidden beneath the moral apothegms. The philanthropist-manufacturer is a direct descendant of Franklin; I'm surprised that this psychological phenomenon has not yet been utilized by a writer of comedies.[5] He is the real Tartuffe of our century, since a *derevyashka* may take any shape, even that of a philanthropist. This guise is the most unendurable to him: he suffocates under it; one correctly calculated advantage may force him into the role of a philanthropist. A manufacturer-philosopher in his odd occupation does only what is necessary, he does not go beyond this limit. He does not penetrate into the real essence of a disaster; he only patches it somehow to make it less obvious. He cares about the prosperity and morals, even about the religion, of his workers, but only inasmuch as it is necessary for the unceasing work in his factory. Such mockery of the loftiest feeling, of Christian love, does not remain unpunished, and the proofs of it are not at all philanthropic manifestations, which you'll find in the reports to the English Parliament on the state of children in factories, and even with the Doctors . . . , those advocates of industrial religion, and finally, daily in the newspapers."

VICTOR: "You forget, however, that it is the philanthropy of manufacturers to which we are indebted for one of the most important claims of the nineteenth century to the admiration of posterity: the reformatory system of our prisons."

FAUST: "I would agree with you if medieval monasteries had not been real reformatory institutions and had not achieved their purpose, and perhaps with greater success than all conceivable reformatory systems of seclusion and silence. Only God knows if they reform anyone, but surely they suffice to make a man go out of his mind.[6] It was thought possible to improve a person as one would a plant, by transplanting it into a hothouse. It seems that they took all the laws of nature that could affect it, like light, air, into precise account—but they forgot one thing: the power of

[5] At the present time there are already many comedies based on this subject.

[6] The system of silence in particular has this result. An imprisoned person, deprived for days of the right to express his doubts or his suspicions to his neighbor, is tormented by the thought that he is denounced, and at this point he loses his mind.

love, which could move mountains. As long as the plant was in the hothouse, it seemed to have been cured, improved; but as soon as it was brought back into its former soil, all the efforts spent on it proved to be wasted because it had not been given real life. Therefore, gentlemen, don't say that it is sufficient to *know* in this world, without concern for the means by which this knowledge is obtained."

THE EIGHTH NIGHT

(*Continuation of the Manuscript*)

SEBASTIAN BACH

Once at a party a man of fifty or so was pointed out to us. He wore a black dress coat, was slender and sad-looking, although his features were fiery and lively. We were told that for a score of years he had had a rather strange hobby. He collected paintings, engravings, works of music. He spared neither time nor money for that purpose. Often he undertook journeys only to find some vague line, which an artist may incidentally have placed on paper, or a sheet scribbled over by a musician. He would spend days arranging his treasures, sometimes chronologically, sometimes according to a systematic scheme, sometimes by author. But most frequently he would carefully examine these painted strokes or these musical phrases; he would put the bits together, note their distinctive character, their similarities and differences. The purpose of all this research was to prove that beneath these lines, beneath these scales there was hidden a mysterious language, which was practically unknown until then but was common to all artists—a language, he maintained, without the knowledge of which one could understand neither poetry in general nor any particular beautiful work, nor the essence of any poet.

Our investigator boasted of his success in discovering the meaning of some of this language's expressions and in explaining through them the lives of many artists. He seriously asserted that one particular turn of a melody indicated the poet's sadness, while another indicated a happy event in his life; one kind of harmony told of delight; a particular curve indicated a prayer; a particular color expressed a painter's temperament, etcetera. The eccentric man quite gravely told us that he had been busy compiling a dictionary of these hieroglyphs and that, utilizing it, he intended later to publish corrected and supplemented biographies of various artists.

"For this task is very complicated and difficult," he would add, with a determined kind of pedantry.

"For the complete knowledge of the *inner* language of the arts, one must study all the works of all artists without exception, and not only those of the famous artists. Because," he would go on, "the poetry of all ages and peoples is one and the same harmonious creation. Each poet adds to it his own sound and word, his own line. Often an idea born in a great poet finds its final expression in a mediocre versifier. An obscure thought born in a common man is often brought into shimmering light by a genius. Separated by time and space, poets often answer each other like echoes among cliffs. The conclusion of the *Iliad* is given in Dante's *Divine Comedy*; Byron's poetry is the best commentary to Shakespeare; you will find Raphael's secret revealed in Albrecht Dürer; the Strasbourg bell tower is an adjunct to the Egyptian pyramids; Beethoven's symphonies are a second set of Mozart's symphonies. All artists work at one thing; they speak one language and therefore understand each other spontaneously. A common man, however, has to learn this language; he has to seek out its expressions by the sweat of his brow. That is what I am doing and that is what I advise you to do."

Incidentally, our investigator hoped to complete his work soon. We persuaded him to tell us of some of his historic findings, and he readily acceded to our request.

His story was just as odd as his occupation. He was animated by one particular feeling, but his habit of combining various feelings, of reliving the feelings of others, led to a confusion of concepts and ideas that were often conflicting. He was angered by being at a loss for words that would make his speech comprehensible to us, and in his explanations used everything that came his way: chemistry and hieroglyphics, medicine and mathematics; from a prophetic tone he descended to sheer polemics, from philosophical reasoning to drawing-room phrases. Everything was mixed together, motley, strange. But despite all his shortcomings, I regret that the printed word cannot convey his sincere conviction in the truth of his words, his dramatic participation in the fate of an artist, his special art of gradually ascending from a common subject to a lofty idea and intense feeling, his sad laughter at the ordinary occupations of ordinary people.

When we had all taken our seats around him, he looked at the gathering with an ironic glance, and began:

*   *   *

I am sure, gentlemen, that many of you have at least heard
the name of Sebastian Bach.[1] Perhaps some of you may even
have had a piano teacher who would bring you a sarabande,
gigue, or some such thing with a name just as barbaric and
would try to prove to you that this music was useful for
straightening out your fingers, and so you would play it over
and over. You would curse both the teacher and the composer and probably ask yourself "What made this German
organist pile one difficult passage on top of another and
mockingly throw them, like Odysseus's bow, into the hands
of his descendants? Since that time, among the brilliant and
resplendent works of the new school, you have forgotten both
Sebastian Bach and his monotonous melodies in the minor
keys, or the mere thought of them chills you, like a commentary to a poem, like a foreword to a novel, a game of whist
during a concert, or Moscow newspapers[2] among foreign
magazines in a pale-yellow vellum cover adorned with pink
leaves. Nevertheless, you encounter an artist with a devoted
heart and a lofty mind, who studies the forgotten works of
Bach in the seclusion of his room, who exalts him as eternally
fresh. . . . And—need I say?—he can not find anyone like him
in the sanctuary of sounds.

You are amazed at this inconceivable predilection. You
scan the works of the immortal one and they seem to you like
the tomb of some Psammetich, covered with hieroglyphs. Between them and you there are centuries and many-colored
clouds of new music. They hide the mysterious meaning of
the symbols used in his works from your sight. You ask for a
portrait of Bach. But art in the tradition of Lafater, the art of
transforming faces of great personalities into caricatures, al-

[1] In Moscow, at the time when this was written, the name of
Sebastian Bach was known only to a few musicians. For me, Bach
was practically my first textbook in music, and I knew most of it
by heart. Nothing could enrage me more at that time than the
naïve comments of amateurs that they had not even heard of
Bach.

[2] At that time the Moscow papers (*The Moscow Herald*) were
printed on poor paper, in an old-fashioned format and with an
amazing sloppiness in all respects. Does the reader know the very
typical anecdote of that time when *The Moscow Herald* enlarged
its format? This innovation much displeased the majority of its
subscribers. One of them wrote from the provinces to the publisher asking whether it would be possible to print the copy of the
newspaper for him alone in its previous format, promising to pay
double the price.

though maintaining every possible likeness, has not yet disappeared among painters—and, instead of Bach, you are shown some snappish old man with a mocking look, with a large powdered wig and the dignity of a high government functionary. You search in dictionaries, in a history of music. Oh, don't look for anything in biographies of Bach. You will be surprised only to find out that Frederick the Great, whose poetic soul searched in music for a shelter from his antipoetic age and from his own thoughts, bent his knee before Sebastian's altar of harmony. Biographers of Bach, as well as of other artists, describe his life as they do the life of any other man. They tell you when he was born, with whom he studied, whom he married. They are ready to prove that Dante belonged to the Ghibelline party, that he was exiled by the Guelfs, and that he wrote his poem as a result; that Shakespeare took a fancy to the theater while holding horses at the entrance; that Schiller poured out his soul in ardent verses because he used to put his feet into cold water; that Derzhavin was a Minister of Justice and therefore wrote *The Grandee*. They overlook the sacred life of an artist, the development of his creative power, this real life, only remnants of which manifest themselves in the artist's daily life. And what do they do? They describe only the remnants of remnants, or how should I express it?—some useless residue that remained in a chemist's still after a mighty force had come from it to start the wheels of a huge engine. Fanatics! They paint the golden curls of a poet and, like Herder, fail to see the sacred forest of Druids, beyond which awful mysteries take place in him. They enter the temple of arts on crutches, as in ancient times sick people used to enter the temple of Aesculapius. There they lapse into an animal sleep, write their dreams on copper plates to deceive the coming generations, and forget about the god of the temple.

There is only one source for the artist's life: his works. Whether he be a musician, a poet, or a painter—in his works you will find his spirit, his character, his face; in them you will find even those events which have escaped the chronological pen of historians. It is difficult to learn about the creator from his creation, just as it is difficult to reveal the mystery of the Supreme Creator in blocks of gneiss and axinite crystals of primeval mountains. But it is only the world that tells us about the Almighty, and it is only the works that tell us about their artist. Don't look for the ordinary man's events in his life—they did not exist. There are no unpoetic moments in the life of a poet. He sees all the phenomena of life illuminated by the never setting sun of his soul; and this soul, like the statue of Memnon, incessantly produces harmonious sounds.

Bach's family became known in Germany around the middle of the sixteenth century. German writers, who collected data on this family, begin its history from the time when the head of the family, Focht Bach, exiled for his faith, moved from Pressburg to Thuringia. Our historians are concerned with grave matters—why then couldn't they prove that Focht Bach belonged to the Slavs, like Haydn and Pleyel (there is almost no doubt of that), and change my moral conviction into a historic one?[3] All they would have had to do would have been to write one article, then another, scatter references in it abundantly, and then refer to the article as proof. Don't they base the first centuries of Russian history on the writings of a monk who for his own amusement copied the Hoffmannesque stories of Byzantine chroniclers? And who had ever doubted the existence of Romulus and Numa Pompilius before Niebuhr? Has the Trojan War been omitted from the introduction to the histories of all the peoples for a long time?

And this, indeed, is worth the effort. Here we deal not with the arguments of small princelings for a dozen wooden huts, not with farthings, but with a numerous family that for several generations had preserved a poetic sense. This is a phenomenon unparalleled in the chronicles of fine arts and physiology.

How much longer, along with a group of merchants who settled in North America and along with European Chinese, usually called Englishmen, will we consider poetry a superfluous element in a political society and weigh the inner essence of life in money, thus proving only that it does not weigh at all, and then wonder, naïvely, at the calamities of our society and the calamities of man?

Indeed, Bach's family was blessed with piety and love for harmony from above. In his quiet abode Focht Bach devoted his uneventful days to his children and to music. In the course of time his children scattered all over Germany. Each

---

[3] It is interesting that this idea, invoked simply by the character of some melodies of Bach, later really found a certain historic support. Bach is not a name, but a *nickname*.

of them established his own family; each led a quiet and or-
derly life, like his father, and each of them elevated Christian souls in a church of the Lord with spiritual music. But
on a fixed day of the year they would all unite, like the individual sounds of a single chord. They would devote the
entire day to music and then again return to their own
occupations.

Into one of these families Sebastian was born. Soon afterward his father and mother died; nature had created them
to produce a great man and then destroyed them like an object which is no longer needed. Sebastian was left in care of
Johann Christoph, his older brother.

Johann Christoph Bach was an important man in his com-
munity. He never forgot that his father, Ambrosius Bach, was
a *Hof-und-Rats-Musicus* in Eisenach, and his uncle, also
Johann Christoph Bach, a *Hof-und-Staats-Musicus* in Arnstadt, and that he himself had the honor of being the organist
of the Ohrdruf church.[4] He respected his art like an honorable old lady and was extremely polite, gentle, and attentive
to it. Buffon imitated Christoph Bach's habit of sitting down
to work in full attire. Actually, Christoph would take his seat
at a clavichord or an organ only when wearing stockings and
shoes, his hair in ringlets majestically spreading over his
orange velveteen coat, between two shining brass buttons. A
septima or a *nona* never burst suddenly from under his fingers extemporaneously. Neither in church nor at home, nor
even out of curiosity, would Christoph permit himself this
effect, which in his youth was considered an innovation, and
which he called disrespect for art. Of musical theory he knew
only Gafurius's *Opus Musicae Disciplinae*[5] and adhered to

[4] Sebastian Bach was born in Eisenach on March 21, 1685, and
died on July 30, 1750 (according to the *Real-Enzyklopädie*, on
July 28). Christoph Bach was his twin brother. His older brother's
name was Johann Cristopf and he was the organist in Ohrdruf—
Reissmann, *Von Bach zu Wagner* (Berlin, 1861), p. 4.

[5] Gaforus or Gafurius, as it is called in the *Valthern Musik-
Lexikon* (Leipzig, 1732), p. 270. This Lexikon is a bibliographic
rarity in itself. An engraving attached to the *Lexikon* depicts an
organist playing on an organ, and behind him a conductor and an
orchestra. What is curious in it is that the bows of violins, or
rather of violas, are not straight but bent, almost like those of the
double bass; also interesting are very long trumpets such as no
longer exist today. On the wall there are a waldhorn, a theorbo,
and something like bugles. All the musicians, of course, are wearing wigs with braids, stockings and shoes.

this discipline with the strictness of a military man. For forty years he was an organist at the same church. For forty years he played almost only one and the same chorale each Sunday; for forty years he played one and the same prelude to it; and only on great holidays would he add a grace note and two trills in certain places, and then the parishioners would say to each other, "Oh, our Bach has gotten quite excited today." However, he was known for his extraordinary skill in composing musical riddles, which in those times musicians used to give to each other to solve. No one could invent a more difficult development for a canon[6] than he; no one could find a more intricate epigraph to go with it. Inflexible even in the choice of conversation, he would usually talk only about two subjects when he was in a good mood: first, about his canon with the epigraph *sit trium series una*,[7] in which voices were supposed to go with a *flea-step* and which all the counterpoint specialists of Eisenach had been unable to solve; and second, the Black Mass (*messa nigra*), the composition of his contemporary Kerll; it was called black because not only white notes but quarter-notes as well were used in it, which was then considered terribly daring. Christoph Bach was amazed at it but called it a harmful innovation which in the end would destroy the art of music completely. These, then, were the rules that he followed while giving his younger brother Sebastian a musical training. He loved him like a son, and therefore did not permit him indulgence. He wrote a prelude on a small sheet of staff paper and made Sebastian play it for several hours a day without showing him any other music. After two years he turned the sheet upside down and made Sebastian play the same prelude in this new version for two more years. And in order to prevent Sebastian from spoiling his taste with some fantasia, he never forgot to

---

I managed to see only two works of Gafurius in the marvelous library of Sergey Alexandrovich Sobolevsky; both are great bibliographic rarities and of the utmost importance for the history of music; one is the *Practica musica Franchini Gafori Londensis* (Milano 1496, in quarto), and the other, *Franchini Gafurii . . . de Harmonia musicorum instrumentorum opus* (Milano, 1518, in quarto).

[6] Those who know music will guess that we are talking about what Germans call a *Räthsel-Canon*; for those who don't know music my explanation of the term would not help.

[7] Those who read Weber's *Cecelia* know that a similar canon was given to the musicians of the nineteenth century to be solved.

lock his clavichord when he was leaving the house. For the same reason he used to hide from Sebastian all the works of the newest musicians, although at this time he himself no longer quite followed Gafurius's rules; but in order to ground Sebastian as firmly as possible in the principles of pure harmony he permitted him to read no other book. Frequently Christoph would interrupt his explanations with sudden outbursts against the Italians. As proof he would point at the *Litaniae mortuorum discordantes*, used as an example by Gafurius, a work that consisted entirely of dissonances. He tried to inculcate a horror of such lawlessness in the young soul of Sebastian. Christoph was frequently heard to boast that this system would, in thirty years, make his younger brother the first organist in Germany.

Sebastian respected Christoph as he would his father, and in keeping with ancient custom he obeyed him in everything with absolute submission. He never even conceived of doubting his brother's wisdom. He played and studied the prelude of his teacher again and again, right side up and upside down. But at last nature took its own course. Once Sebastian caught sight of a book in which Christoph used to copy various gigues, sarabandes, and madrigals of Froberger, Fisher, Pachelbel, and Buxtehude, who were then famous. It also contained the famous Black Mass written by Kerll about which Christoph could not speak with indifference. Often Sebastian would listen in rapt attention when his brother would practice these sacred works, slowly, pondering each note. Once, unable to contain himself, he could no longer stand it and shyly and hesitantly asked Christoph to let him try his skill with these hieroglyphs.

Such a request coming from a young man seemed an unpardonable presumption to Christoph. He smiled contemptuously, gave a shout, stamped his foot, and put the book in its usual place.

Sebastian was in despair. Day and night unfinished phrases of the forbidden music rang in his ears. To unravel the meaning of their harmonic combinations became a passion, a disease in him. Once, late at night, unable to fall asleep, he began humming softly some snatches from the sacred book, trying to imitate the sounds of the muted harpsichord. He remembered some of the phrases, but there was so much he could not understand or remember. At last, quite exhausted, he resolved to do an awful thing. Silently he left his bed and in the bright moonlight, on his tiptoes, he stole down to the bookcase, pushed his little hand into its latticed door, pulled out the mysterious notebook and opened it. . . . Who could describe his joy? Dead notes began to sound for him; they explained to him clearly what he had desperately been trying to find in the hazy vision of his memory. He spent the entire night thus occupied, avidly turning sheet after sheet, humming, playing with his fingers on the table, as upon a keyboard, increasingly carried away by his youthful, ardent impulse, and at the same time increasingly fearing each louder sound that occasionally would escape him and that might awaken the strict Christoph. Toward morning he put the book back in its place, having promised himself to repeat this pleasure again.

He could hardly await the next night, and as soon as Christoph finished smoking and tapped his porcelain pipe against the table, Sebastian again went to work. The moon was shining; one leaf was turned after the other; fingers played on the wooden board; the trembling voice hummed majestic tones intended for an organ in all its infinite greatness. . . . Suddenly it occurred to Sebastian to make this enjoyment even more accessible; he got some notepaper and by the weak light of the moon began to copy from the sacred book. Nothing could stop him; his young eyes did not feel the strain; his young head did not bend from want of sleep; only his heart was pounding and his soul was fervently yearning for sounds. . . .

Oh, gentlemen, this was not the joy that we may experience at the end of a good dinner and that passes with digestion, not the joy that our poets call fleeting: Sebastian's joy lasted six months, because he spent six months doing his work. And during all this time, each night the familiar delight came to him, like a passionate maiden: it did not burst into flames nor did it die down. It glowed with a quiet, even, but intense fire, as metal glows in a foundry before it becomes pure. Sebastian's inspiration at that time, as during his whole life on earth, was an inspiration raised to the level of endurance.

The work, which had already exhausted his strength and damaged his eyesight for the rest of his life, was approaching its end, when once, as Sebastian wanted to feast his eyes upon his treasure in the daylight, Christoph entered the room. As soon as he glanced at the book he guessed Sebastian's stratagem and, disregarding his entreaties and his bitter tears, the cruel man coldbloodedly threw the poor boy's long and difficult work into the fire. Now, gentlemen, try to be amazed at your mythological Brutus. Here I am telling you not about some dead fiction, but about the reality of life, which is loftier than fiction. Christoph loved his brother tenderly; he understood how much he would hurt the genius of his soul in depriving him of the fruit of his long and painstaking work; he saw his tears, heard his moans—yet he happily sacrificed all this to his system, to his rules and way of thinking. Is he not greater than Brutus, gentlemen? Or, at least, isn't this deed equal to the most famous deeds of pagan virtue?

But Sebastian did not have our high concept of social virtues; he did not understand all the greatness of Christoph's action. The room began to turn all around him; he was about to let his work be followed by the copy of this damned Gafurius who was the cause of all his trouble. And I must inform the gentlemen bibliomaniacs that that copy, which was in such apparent danger, was nothing less than the one published in Naples *per Franciscum de Dino, Anno Domini 1480 in quarto*, that is, the *editio princeps*, and that perhaps it was the same, and probably the only, copy, which has been preserved till now. But the god of bibliomaniacs, unknown to ancient people, saved this precious edition and turned Nemesis upon Christoph, who died shortly after this event, as we shall see later. This is also something like the story of Brutus, and I am convinced that it will find its way into some anthology among the number of instructive historic examples.

Shortly before Christoph's death occurred the day when Sebastian had to undergo what the Lutheran Church calls Confirmation. Christoph Bach wanted this important event to take place near the resting-place of their father, to make it, so to speak, the proof that the older brother had fulfilled the parental duty thoroughly. Sebastian's hair was curled and powdered for the first time; a hairnet was affixed to it; a striped French coat was made for him out of his grandmother's old housecoat, and he was brought to Eisenach.

Here Sebastian heard the sounds of an organ for the first time. When the full, overpowering harmony descended from Gothic vaults, like the rush of a storm, Sebastian forgot everything around him. The harmonies seemed to stun his soul. He saw nothing—neither the beautiful church nor the young communicants, the girls who stood next to him. He hardly understood the words of the pastor; he answered without participating in his own words at all. It seemed as if all his nerves were filled with these airy sounds, as if his body

were involuntarily lifted from the ground . . . he could not
even pray. Christoph was angry, and could not understand
why his diligent, humble, and even shy Sebastian, who had
mastered the catechism in Ohrdrul so well, answered the pastor of Eisenach worse than anyone else, and as if in spite. He
could not understand why Sebastian sullied his coat against
the wall, left a shoe unbuckled, was absentminded, impolite,
pushed his neighbors, did not offer a place to older people,
and could not utter any of those long, fancy phrases by which
Germans used to measure the degree of respect at that time.
In Christoph's mind, music was inseparable from all family
and social duties: a false fifth and an impoliteness were one
and the same for him, and he was quite convinced that a
person who did not observe the accepted customs, who was
impolite, carelessly dressed, could never be a good musician,
and vice versa—and the good Christoph began to have sad
doubts: Was it possible that his system was wrong, or rather,
was he mistaken in his brother, and nothing worthwhile
would come of Sebastian?

This last notion became a certainty when after the mass he
took Sebastian to Bandeler, a famous organ builder of that
time and a relative of Bach's. After dinner the gay Bandeler,
according to custom, proposed that his companions sing the
Quodlibet—a kind of music that was very popular at that
time. It consisted in the participants singing folksongs all together, but each singing his own song. It was considered a
great art to sing in such a way that despite the many voices
one would be in perfect harmony with the others. Poor Sebastian constantly erred and sang false fifths, and no wonder: he
was gazing, and gazing intently, alas, not at the shy and
beautiful Annchen, Bandeler's daughter, whose actual portrait
you can see now in Hermitage, painted as a young girl by
Lucas Cranach. Sebastian was gazing at the huge wooden
and lead pipes, keyboard, pedals, and other parts of an unfinished organ that stood in the dining room. His young mind,
amazed at the sight of this chaos, tried to solve the problem
how it was possible for such low objects to create such a
majestic harmony of sounds? Christoph was in despair.

After dinner the old men became quite gay and began to
talk. Christoph Bach had already smoked his tenth pipe, for
the tenth time he was retelling the anecdote about his canon
and about the organists of Arnstadt, and for the tenth time
all those present were ready to laugh wholeheartedly—when
they noticed that Sebastian had disappeared. There was gen-

eral confusion. They looked here, they looked there—Sebastian was nowhere to be found. At first Christoph thought that Sebastian, feeling tired after the busy day, had gone to bed. But he was wrong: Sebastian did not return. Not having found him at home, Christoph grew angry, smoked his pipe to the end, and fell asleep at the usual time.

And it's no wonder they could not find Sebastian. No one could have suspected that at this time he was walking along the narrow streets of Eisenach toward the church. It had occurred to Sebastian to find out from where and how the enchanting sound that had taken possession of his soul this morning came, and he had decided to secure this pleasure for himself no matter what.

For a long time he looked for an entrance to the church. The main door was already locked. Sebastian was ready to climb up the outer wall and into the open window, about fifteen feet above the ground, not afraid of breaking his neck, nor of being suspected of sacrilege, when suddenly, to his great joy, he noticed a low, unlocked door. He pushed it, and the door opened. A small winding stairway was before him.

Trembling with joy and fear, he quickly ran upstairs, several steps at a time, and finally found himself in some narrow place. . . . In front of him were rows of columns, bellows of different sizes, and Gothic ornaments. The moon, which was still protecting him, shone suddenly through the stained glass of the semicircular windows, and Sebastian almost shouted with rapture, when he noticed that he was in the very place where he had seen the organist in the morning. He looked—in front of him was a keyboard, which seemed to tempt him to try his youthful strength. He rushed to it, struck the keys firmly, and waited for the full sound to rush against the vaults of the church. But the organ emitted a distorted chord into the church, like the groan of an angry man, and grew silent. In vain Sebastian tried first one chord then another; in vain he touched one key after another; in vain did he pull and push the handles nearby—the organ was silent, and only the dull wooden sound of the keys that set the valves of the pipes in motion was heard, as though it were laughing at the youth's efforts. A chill ran through Sebastian's veins. He thought that God was punishing him for his sacrilege and that the organ was destined to keep silent under his fingers forever. This thought almost made him lose consciousness.

Finally he remembered the bellows he had seen, and, smiling to himself, understood that without moving them the organ could not play, and that the first sound he had heard was caused by a small amount of air that had remained in one of the air ducts. Vexed by his ignorance he rushed to the bellows. With his strong hands he made them move, and then rushed headlong again to the keyboard to make use of the air that had not yet escaped the bellows. But it was in vain; the pipes emitted only distorted sounds, and Sebastian grew weak from his efforts.

So as not to have made his nocturnal trip in vain, he decided at least to examine this wonderful creation of art. Using the narrow ladder that stood leaning against the second level of the organ, he got inside. With amazement he looked at everything around him: here the huge rectangular pipes, like the remnants of an ancient Greek building, formed tiers, one stretching above another, and around them rows of Gothic towers raised their pointed metallic columns; with curiosity he examined the air ducts, which like the veins of a huge organism connected the pipes with the numerous valves of the keys; he stared at the marvelously built instrument which did not even emit any particular sound, but rather loud vibrations of air in which all sounds were fused and which no other instrument could imitate.

Suddenly he saw rectangular columns rising from their places, joining the Gothic columns, forming tier after tier, again and again . . . and before the eyes of Sebastian appeared an infinite, beautiful edifice which could not possibly be described consciously in the barren language of man. Here the mystery of architecture joined with the mysteries of harmony. Above the huge rafters, diverging in all directions from one's sight, full harmonies crossed each other in the shape of airy vaults and rested upon the numerous rhythmic columns. A fragrant mist rose from thousands of censors, and filled the inside of the church with a shimmering rainbow of light. Angels of melody floated on its light clouds and disappeared, joined in mysterious embraces; in graceful geometric shapes arose the combinations of musical instruments; above the sanctuary ascended choruses of human voices; variegated veils of contrasting sounds coiled and uncoiled in front of him, and a chromatic scale like a playful bas-relief rippled down the cornice. Everything here lived a harmonious life, each rainbow-like movement emitted a sound, and each sound was fragrant—and an invisible voice clearly pronounced the marriage of religion and art.

This vision lasted for a long time. Wonderstruck by fervent

awe, Sebastian fell to the ground, and instantly the sounds became louder; they thundered and the earth began to tremble under him, and Sebastian woke up. The majestic sounds still continued, and the sound of voices joined them. Sebastian looked around: daylight struck his eyes—he saw himself inside the organ where yesterday he had fallen asleep exhausted by his exertions.

Sebastian could not convince his brother that he had spent the night in the church playing the organ. Christoph could not comprehend the impulse of the soul that had taken possession of Sebastian in this case. In vain Sebastian told him about this inconceivable feeling that had carried him away, about his impatience, about his rapture. Christoph answered that all this was known to him too, that, indeed, a musician must know of rapture, even Gafurius said so, but that one should choose appropriate moments for rapture. He used convincing arguments and examples to prove that every rapture, every passion must be based on the principles of reason and proper conduct, just as every musical idea is based on the principles of counterpoint and not on the violation of all principles, on decency and customs; that only an immoral and ill-bred man would let himself be carried away by an emotion, no matter what kind. Immediately after that, he began to reproach Sebastian with renewed vigor, reminding him that neither his father nor his grandfather nor his great-grandfather had ever spent a night outside their homes. To conclude, he attributed everything that had happened to Sebastian to the contrivance of a young man who wanted to cover up some improper pranks.

This incident confirmed Christoph's notion that Sebastian was a lost man, and it grieved him so much that he became ill and shortly afterward passed into eternal life. Sebastian was horrified when he found his heart devoid of sincere regrets at the loss of his teacher.

Sebastian did not return to Ohrdruf anymore, but remained in Eisenach and devoted his life to the development of his musical talent.[8] He would reverently listen to what many

[8] During one of my trips abroad I purposely stopped in Eisenach and, of course, first of all inquired where Sebastian Bach's house was. The tavern servant did not return for a long time. Finally he came and told me that Mr. Bach was no longer in Eisenach. "Where is he then?" I asked. *"They say* that Mr. Bach is dead," answered the precise servant.

famous organists of that town had to say, but none of them
could satisfy his insatiable curiosity. In vain he besought his
teachers to reveal the secrets of harmony to him; in vain he
asked them how our ear could comprehend the combination
of sounds, why musical impression could not be verified by
any other physical sensation, why one combination of sounds
would make one ecstatic while another would offend one's
ear? His teachers would answer him with the conventional
artificial rules which could not satisfy Sebastian's mind: the
feeling about music his mysterious vision had left in his soul
was more comprehensible to him, but he was unable to formulate it into words for himself.

Not for a moment could Sebastian forget this vision; he
would not even be able to relate it completely, yet the impression created by that feeling was still vibrant and became
part of all his thoughts and feelings, enveloping them in a
rainbow-like veil. Old Bandeler, whom he did not stop seeing
after the death of Christoph, and to whom he told this,
laughed and advised him not to think of dreams, but rather
to use his time learning the art of organ building, which
could surely give him a comfortable livelihood for the rest of
his life.

In the simplicity of his heart Sebastian almost believed
Bandeler, and was annoyed that his dream would take hold
of him so often and against his own will.

Soon Sebastian moved to Bandeler's house and began to
learn his craft with great eagerness and later even to help
him. Zealously he chiseled keys, measured pipes, attached
pistons, bent wires, pasted valves. But often the work would
drop out of his hands, and he would think bitterly of the
immense gulf between the feeling aroused in him by the
mysterious vision and the craft that was about to become his.
The workers' laughter, their trivial jokes, squeaks of organs
being tuned would wake him up from his meditations, and,
reproaching himself for his childish dreams, he would set to
work again. Bandeler did not notice these bitter moments of
Sebastian's. He saw only his pupil's diligence, and other
thoughts took shape in his mind: he would often be kind to
Sebastian in the presence of his Annchen, or caress his
daughter in the presence of Sebastian. He would talk about
her ability to handle money, her art in housekeeping, then
about her piety and even about her charm. Annchen would
blush, smiling sweetly at Sebastian, and it was noticeable that
for some time she began to starch and press her cuffs more

zealously and to spend more time than she previously had in the kitchen and on household accounts.

Once Bandeler announced to his household that he had invited his old friend Johann Albrecht, an organ builder from Lüneburg who had recently come to Eisenach, home to dinner. "I still love him," said Bandeler; "he is a kind and quiet man, a true Christian, and he might even have been a famous organ maker, but he is strange. He tries his hand at everything: organs alone are not enough for him, no! He wants to make organs and clavichords, violins and theorbos. He toils and plods over these instruments, and you know what happens? Just listen, you younger men! Somebody would order an organ from him—he would start working on it, and he would really work hard, not a month or two, but a year, or even longer. Then, all of a sudden, he would put some new fixture into it, some gadget to which our organists are not accustomed. So, of course, the organ remains on his hands, and he is only too happy to sell it at half-price. The same with violins . . .

"Now, you take our neighbor Klotz. He found the way: he takes a violin of the old master Steiner, measures it, cuts the wood with precisely the same dimensions, makes a bridge and a neck, puts in pegs, everything according to measure, and a perfect violin comes out. That's why his violins sell like hotcakes, and not only in our blessed Germany but also in France and in Italy. Just see what a beautiful house our neighbor has built for himself. But old Albrecht? Do you think it would occur to him to copy an old violin? No, he would calculate and measure, look for some kind of mathematical proportion in a violin: he would take the fourth string off, then he would replace it; at one time he would curve the sounding board, then he would straighten it out; now he would make it convex, then flatten it again—busy, busy, all the time, but nothing comes out of it. Would you believe it? In twenty years he has not succeeded in making one decent violin. Meanwhile, time goes on but his business is at a standstill: it looks as if he had just opened his shop. Don't follow his example, young men! Don't expect anything good of someone who outsmarts himself. Innovations and philosophizing aren't worth anything in our business, or in any other. Our fathers were really clever. They invented everything that is good, and didn't leave anything for us to invent. May God grant us to go as far as they did!"

At this moment, in came Johann Albrecht.[9] "You've come just at the right moment, my dear Johann," said Bandeler, embracing him. "Just now I was berating you and advising these young men not to follow your example."

"That was wrong of you, my dear Karl," answered Albrecht, "because I'll need them very much. I've come to ask you to supply me with assistants for a new and difficult project. . . ."

"Well, it is probably another one of your inventions!" Bandeler burst out with a laugh.

"Yes, an invention in which I've succeeded, to your surprise. . . ."

"As with all your violins . . ."

"Something more important than violins; I am speaking of an entirely new register[10] on the organ."

"So! I knew that you would come up with something like that. Won't you tell us about it? We'd be happy to learn from you at least once."

"You know that I don't like idle talk. We can discuss it during dinner, at our leisure."

"Well, well, let's see."

Several organists and musicians of Eisenach came to dinner. They were, according to the old German custom, joined by all Bandeler's pupils, and so there was a rather large gathering at table.

Albrecht was reminded of his promise.

"As you know, my friends," he said, "I've been trying to penetrate into the mystery of harmony for a long time, and to that end have repeatedly made various experiments."

"We know, we know," said Bandeler. "We know only too well."

"Whatever you say, I consider such experimentation indispensable to our craft. . . ."

"That's exactly your trouble. . . ."

"Just be patient until I've finished!

[9] In musical histories there are three Johann Albrechts, but they came later. Which of them our narrator is talking about is not known. He seems to have his own chronology. We will leave it to the reader to verify it himself.

[10] The organ, as is well known, is composed as it were of several orchestras or groups of many different instruments. Wooden pipes compose one group, metal pipes another; each of these groups has many subdivisions, each having its own name: *Vox Humana, Quintadena,* and so on. And these subdivisions are called *registers.*

"Not so long ago, while doing the Pythagorean experiments with a monochord, I sharply pulled the thick, long taut string, and—imagine my surprise: I noticed that the sound it emitted was joined by other tones. I repeated my experiment several times, until I made quite certain what these tones were: I heard a fifth and a third. This observation made it clear to me that everything in this world leads to unity—and that's the way it should be! In each sound we hear the whole chord. Melody is a series of chords. Each sound is nothing else but a full harmony. I began to think about it; I thought again and again until I decided to supply the organ with a new register, each key of which opened several little pipes tuned into a full chord, and I called this register *Mystery*,[11] because, truly, a very important mystery is concealed in it.

All the old men began to laugh and the young ones to whisper to each other. Bandeler, unable to restrain himself, jumped up from his seat and opened the clavichord: "Listen," he cried, "what discovery your dear Albrecht offers us," and began playing some comical folksong, using false fifths. The laughter redoubled; only Sebastian took no part in it; he only stared at Albrecht, impatiently waiting for his answer.

"Laugh as much as you want to, gentlemen, but I must say that my new register gave a power and greatness to the organ that it never had before."

"It's really too much!" muttered Bandeler, and having made a sign to the others to keep silent, didn't mention the subject again throughout dinner.

When the dinner was over, Bandeler took Albrecht aside, away from the young people, and said:

"My dear, beloved Johann, listen to me, please. Don't be mad at me, your old friend and schoolmate. I didn't want to say this in front of my pupils, but now that I'm alone with you, I ask you, as an old friend of yours: come to your senses, don't put your gray head to shame. Do you really want to add your ridiculous register to the organ?"

"What do you mean, 'to add'?" shouted Albrecht. "It has been done already, and let me repeat to you, no organ in existence can ever compare with mine. . . ."

"Look, Johann! You know that for fifty years now I've been building organs; for some thirty years I've been a master in this craft. My neighbor Hartmann, too. Our fathers and

[11] In present-day organs this word has changed into a prosaic one: *Mixturen.*

grandfathers built organs—how do you intend to convince us of something that goes against the fundamental principles of our craft?"

"Yet, it does not go against nature!"

"For goodness' sake, here you have not only false fifths but complete nonsense."

"And yet these false fifths create a majestic harmony in the organ."

"But the false fifths—"

"Do you really think," Albrecht interrupted, "you gentlemen who for fifty years have been chiseling pipes just the way your fathers and grandfathers had chiseled them before —do you really think that this occupation enabled you to comprehend the mysteries of harmony? These mysteries are not revealed through hammer and saw: they are rooted deep down in one's soul, as in a covered vessel. God brings them forth into the world; they are endowed with a body and shape, not by the will of a man but by God's will. Are you the ones to stop it because you do not understand it? . . . But that's enough. I repeat again that I came here to ask you for help, you, Karl, and you, Hartmann. I'm overloaded with work now; I need assistants. Lend me some of your pupils."

"What are you talking about?" said Bandeler, enraged. "Who among them do you think would consent to become your pupil after the things you've said here?"

"If I might . . ." softly muttered Sebastian.

"What? You, Sebastian? My best, my most diligent pupil . . ."

"I would like to hear Mr. Albrecht's new organ. . . ."

"To hear false fifths—do you really believe that something like that is possible?"

"Doubting Thomas!" Albrecht cried out. "Go to Lüneburg yourself. Then at least you'll believe your own ears. . . ."

"Who? I? I should go to Lüneburg? What for? To make people say that I don't know anything about my craft, that I am just as odd as Albrecht, that I believe his inventions which only a boy might believe, to make myself everybody's laughingstock?"

"Don't worry, you will be in such company that no one would dare to laugh. The Emperor visited me, on his way through Lüneburg."

"The Emperor!"

"You know what a profound connoisseur of music he is. He heard my new organ and ordered one just like it for the

Vienna Cathedral. Look, here is the contract for ten thousand gulden; here are other orders for Dresden, for Berlin. . . . Do you believe me now? I didn't want to mention it before; I expected you to believe the words of your old Albrecht. . . ."

The men around him were astonished. After a moment of silence Klotz went up to Albrecht, bowed low, and said: "Although I am not of your guild, such an important discovery makes me ask you, Mr. Albrecht, for permission to look at your new register, and learn." Hartmann, without a word, went home immediately to prepare for his departure. Bandeler alone remained undecided. He let Albrecht take some of his pupils, among them Sebastian; but he himself did not go to Lüneburg.

Sebastian had not been working long at Albrecht's as his assistant. Once, on a holiday, when the youth, seated at the clavichord, was singing religious songs, the old man entered the room unnoticed and stood there listening for quite a while. "Sebastian!" he said finally, "Only now do I recognize you. You are not a craftsman. It is not your job to chisel keys: another, higher task is destined for you. You are a musician, Sebastian!" cried out the ardent old man. "You are meant for this high calling, the importance of which only a few can understand. Providence endowed you with the language in which man can understand the divine and through which man's soul reaches the throne of the Almighty. We shall talk more about it later. Now leave your work as a craftsman. I lose a dependable helper in you, but I do not want to oppose the will of Providence. It has not created you in vain."

After a moment's silence he went on: "It will be difficult for you to find a position as an organist here. But you have a good voice, and you must train it. Magdalena is taking singing lessons with the local pastor; you can go along with her. Meanwhile, I'll try to get you into the church choir of St. Michael's—that will provide you with a means of living. But for the present, study the organ, this magnificent likeness of the world of God: both of them contain many mysteries; only persistent study can reveal them."

Sebastian threw himself at Albrecht's feet.

From then on, Sebastian was one of the family in Johann's house.

Magdalena was an unaffected and beautiful girl. From her Italian mother she inherited her black, shiny hair, curling in ringlets above her northern blue eyes. But this was the only thing that set her apart from the girls of her age. She lost her mother before she was three, and was brought up in the simple, ancient German ways, and she therefore knew nothing except her own little world. In the morning there were things to be done in the kitchen, flowers needed watering in the garden; in the afternoon she would sit embroidering at the window; on Saturday she would work in the laundry, and on Sunday go to the pastor. Lüneburg musicians those days used to say of her that she resembled an Italian theme developed in the German manner. Sebastian attended singing lessons with her as though she were a comrade. Neither the beauty nor the innocence of the girl affected the inexperienced youth, whose soul was set on fire by Albrecht's words. There was no place for earthly emotions in his pure soul: it was full only of sounds, of their wonderful harmonies and their mysterious affinities to the world. On the contrary, the proud youth would even grow impatient with the beautiful girl and scold her whenever her immature voice would break on the note needed for a chord, or when she would innocently ask for an explanation of musical problems that seemed so easy for Sebastian.

Sebastian found himself in his real element. Albrecht's huge collection of books and music was open to him. In the morning he would exercise his skill on various instruments, particularly on the clavichord, or he would sing. Then he would get a key to the church organ from his friend, the organist, and there, alone, under the Gothic vaults he would study the secrets of the wonderful instrument for the rest of the day. Only the Altar of God, covered with a cloth, heeded him in majestic silence. Then Sebastian would recall the event in the church of Eisenach; the vision of his childhood would again rise from the gloomy recesses of the church. With each new day he understood it more and more—reverent awe would descend upon the soul of the youth, and his heart would flame up. In the evenings, at home, he would see Albrecht, tired from his daily work, sitting among his pupils. He talked to them softly, and lofty words adorned with playful allegories would pour out from his lips. However, gentlemen, don't think that Albrecht was one of those eloquent rhetoricians who would first sketch a naked skeleton and then, to please the honorable audience, proceed to adorn it with metaphors, allegories, metonymies, and other confections. Common language seldom issued from Albrecht's lips because he could not find words in it to express his thoughts: he felt forced to search through all nature for things that might express his feelings, which were inexpressible in words. There is a language used by a half-civilized man, who has just attained the first stage of enlightenment, when he is struck by a new, hitherto undreamed-of, idea. Such, too, is the language of the man who has entered the sanctuary of secret knowledge and who tries to give shape to objects for which the human language does not suffice. Albrecht, who was perhaps a combination of both, spoke in such a language. Only a few sympathized with Albrecht and understood him. Others tried to find in his words some sort of advice to be followed in their craftsmanship. The rest of his pupils listened to him only distractedly, and out of respect.

"There were times," Albrecht used to say, "from which not a sound, not a word, not a trace is left: mankind had no need of *expression* then. Peacefully it rested in its innocent cradle, and in its carefree dreams it understood God and nature, the present and the future. But then . . . the infant's cradle shook: a tender being, unfledged, like a butterfly in its scarcely opened cocoon, was confronted with stern and inquisitive nature. In vain did a youthful Alcides strive to chain nature's huge and varied forms in his childlike babble. With its head, nature touched the world of ideas; with its heel, the coarse instinct of crystals, and it challenged the man to measure up to its strength. It was then that the two constant and eternal but also dangerous and treacherous allies of the man's soul were born: *thought* and *expression*.

"No one knows how long this primordial strife went on: on the battlegrounds there have remained only the pyramids scattered in the sands of Egypt, magnificent silt-covered castles, a testimony to ancient power. There have remained also the diseases of man, whose heavy chain vanishes in the darkness of ancient times. Defeated, but as strong as he was formerly, man continued this struggle, fell, and with every new fall, like Antaeus, he gained new power. It seemed for a while that he had subjected the unconquerable to his power —but then, suddenly, man's soul encountered a new enemy, more terrible and demanding, more importunate and dissatisfied—*man himself*.

"With the appearance of this new combatant, the temporarily pacified forces of nature rose anew. Terrible, relentless enemies fiercely rushed upon the man, and like the Titans in their fight with Zeus, they began to crush him with the weight of awful questions about life and death, will and necessity, motion and rest, and it would have been vain till this very day for a philosopher to evade the issue behind the shield of logical conclusions, or for a mathematician to hide in the crevices of spirals and conchoids—mankind would have perished if the heavens had not sent him a new champion: *art!* This great, invincible power, this reflection of the Creator, subdued both nature and man. Like Oedipus, it guessed all the symbols of the two-headed Sphinx—and people named this solemn moment in the life of mankind Orpheus, who subdued stones by the power of harmony. With the help of this life-giving creative force man erected an edifice of hieroglyphs, statues and temples, Homer's *Iliad*, Dante's *Divine Comedy*, the Olympic hymns and the psalms of Christianity: he fused the mysterious forces of nature and his own soul in them. However, imprisoned in their magnificent but narrow cells, these creations long for freedom, and therefore at the sight of Dürer's *Cecilia*, of the Medici Venus, or from the vaults of the Strasbourg bell tower we feel the stormy breath that chills the veins and immerses the soul in sublime thought.

"But there is still the highest state of man's soul, which he does not share with nature, which eludes the sculptor's chisel, remains unrevealed by the passionate lines of the poet. This is the state when the soul, proud of its victory over nature, in the full blaze of its glory, grows humble before the Almighty and, suffering bitterly, yearns to prostrate itself at His throne and, like a stranger amid the luxurious delights of a foreign land, sighs for his fatherland. People called the feeling that springs from this lofty state of the soul *the ineffable. Music* is the only language of this feeling. In music, in this highest sphere of human art, man becomes oblivious to the storms of his earthly wanderings. In it, as at the peak of the Alps, there radiates a cloudless sun of harmony. Only the inexplicit, boundless sounds embrace the infinite soul of man; only they can unite the elements of joy and sorrow, sundered by the fall of man; only they can rejuvenate the heart and transport us into the innocent first cradle of the first innocent man.

"Do not weaken, my young friends! Pray, concentrate all the knowledge of your mind and all the strength of your heart in the perfection of the medium of this wonderful art. Its simple, crude pipes conceal the mystery of inciting the loftiest feelings in man's soul. Every new step toward improvement brings them closer to that spiritual force whose expression they should be. Every new step means a new victory of man over life, over this phantom which, sneering at intellectual effort, becomes more awful every new day and threatens to reduce to ashes the scanty vessel of man."

Thus Albrecht often talked to his pupils. Profound silence reigned around him. Only from time to time a flickering coal would blaze up in the dying hearth, casting its momentary glow on the old man's silvery hair, on the young and fresh faces of the German youths, on Magdalena's black curls and the shining, scattered pieces of unfinished instruments. The voice of a night watchman would be heard; the old man would bless the youths and end a harmonious day with a solemn, sonorous prayer.

Albrecht's words sank into Sebastian's heart; their mystery frequently bewildered him. He would not be able to repeat them, but he understood the feeling they expressed. Through this feeling his soul unconsciously grew and gained strength in ardent inner activity.

Years passed. Albrecht finished building organs, distributed the money he had earned among his pupils, or used it for new experiments, and without giving a thought to increasing his own estate he again began to work at perfecting his favorite instrument. It was said that he had been dreaming of fusing in it the expressions of all the elements of the world: fire and water, earth and air. Meanwhile, people in Lüneburg talked of nothing else but the young organist Bach. Magdalena's voice developed with the years: now she could read a score at sight; she sang and played Sebastian's music.

One day Albrecht said to the young musician: "Look, Sebastian, there no longer is anyone in Lüneburg from whom you could learn. You have left all the local organists far behind. But art is infinite. Now you have to meet the men you will be replacing in the musical world in the days to come. I've procured for you a position as a court violinist (sic) in Weimar; it will bring you money—an essential thing on earth, and money will enable you to visit Lübeck and Hamburg, where you'll get to hear my famous friends Buxtehude and Reinken. There's no need to dally in this world; time flies. Get ready and be on your way."

At first this proposal delighted Sebastian: to hear Buxtehude, Reinken, whose works he knew almost by heart; to assure himself that he had understood their lofty ideas correctly; to hear their brilliant improvisations which couldn't be fixed on a sheet of paper; to learn about their method of com-

bining registers; to display his own talent before these cele-
brated judges; to spread his own fame—all this immediately
captured the imagination of the youth. But to leave the house
in which his young talent had developed, the house where
harmony lived and breathed in everything; not to hear
Albrecht anymore, to find himself again among cold people
who do not understand the divine nature of art! . . .

Then he remembered Magdalena with her black curls, blue
eyes, and shy smile. He had got so used to her soft velvety
voice that all Sebastian's favorite melodies seemed to have
become entwined with it; she was of great help in learning to
play new scores; she listened to his compositions with such
understanding that he loved to see her before him when,
immersed in a reverie of improvisation, his eyes would stare
fixedly at one spot. Not long ago, realizing that Sebastian's
fingers could not reach all the sounds needed for the chord,
she got up, bent over the chair, and placed her little finger
on the key. . . .

Sebastian began thinking, and the more he thought, the
more he realized that Magdalena was part of his musical life;
it amazed him that he had not noticed it until now. . . . He
glanced around him: here was the music she copied for him;
here lay the pen she sharpened; here was the string she was
trying to fasten in his absence; here was the music sheet on
which she wrote down his improvisation that otherwise would
have been lost forever. . . . All this made Sebastian conclude
that Magdalena was indispensable to him; but, looking
deeper into himself, he finally realized that the feeling he had
for Magdalena was what is usually called love.

This discovery surprised him very much. Working daily,
turning in the very same sphere of ideas and sensations, in
the serenity so natural and so much in keeping with Sebastian's character, even the monotonous order of activities in
Albrecht's house—all this had accustomed the young man's
spirit to a quiet and harmonious existence. Magdalena was
such a melodious, indispensable sound in that harmony that
their very love was born and had passed all its stages almost
unnoticed by the young people themselves, it fused so perfectly with all the events of their chaste lives. Perhaps Magdalena had begun to understand this feeling earlier; but only
a parting could explain it to Sebastian.

"Magdalena! my dear sister!" said Sebastian, stammering
when the girl entered the room, "your father is sending me to
Weimar. . . . We are not going to be together. . . . Maybe we

won't see each other for a long time: do you want to be my wife? Then we shall always be together."

Magdalena blushed, gave him her hand, and said, "Let us go to tell Father."

The old man met them with a smile: "I've anticipated this for a long time," he said. "Evidently it is God's will," he added with a sigh. "God bless you, my children; art has united you, and may it be a strong bond for your entire life. Only, don't get attached too much to singing, Sebastian; you sing too often with Magdalena: the voice abounds in human passions; unperceptibly, in the moments of purest inspiration, sounds of another, impure world break into it; the human voice still carries the imprint of the first sinful wail! . . . The organ subjected to your control is not a live instrument, and therefore is not privy to delusions of your will: it is eternally quiet, impassive, like nature itself. Its smooth harmonies do not obey the whims of worldly delights. Only the soul immersed in a silent prayer gives a soul to its wooden pipes; and they, solemnly ringing through the air, display its own greatness before it. . . ."

I won't go into the details of Sebastian's wedding, gentlemen, or of his trip to Weimar, of Albrecht's death, which followed soon after it; of various posts Sebastian held in various cities, or of his acquaintanceship with many famous men. All these details you'll find in various biographies of Bach; I don't know about you, but I am more curious about events in Sebastian's inner life. There is only one means to learn about these events. I advise you to play all Bach's music from beginning to end, as I did. It is a pity that my talkative old Albrecht is dead: at least he related what Sebastian felt. When Sebastian listened to Albrecht, he always thought that he was listening to himself. Verbal language was not his chief medium of communication—he expressed himself only through the sounds of an organ. And you cannot imagine how difficult it is to translate from this divine, infinite language into our language, which is limited and mixed with the clay of life. Sometimes I have to write a volume of commentary to four notes, and yet these four notes speak more clearly to one who knows how to understand them than my whole volume.

Indeed, Bach knew only one thing in this world—his art; he understood nature and life with its joys and griefs only when it penetrated the sounds of music. They moved his thinking, his feelings; he lived for them; everything else was superfluous and dead to him. I can well believe that Talma in a moment of deep grief unconsciously approached the mirror to see what lines it made on his face. That's what an artist should be like—and that's how Bach was. Once, signing some financial transaction, he noticed that the letters of his name composed an original, rich melody, and he wrote a fugue based on it.[12] When he heard the first cry of his first child, he was very happy, but he immediately had to figure out what key the sounds he heard were in. When he learned of the death of his dear friend, he covered his face with his hands, and a minute later began writing a funeral motet. Do not accuse Bach of insensitivity—perhaps he felt more deeply than other people, but he did so in his own way; these were human feelings, but in the world of art. He valued his own frame just as little: in Hamburg it is said that when the hundred-year-old organist Reinken heard Bach, he burst into tears and said, "I thought that my art would die with me, but you are resurrecting it." In Dresden it was said that a well-known organist of that time, Marchand, challenged to compete with Bach, became frightened and left Dresden on the very day of the concert. In Berlin, people were surprised that Frederick the Great, when he read through the list of guests arriving in Potsdam before his house concert, became obviously worried, and said to those around him, "Gentlemen! Bach the senior has arrived." Thereupon he humbly put his flute away, immediately sent for Bach, and made him, still in his traveling suit, go from piano to piano, placed in all the rooms of the castle in Potsdam. He gave Sebastian a theme for a fugue, and listened to him with reverence.

But Sebastian, when he returned home, told Magdalena only about a happy melody that had occurred to him during the improvisation before Reinken, how the cathedral organ in Dresden was constructed, and that, while entertaining King Frederick, he took advantage of an out-of-tune key in the piano to make an enharmonic passage—and nothing else! Magdalena asked nothing more, and Sebastian at once took

---

[12] Bach's fugue on the following motif is well known:

 b, a, c, h.

his seat at the clavichord and played or sang with her his
latest compositions: this was the usual mode of conversation
between the couple; they rarely spoke to each other differently.

And all the days of his life were like this. In the morning
he composed; then he would discuss the mysteries of harmony with his sons and other pupils, or perform the duties
of organist in the church. He spent his evenings at the
clavichord singing and playing with his Magdelena; then he
would fall asleep quietly, and in his dreams he would hear
only sounds, see only progressions of melodies. When he
felt distracted, he entertained himself by studying new music
ad aperturam libri, or improvised pieces on a ground bass or,
listening to the trio performing, would sit down at the
clavichord to add another voice and thus change the trio
into a real quartet.

Frequent playing on the organ, constant thinking about
this instrument contributed to the development of Bach's
even, quiet, and majestic character. This character was reflected in his whole life, or rather, in all his music. In his
early compositions certain sacrifices to the predominant taste
of that time are still audible, but later Bach shook these
remnants off, ridding himself of the bonds that tied him to
everyday life, and his peaceful soul found perfect, even, and
formal expression in his magnificent melodies. In other words,
he became the church organ raised to the level of man.

I told you that inspiration did not come to him in bursts;
it glowed quietly in his heart: home at the clavichord, in a
chorus among his pupils, in a conversation with his friends,
at the organ in church, he was faithful to the divine art, and
never did an earthly thought or passion burst into his sounds;
that is why now, when music has ceased to be a prayer,
when it has become an expression of restless passion, a toy
for diversion, a lure for vainglory—Bach's music seems cold
and lifeless. We do not understand it, as we fail to understand the impassivity of martyrs burned at the stake by
pagans. We look for something comprehensible, something
that approximates our indolence, our comforts in life. We
are afraid of profound feeling, as we are of profound
thought. We are afraid to plunge into our innermost souls
lest we reveal our own ugliness. Death has chained all the
impulses of our heart—we are afraid of life! We are afraid
of things for which there are no words: and what can you

express in words? . . . This was not what Bach felt, when absorbed in the creation of his musical fantasies: his soul was in his fingertips; obedient to his will, they expressed his feelings in innumerable forms; but the feeling was one, and the simplest of its expressions was contained in just a few notes. This was the unity of a prayer, which bestowed upon people such manifold gifts.

This was not what was felt by those happy people who heard Bach play the organ. Their feeling of reverence was not dissipated by playful displays. At first, it was expressed by a plain melody, like the first feeling of a childlike heart; then, slowly, the melody grew, matured, produced another harmonizing melody, and then a third; they would all at times merge into a brotherly embrace, at others scatter into various chords. But the original feeling of reverence was not lost for a moment; it touched all the impulses only lightly, all the corners of the heart, in order to enliven all spiritual forces with a beneficial dew. When all their variegated images had been expressed, the theme appeared in plain but great, full chords, and the listeners left church with a purified soul, called to life and love.

Bach's biographers describe this sacrament of harmony, now lost, as follows: "During the service," they write, "Bach took up one theme, and developed it so skillfully on the organ that he could play for two hours. First this theme was heard in the *Vorspiel*, or prelude; then Bach presented it as a fugue; then, by means of various registers he turned that same theme into a trio or quartet; this was followed by a chorale, where the same theme was again utilized in three or four voices; finally, he concluded by playing another fugue, still on the original theme but developed in a different manner, and with the addition of two other themes. That was the real art of the organ!"

That's how these people translate a musician's religious inspiration into their own language!

Once, during the service, when Bach was at the organ, completely immersed in the feeling of reverence, and the chorus of voices blended with the magnificent harmonies of the divine instrument, the organist suddenly stopped; a moment later he continued playing, but everyone noticed that he appeared worried, that he was constantly turning around and looking at the crowd with troubled curiosity. In the midst of the singing Bach had noticed that the chorus had been joined by a beautiful, pure voice that sounded very strange, and unlike the usual singing. Now it broke out like a cry of pain; now it was sharp, like the wild shouting of a joyous crowd; now it seemed to be bursting out of the dark recesses of the soul; in short, this was not a voice of reverence or prayer—there was something tempting in it. Bach's experienced ear immediately noticed this new kind of expression; he perceived it as a bright, dazzling shaft in a painting; it destroyed the general harmony: the fervent feeling of reverence ceased to be chaste; the spiritual, light-winged prayer became heavy; there was a certain mockery at the general sacramental peacefulness in the church. It troubled Bach; he tried not to hear it; he tried to drown these earthly impulses in thunderous chords. All was in vain: the passionate voice proudly floated above all the others, and, it seemed, defiled every harmony.

When Bach arrived at his home, a stranger entered after him, saying that he was a foreigner, a musician, and that he had come to pay his respects to the famous Bach. He was a tall, young man with black southern eyes. Unlike the Germans, he did not use powder. His black fair fell on his shoulders, framing his dark, emaciated face, which was constantly changing its expression; a kind of restless thoughtfulness or absentmindedness was its main characteristic. His eyes kept darting from one object to another without stopping at any one of them; he seemed to fear attracting anyone's attention.

"I am from Venice and my name is Francesco," said the young man. "I am the pupil of the famous Abbot Oliva, the follower of the glorious Cesti."

"Cesti!" said Bach. "I know his music; I have also heard about the Abbot Oliva, although little; I'm very glad to know you."

The simple, sincere Bach, who was always kind to visiting foreigners, was kind to the young man. He asked him about the present state of music in Italy, and finally, although he disliked contemporary Italian music, invited Francesco to acquaint him with his teacher's recent compositions.

Francesco confidently took his seat at the clavichord and began singing—and at once Sebastian recognized the voice that had taken him by surprise in church. However, he did not show his displeasure, and continued listening to the Venetian in his usual quiet, simple manner.

At that time a new era was beginning in Italian music, the latest development of which we see in Rossini and his followers. Carissimi, Cesti, Cavalli wanted to discard the somewhat antiquated forms of their predecessors' music, and set the voice free. But the followers of these talented men went still further: singing became furious shouting; some passages were now adorned, not for the sake of music itself, but to give the singer a chance to display his voice; invention diminished, and playful roulades and trills replaced well-developed, full harmonies. Bach had some knowledge of Cesti's and Cavalli's operas, but the new manner in which Francesco sang was quite unfamiliar to the organist of Arnstadt. Imagine Bach in his dignity, used to melodious tranquillity, used to a mathematical necessity for every note, now listening to the outpouring of unusual sounds made disquieting by the Italian mode of expression, which was unknown in Germany. The Venetian sang a few arias (this word was being then introduced) of his teacher, then some folk canzonettas arranged in the new mode. The humble Bach patiently listened to all this, and with false modesty said that he was not capable of writing anything of that kind.

But what was happening to Magdalena? Why did the color disappear from her rosy cheeks? Why did she look so fixedly at the stranger? Why was she trembling? Why were her hands so cold and tears streaming down her cheeks?

The stranger finished playing, said good-bye to Bach, and asked for permission to visit him again. Still Magdalena stood motionless, leaning against the half-open door. The stranger glanced at Magdalena as he was leaving, and she felt a chill.

After the stranger left, Bach, who had noticed nothing, was about to make fun at the expense of his self-confident visitor. But suddenly he saw Magdalena rush to the clavichord and try to repeat the melodies, the phrases she could still remember. At first Sebastian thought that she was making fun of the Venetian, and he was about to burst out laughing. But he was astonished when Magdalena covered her face with her hands and cried: "That's real music, Sebastian! real music! Only now do I understand music! How often I tried to recall, as if in a dream, the melodies my mother used to sing to me, rocking me in her arms, but they had vanished from my memory. In vain did I try to find them in your music, in all the music I heard every day! I felt that it lacked something, but I couldn't explain to myself what it was. It was a dream the details of which were forgotten and which had left in me only sweet memories. Only now do I realize what your music lacked; now I remember the songs of my mother. . . . Oh, Sebastian!" she cried out, and, with an unwonted gesture, threw herself into his arms, "throw all your fugues, all your canons into the fire! Write Italian canzonettas; for my sake, write them!"

Sebastian seriously thought that his Magdalena had lost her mind. He seated her in a chair, did not argue with her, and promised everything she asked.

The stranger visited the organist a few more times. Though Sebastian was impatient to be rid of him, when he saw how happy these visits made Magdalena, he was unable to be unkind to him.

Sebastian was surprised to notice that Magdalena began to add certain refinements to her dress, that she hardly took her eyes off the young Venetian, hanging on his every word. It seemed strange to Sebastian, after twenty years of married life in peace and harmony, to feel jealous of a man his wife hardly knew. But he was worried, and Albrecht's words, "The voice abounds in human passions," rang in his ears.

Unfortunately, Bach had a right to be jealous, in the full sense of the word. Italian blood, in the course of forty years—forty years!—suppressed by education, way of life, habit, suddenly was awakened by its native sounds; a new, unsuspected world opened before Magdalena. Southern passions, which had long been confined in her soul, now broke loose with all the ardor of fiery youth. To their agony was added the agony experienced by a woman who has understood love only during the decline of her beauty.

Francesco did not fail to notice the effect he exercised on Magdalena. It was amusing and entertaining to make the wife of the famous organist fall in love with him. It flattered his vanity to elicit such attention from a woman among the northern barbarians. His heart delighted in avenging the music of his school, which had been ridiculed by German musicians, in the home of Germany's greatest genius. And when Magdalena, leaning on the clavichord, beside herself with ecstasy, oblivious to her husband and her duties as the mother of the family, fixed her passionate gaze on him, the derisive Venetian did not spare his alluring southern eyes. He tried to remember all the melodies and phrases that would enrapture an Italian soul—and poor Magdalena, like a Delphic priestess, would find herself in a terrible, frenzied trance.

Finally, this comedy bored the Italian, and he departed.

Bach was beside himself with joy. Poor Sebastian! It was true that Francesco did not take Magdalena away with him, but he removed peace from the quiet home of the humble organist. Bach no longer recognized his wife. The woman who had been so cheerful and active before, who had cared deeply about her household, now spent her days sitting with her hands in her lap, deep in thought and softly humming Francesco's canzonettas. In vain did Bach write joyful minuets, mournful sarabandes and fugues *in stilo francese* for her. Magdalena remained indifferent; she would listen to them almost resentfully, and say, "Wonderful! yet it is not the real thing!" Bach was vexed. There were not many people who could appreciate his music even then. Completely devoted to his art, he did not value people's opinions, and thought very little even of the praise of those who were partial to him. He sought to reveal the secrets of art by his own deep perception of it rather than by a passing fashion. But he had become accustomed to Magdelena's participation in his musical life, and her approval was gratifying to him; it increased his self-confidence. To see her indifference, her opposition to the aim of his life, and this in his own family circle, in his own wife, in a being who had felt and thought and sung in unison with him for so many years—this was unbearable for Sebastian.

Other things added to his distress: the order to which Sebastian was accustomed in his house was gone. Formerly he could devote himself entirely to his art, knowing that Magdalena would take care of all the material aspects of their life together. Now Sebastian, in the fiftieth year, had to learn household tasks. Right in the middle of his musical inspiration he had to think of his clothing. Bach was vexed, indeed.

Frequently Magdalena was in agony too, but for other reasons. She would wipe away her tears, remembering her duties, or she would open Bach's scores—but Francesco's eyes would appear before her, his passionate melodies would resound in her ears, and she would put aside her husband's formal music with distaste. Often her agony became a frenzy: she was ready to forget everything, to leave her home and run after her charming Venetian, to throw herself at his feet and offer him her love along with her life.

Then she would glance into the mirror: the impartial glass showed her the wrinkles of a woman in her forties and made her realize that her day was over. Crying bitterly, Magdalena would throw herself on her bed, or go to her husband and beg him to write an Italian canzonetta for her. The poor woman thought that she could thereby transfer her sinful love for Francesco to Sebastian.

Bach, listening to her, could not help laughing. He took her words for a feminine whim; but was it for a feminine whim that Sebastian should humiliate his art, bring it down to the level of buffoonery? Magdelena's requests were both ridiculous and insulting to him. Once, just to be rid of her, he took a sheet of paper and wrote a famous theme that later was used by Hummel:

but immediately he noticed how easily it could be developed into a fugue. Indeed, there was a C sharp major fugue missing in his *Well-Tempered Clavicord* which he was composing at that time; he put six sharps after the clef—and the Italian canzonetta became a fugue to be played for practice.[13]

Meanwhile, time passed. Magdalena stopped asking Sebastian for Italian canzonettas, and again took up her housekeeping. Bach was content: he could again devote himself to perfecting his art—and this was the only thing he needed in life. He assumed that Magdalena's caprice had completely disappeared; and, although from time to time she would go through his scores with him rather unwillingly, Bach got used to her indifference. At that time he was composing his famous *Passion's-Musik*; he was satisfied with it, and asked for nothing more.

At that point a new circumstance occurred to bring a peaceful atmosphere into the family, although in a very deceitful manner. As a result of incessant work, Bach's eyesight began to weaken. First, he could not work at night; then, daylight was too strenuous for his eyes, and finally,

[13] See *Clavecin bien tempere par S. Bach*, I partie.

he could not see the daylight itself anymore. Sebastian's
illness awakened Magdalena to his need for her; she took
tender care of the poor blind man, wrote music that he
dictated to her, played it for him, and led him to the
church to play the organ. It seemed as if Francesco had
vanished from her memory for good.

But the fire that had flamed up in Magdalena was now
only banked. Though it did not burst out into the open, it
burned deeper inside her heart. Magdalena no longer shed
tears; gone was the poetic vision in which the charming
Venetian had appeared to her. She did not allow herself to
sing his songs any more. In short, everything beautiful that
sweetened the agonies of love had left Magdalena; in her
heart there remained only bitterness, only the conviction
that her happiness was unattainable, and that the grave was
the only solution to her sufferings. And as the grave approached her, its pernicious air dimmed the glow of her
cheeks, penetrated her breast, furrowed her face, and wasted
her away.

Bach discovered this only when Magdalena was on her
deathbed.

This loss affected Sebastian more than his own affliction.
With tears in his eyes he wrote a funeral song and accompanied Magdalena's body to the graveyard.

Sebastian Bach's sons were now respected organists in
various cities in Germany. Their mother's death brought the
whole family together: all came to see the famous old man,
trying to console him, entertaining him with music and
stories. The old man listened attentively to everything, trying to recapture his former life and its beauty in these stories,
but now, for the first time he felt the need of something else.
He wanted someone to sit beside him, someone in whom he
could confide his own bitterness, without irrelevant questions. . . . But such ties did not exist between him and the
members of his family. They told him of the praise his
music was gaining throughout Europe; they asked him
technical questions about chord progressions; they explained
to him the advantages and disadvantages of the duties of a
conductor. . . . Soon Bach made a terrible discovery: he
found out that in his own family he was only a professor
among his pupils. Life had granted him everything—enjoyment of art, fame, admirers . . . everything except life itself;
he had not found a being who could understand him, who
would anticipate all his wishes—a being with whom he could

talk about things other than music. Half of his soul was dead!

Though Bach was unhappy, the sacred flame of art still burned in his soul, still filled the world for him. He continued to teach his followers, to give advice in building organs, and to perform his duties as an organist.

But soon Bach noticed that his thoughts had lost their former lucidity, that his fingers had lost their agility. What seemed so easy before became insurmountably difficult, his even, light touch vanished, his fingers asked for rest.

He would frequently ask to be taken to the organ, where, as before, by the power of his will he sought to awaken his slumbering inspiration with thunderous harmonies. Sometimes he remembered with ecstasy the vision of his childhood: now it was clear to him; he well understood its mysterious forms. Suddenly, he would try to recall Magdalena's voice— but to no avail: in his imagination he heard only the impure, enticing melodies of the Venetian, and Magdalena's voice echoing them in the deep recesses of the vaults—and Bach would fall, exhausted and unconscious.

Soon he was no longer able to leave his chair; surrounded by eternal darkness, he sat with his hands folded, his head bent—without love, without memories. Accustomed to experiencing unfailing inspiration, he waited for its exhilarating dew again, as an addict craves opium. His imagination despaired, seeking sounds, the only language in which he understood both the life of his soul and the life of the world. But all was in vain. His imagination was old and impaired now; it showed him only the keys, pipes, and valves of the organ. Dead and lifeless, they no longer stimulated his interest: the magic light that enveloped them in a rainbow shimmer had faded forever.

THE NINTH NIGHT

The evening sun shone above the stately river; scarlet clouds were floating in the gray-blue skies, and each of them glowed on the side turned toward the sun, while the other side was disappearing in fog. Faust sat by the window, now turning the pages of an old book, now looking at the crimson reflection from the waves on the river spreading on the walls of his room and imparting quivering life to paintings, statues, and every inanimate thing. Our philosopher was more meditative than usual; his face did not show that constant but not evil mockery with which he used to accompany the riddles he liked to set his young friends, whose contradictory thoughts so little resembled the serenity of conviction our good eccentric seemed to possess. At this moment Faust was not disposed to joke; his meditation seemed to be of grave import. As he scanned the pages of the old book, brightness came again into his look; but whenever he turned his eyes away from it, as if trying to concentrate within his soul the meaning of what he had read, mournfulness appeared again on the philosopher's face.

The door opened; in came young Rostislav, always absent-minded, always remote from the present moment.

ROSTISLAV: "Today, as I was about to come to see you, I recalled all our recent discussions interwoven with your manuscript . . . what an encyclopedia! How many various questions we have discussed!"

FAUST: "And how many of them have we solved, you want to say."

ROSTISLAV: "Exactly! If anyone had listened to us and heard our talks, what would people think of us?"

FAUST: "Thinking people would have said that at least our conversation was not false; pedants would have proved to us quite convincingly that our conversation was nothing but a dissertation, logically developed in dramatic form."

ROSTISLAV: "What if we really chose a definite subject for each evening, decided each one's turn to speak, and made it

a rule not to deviate from a subject until we examined it in
all its details?"

FAUST: "By so doing we would have expressed a claim to a
full harmonious philosophical system, for which one perhaps
has to have a right that I cannot admit in us so far. It seems
to me that we are like wanderers who reach at night a strange
land about which they have only general, incomplete information. They must live in this land and therefore they must
study it. But at that moment, any systematic effort would be
beyond their strength, and consequently a source of delusion.
All they know about this land is that they do not know it. At
that moment they might more easily be saved by a guess—a
spontaneous, unconscious, instinctive, to a certain degree poetic guess. At that moment the most important thing is the
sincerity of their will; later, perhaps, they would notice their
errors, evaluate their guesses, and would perhaps ascertain
that one of them contained the truth they were after. But
until that time, if they were to subject themselves to systematic effort, the wanderers would become slaves of their own
word—actors. Discussions would lose all their sincerity, and,
if you wish, all their usefulness; they would become a stage
on which no one speaks what is spontaneously, unconsciously
suggested by the words of another person, but tries to give
his own thought the most comely form, and by means of the
clever concatenation of words, always more or less vague, to
protect his speech against contradictions at any cost. That's
how it is with us, too! Besides, there is another considerable
difficulty which just occurred to me: words like 'unity' and
'subject' are usually encountered in the first paragraphs of
every philosophical book, as terms completely known and
understandable to anyone, but I must say they are the ones
that stop me. Is there anything more indefinite than the word
'unity'? or a word more confusing than *'subject'*? The combination of these two words creates something quite inconceivable to me."

ROSTISLAV: "I don't understand your objections; suppose
we chose as a subject the definition of a tree . . . and kept to
this question without touching upon stone or animal or art,
and so on."

FAUST: "Futile hopes! Where do we begin, in order not to
move a step from the chosen subject? One begins to speak of
the life of a tree; others object that he is departing from the
subject, since the life of a tree is only one of the phenomena
of this object, and that it is necessary to determine before-

hand what the word 'life' means. Another person suggests that we begin with the description of the parts of a tree. This raises new questions: Where to begin? with the roots, as the organs of feeding? or with the leaves, the organs of respiration? One person assures us that it is necessary to begin with the bark, as an outer cover which first of all strikes our senses. Another one just as thoroughly proves that we should begin with the core, as the central part of a tree. This brings up the question of what a central part is and whether it exists in a tree. In order to put an end to these arguments, it is suggested to proceed negatively, that is, to show first of all why a tree is neither a stone nor an animal. But this naturally leads to the question What is a stone? or What is an animal? and with each new object the same story begins as with a tree. And neither centuries nor the lives of millions of people will suffice to determine where to begin in order to speak about a tree, because this question will involve all sciences, all nature. And that is apparently why all arguments which have been arising in mankind for centuries lead to one and the same question: Where to begin? or, better to say, to a still higher one: What is the beginning? What is knowledge? and finally: Is knowledge possible? And this question is the limit of the science called philosophy."

ROSTISLAV: "Even so, should we be afraid of this question, we, half of whose lives have been spent working at this fearful but delightful science?"

FAUST: "I agree; apparently we are doing just that. But whether what we call harmonious logical form is as possible for this science as for any other is another question."

ROSTISLAV: "Consequently, you don't admit the possibility of a logical structure of thoughts?"

FAUST: "I don't admit yet that people speaking to one another understand one another completely. I can't discuss here the principles on which this conviction is based *for me*; but apparently it can be reached in other ways too. I'll try. Condillac had it easy: for him all philosophy meant an *art of reasoning*; he forgot only one thing: that fools and madmen frequently reason very logically; there is only one thing they cannot prove to themselves logically: a madman, that he is mad, and a fool, that he is stupid. Unfortunately, I don't know how each one of us can prove to himself that he is really in his right mind, that, for instance, he does not take a part for the whole or the whole for a part, motion for rest and rest for motion, just like a certain crank who, walking up and down his room, held onto the wall, thinking that he was constantly on a ship in stormy weather. Until that means of proof has been found, each discussion, each speech is a delusion into which we ourselves fall and draw in others; we think that we are speaking of the same subject, whereas instead we speak of completely different subjects."

ROSTISLAV: "But then it would be impossible for two people ever to agree on anything, and yet that happens."

FAUST: "Very seldom, and even if it happens, then apparently it does so in a very different way and not at all logically. Two people can be in accord in believing, or, if you wish, they can *feel* the truth, but they can never *think* about it in accord, much less express their accord in words. I'll explain it to you with a quite simple example. Who doesn't know what metal is? Everyone, even if he hasn't studied mineralogy or chemistry, knows what is meant when someone says, 'Such and such a substance is a metal.' In old books of chemistry there were quite detailed definitions of metal and its distinctions from other minerals. Currently chemists have been forced to relinquish the definition of a metal. Indeed, it is impossible: how does metal differ from other substances? By its strength—but diamond is stronger than metal. By its malleability—but where should we place mercury, then? By the fact that it is a simple substance—but there are more than half a hundred simple substances. By its luster? But sulphur and mica have a metallic luster under certain circumstances. Finally, to add to the problem, there was discovered a substance having all the properties of a metal in its compounds, and yet no one has seen this body. Chemistry cannot isolate it; it almost does not exist—this, as you know, is the metal *ammonium*. And yet we understand each other when we speak of metal, and we never confuse this body with others.

"What does this mean, then? That to this word we add also *some sort* of concept not expressed in words, a concept imparted to us not by an external object, but originally and undoubtedly stemming from our spirit. I took a simple word as an example, and it denotes a simple object. But what must take place in our words when we speak of intangible concepts, of concepts including in themselves thousands of other concepts, as, for instance, moral concepts. A regular Babylonian confusion of tongues! Hence in part stems my conviction that we speak not in words but in something that is outside the words, for which words are only riddles which sometimes, but by no means always, lead us to a thought, force us to *guess, awaken our thought within us,* but by no means express it. Therefore, the more we want to expound some concept in detail, the more words or vague signs must we use. In a word, the clearer, that is, the more materially we want to express our thought, the more it loses its definition.

"Perhaps it was in this sense that Socrates said, 'All I know is that I know nothing,' and not at all in a spiritual sense, as it is usually assumed. Because inner speech is always comprehensible for people who are to a certain degree attuned to each other. Socrates, too, was convinced of that, and the proof of it is that he did not keep silent. There is one condition for understanding one another: to speak sincerely and from the fullness of one's heart. Then each word obtains clarity from its higher source. When two or three people speak from the *bottom of their hearts,* they don't worry about greater or lesser fullness of their words. An inner harmony is formed between them; the inner power of one excites the inner power of another. Their unity, like the unity of organisms in a magnetic process, increases their power. In a friendly spirit they journey through entire worlds of various concepts incalculably quickly, and in harmony reach the thought they were in search of. If this journey were expressed in words, their imperfection would hardly denote its limits: the point of departure and the point of rest; the inner thread connecting them is inaccessible to words. Therefore, a live, open, and sincere conversation seems to lack any logical connection, and yet, only this harmonious agreement of man's inner powers unexpectedly begets the profoundest observations, as Goethe says in passing.[1]

"It is even more difficult to explain this harmonious process in words than to explain what metal is. This process is usually disregarded, and yet it is so important that without a preliminary study of it any philosophical concept expressed in words is nothing but a simple sound which may have thousands of arbitrary meanings. In a word, without a preliminary study of the *process of expressing thought* no philosophy is possible, because at the very first step it must avail itself of this process; nevertheless, phenomena identical with this process to a certain degree confront us daily. Here is the simplest example. Everyone knows that the best method of persuasion is not logic but so-called moral influence. Hence the difference between an improvised and a read speech; hence

[1] *Wilhelm Meisters Lehrjahre.*

the simple word 'forward,' exclaimed by an experienced general, affects soldiers more than the best dissertation could; hence, for instance, the wonderful affect of Napoleon's speeches, which in reading are mere pompous verbiage; hence, finally, the fascination of a friendly, sincere conversation and the intolerable boredom of a stiff conversation."

ROSTISLAV: "Do you realize that with your words you destroy the feasability of any science, any learning?"

FAUST: "No, I am protecting science from the stumbling block thrown under its feet by skepticism and dogmatism. By the way, it was not I who began. Schelling, in the first year of the present century, cast into the world a profound thought as a problem for the young century, the solution of which must leave a characteristic imprint on this century and express its inner meaning in the ages of the world much more precisely than all the steam engines, propellors, wheels, and other industrial toys imaginable. He distinguished the unconditional, original, free self-contemplation of a soul from the perception of a soul which subjects itself, for instance, to mathematical, already *constructed* figures; he recognized inner feeling as the basis of all philosophy, he called the action of our soul when it turns upon itself and becomes an object and an observer at the same time the first act of knowledge;[2] in a word, he established the first and the most difficult step of the science on the most irrefutable, the most obvious phenomenon, and thus, as if by intuition, forever blocked the way for all artificial systems which, like Hegelianism, begin

[2] Here are Schelling's original words: "The only subject of transcendental philosophy is *inner feeling*, and this subject can never be an object of external perception (*Anschauung*) as in mathematics. The subject of mathematics is just as much beyond knowledge as the subject of philosophy. The whole existence of mathematics is based on perception; it exists only in perception, but in an *external* perception. Therefore, a mathematician is not preoccupied with self-perception (an act of construction) but with what has been already constructed, which manifests itself externally, whereas philosophy deals only with the very act of construction, an *inner* act.

Besides, the subjects of the transcendental philosophy exist only when they are original, free creations. One cannot be forced to an inner perception of these subjects, as one may be forced to perceive externally a mathematical figure: the reality of a mathematical figure is based on an external feeling, just as the reality of a philosophical concept is based on an inner one.—*System des transcendentalen Idealismus*, § 4 (Tübingen, 1800).

the science not with the real fact but, for example, with a *pure* idea, with an *abstraction of an abstraction.*[3] "I don't know if I am right, but it seems to me that the great thinker pronouncing the great thought keenly felt the disagreement between thought and word which, I am convinced, plays such an important role in the life of mankind. 'The accusation of obscurity leveled at philosophy,' he says,[4] 'does not originate in its actual obscurity but in the fact that not everyone is given the organ by means of which it can be embraced.' If this is so, what does a word we use to express a thought mean? A changeable form, clear to one, less comprehensible to another, completely incomprehensible to the third!"

ROSTISLAV: "All right! I agree with you so far as the higher levels of philosophy are concerned, but in other subordinate sciences—"

FAUST: "Philosophy is the science of sciences; its basic position cannot be completely expressed in words, because no matter how perfect these words may be, there will always be a minimum difference between them and the thought, which will vary according to the philosophical organ mentioned by Schelling; to reduce this minimum difference to zero is the highest task of philosophy at present. Until this problem is solved, whatever position may be taken as the primary one (and the higher it is, the more difficult), so long as it is shaped into words will have as many meanings as there are human heads. This position adapted to any individual branch of human knowledge will bring its changeable, unstable character into it as well. Hence the logical construction of this individual branch becomes false, delusive, based on an unstable meaning of the words used."

ROSTISLAV: "It follows once again that in your opinion no science, no knowledge is possible."

FAUST: "No! my saying this would mean arguing against reality; all knowledge is possible because primary knowledge is possible, that is, the knowledge of the act of self-perception; but since this knowledge is an inner, instinctive knowledge conceived not from the outside, but within the actual substance of a soul—so all knowledge of man must then be so. Therefore, I do not admit the existence of a science artificially constructed by scientists; I do not understand sciences called philosophy, history, chemistry, or physics—these

[3] See Hegel's *Encyclopedie der philosophischen Wissenschaften im Grundrisse,* § 19 and § 24 (Tübingen, 1827).

[4] Schelling, *System,* p. 51.

are the segmented, mutilated parts of one harmonious organism, of one and the same science which lives in man's soul, and whose form must vary according to his philosophical organ, or, in other words, to the substance of his spirit. This science must combine all sciences existing under various names as a bodily organism combines all forms of nature, and not just the chemical or the mathematical or any other alone. In a word, each person must form his science out of the substance of his own individual spirit.

"Consequently, learning must not consist of logical construction of one knowledge or another (that's a luxury, an aid to memory—and nothing more, perhaps not even an aid); it must consist of an incessant *integration* and elevation of one's spirit, in other words, increasing its original activity. The question to what extent and how this elevation is possible, and how it could shed light on all the infinite realms of knowledge, is a very important question, and I cannot answer it fully now; I shall point out only some individual solutions to it.[5] Thus, for instance, it is completely clear to me that this activity can not be stimulated by one fact or another, by one syllogism or another, because you can prove with syllogisms, but you cannot convince. But that this activity can be stimulated in an *aesthetic* manner, that is, 'by means of an incomprehensible principle,' as Schelling says,[6] 'which is involuntary and intuitively combines objects with knowledge.' Aesthetic activity penetrates the soul not by means of an artificial logical construction of thoughts, but *directly*; its condition is that particular state called *inspiration*, a state comprehensible only to those who possess the organ for this state, and which has the inexplicable privilege of acting also upon those who have this organ at a lower level. The lower levels surmise the existence of the higher levels of this wonderful spiritual process —and Schelling—"

(*Enter* Vyacheslav and Victor.)

[5] Differentiation in the simplest sense is the road from a polygon to a circle; integration, the way from a circle to a polygon. Faust uses these expressions purposely: in mysticism everything sensual is expressed by a circle; the spiritual, by a unit which manifests itself in a line and a triangle and plays such an important role in mystical books. Hence, in cabalistics the meaning of numbers 6 and 9, which we constantly encounter in St. Martin; six ♂ is a triumph of the one over the circle, the destruction of the sensual; nine ♀ is a triumph of the sensual over the spiritual, the destruction of the spiritual.

[6] *System*, p. 457.

VYACHESLAV: "So, they are discussing Schelling! Congratulations, gentlemen, Schelling has changed his system; you'll have to study him again."

FAUST (*to Rostislav*): "Wasn't I right, when I said that human language is the betrayer of his thought and that we do not understand each other? You say Schelling has changed his ideas altogether, right? And you believe it?"

VICTOR: "In all the journals, even in your philosophical ones . . ."

FAUST: "I know! I know! There are people to whom each failure gives real enjoyment; they rejoice at a misprint in a luxurious edition, at a false note played by an excellent musician, at a grammatical mistake in an artful writer; where there are no failures, in the kindness of their hearts they assume it to be there—just to feel better. Calm down, gentlemen, the great thinker of our century hasn't changed his theory. Words have deceived you: words are like a spyglass which sways in the hands of the man on the deck; this telescope provides a certain limited field for the eye, but in this field objects change incessantly, according to the position of the eye; it sees many objects, but not one of them clearly. Unfortunately, our words are worse than this optical instrument—there is nothing on which to support them! Thoughts glide under the focus of a word! The thinker says one thing—the listener hears something else; the thinker chooses the best word for the same thought; he tries to chain this word to the meaning of his thought by threads of other words—and you, gentlemen, think that he has changed the thought itself as well! It's an optical illusion! An optical illusion!"

VYACHESLAV: "This may be very consoling to your self-love, gentlemen-philosophers, but it must still be proved."

FAUST: "I promise to prove this conviction as soon as Schelling's new lectures are published."

VICTOR: "Well, and how about the famous manuscript? What other stories will your eccentric travelers tell us?"

FAUST: "The manuscript is finished."

VYACHESLAV: "What? Finished? So it was just a *bluff*! These gentlemen undertook, apparently, to clarify all the secrets of the spiritual and material world, and the whole affair ended with some ideal biographies of certain cranks who could have remained unknown without any loss to human history."

FAUST: "It seems to me that my friends saw an uninterrupted living connection between all these persons—ideal or not—that does not matter."

VICTOR: "I confess my lack of insight: I failed to notice this connection."

FAUST: "To me it seems rather obvious; but if you doubt its existence, I'll read you a few more sheets, which I didn't feel like reading before, because they are nothing else than an offering to the systematic character of the century, which is not satisfied with an endless, indefinite thought, but needs something palpable. Listen, then! Here you have a systematic heading for the entire manuscript, and even an epilogue to go with it."

Faust reads:

THE COURT
Defendant! Did you understand yourself? Did you find yourself? What did you do with your life?

PIRANESI
I went around the world; I set off to the East, and returned from the West. Everywhere I searched for myself. I searched for myself in the depths of the ocean, in the crystals of the firstborn mountains, in the sunshine—I embraced everything in my powerful arms, and struck by my own strength I forgot about people and didn't share my life with them!

THE COURT
Defendant! Your life belonged to the people, not to yourself!

THE ECONOMIST
I gave my soul to the people, my life blossomed into a luxurious splendid flower—I gave it to the people: the people tore it off and into shreds, and it disappeared before I could breathe in its entrancing fragrance. In my passionate love for them I descended into the dark well of science; I exhausted it till I broke down thinking of quenching the thirst of mankind; but there was a vessel of the Danaides before me! I didn't fill it—I only forgot myself.

THE COURT
Defendant! Your life belonged to you and not to the people.

A CITY WITHOUT NAME
I was preoccupied with my life; I calculated it according to a mathematical formula; and having noticed that neither

lofty feeling nor poetry nor enthusiasm nor any belief entered my equation, I took them for zero, and in order to live peacefully and comfortably, I thought it necessary to do without them; but feeling, which I have refuted, burned me, and I realized only too late that an important letter was left out in my equation. . . .

THE COURT

Defendant! Your life belonged not to you, but to feeling.

BEETHOVEN

My soul lived in sonorous harmonies of feeling; in it I thought to gather all the forces of nature and to re-create man's soul—I became exhausted by the inexpressibility of feeling.

THE COURT

Defendant! Your life belonged to you, not to feeling.

THE IMPROVVISATORE

I loved my life passionately—I wanted to sacrifice to my life science and art, poetry and love; hypocritically, I bent my knees before their altars and their flames burned me.

THE COURT

Defendant! Your life belonged to art, and not to you!

SEBASTIAN BACH

No! I was not hypocritical toward my art! I wanted to concentrate my whole life in it; I sacrificed to it all the gfits bestowed only by Providence, gave up all family joys, everything that amuses the lowest commoner.

THE COURT

Defendant! Your life belonged to you, not to art.

SEGELIEL

What kind of entertaining court is this? Why, it's unheard of. It contradicts itself at every step: live for yourself, live for art; live for yourself, live for science; live for yourself, live for the people. It simply wants to delude us! Whatever you may say, however you may call things, whatever guise you may appear in, the *I* always remains the *I* and everything is done for that *I*. Gentlemen, do not trust this court; it doesn't know itself what it wants from us.

THE COURT

Defendant! You are concealing yourself from me. I see your symbols, but you, you, I do not see. Where are you? Who are you? Answer me.

A VOICE FROM THE INFINITE ABYSS

I cannot be expressed fully!

EPILOGUE

ROSTISLAV: "That means, these gentlemen by various round-about ways got back to the point of departure, that is, to the fateful question about the meaning of life."

VYACHESLAV: "No, apparently they intuitively wanted to prove Faust's favorite idea that we can't express our thoughts and that we do not understand one another when speaking."

FAUST: "Your words may serve as a proof of what you call my favorite idea. I often turn to it, but apparently I do not express myself clearly enough, despite all my efforts: and no wonder—I must use the same instrument to prove that this instrument is of no use. That is like testing an incorrect yard-stick by the same yardstick, or letting a hungry man feed upon his hunger. No, I don't say at all that our words are useless in expressing our thoughts, but I maintain that the identity between a thought and a word exists only to a certain degree; it is impossible, indeed, to determine this degree by means of words—one must feel it in himself."

VYACHESLAV: "Then why don't you arouse this feeling in me?"

FAUST: "I can't—if it does not arise within you by itself; a person can be lead to this feeling by means of pointing at various physiological and physical phenomena; but it is impossible to create this feeling in another person without his own inner process. One can lead a person to the idea of beauty, perfection, harmony; but it is impossible to make him feel this idea, because one cannot find the full expression of this idea in nature—it exists only in the heads of Raphael, Mozart, and other people of that kind."

VICTOR: "If such is the situation, none of your physical phenomena can serve as an expression of a thought, but once you said that in nature letters are constant, stereotyped. Say what you like, a word or a number is always clearer to me than all these comparisons and metaphors you and your manuscript so liberally have thrown at us."

FAUST: "You shouldn't accuse me of contradiction; letters in nature are in fact more constant than those invented by man, and here is the proof: in nature a tree always expresses its word clearly and fully, regardless of names under which it exists in a human language; however, not without a blow to our pride, there is not a word we pronounce that does not have thousands of different meanings, and would not cause arguments. A tree has been a tree for everyone from the beginning of time; but give me a single word expressing a moral concept whose meaning has not changed almost from year to year. Did the word 'elegance' mean the same thing to people of the past century as to the people of our century? The virtues of a pagan would be a crime in our day. Just remember the abuses of words such as 'equality,' 'liberty,' 'morality.' And that's not all: a distance of a few yards and the meaning of words changes: 'baranta,' 'vendetta,' all sorts of bloody vengeance in some countries mean: 'duty,' 'courage,' 'honor.' "

VICTOR: "I agree that this vagueness of expression exists in metaphysics, but who is to blame for it? Why doesn't this vagueness exist in exact sciences? Here every word is definite, because its object is definite and tangible."

FAUST: "That's quite true—and here is proof. For example, 'infinity,' 'infinitely large and infinitely small magnitudes,' a 'mathematical point,' in a word, all the basic concepts with which mathematics should begin; in chemistry I recommend words such as 'affinity,' 'catalysis,' 'simple body'; not to speak of other sciences, dealing with living nature. Remember the words of Bichat, the great experimenter and experienced physicist, killed in an anatomic experiment, whom someone placed on a par with Napoleon, and not quite without reason. Bichat had to admit that a new language should be invented for organic bodies, because all the words we transfer from physical sciences into the animal or plant economy remind us of concepts which do not correspond to the physiological phenomena at all.[1] When we speak, each word raises the dust of a thousand meanings given to this word during the centuries and by various countries, and even by individual people. That does not happen in nature, since there is no will in nature; it is the creation of eternal necessity; a plant blossomed a thousand years ago as it blossoms today. Therefore, when we want to give our word a definite character, we instinctively reach for a certain letter in nature, as the constant

[1] Bichat, *Recherches physiologiques sur la vie et la mort* (Paris, 1829), p. 108.

symbol of a living thought, identical with our thought. We try to give our thought the solid garment that we can't create ourselves, because we don't know how to direct our will along such firm laws as govern the acts of nature."

VICTOR: "Another contradiction: didn't you yourself try to convince us quite recently that works of nature are much lower than works of man? Now, on the contrary—"

FAUST: "Again disagreement in word usage! Please note that I said *such*, but not *the same* laws of nature; as soon as man wants to imitate nature he is always lower than nature; but he is always higher when creating by his inner power. It doesn't matter if he employs for his needs conveniences he finds in nature! A rich landowner has huts, ruins, and meadows in his park, but it doesn't follow therefrom that he sleeps on the grass or lives in a hut; he has his own palaces—and the main thing for the landowner is to be rich himself."

VYACHESLAV: "What, then, makes his wealth, or, leaving comparisons aside, when can man express his thought completely?"

FAUST: "When his will has reached that height where *it is sure of its sincerity*."

VYACHESLAV: "But what makes it sure of this sincerity?"

FAUST: "The same process which assures a mathematician that a may be equal to b, because he can't prove this axiom by anything existing in nature; in nature man can find only *likeness*, but never *identity*; that idea undoubtedly exists in man."

VICTOR: "What? There is no identity of two objects in nature? I see two leaves in a tree: I see that they are both green, both pointed, both grow on a tree—and I conclude that they are identical; I apply this identity to other objects, and so on. . . ."

FAUST: "By what right? You cannot fail to see that no matter how similar the two leaves may be, they are not mathematically identical, that there is a minimum of difference between them."

VICTOR: "I agree."

FAUST: "If you see this minimum of difference, you consequently notice yourself that there is something in an object that contradicts the idea of perfect identity; consequently, you have taken something from nature that you didn't observe in it; and I ask you again: by what right? In other words: from where?"

VICTOR: "By means of abstraction."

FAUST: "But abstraction is a process by means of which we compress into one form thousands of an object's various properties. One cannot compress something non-existent; if there is no perfect identity in nature, then it cannot be introduced into your abstraction from anywhere. Suppose you want to make an accurate abridgement of some book; if you have added to the abridgement ideas that are not in the original, your abridgement is inaccurate; you have deceived both yourself and others. The same thing holds for all so-called abstractions. They compress a few individual concepts and add a new one to them—where did it come from? In a word, if we have an idea of identity, of beauty, of the perfect good, and so on, then they exist within us by themselves independently and we use them only as a measure for other, visible objects. Plato discussed this, and it's beyond me how one can still argue about such an obvious matter."

ROSTISLAV: "We got off the subject; we were talking about the expression of thoughts. I admit, Faust's conviction rather disturbs me; it shakes the entire edifice of our sciences, because they are all expressed in words."

FAUST: "Most of them, yes, but not all."

VYACHESLAV: "What do you mean, 'not all'? How, then? Can't we do without riddles?"

FAUST: "The question whether there could be a science expressed not in words would lead us too far. At the moment I insist only that we do not trust our words too much and that we do not think that our thoughts are *fully* expressed by words; it's not in vain that this insistence frightens Rostislav; it is an important matter and causes many sorrows on earth."

VYACHESLAV: "Voltaire said it a long time ago."

FAUST: "Volaire had an irresponsible and criminal purpose in mind, and therefore he saw only one side of the question, namely, whatever he could use as a weapon against the object of his hatred. However, no one has ever used the ambiguity of words to the extent Voltaire himself did; all his opinions are wrapped in it. Here we are dealing with something else. The *ambiguity* of words is a great inconvenience, but their *senselessness* is of still greater consequence, and words of this latter category are much more frequent in use, thanks to Voltaire, too, by the way."

VYACHESLAV: "Aren't you too harsh, particularly in respect to a person whose genius cannot be denied?"

FAUST: "I know of a being who cannot be denied the right to be called genius even more."

VYACHESLAV: "Who is it then?"

FAUST: "He is sometimes called Lucifer."

VYACHESLAV: "I don't have the honor of knowing him."

FAUST: "The worse for you; mystics say that he's acquainted most of all with those who don't know him."

VYACHESLAV: "Didn't we agree to do without mysticism?"

FAUST: "Joking aside, I don't know anyone except that gentleman who could so skillfully send into the world the following senseless words: *fact, pure experiment, positive knowledge, exact sciences,* and so on. Man has been playing with these words for many centuries without giving them any meaning. For instance, in education they say: Please, no theories, give us facts and more facts; and the child's head is stuffed with facts; these facts crowd in his young brain without any connection; one child is stupid; another, trying to find some sort of a connection in this chaos, makes up his own theory, and what a theory! People say, 'He was badly educated!' and I agree with them completely. In the learned world you constantly hear: Please don't speculate; use experiments, pure experiments. However, we know of only one pure experiment, without the slightest admixture of theory, and quite worthy of being called an experiment. One doctor was treating a tailor of fever; on his deathbed the patient asked for ham, as his last treat; the doctor, seeing that the sick man could not be saved, granted him his wish; the patient ate some ham—and recovered. The doctor carefully entered the following observation into his notebook: 'Ham is a successful remedy for fever.' Some time later the same doctor happened to treat a cobbler, also of fever; guided by his *experiment* the doctor prescribed ham for his patient—the sick man died; the doctor, faithful to the rule to note down facts as they come, without any speculations, added the following remark to the previous note: 'The remedy is useful only for tailors, not for cobblers.' Tell me, don't these gentlemen require observations of the same kind when they speak of *pure experiment*; if an *experienced* observer were to continue collecting his *expert* observations—in time he would have constructed what is now called science."

VICTOR: "A joke is not a deed."

FAUST: "Nor is a deed a joke, and I think that these gentlemen are simply joking."

VICTOR: "But please! You can't compare all the people doing experiments with a fool who would write down indiscriminately anything that struck his eyes."

FAUST: "Excuse me! Discrimination already presupposes some theory, and since you think that a theory can only be the result of *pure experiment*, my doctor had every right to enter his observations in his notebook. I do not compare empiricists with this doctor, because they don't practice what they preach. Each of them, contrary to his theory, had a theory, so that, indeed, the *pure experiment* they talk about is a meaningless word. But let's go further: frequently a word contains a thought, let us even assume that it is clear and comprehensible to everyone. After a certain time, the meaning of the word changes, but the word itself remains. Such, for instance, is the word 'morality.' This word was lofty when spoken, let us say, by Confucius; what did his descendants do with it? The word has remained—but there it means now nothing else but the external form of propriety. After that— deceit, perfidy, depravity of every sort became something foreign. That country is interesting in general, and serves as a very important pointer to formalists. There was good reason for philosophers of the eighteenth century to delight in it; it fitted exactly into their destructive teaching; everything was said there, everything was expressed; there was a form for everything. There was a form of enlightenment, a form of military art; even a form of gunpowder and firearms—but the core had rotted, rotted to the extent that a country of three hundred million people may collapse from the slightest European impact.[2] Look at history, that cemetery of facts, and you'll see what mere words mean when their meaning does not rest upon the inner dignity of man. What do all these crowds of people mean, their domestic quarrels, rebellions, if not an argument about words without meaning, as, for example, social form. One does not have to go far—just remember the French Revolution; people rose against oppression, against despotism, as they called it. Rivers of blood were shed, until finally the dreams of Rousseau and Voltaire came true; to their great satisfaction the people attained a republican form of government, and along with it they got Robespierre and other gentlemen of the same kind, who, under the protection of the same forms, proved in deed and not merely in words what oppression and barbarism mean. These, then, are the jokes played in this world thanks to words! The kingdom of falsehood thrives on them!"

[2] The easy victory of the English over the Chinese proved the correctness of this remark, written in 1838.

VYACHESLAV: "Wonderful! But if there is falsehood on one side, there must be truth opposite it, on the other side. Therefore, I would be very interested to find out how man could do without words. For example, I should like to know what was attained by your friends who wrote the manuscript you read, and who were likewise convinced of the harm of this means. What did their jumps across human language lead them to?"

FAUST: "My young friends were people of their own time. Today, among their papers, I opportunely found a sort of conclusion of their journey; it is not long, but rather remarkable, as to the point of view reached by my dreamers—also the victims of words! They have the honor of having detected the enemy, although it was not their business to conquer him, and perhaps it is not ours, either. Now, listen:

"We will be asked, 'How did your journey end?' By journeying. Before we ended it we became old with that old age which begins in one's cradle in the nineteenth century—with suffering. Nothing could save us from it: both the exact science of one of us and the indefinite art of another were futile. We measured the desert of the human soul with our steps in vain; full of faith we moaned and cried on the steps of its temples in vain; bitter with our scorn we examined their ruins in vain—the desert remained silent and the veil of the sanctuary was not yet rent. We stopped passersby; we asked them about the famous messengers of heaven, who used to appear on the earth for a moment. They pointed at the invisible clock of the centuries and answered, 'Suffering! Suffering!' In the distance the dawn of some inconceivable sun glowed, but the wind of midnight was blowing around us; cold penetrated to our bones, and we, too, repeated, 'Suffering!' This dawn was not for us; this sun was not for us! It could not warm our benumbed hearts! We had only one sun—suffering! These pages are scorched by its burning warmth!

"There was a time when skepticism was considered the most horrible idea ever invented by man's soul. In its own day this idea killed everything: faith and science and art. It troubled nations as the sands of the sea. It crowned the slanderers of Providence along with the saints of the world with cypress wreaths; it compelled people to seek destruction, evil, and nothingness as reliable havens. But there is a feeling more horrible still than skepticism. Perhaps it is more beneficial in its consequences, but also more tormenting for those who are condemned to experience it.

"Skepticism is, in a certain sense, a world of its own kind, a world with its own laws, in a word, a self-contained and to a certain degree peaceful world.

"Skepticism has the satisfied desire to desire nothing; it has the fulfilled hope not to hope for anything; the impassive activity not to search for anything; it has also its faith—not to have faith in anything. But the distinctive character of the present moment is actually not skepticism, but a desire to get away from skepticism, to have faith in something, to hope for something, to search for something—an unsatisfiable desire and, therefore, unspeakably tormenting. Wherever a friend of mankind turns his sad glance, he sees that everything is refuted, desecrated, ridiculed; there is no life in science, nothing sacred in art! What we maintain is that there is no opinion, the contrary of which could not be affirmed with all the proof possible to man. Such unfortunate epochs of contradiction end by what is known as syncretism, that is, the union of all the most contradictory opinions into one hideous system in defiance of human reason; such periods are not rare in history. When, in the last centuries of the ancient world, all systems, all opinions were shaken, the most enlightened people of that time with a clear conscience combined the most contradictory statements of Aristotle, Plato, and the Hebrew legends. In old Europe today we observe the same thing.

"What a bitter and strange sight! One opinion against another, power against power, throne against throne, and around all this contention—a deadly mocking indifference! Sciences, instead of striving to attain the unity which alone could restore their power, have crumbled into flying dust; their common bond has been lost; they lack organic life. The old Western World, like a child, sees only parts, only signs—the whole is unattainable and impossible for it; individual facts, observations, secondary causes accumulate in immeasurable quantities—what for? For what purpose? Already in Leibnitz's time it was impossible to recognize them, let alone to study or verify them. What can be done now?—now, when the study of a hardly noticeable insect will soon be called a science, when man will soon dedicate his life to it, forgetting everything else under the sun. Scholars have repudiated the all-uniting power of human mind. They have not yet become bored of observing and watching nature, but they believe

only in chance—from chance they expect the inspiration of
truth; they pray to chance. *Eventus magister stultorum.* They
see the eminence of science already in its having become a
craft! . . . and the words of a pagan, 'We know nothing!' have
left a deep impression on all the works of our century! . . .
Science is perishing.

"Art lost its meaning long ago; it is no longer carried away
into the wonderful world where man used to rest from the
sorrows of this world; the poet has lost his power; he has lost
faith in himself—and people no longer believe in him; he
mocks his own inspiration, and only with this mockery can he
attract the attention of crowds. . . . Art is perishing.

"Religious feeling in the West? It would have been forgotten long ago if it had not been for its external language,
which remained as an adornment, like Gothic architecture, or
hieroglyphics on furniture, or for the selfish ends of people
who use this language as a novelty. The Western Church is
now a political arena; its religious feeling, a conventional sign
of small parties. Religious feeling is perishing!

"The three main forces of social life are perishing! Let us
dare to pronounce the word, which may perhaps seem
strange to many now, but will be all too simple later on: The
West is perishing!

"Yes! it is perishing! While it is gathering its petty treasures, while it is given to its despair—time goes by, and time
has its own life, different from the life of nations; in its flight
it will soon overtake old enfeebled Europe and cover it with
the same layers of immovable ashes with which it had covered the huge buildings of nations in ancient America, nations without names.

"Can such a fate really await this proud center of ten
centuries of enlightenment? Can the wonderful creations of
ancient science and ancient art really vanish like smoke? Can
the living plants sown by men of genius, the enlighteners,
really be smothered without having blossomed?

"Sometimes, during happy moments, Providence itself
seems to revive man's dead feeling of faith and love for science and art; sometimes, for a long while, and away from
worldly storms, it nurses a nation, which will have to show
the way from which mankind had deviated and which then
will occupy the first place among other nations. But only a
young and innocent nation is worthy of this great mission; in
it alone, or through its mediation, the conception of a new

world embracing all the spheres of mind and social life is possible.[3]

"When Asian powers, whose names we see on the pages of history as terrible apparitions, were fighting bloody battles for their superiority in the world—the light of truth was quietly rising in the Hebrew desert; when the art and sciences of Egypt were dying of debauchery—Greece restored their power in its embraces; when the spirit of despair had contaminated all the social elements of proud Rome—Christians, this nation of nations, saved mankind from destruction; when at the end of the Middle Ages weakened spiritual activity was ready to devour itself—new parts of the world gave new food and new strength to the feeble old man, and prolonged his artificial life.

"Oh, have faith! The chosen one will be a young nation, fresh and not privy to the crimes of the old world! It will be worthy of fostering a lofty secret in its soul, and of replacing the lamp in its holder, and travelers will be amazed at how close and how obvious the solution of the problem was and how long it was hidden from human sight.

"Where is this sixth part of the world destined for the great deed by Providence now? Where is the nation that contains in itself the secret of the world's salvation today? Where is the chosen one? . . . Where is it? Where has our lofty feeling of national pride carried us? Did not all nations speak this way when they began their existence? They, too, dreamed of seeing in themselves the solution of all man's secrets, the embryo and the pledge of the world's bliss!

"What if? . . . an awful thought! But let's forget about it! When getting ready to fight a deadly battle, a general does not talk of death! He thinks of the words of wise men, and of errors of those who failed.

"Many kingdoms came to rest in the broad bosom of the Russian eagle! In the year of fear and death, the Russian sword alone cleaved the knot which had tied trembling Europe—and the glitter of the Russian sword has been shining sternly amidst the somber chaos of the old world to this day. All phenomena of nature are symbols of one another: Europe called the Russian *a savior*! This name contains in itself another, still loftier calling, the power of which must penetrate

[3] The careful reader will notice that these lines contain the entire theory of *Slavophilism*, which appeared in the second half of the present century.

all the spheres of social life: we must save not only the *body* of Europe, but her *soul* as well!

"We are placed on the border of two worlds: the past and the future; we are young and fresh; we are not privy to the crimes of the old Europe. Its strange, mysterious drama unfolds before us, the clue of which perhaps lies hidden in the depth of the Russian spirit; we are only the witnesses; we are indifferent, because we are accustomed to this strange sight; we are impartial, because often we can frequently guess the ending, because we frequently recognize the parody together with the tragedy. No, Providence takes us to these saturnalia purposely, as Spartans used to take their youths to look at drunken barbarians!

"Great is our calling and difficult is our task! We have to revive everything. We have to enter our spirit into the history of human mind, as our name is entered on the rolls of victory. Another, higher victory—the victory of science, art, and faith —is awaiting us on the ruins of enfeebled Europe. Alas! Perhaps this great task is not for our generation to perform! We are still too close to the spectacle we have witnessed! We still hoped, we still expected the beautiful from Europe! Our clothing still carries the traces of dust stirred up by her. We still share her suffering! We have not yet isolated ourselves in our own way of life. We are an untuned string—we have not yet understood the sound which we have to contribute to the general harmony.[4] Are all these sufferings the fate of the century, or the fate of mankind? We don't know yet! Woe to us, we are even ready to believe that such is the lot of mankind! What a frightening, chilling thought! It persecutes us; it has penetrated into our blood; it grows and matures along with us! We are contaminated! Only death will cure our contagion.

"The new sun is waiting for you, new generation, for you, you!—and you will not understand our sufferings! You will not understand our age of contradictions! You will not understand this Tower of Babel with its confusion of all concepts and where each word has acquired a contrary meaning! You will not understand how we lived without beliefs, how we lived with suffering alone! You will laugh at us! Do not despise us! We were but a frail vessel which Providence thrust into the initial furnace to cleanse the sins of our fathers; for you it has reserved an artful die, to raise you to its feast.

---

[4] Today other Slavophiles will perhaps not agree with this, but *at that time* doubt was permissible.

"Unite, then, in yourselves the experience of an old man with the strength of a youth; do not spare yourselves; carry the treasures of science out of Europe's shaking ruins, and, fixing your eyes on the last convulsive movements of the dying one, look deep into yourself! Look for inspiration in yourself, in your own feeling, bring out into the world your own, not an induced activity, and in the sacred triad of faith, science, and art you will find the peace for which your fathers prayed. The nineteenth century belongs to Russia!"

"It would be fine if things turned out as they claimed," said Rostislav.

"Of course," interjected Vyacheslav, "but do you see, gentlemen, what pathos!"

"Phrases, phrases, that's all!" said Victor in a dictatorial tone.

"I agree that these are phrases," answered Faust, "but my late friends lived in the age of phrases—people did not speak differently at that time. Today we have the same phrases, but with a pretense at brevity and compactness. God knows whether this has made them clearer. From Bentham's time phrases gradually became more and more compressed, until finally they turned into one vowel: I. What can be shorter? But the phrase in this shape hardly became clearer than ten volumes of Bentham, where it is encountered on each page as a long period. I admit, I like phrases; in phrases a person occasionally forgets his craft of an actor and speaks from his heart, and what is spoken from one's heart is often truth, although the speaker himself doesn't notice it."

VICTOR: "But where is the truth in this philippic of your late friends? Is the West really dying? What nonsense! On the contrary, when, in what epoch, was it as rich in strength and means of life as it is at present? Everything there is in motion; railroads cross it from one end to another; industry produces marvels; war has become an impossibility; personal security is guaranteed; schools are multiplying; prisons are getting less harsh; the progress of sciences is gigantic; conferences of scientists make the smallest discovery the property of all Europe; and its power, its material power is such that the entire world bows before the West. Where are the signs of its fall, its death?"

FAUST: "I could answer this question along with naturalists, men of politics and medicine, that the highest development of any power, of any organism is the *beginning* of its *end*; but I would rather agree with you in the view that my friends' opinion of the West is exaggerated; actually, I don't see any sign of its imminent fall, but only because I don't see that highest development of power of which you speak. Let's wait for a balloon, then we shall see. As to the evaluation of the present time, I'll be even less polite than my friends were. They characterized the present epoch as *syncretic*, I dare to say that its character is simply—*falsehood*, unprecedented in the world's history."

VICTOR: "Don't stand upon ceremony! Schlözer in his book for children said before you that 'mankind, generally speaking, is still very stupid.' "[5]

VYACHESLAV: "That is to say, with these words Schlözer felt like saying 'Look, how intelligent I am,' or, 'I alone am intelligent.' "

ROSTISLAV: "That is the secret meaning of each word uttered by man."

VYACHESLAV: "That's why Faust, too, is convinced that he alone is sincere in this world."

FAUST: "No, unfortunately, I am still far from this conviction, and have no right to possess it yet, because I consider this conviction the highest blessing attainable by man. Falsehood envelops him with so many covers from the moment of his birth, that struggle with it devours all his strength. These covers with bloody veins adhere to the human organism. Frequently you tear them out of your inner organs with cries and groans after long, immeasurable sufferings; exhausted and powerless, you think you have reached the core of your soul—not at all! There is a new cover, bloody, ugly, staining the purity of your will—and you have to start all over again. I lay a claim to only one privilege: I would *wish* not to deceive and not to be deceived; but I'll say again, I don't know if I have any right to have this privilege!"

VYACHESLAV: "Don't worry. You have this privilege and you share it with all mankind."

FAUST: "Is that really so? Man has always deceived himself and deceived others, but only in our time did he reach such perfection that he *wants to be deceived*."

VICTOR: "In our time? On the contrary! When, during what epoch, were reality, the obvious, the truth, in such demand

[5] Schlözer's *History for Children*, Book 2.

as they are now? Now you can't win anything by superficial speculations, analogies, approximate observations: exactness, numbers, facts are required; now they alone attract attention."

FAUST: "That is, having tired of discussing how to improve their eyesight and clean their glasses, afflicted men reject this vexing, troublesome suspicion and simply decide that their sight is perfectly normal, and their glasses quite clean; one of them sees all objects green, another red, until the third man comes and tries to convince them that the objects are neither green nor red, but blue. Then comes a man who either carefully accumulates all this evidence, just for the sake of information, or he concludes that an object contains in itself both green and red and blue; they are both fully convinced that the combination of many lies can finally make truth, just as physicists of the past century tried to prove that the sun's light consists of all the crude colors they created. In this I see the source of trouble; no one is more dangerous than a madman who doesn't suspect that he is mad. No one is more dangerous than a liar who has the appearance of a sincere person."

VICTOR: "But where do you see these lies? And do they predominate in our age?"

FAUST: "I repeat: not only do people deceive one another; they even know that they are being deceived."

VICTOR: "At least you don't refuse our century this knowledge?"

FAUST: "That is our trouble, and not a joke. We have discovered the art of deceiving and, what is still worse, to be deceived—consciously. There was a time when a person insulted by another would fight with his enemy and they would simply kill each other. Now, in our century, enlightened people insult one another too; they fight and kill in the same manner, but with an addition: though one considers the other a scoundrel, on challenging him to a duel he assures him of his sincere *respect* and *devotion*. There was a time when a man would get drunk on wine and opium without knowing about their harmful effect upon health; now man knows it all too well, and yet he gets drunk with one and the other. An ancient Greek or a Roman would believe an oracle, Pallas or Zeus, or not. Now we know that the oracle lies, and yet we believe him. Nine out of ten so-called Roman Catholics believe neither in the infallibility of the Pope nor in the honesty of Jesuits, and yet all of them are ready to fight with knives for both. We have become so accustomed to lies that these phenomena do not seem strange to us.

"Do you care to see their brothers and sisters elsewhere on earth? For instance, at least in respectful countries—not to speak of others—they speak only of the people's will, of the common wish; but everybody knows that this is the wish of only a few profiteers; when the common good is mentioned everybody knows that it concerns only a few merchants, or, if you wish, shareholders and other corporations. Where does this crowd of people rush?—to elect their legislators. Whom will they elect? Don't worry, everybody knows it—the one for whom most money has been paid. What sort of gathering is that? They speak about abuses, about the necessity of new measures . . . about their country going to ruin. The crowd surges around the orators . . . don't worry! They are doctors without patients and lawyers without cases; they have nothing to live on: should the bloody battle ensue, perhaps they would get their share, too. Both the orators themselves and the crowd know it. Where do these respectable men go? Into faraway countries, to enlighten semi-barbarians. What a selfless deed! Nothing of the sort: they go to sell a few dozen cotton stockings more—everybody knows it, even the missionaries themselves.

"There you hear an eternal, mutual oath pronounced: an awe-inspiring matter. Don't worry, everybody knows that matrimonial rites have purposely omitted something without which marriage occasionally can be considered non-existent. A people's judge caught some men in a tavern, but everyone is calm because they know that the witnesses in this case are relatives of the judge and receive a set payment for their appearance, and that this was the reason for all the trouble. Somewhere they speak excitedly about the necessity for supporting the bread industry, with what facts! what arguments!—but everybody knows that the affair concerns only the profit of a few monopolists, whose neighbors are dying of starvation. A university professor promises to disclose the whole truth, but everybody knows that he doesn't know it and couldn't tell it, and yet students listen to him. A married couple, their brothers and members of the family appear in a drawing room and say the nicest things about each other, but they and everyone else know that they can't stand one another and can hardly wait to learn, as Pushkin said, 'When's the devil going to take you?'

"A journalist exhausts himself assuring people of his impartiality, but all his readers know very well that in yesterday's shareholders' meeting the journal was instructed to be of one particular opinion and not another.[6] A person who was helped by ignorant crowds to the first place in the country pays improbable compliments to these crowds—but everybody knows that this is not true; everybody knows that he speaks this way only because he wouldn't be able to keep his position otherwise, and yet they listen to him with pleasure. A friend of mine said jestingly: 'What a flatterer this B is; he flatters me unashamedly to my face; but what can you do! I know that these are lies, but it's pleasant to hear them.' These words contain all the characteristics of the century.

"When necessity drives one to frankness, just for the sake of decency he covers its nakedness with words which often have a contrary meaning. A statesman once said: 'Our fathers approached this question with such wise *tolerance* that until now it has never disturbed the general peace, and I, likewise, will not permit any reforms in this matter.'[7] What did he mean by this beautiful word *tolerance*? You may think he meant religions, or something similar. No! he simply meant the disgraceful slavery of Negroes and the merciless arbitrariness of southern American planters toward American Negroes! *Tolerance* in this sense! An example of ingenuity! An invaluable play on words, and unfortunately neither the first nor the last. Gentlemen, if all this is not *lies*—then we understand different things by this word."

VICTOR: "No! but you confuse lies with the word 'decency,' which, of course, plays an important role in our century— and all the better—this is the sign of its enlightenment."

VYACHESLAV: "An intelligent person once said: 'Hypocrisy is an involuntary tribute of respect which vice pays to virtue.' "[8]

FAUST: "I know an even better expression: 'A tongue is given to man to hide his thoughts.' "[9]

VICTOR: "Speaking of quotations—I'll remind you of a rather profound thought, which has now become commonplace: *Toutes les vérités ne sont pas bonnes à dire*—I don't

[6] A hint at the *Times*.
[7] Proclamation of Van Buren of March 4, 1837.
[8] Rochefoucauld.
[9] Talleyrand.

know how to translate it into Russian; it is translated as: *Not every truth is to the point*, but it is not the same."

FAUST: "Fortunately not the same! Our virgin language did not allow itself to become corrupted by this absurdity;[10] it did not accept its incontestable general meaning. Our language, having accepted the foreign guest, compressed it into the notion of chance: *'Not to the point, not at the right time'*—and thus has carefully preserved its original, inborn, profound, although simple word: 'accept hospitality, but be truthful.' This proverb can serve as a basis for an entire course in morality, which, of course, will not fit into Bentham's framework; the latter can accommodate only the first, hospitable part of our honorable proverb. So, this is what you've attained, you empiricists, fact-lovers, and positive people! You hide the word *lie* under the word *decency*, as a child hides his head in a pillow and thinks that no one can see him! What is the use of a word, if its meaning humiliates and frightens man's soul? Where is your love for the obvious, for clarity, for facts, for numbers? This love extends only to a certain point, and beyond that—welcome lies! Oh, you are right! Hide your lies away, lock them up, paste and paint them over, because, if someone should put you face to face with them, you would hate yourself for your ugliness."

VICTOR: "Everything that you say is quite true in a certain sense."

FAUST: "In a certain sense! That's another dress to cover a *lie*! Dress it up as you please, gentlemen, your pupil, or rather your teacher."

VICTOR: "Call it whatever you wish: lie, decency, the spirit of the times—it does not make any difference; what matters is that by means of this drug the West has left the obscurity of the Middle Ages and has lifted itself to the level on which we can see it now; it has become the hotbed of inventions, of arts and sciences . . . the main thing is the purpose, not the means."

FAUST: "At least you agree that this hotbed came to be by means of a *syncretic drug*, to put it politely—that's a good sign! You say, the purpose is achieved?"

VICTOR: "It is being achieved."

FAUST: "Let's see, what has been achieved—the tree is

[10] In his enthusiasm Faust forgets that our language has accepted such expressions as: "legal bribe," an "honest income"; he forgets also the entire terminology of serfdom.

recognized by its fruit. I repeat again, my late friends' thoughts about the West are exaggerated—but listen to what Western writers say themselves; take a careful look at the facts in the West, not at one of them but at all of them without any exception; bend your ears to the cries of despair which resound in its contemporary literature."

VICTOR: "That doesn't prove anything; how can one refer to the evidence of the most talkative people in the world, of literary men? Of course, what they need is to create an effect by whatever means they can—by truth or lie."

FAUST: "Right! But you can't deny that literary works, novels in particular, reflect if not a social life then at least the spiritual state of writers, who, although they are talkative, as you say, nevertheless constitute the flower of society."

VYACHESLAV: "Oh, of course, whatever one may say, the press is a great thing; it is a touchstone and a very dependable one! How many people were considered intelligent by the world, taken for men of genius—they had all apparently digested earthly wisdom; but their mask fell off, as soon as their first lines were published; unexpectedly it was revealed that their supposedly profound thoughts were nothing else but a few childish phrases, their wit, strained verbiage; their scholarship, below a high school course; and their logic, chaos."

FAUST: "I agree with you to a certain extent . . . but let's leave that aside; I spoke of literature as one of the thermometers of a spiritual state in society; this thermometer shows an insuperable boredom (*malaise*) prevailing in the West, the lack of any general belief, hope without hope, denial without any affirmation. Let's take a look at other thermometers. Victor spoke of industrial marvels of our century. The West is the world of manufacturing. The honest statistical tables of Quételet involuntarily made him reach the following conclusions: first, that the number of crimes is much higher in industrial than in agricultural regions;[11] second, that poverty is greater in manufacturing countries than anywhere else, because the slightest political circumstance, the slightest depression in trade plunges thousands of people into poverty and leads them to crimes.[12] Contemporary industry really produces marvels: factories, as you

---

[11] Quételet, *Sur l'Homme, ou Essai de Physique sociale* (Bruxelles, 1836), T. I, p. 215.
[12] *Ibid.*, T. II, p. 211.

know, employ a great number of children below the age of eleven, down to six, simply because they don't have to be paid so much. Since it's not profitable to stop a factory machine at night, because time is money, factories work day and night; each shift works eleven hours a day; toward the end of these hours poor children are so exhausted they can't stand on their feet; they collapse and fall asleep so soundly that only a whip can wake them up; our honest industrialists tried to eliminate this inconvenience and made a marvelous invention: they invented tin boots, which even prevented the poor children from falling down of exhaustion."

VICTOR: "This is an individual case, which doesn't prove anything."

FAUST: "Just be patient and scan at least the parliamentary inquiries from 1832 to 1834 and other documents;[13] this won't be the only thing you'll find there. The answer is the same everywhere: ten-year-old children work eleven hours a day; fatigue to the point of exhaustion; swollen feet; backaches; lack of sleep, hence the constant state of semi-somnolence;[14] finally, what's most important—impossibility of bringing up the children, impossibility of any education, least of all moral education, because there is no time for school after eleven hours of work. And even if children would find the time, their physical and moral state is such that learning is useless to them. Parliamentary commissioners have discovered that the large majority of factory workers don't know how to read or write, and the weakness of old age strikes them before its time; this is not a fairy tale, but an official fact."

VICTOR: "However, Dr. Ure has proved that the very presence in a factory is an educative factor for workers."

FAUST: "I remember that passage—it is such a bluff that you can't read it without laughing and without regret. The much learned Dr. Ure is a passionate champion of cotton skeins, and he takes up anything to protect the object of his adoration: he speaks of the necessity for a worker to look at a thermometer which 'along with a hygrometer supposedly reveals to him the secrets of nature inaccessible to other

[13] Factories inquiry: First Report; Second Report; Supplementary Report 1832–1834, 4 vols. in folio.

[14] It seems that this semisomnolent state is very useful to factories. Recent newspapers contain many descriptions of the composition of *sleeping drugs*, by means of which Western manufacturers calm down children who are too lively.

people; every day he has an opportunity,' continues the philanthropist-manufacturist, 'to observe the expansion of solid bodies, which takes place during a rise in temperature, by observing the huge steam pipes that heat the workrooms . . . to obtain information in practical mechanics from the weaving loom itself.'[15] That's an example of positive thinking. The manufacturing philosopher thinks that knowledge can be screwed into man's head like a screw into the wall, without any preliminary preparation, which could develop man's intellectual concepts to such a degree that individual facts of knowledge would become accessible to him."

VICTOR: "But you must admit that daily contact with machines and with a thermometer can develop the intellectual abilities of man somewhat."

FAUST: "Yes, if he is a genius; others may have a wheel turning and a thermometer hanging in front of them all their lives—and they wouldn't understand anything in either. Thousands of people had been looking at a teapot lid being lifted by steam, but only Watt was led by this observation to the steam engine. The Englishman Hales, one of the most famous seventeenth century craftsmen in chemistry, even invented a device for gathering gases; he touched them, so to say, with his hands, but didn't recognize them; he took them for the same air with some admixtures. A man of genius does not need a school; but all who *lack genius* cannot do without at least a primary education.

"But all this is just daydreaming! Take a look at a weaving plant! Do you know whether a man who must look after hundreds of tearing threads every minute has a chance to conduct observations on a thermometer or to get an insight into mechanics? To say nothing of the unfortunate ones whose sole occupation all day long is to crawl on their fours under a loom gathering cotton—because this is the work that children do; how, at the same time they can perform thermometric and hygrometric observations is known only to Dr. Ure! It seems, however, that profound reflections over the screws and wheels of an automatic loom haven't revealed secrets of nature well known to other mortals or even to Dr. Ure himself. Answering the remark of an intelligent

[15] *Philosophie des manufactures* par Andrew Ure. 2 vols. in 12 (Bruxelles; traduit sous les yeux de l'auteur), Chap. I, p. 36 *et seq.*

doctor in London, who unceremoniously said that *night* work is harmful to one's health, and, particularly in childhood, inhibits the normal development of the body, Dr. Ure scornfully and with a feeling of insulted dignity tried to prove to the medical school that machines are brightly lit by gas and, consequently, night work could not harm children."

ROSTISLAV: "Aren't you joking?"

FAUST: "Take a look at the second chapter of the second volume of *The Philosophy of Manufacturing;*[16] this answer shows that Dr. Ure doesn't know one of the simplest questions of physiology about the effect of night upon living organisms at all. Only a manufacturing philosopher can be excused of such impossible, unforgivable ignorance—but to make up for it, Dr. Ure is a positive man and is considered an authority in the weaving and in the general manufacturing world."

ROSTISLAV: "Does he at least mention the moral education of these unfortunate children in factories?"

FAUST: "In general he praises moral education in factories very much, and here is the evidence I found in his work: 'If the foreman in a wool factory,' he says,[17] 'is a sober and decent man, he doesn't need to harass his little helpers . . . but if he is given to strong drink or is hot-tempered, he treats them tyrannically. . . . When, coming from a tavern, he is late to work, he tries to make up for it by running the machine so fast that his helpers cannot help him . . . then he hits them mercilessly with a long roller (*billy rouleau*). . . .' Isn't this education? Poor children are entirely at the mercy of an adult drunken scoundrel—but that's only for eleven hours a day! By the way, Dr. Ure seriously maintains that this happens only in wool, but never in cotton, factories[18] and hopes that new improvements in wool factories will eliminate this little inconvenience."

VICTOR: "But you take up only individual cases."

FAUST: "These individual cases exist in all the factories of the West."

VICTOR: "You point out only one side."

FAUST: "You wish to learn about another side; here it is: Charles Dupin solemnly announced from the parliamentary

[16] *Ibid.,* p. 149.
[17] *Ibid.,* T. I, p. 13.
[18] *Ibid.*

tribune that for every 10,000 recruits in manufacturing de-
partments in France there are 8,900 sick people and cripples,
whereas in agricultural ones there are only 4,000."[19]

VICTOR: "This is still the dark side; you must also consider the force of circumstances, as for instance the West's
huge productiveness which, naturally, lowers the prices of
manufactured things and forces factories to make them
cheaper and in less time; that accounts for all this night
work, employment of children, exhaustion—without that, the
greatest part of manufacturers would be ruined."

FAUST: "I don't see any need for this excessive productiveness."

VICTOR: "For pity's sake! You want to limit the freedom
of industry."

FAUST: "I don't see any need for limitless freedom."

VICTOR: "But there wouldn't be any competition without
it."

FAUST: "I don't see any need for so-called competition.
What? People who are anxious to profit try with all their
might to drown one another in order to sell their product,
and for that they sacrifice all human feelings, happiness,
morality, the health of entire generations—and only because
it occurred to Adam Smith to call this trick 'competition,' 'the
freedom of trade'—people do not even dare to touch this
sacred thing? Oh, what a shameful disgraceful lie!"

VICTOR: "I admit that the present state of Western industry
is quite strange and sad, but the West is not contained in it
alone. Remember that the West is the cradle of our enlightenment, that people go to the West to study, that the
West is truly a temple of the sciences."

FAUST: "That's an immense problem! We could talk about
it till tomorrow night! In order not to go too far, I shall only
ask you what sciences, precisely, have made progress in
this temple? I see activity in the West; I see an enormous
loss of effort; I see many useful and useless methods—it
wouldn't harm to learn them; but to think that the new
science has left the ancient one far behind, that is another
question. Did the new science increase man's welfare even
a hair'sbreadth—that is a third question."

VICTOR: "Listen, it's impossible to deny the enlightenment
of the West; you won't be able to prove it."

FAUST: "I don't deny it; I even realize that we still have a

[19] See the newspapers of the thirties.

lot to learn from the West, but I wanted to assess the value
of this enlightenment realistically. We have already seen their
success in political economy and social organization, and we
keep seeing it every day; things have gone so far that one
goodhearted eccentric suggested that we change the entire
social way of life around and try whether it wouldn't be
better to let passions have their way, even inciting them,
rather than curbing them, and this eccentric was not a fool;
the absurdity at which he arrived proves that there is no
longer any way out of the circle in which Western science
now finds itself. Physical sciences have many applications,
but exactly what belongs to the new century is uncertain."

VICTOR: "To ascribe all inventions to the ancients is a very
old idea; hundreds of books have been written about it."

FAUST: "That means that there is something right about it;
you know my conviction: I can't believe that science is able
to progress much when scientists push it in various directions! In this progressing they can come across something
new, but they can only come across it; the ancients apparently pushed it into one direction and the cart went
faster."

VICTOR AND VYACHESLAV: "Proof, proof, please!"

FAUST: "You know the book which occupies me at present;
its purpose is to remind people about forgotten knowledge,
something like the work of Panciroli, *De rebus deperditis*;
parenthetically, and unexpectedly to myself, it proved that
alchemists, magi, and other people of that sort were already
acquainted with all our physical knowledge and that it was
known in the Eleusinian temple and by Egyptian priests. I'll
limit myself to only a few remarks at present. When we
know for sure that one object or another existed at a given
time, we must conclude that there must also have existed
the means to produce it; when we see a wooden house, we
conclude that squared beams were made of trees, that they
were cut by iron, that iron was forged, that it was obtained
from iron ore, that the ore was worked upon, and so on.
All the most important chemical compounds, without which
our science would stand still, came to us from alchemists;
alcohol, metals, all important acids, alkali, salts; their existence necessarily presupposes knowledge at least as extensive as that of our time, even if the very processes and
devices were not described in detail; that's as clear to me as
two times two make four."

VICTOR: "A story of one invention has been preserved

which may serve as a clue to how many others were done without the aid of particular knowledge. Phoenician merchants discovered glass quite accidentally and without any chemistry while making a fire on the seashore for their dinner."

FAUST: "Pliny wrote down this legend, along with many others. According to him, 'merchants used pieces of *nitrate*[20] which they had on their ships for their tables. Nitrate, under the action of fire along with the sea sand, began to flow in transparent streams, and such was the origin of glass.' Actually, that could never happen, Pliny notwithstanding. Glass could never form at such a low heat in the open air for this reason: to melt glass one needs the temperature of a smelting furnace, not that of an open fire. Whatever you may say, the existence of glass in ancient times points to an enormous preliminary knowledge, which alone could lead to glass manufacturing. As far as I can see, thousands of experiments must have preceded the discovery of the composition of glass, and the discovery of the proportion of substances contained in it; and let's not forget an elastic glass, unknown to us, but mentioned by Pliny and apparently by Suetonius, too."

VYACHESLAV: "To elevate the ancients, and to lower the new people was in fashion, but now it is passé!"

FAUST: "I do not maintain that every possible discovery belongs to the ancients, but I can't forget, for instance, the legend about Numa Pompilius, a pupil of the Pythagoreans, who is supposed to have brought thunder to the earth by means of mysterious rites; the name of Jupiter the Elicitor, that is, the one who evokes;[21] the story by Titus Livy[22] about Tulla Hostilius, who having forgotten something in the rites was struck by lightning while imitating Numa. This story reminds one exactly of Rickman's death during his experiments with a lightning rod, as described by Lomonosov. One should also not forget the circumstances which accompanied Egyptian initiations, and which explain Aeschy-

[20] "Glebas nitri"—Pliny, *Hist. natur.*, lib. xxxvi, 65, saltpeter? potash? nitrate?

[21] Eliciunt coelo te, Jupiter; unde minores
    Nunc quoque te celebrant, Eliciumque vocant.

says Ovid, lib. 3, v. 328. Jupiter Elicius—ab eliciendo, sive extrahendo. Cf. Dutand.

[22] Lib. I, p. 20, Cf. also Pliny, lib. I, p. 53, de fulminis evocandis.

lus's words:[23] 'Only Minerva knows where the thunder is hidden'; embalming, described by Herodotus, indicates that Egyptians knew about creosote, which we barely managed to obtain after many years' efforts. Distance in time, destruction and distortion of written monuments prevent us in this case from realizing the truth; but I maintain at least that we haven't progressed a step in our knowledge of nature from the time of the disastrous state of sciences, created by Bacon of Verulam, and even more by his followers. Whoever has patience to read through the works of the alchemists will easily be convinced that this statement, so strange at first glance, is true. The entire present knowledge of chemistry is found not only in works of Albert the Great, Roger Bacon, Raymond Lully, Basilius Valentinus, Paracelsus, and other wonderful people of the kind, but this knowledge was so elaborated that one can find it also in alchemists of lesser importance. For instance in the *Cosmopolitan*[24] you'll find an experiment on freezing water by means of sulphuric acid, which presupposes the existence of projectiles, which in their turn presuppose vast experience. Nitrogen was known to Roger Bacon; even in the book which bears the name of Artephius[25] one can detect knowledge of the property of gases; not only Basilius Valentinus but Hildebrandt[26] also describes metals with such details as you will not find even in many recent works; Heinrich Kundrat[27] felt the importance of analyzing organic substances. . . ."

VYACHESLAV: "Be merciful . . . what names are these? What could such barbarians know?"

FAUST: "I purposely mentioned people who were not particularly famous even in their own time, and yet we attain the state of their knowledge only with effort."

VICTOR: "But won't you leave something for our own time: for instance, the knowledge that water is not a primary element, as the ancients thought, despite all their wisdom."

FAUST: "That too is one of the tales which placates our

[23] In the last part of the Trilogy on Orestes, *The Eumenides.*

[24] In the newest translation of 1723: *Cosmopolite ou nouvelle lumière chymique,* p. 26.

[25] *Artephii antiquissimi philosophi de arte occulta atque lapide philosophorum liber secretus,* in quarto, 1612.

[26] *Magiae naturalis,* P. II. Hortus deliciarum—durch Wolfgang Hildebrandum, in quarto, 1625.

[27] *Amphiteatrum sapientiae eternae solius verae,* in folio, Lipsiae, 1602.

pride as experimentalists; the ancients never took water for
a simple matter, at least from the time of Plato, who states
in the *Timaeus* that 'water may be *divided* by means of fire
and produces a fiery substance or two air-like substances.'
Isn't it clear that he meant oxygen and hydrogen, the discovery of which makes us so proud? I have no doubt that
by the names of the elements fire, air, water, and earth the
ancients understood the concepts corresponding to our four
simple substances: oxygen, nitrogen, hydrogen and carbon;[28]
we can find hundreds of proofs for that: it is worth remembering the Eleatics, to say nothing of the Pythagoreans! When
modern chemists testify that all organic bodies are formed
of the gases constituting air, I take my hat off and bow to a
rather old acquaintance—the contemporary of Anaximenes.
It should also not be forgotten that all the most important
gases were known to the alchemist Van Helmont and that
even the word *gas* belongs to him."

VICTOR: "At least steam power—"

FAUST: "It was used *practically* by Hieron of Alexandria
120 years B.C.; Blasco offered it to Karl V; between these
two epochs, as you know, Roger Bacon spoke about it—and
now all this has been made clear by proof."

VICTOR: "At least balloons—"

FAUST: "They were known to the same wonderful Bacon,
and one of the alchemists left a quite detailed description of
a balloon a hundred years before Montgolfier, and suggested
building it exactly as it was *thought of* rather recently, that
is, of copper.[29] Look, here is a picture: spheres, and a boat,
and a sail; these barbarians, as Victor says, have great un-

---

[28] Here is this interesting passage in Plato, barely noticed till
now, in Ast's translation: "terra quidem concurrens cum igne dissoluta ab ejus acie fertur, sive in ipso igne soluta fuerit (metal?),
sive in aëris oxide?), sive in aquae mole (salt?), dum concurrentes
forte ejus partes rursusque inter se ipsae copulatae terra evadant:
neque enim in aliam umquam speciem transeant. Aqua autem ab
igne vel etiam ab aëre divisa potest fieri composita *unum ignis
corpus et duo aëris*. De aëris vero particulis ex una parte dissoluta
duo existent corpora ignis—Plat. op., t. 5, p. 197, Ed. As., 1822.
Here I make bold to remark that δέ in the words: δύο δὲ ἀέρος
may mean *or*, Slavic же , despite μέν .

[29] Francesco Lana, *Prodromo all'arte maestra* (Brescia, 1670, in
folio), cap. 6, pp. 52-61: "Fabricare una Nave, che camini sosten-
tata sopra l'aria a remi et a vele, quale si dimostra poter riuscire
in prattica."

touched treasures, some of which we attain by chance, some we are afraid to touch, of some we do not know. All these marvels were not the product of a painstaking sensual experimentation, but of a view of nature we do not even dream of in this mousehole into which we have fallen thanks to Bacon of Verulam."

VYACHESLAV: "I don't know why you should blame Bacon in particular; if the experimental direction was abused one should rather blame the followers of Bacon: Locke, Condillac, and others."

VICTOR: "But I still do not see what there is in common between the discovery of one acid or another and one metaphysical idea or another?"

FAUST: "In the temple of philosophy, as in a supreme court, are determined problems which in a given epoch are worked out in the lower spheres of human activity. One cannot help noticing an obvious parallelism between the most abstract metaphysical concepts of the century and the activity of applied sciences, which form the entire social, familial, and individual life of man in that century. Thus, for example, it is rather interesting that the gradual fragmentation of natural sciences, or better to say, their diminution, in other words, their turning into crafts, which, in my opinion, is their gradual fall—corresponds precisely to that disastrous epoch when philosophy, having slipped in Bacon, passed Locke, and descended to Condillac, despite all the great Leibnitz's contradictions, that is, from the second half of the seventeenth century till the beginning of the nineteenth. From that moment on, as if by some sort of sorcery, basic discoveries, which had formed the huge arsenal of physical sciences and which we have been using until now—ungratefully laughing at the ancients, no longer take place; now we see on our stage only industrial applications of what had been discovered before. As for Bacon, he himself probably did not anticipate the absurdities his followers would reach; he attacked the experimental methods of the crowds of his time, 'blind and senseless ones,' as he called them. He demanded that experiments be conducted in a certain order and with some method; but on Bacon rests the heavy responsibility for having trained investigators to stop at *incidental, secondary* causes, leaving the *inner essence* of phenomena aside. He pronounced the unfortunate words, which had been the precious insignia of the scientific world for two centuries, and which have now been dissipated in trifles: 'The best of all evidences is, of course, an experiment, but an experiment where you consider only the fact which is before you. . . .' and further: 'Having accumulated many facts of all sorts one must extract from them the knowledge of causes and principles.' "[30]

VICTOR: "But what did your alchemists do? Weren't they poisoned by charcoal fumes beside their furnaces? Didn't they gather facts? Even if Egyptian temples were nothing but physical laboratories, they probably followed Bacon's laws there, too."

FAUST: "With the only difference that the ancients, as well as the majority of alchemists, knew where they were going: for them the material experiment was the last step in their search for truth. Since Bacon's day people begin with this step, and they go, as they say, headlong, without knowing where and what for. That's why alchemists made all their discoveries, without which we can't move, just so, among other things—whereas we are only screws and wheels for cotton caps."

VICTOR: "All right! Let's assume that all our present knowledge was also known to the ancient world and to the Middle Ages, that we gather only crumbs from their rich table, but the thing is that this table was set *for a few*, for very few, whereas now science is like a common table in a fine hotel, open to everyone."

FAUST: "I agree with that, but I want to remark that the doors of this hotel are not wide enough and not everyone can afford to sit at this table. Indeed, in ancient times and in the Middle Ages science was a secret, known only to priests or their adherents; and secrets exist until now in various technical processes for a quite simple reason: for the self-interest of inventors. You know how long (from the beginning of the eighteenth century) the composition of laundering blue remained a secret, although it was widely sold. Only at the end of the eighteenth century Schell and Bertholet made the composition of hydrocyanic acid known to the public; for the ancients this secrecy was a necessity: they understood the strange inscription in Isis's temple: 'Do not disclose the secret for fear of punishment by a peach,' and they knew why a peach tree is dedicated to the God of silence—which, by the way shows that the ancients also knew

[30] *Nov. Org.* 1, I, p. 70.

hydrocyanic acid before us.[31] Plato constantly stops and makes a slip when touching upon subjects known to him as an *initiated* man; the necessity of keeping a secret was so important in the Middle Ages that Roger Bacon, the most outspoken of alchemists, having named saltpeter and sulphur as components of gunpowder, hides the word carbon under a rather obscure anagram: *luru vopo vir can utriet* (which is read: *carbonum pulvere*). Finally, almost in our day some-one in London who expressed his intention of disclosing the secret of the composition of gold was found killed in his room.[32] But the smaller the circle of these people was, the more amazing is the fact that they, without all our resources, books, dictionaries, instruments, journals, and conferences, made all our discoveries before us. . . ."

VYACHESLAV: "I don't see anything amazing in that: alchemists were looking for nonsense, the philosopher's stone, and by accident came across various discoveries. . . ."

FAUST: "Do you know what's needed to find something accidentally?"

VYACHESLAV: "A series of experiments."

FAUST: "And *eyes*—in the fullest sense of this word! Other-wise we would resemble workers taught by Dr. Ure's system."

VICTOR: "Whatever you say, it is impossible that all these thousands of special experiments, which are now conducted by thousands of people all over the world, in all branches of natural sciences, should not finally lead to the real theory of nature."

FAUST: "I have proof for this as well: meteorology. We are witnesses of all of its manifestations; observations of this kind are possible every day, every hour—and how far has it got? To a negative answer. Meteorologists can prove only one thing: that all preceding explanations (the result of direct experiments) are false and that we, at the present state of the science, are unable to explain even the formation of snow, hail, rain, direction of wind, and so on.[33] Considering

[31] Prussic acid; it is known that this terrible poison can also be obtained from peach stones, fortunately only with great effort. (See Hoefer, *Hist. d. 1. Chim.*)

[32] See *Geschichte der Alchemie* Schmieder (Halle, 1832). Hoefer, *ibid.*

[33] Poulier, Kemtz, Arago. This book is not a scholarly disserta-tion; to give quotations at each step would mean to burden it superfluously; even as it is, there are many references, although

the present trends and following meteorology, all other sciences also strive toward the same result. Somebody remarked quite justly that these gentlemen resemble a physiologist who would draw all the blood out of a man to the last drop the better to explain to him the composition and action of blood.

"Disbelief in the possibility of general principles, the habit of being satisfied with secondary, incidental causes, and being unaccustomed to the higher movements of spirit produced two evils. The first evil is the conviction that the feeling of a soul really exists only when it can be expressed in words; thus, whatever does not fit into one material form or another is called a dream. This conviction is so strong that everyday phenomena, obviously contradicting it, are unable to shake it. Who doesn't discuss the *medical eye* (*coup d'oeil medicinal*)? Ask a man of medicine who is endowed with this gift how he hit upon the cause of illness. Why did he prescribe exactly one method of treatment rather than any other?—and frequently you'll embarrass the most learned doctor. Only in China is it required that a doctor find the disease of his patient in official medical books and treat him exactly according to these books. I consider it rather logical: if everything can be expressed in words, one need only follow these words and everything will be all right.

"Wasn't there a time when it was thought that by means of poetics and rhetorics a person could be taught to write poetry! The Academy of Paris demanded quite recently that it be given to feel the action of animal magnetism; whoever protests against such demands goes against logic. The second evil: destructive *specialization*, which now is considered the only road to knowledge, and which turns man into a camera-obscura, forever directed to one and the same object. For years it keeps reflecting it without any realization of why and for what and in what connection this object is with other ones.

"To this day you'll find people who are convinced that the marvels of English industry are due to the fact that if a person makes a screw, he keeps making it his entire life and

---

the author limited himself to quite necessary ones. Those readers who believe the author will not need quotations; for others, he can later disclose a whole arsenal of quotations, upon which the statements contained in this book are based.

doesn't know about anything in the world except this screw. *Concentration of attention*—the highest spiritual power, which can draw entire nature into its sphere, and which is attainable by the highest spirit only—for these gentlemen is nothing else but a machine which strikes the same place for years. These two evils cause *dissension* and *lack of co-ordination* in sciences and in life; they cause anarchy, infinite arguments and disconnected efforts; they make man helpless before nature. Take any subject you want, the most abstract or the most ordinary one from our daily life; collect the *specialists'* answers—these graduates of I-can't-know, as Suvorov used to say; this indiscriminate search may be quite interesting:

" 'Please tell me the chemical composition of these or other substances used in food, how can it effect the human organism, and, consequently, one of the sources of social wealth?'—'Excuse me, that's not in my line, I'm interested only in financial knowledge.'

" 'Tell me, can one not explain certain historical events by the effect of chemical composition of the substance used by man as food at different times?'—'Excuse me, I can't be bothered with studying history. I'm a chemist.'

" 'Tell me, is it true that fine arts, and music in particular, have such a strong influence upon moderating of tempers—and precisely what kind of music?'—'For pity's sake, music is just a distraction, a toy. When do I have time for it? I am a lawyer.'

" 'Tell me, can your present-day music, always passionate or brilliant, disturb the equilibrium of moral elements on which the making of a society depends?'—'Excuse me, this question is too remote from me. I'm a violinist.'

" 'Can you explain the meaning of the rites observed in ancient times by the priests of Cybele or the earth?'—'Excuse me, I'm not concerned with philology. I'm an agronomist.'

" 'Tell me, are there among ancient agricultural processes any experiments now forgotten which would be worthwhile to repeat?'—'Excuse me, I'm not a farmer; I'm a philologist.

" 'Would you know what the cause of a particular propagation and frequently an appearance of one insect or another in a particular year may be? Have certain periods in these phenomena been observed in history? Is there any mention of it even in obscure legends, during the climacteric years discussed by astrologists?'—'Excuse me, cosmology is not my field. I examine insects in a microscope, and, I admit, quite successfully: I have discovered a dozen completely new species.'

" 'Tell me if you have noticed the relation between the deviation of the magnetic needle and an unusual harvest of one plant or another, or particular mortality among animals.' —'Excuse me, I can't worry about such details. I've dedicated myself to purely magnetic observations.'

" 'Tell me, sir, to what extent can the spreading of a theory *pro* and *contra* inborn ideas in Plato's sense have an influence upon administrative measures in one country or another?'—'What a strange question! It's too remote for me. I'm an employee, a civil servant.'

" 'And you, sir, can you tell me to what extent a harmonic construction of the human soul must be considered in organizing a city police force?'—'This apparently belongs to legislative sciences, and I teach logic and rhetoric.'

" 'Tell me, is it possible to determine the inner properties of a plant by its external forms, as Raymond Lully wrote, for example, one or another of its medical properties?'— 'Actually, this is a medical subject, and I do only botanical classification; as to Raymond Lully, I have not had a chance to read him—I'm not a bibliomaniac.'

" 'Have you noticed any analogy in the external form of plants having identical medical effect? Can this phenomenon be of assistance in compiling a more accurate, more consistent system of the plant world, and on the basis of such a system couldn't one search directly for a still-undiscovered plant, or for one substance or another in a given plant, instead of doing so by chance?'—'That would greatly increase our means. Take cinchona for example, which is much more convenient to use than quinine itself; as to the analogy you mentioned, one cannot help noticing it; thus, for instance, the majority of poisonous plants have something in common in their physiognomy. However, I can't take up working on this subject: that is a job for botanists. I am a practicing doctor.'

" 'Tell me at least, what is ginseng, this strange plant, which in China is worth its weight in gold, and to which is ascribed such a marvelous power?'—'I can tell you that: it is *Panax quinquefolium*, of the *diospiri* family. Ask a chemist about the properties of this plant; I'm a botanist!'

" 'Tell me, what is the composition of this strange plant? What is its effect upon an organism and how is it used?'—

'Most probably it consists of oxygen, hydrogen, carbon and, maybe, nitrogen. As to its effects, ask Orientalists or travelers about it.'

" 'You, sir, are one of the few people who spent a long time in China; you are an educated man. Tell me, what is this plant, and how is it used?'—'I heard that there are several kinds of it; one is quite common and does not produce any effect, but another is very rare, and as I saw myself, it really saves people most critically ill. What the difference between these two kinds is, and in what cases one or the other is used, I was unable to learn because I do not occupy myself with natural sciences. I am a linguist and an Orientalist.'

" 'Sir, you write so well. Could you not write a book in a human language which would make physical knowledge attractive and accessible to everyone?'—'What can I do? That is not my subject! I'm interested only in belles-letters.'

" 'You, sir, you have such a profound knowledge of physics and natural history. Couldn't you reform the barbaric physical nomenclature which alienates readers and makes the best works of physics incomprehensible to anyone but a physicist?'—'I can't help you! That is not my subject! I am not a literary man.'

" 'Sir, I heard that you have published your book on differential and integral calculus; they say that the insight in your formulas provides an explanation of almost all physical, chemical, and ethnographical phenomena! How glad I am that you finally published your book!'—'What's the use! There will hardly be ten persons who will read it—and hardly three in the whole world who will understand it.'

" 'And you, sir, you, who by the nature of your science must have information on everything, tell me, why do all scientists go in different directions and why does each speak a language incomprehensible to the others? Why is it that, having learned and described everything, we know almost nothing?'—'Excuse me, this is not my subject; I collect only facts: I am a statistician!' "

VYACHESLAV: "Enough! Enough of that! If you intend to collect all the reservations of the scholarly world, you can keep talking till the end of the world."

FAUST: "I am trying to find out if the droplets of blood which are so zealously drawn by these gentlemen from all veins of nature, by each from his own, will not merge somewhere."

VICTOR: "Don't worry! They begin to merge: for instance, the identity of electricity, galvanism, and magnetism has been established."

FAUST: "High time! Schelling discussed it thirty years ago. . . . What next?"

VICTOR: "You still want the philosopher's stone! Unfortunately, our century cannot satisfy you in this respect, just as it can give you neither magic nor the cabala, nor astrology."

FAUST: "Ask Berzelius, Dumas, Raspail, and other chemists if they would take metals for simple bodies and if they would laugh at someone who began to search not for a philosopher's stone—no! How could one in the nineteenth century! No! but to search for the *radical of metals*—that is, precisely, what alchemists were after! True, they gave very strange names to the objects of their research: mercury, quintessence, virgin soil, which is quite unforgivable on their part. I'll tell you a little secret, gentlemen, only keep it to yourself; otherwise people may say that I am seriously given to alchemy. Contemporary chemistry has one unfortunate simple substance called nitrogen; this substance serves as a purifying scapegoat for all sins in chemistry; when a chemist doesn't know what he has found—he calls this *I don't know* either a *loss* or *nitrogen*, depending on the circumstances. Nitrogen is a completely negative substance in our time, despite the fact that it is constantly discussed. If chemists come across a gas which doesn't have the properties of any gas they know—they call it nitrogen. And here is my secret: it seems to me that not only was nitrogen well known to alchemists but that they even considered it a *complex body*. When our chemists become convinced of it—only one step will remain to a metallic gas, or what is today called, with a grimace, the *radical of metals*. Now I can say, as formerly alchemists used to say at the end of a mysterious page: 'My son! I have revealed an important secret to you!' All this is fine, only one thing is bad: when this happens, I am afraid people will laugh at our atoms, isomers, catalytic power, perhaps even at our oxides, peroxides, and other elegant names, just as we laugh at mercury, the alchemists' green and red dragon."

VYACHESLAV: "Of course, the sciences are perfecting themselves—and how do we know where they are going to stop?"

FAUST: "The illusion of words, at least in our century. I see one thing in it: with all our efforts we attained what was known before us. I think there was no reason to go that far."

VICTOR: "At least we'll leave to our heirs rich materials and experiments made with the help of instruments whose refinement our predecessors could not have conceived."

FAUST: "I don't know what purpose was served by an exhibition of these beautiful, polished toys called physical instruments. Archimedes had a very unimposing device for determining the specific gravity of bodies—water; Galileo's instrument in discovering the laws of pendular motion was a chandelier which hung in a church; for Newton, it is said, it was an apple."

VYACHESLAV: "At least out of pity you ought to leave something for our time. Can it be that all the scientists who have worked during the last century and a half aren't worth the slightest attention?"

FAUST: "Oh, no! I don't say that! One cannot help respecting scientists! One cannot help respecting the efforts and sufferings of a few eminent figures who felt in themselves the necessity for uniting sciences and who remained unappreciated by their contemporaries. One can only be amazed at the courage with which even those in the lower spheres of endeavor frequently sacrifice their efforts, their peaceful life, and life itself to science! A scientist for me is the same as a warrior. I want to write an interesting book: *on the courage of scientists,* beginning with a humble antiquarian or philologist, who slowly, day by day, absorbs the germs of diseases threatening his secluded life—and progressing up to a chemist who, despite all his experience, can never guarantee that he will leave his laboratory alive; from Pliny the Elder, killed while fighting a volcano, to Rickman, killed by a lightning bolt; Dulon, who lost his eye fighting with chlorine; Parent-Duchatelet, who spent weeks up to his knees in stagnant pits that were contaminating the whole city; to Alexander Humboldt, who descended into mines in order to experience for himself the effect of asphyxiation; who affixed Spanish flies to himself for galvanic experiments, to all the victims of hydrofluoric, hydrocyanuric acid—and I assure you, I will not forget anyone.

"But the more I respect scientific work, the more—I repeat again—I regret this immeasurable and futile effort of fragmented strength, which is now noticeable in the West; and I regret it all the more since science stubbornly wanders along a difficult, thorny road for more than a hundred years and attains only insignificant industrial applications which, following another road, would have come by themselves; or they attain the simple mechanical noting of facts, without purpose, almost without hope, as in meteorology—I regret that we haven't yet left the swaddling of the eighteenth century, that we haven't cast off the shameful yoke of the encyclopedists and materialists, that the general, living bond among the sciences was lost, and that the true principle of knowledge is being forgotten more and more."

VYACHESLAV: "At least you will not deny success to history in our time, because without it you wouldn't have been able to take a single step in attacking our century. . . ."

FAUST: "History! History doesn't exist yet."

VICTOR: "Permit us to doubt that at least! When, in what century was history paid more attention? When did the treasures of history undergo such intensive investigation?"

FAUST: "And yet history as a science does not exist! The main condition for any science is to know its future, that is, to know what it should be upon reaching its goal. Chemistry, physics, medicine, despite all their present inperfection, know what they could become, consequently, what they are striving for. History does not even know that. Like botany, meteorology, statistics, it mounts one stone upon another, without knowing what the building will be like, a vault or a pyramid, or simply a ruin, or nothing."

VYACHESLAV: "You're confusing history with chronology, with chronicles. The time of chronicles is gone; what historian since the time of Voltaire's *Essays on Peoples' Rights* (*Essai sur les mœurs*) does not attempt to combine historical facts so as to make general conclusions possible?"

FAUST: "True! The necessity of one general living theory is felt more and more with each day by the best minds of the century, everywhere: in history as well as in other sciences. But the same thing happened in history as in meteorology. It described in detail that lightning is an electric spark accompanied by thunder; on the other hand, an experiment showed the distance covered by sound. These facts led to well-founded conclusions: that the farther away a thunderstorm is, and the more time passes between the appearance of lightning and the sound of thunder, the less dangerous it is for a man. This theory became an axiom; people began explaining all the phenomena they encountered by means of it. Good people, who studied sciences, even until now count by their pulse the time which passes between lightning and thunder, and with assurance inform an amazed commoner that the thunderstorm is so and so many miles away from him! Wonderful! What could be better! That's a correct observation of facts and of a theory based on facts, and not on dreams!

"But here is what badly disappointed our experienced theorists: they came across other facts, namely: people, animals, buildings were struck by a thunderstorm without the slightest sign of lightning or thunder! What should be done with the proved theory? Now it was all upside down! 'Never mind,' said the observers, 'we will add these facts to the other, contradictory ones—that's all; but to satisfy theorists, we'll find some name for these surprising facts; let's call them a return shock (*choc de retour*)!' The same theory, based on numbers and statistical conclusions, declared that thunderstorms happen more often in warm countries than in cold ones, and explained this law very precisely by means of electric fluid. But, unfortunately, a little supplement was added to these statistical tables, stating that Lima, Peru, and Cairo almost never have thunderstorms, whereas in Jamaica they occur daily from November till April.[34] Apparently, the latter country has the privilege of possessing electric fluid which the first ones lack.

"In history, and particularly in so-called philosophical history, the same thing happens. Nothing could be more interesting than a compilation of historical conclusions concerning causes of events, and evaluation of historical personalities. One says a certain country survived because, despite unfavorable circumstances, it decided to preserve its nationality; another says a certain country perished because, despite the same circumstances, it wanted to resist. A certain general, despite all admonitions made haste and because of that lost a battle; but another general, under the same circumstances, despite all admonitions, didn't want to be tardy, and won the battle. Barbarians attacked Romans, but had to yield to their military discipline; barbarians attacked Romans and the Roman Empire collapsed, despite its military discipline. John Huss died because, relying upon a safe-conduct, he gave himself into the hands of his implacable enemies. Luther triumphed because, despite the example of John Huss, he went right into the midst of his implacable enemies. Here

[34] See *Meteorology* by Kemtz.

then are the lessons of the so-called school of nations—
history. Ask it whatever you want to; it will give you an
answer to everything, both affirmative and negative; there
is no absurdity which cannot be supported by indications in
the faithful records of history, and the less mendacious they
are, the easier they bend to fit any conclusions.

"Why does this strange, ugly phenomenon exist? Because
historians, like meteorologists, thought it possible to stop at
the secondary causes; they thought that a series of facts
could bring them to some general formula! And what do we
see at the present moment? Historians, realizing constantly
that the same causes create completely contrary results, decided to become chronicle writers again. I find it completely logical! Gentlemen, pour all sorts of medicine into
the same bottle—perhaps something will come out of it after
all!"

VICTOR: "In attacking contrary inferences from identical
events, you forgot that it is necessary to consider various
circumstances, as, for example, the geographical situation,
climate."

FAUST: "England is a little bit larger than Iceland, and
their physical setting is almost alike. Why is there such a
difference in the fate of these two islands? Climate? Why
haven't Englishmen who resettled in North America turned
into Indians, and Indians into Englishmen? Why haven't
the Jews and gypsies accepted the customs of all the climate
zones where they lived and live?"

VICTOR: "The reason for this is quite simple: the national
character, the spirit of the time."

FAUST: "You have spoken two important words, but one is
incomprehensible to me, and the other requires an explanation. For instance, what is the spirit of the time? I have encountered this word very often, but nowhere have I seen
its definition."

VICTOR: "It is difficult to define this word, but its meaning
is clear enough. The spirit of time designates the distinguishing character of all human activity in a given period
of time, a general direction of mind toward one subject or
another, toward one way of thinking or another, a general
conviction; finally, something corresponding to the age of an
individual person, something indispensable, unavoidable."

FAUST: "You have apparently defined it rather correctly;
but here is a question: where does this general direction, this
general conviction come from? Does it depend on one power-

ful reason, or on several various principles? If the spirit of the time stems from one basis, it must create one general conviction, excluding all other convictions; if the spirit of time stems from various bases, the conviction created by it can't be general, because it will divide itself into several various convictions, each of them claiming superiority, and then, good-bye necessity. Here is an individual example: What, for instance, is the character of the present century in your opinion?"

VICTOR: "Industrial, positive; that's as simple as two times two make four."

FAUST: "Very well; that, then, is the indispensable inclination of our century, right? We look for a positive, tangible usefulness in everything, right?"

VICTOR: "Of course!"

FAUST: "If that is so, please explain to me how music can exist in our century? In our positive epoch it is an utter impossibility, an absurdity! Every other art at least has some remote usefulness; poetry has found its own little corner in so-called didactic and anacreontic poetry; by means of verse, for instance, one can be taught to wind thread; De Lille wrote a manual for gardeners; I don't remember who, a poem on bookbinding. Painting reminds one of material objects, and can be useful for depicting machines, houses, localities and other useful things; to say nothing of architecture. But music? Music cannot be of any usefulness whatsoever! How did it survive in our century, where each step is accompanied by the question What is it useful for? In other words, What financial operation is it good for? If people were unfortunate enough to be perfectly logical, they should have thrown music out of a window, as old rubbish. The man who once said while listening to music: 'Sonate! que me veux-tu?'[35] was a completely logical man, because you really cannot even ask for a glass of water through music. How did this useless art make its way into our education? Why does a respectable manufacturer want his daughter to strum the piano? Why does he spend money for music lessons and instruments which could be spent for more useful things instead?"

VICTOR: "Don't worry, the reason for such an extravagance is obvious: nothing else but vanity!"

FAUST: "I agree! Music really made its way into modern

[35] Sonata! what do you want from me?

society in one of its fancy dresses protected by vanity, but
why did our vanity make friends precisely with music? Why
not with the kitchen, for instance, which would have been
much easier and more useful? Something rather strange and
interesting happened here. It never occurred to our respectful manufacturer, who made his daughter play brilliant
variations on *di tanti palpiti*, that a few frivolous philanthropists, interested in a reformatory system, came across a
quite incomprehensible fact: they noticed that only those
criminals were inclined to reform who showed a disposition
to music.[36] What a strange thermometer!"

VICTOR: "As you wish—but I can't understand what a
connection there can be between a roulade and the moral
acts of man."

FAUST: "It is strange, indeed! And yet, it is a fact, *un fait
acquis à la science,* as the French say. Involuntarily one
thinks of someone's intervention in the world of human
activities; music, I repeat, made its way into this world,
despite the spirit of the age! You see, I admit the existence
of this spirit, but I give it another meaning, which utilitarians perhaps will not like. In my opinion, the spirit of the
age is in an eternal struggle with the inner feeling of man;
this spirit has been forced to accept into its bosom music,
which is so distasteful to it, yielding to some obscure human
feeling, which unconsciously guesses the lofty meaning of
this art."

VYACHESLAV: "I'm glad to know that: in the future, when
some singer or Signor Castratto starts on *di tanti palpiti* at a
concert, I'll shout, 'Silence, gentlemen, this is a lesson in
morality!'"

FAUST: "Your mockery is to the point, but you made a
mistake in the aim, and thus hit the spirit of the age, not
music. This spirit very much feels like changing the art so
hostile to it to its own taste; in order to do so it has pushed
music onto a carefree road, where it now staggers from side
to side. The material spirit of the age made hymns, expressing the inner man, take up a character of contradance; it
has debased hymns by making them express unusual passions,
spiritual lies; it has covered the unfortunate art with glitter,
roulades, trills, and all sorts of tinsel, so that people wouldn't
recognize it, wouldn't discover its profound meaning! All

[36] See Appert, *Des bagnes et prisons,* 3 vols. in octavo, and
many other books on this subject.

so-called bravura music, all modern concert music is the result of this trend; one more step, and the divine art would simply have turned into jugglery—the dark spirit of the age was already near its triumph, but it was proved to be wrong: music is so strong in its own power that jugglery doesn't last long in it!

"And something strange happened: everything that musicians wrote to please the spirit of the age, for the present moment, for effect, falls into decay, becomes boring, and is soon forgotten. Who wants to listen now to Pleyel's tender passages and the roulades of Cimarosa's time? Rossini's brilliance has already gone! Only a few of his melodies, imbued with sincere feeling, have remained. Everything that he wrote to order, for singers of one voice or another, for one kind of public or another, is vanishing from people's memory; the singers are dead; the forms have become old-fashioned. Bellini, whose music is far below Rossini's, still lives because people haven't had time to become tired of him, and because his operas contain two or three sincere melodies.

Jugglery in modern concert music has become extremely annoying: performers are concentrating on surprising the public with something new: the violin asks for the role of the piano, the piano is dying to sing, the flute tries to play pizzicato; people come, they listen full of amazement, and, by some obscure, unconscious feeling, begin to yawn; the next day everything is forgotten: both their yawning and the music. Before a quarter of a century passes the question 'What do you think of Pacini's or Bellini's operas?' will be just as strange as the question 'What do you think of Galuppi's or Carafa's operas?' is now, although the latter is even our contemporary.

"Meanwhile, old Bach is still alive! Among us we still have wonderful Mozart! In vain does the spirit of the age whisper into people's ears: 'Don't listen to this music! This music is neither gay nor tender! It contains neither the contradance nor the gallop. I'll tell you something even more horrible: this is learned music!' But veneration toward great artists does not cease; as before, their music enraptures; music is studied in their works; their works are being supplied with scholarly commentaries, like Homer's *Iliad*, like Dante's *Comedy*.[37] Isn't that an anachronism in our century? Once

[37] See hundreds of volumes on Sebastian Bach and on Mozart, on the latter in particular, the work of our compatriot Ulybyshev,

we have penetrated into this strange phenomenon (and there are thousands of them), we have a right to ask whether the so-called spirit of the age isn't a combination of contradictions."

VYACHESLAV: "You took only our century as an example."

FAUST: "You'll notice these contradictions in every century: romanticism in the century of ancient classicism,[38] reformation in the century of papism. There are endless examples. What do these contradictory phenomena mean? Can they be reconciled with the concept which is usually held of the spirit of the age? Is it really a necessary form of human activity? Isn't there another, stronger agent in all the historical phenomena?"

VICTOR: "I have already mentioned national character."

FAUST: "I understand this expression somewhat, but I don't know whether in its usual sense."

VYACHESLAV: "It is very simple to define it: the character of a nation is the sum total of its differences from other nations."

FAUST: "Very clear! John is not Cyril, and Cyril is not John; only a trifle remains to be determined: what is John and what is Cyril?"

VYACHESLAV: "This can never be determined."

FAUST: "I don't know."

VICTOR: "Try."

VYACHESLAV: "*A la preuve, monsieur le détracteur! à la preuve!*"

---

which surpasses all books written before him on this subject, both by its profound ideas and knowledge of the matter, by its scholarship and passionate love for the art: *Vie de Mozart*, 3 vols., in octavo. Our journals hardly mentioned this remarkable book. Unfortunately, the book on Beethoven written later by the same author is beneath any criticism.

[38] Shevyrev, in his *Theory of Poetry* (Moscow, 1836, pp. 108, 109), made a rather witty, new, and profound remark, which shows the ancient world from a completely different point of view than the one we are accustomed to. He found "that the examples chosen from pagan writers by Longinus in his work all distinguish themselves by a particular loftiness of *idea*, and not so much with the ancient style, as much with our romantic style. . . . Longinus searches in pagan writers for these very ideas, which are closer to our spirit of time, our Christian tendencies, and he discovers in them a completely new aspect, with which we are more familiar." Shevyrev's book itself supports this opinion by irrefutable indications.

FAUST: "Gentlemen, you place me in a most difficult position. You do not realize how difficult it is to bring into the open a thought which you consider new! What roundabout ways one must go, with how many detours, how much old knowledge has to be reviewed, with how much regret one must destroy everything that may stand in the way of its existence. At the present state of minds, the explanation of any idea must begin with the alphabet, because people are interested only in conclusions, whereas what really matters is the basis. Yet, frequently, this idea consists of four words, and what's worse, sometimes this idea isn't new at all; it is already lodged in the heads of contemporaries—but you have to hammer their skulls to let the locked prisoner out; what's even worse, someone's skull may break without his noticing it!"

VICTOR: "Oh, oh! our humble philosopher! What self-assurance!"

FAUST: "No! A man cherishing an idea is like a loving mother with grown-up daughters; it's time to get them married off, and they have to be given a chance to go out; they have to be properly dressed up; now they have to be praised, now their girl friends of the same age must be criticized. Unfortunately, quite frequently, despite all motherly care—"

VYACHESLAV: "The young ladies don't find bridegrooms! Take care that your dear daughter does not remain an old maid all her life."

VICTOR: "Keep to the point, to the point, please! Don't make any excuses! One cannot with impunity accuse an entire epoch of madness and not show what's not madness."

FAUST: "Seriously, gentlemen, I am in a great difficulty because I, too, belong to our century, and therefore I may have to replace one kind of madness by another. We all resemble people in a huge library: one reads one book, another a second book, a third only looks at the binding. . . . They begin to talk: each speaks of his book—how can they understand each other? Where should they start in order to understand each other? If we all read one and the same book, conversation would be possible—each of us would know where to begin and what to discuss. To give you *my* book to read first is impossible! It has forty volumes, in fine, painstaking print! To read it is an unbearable, inexpressible torture; its pages are in disorder, torn by the pain of despair, and, what's more annoying, the book is far from

finished; much of it has remained incomplete, mysterious. . . .
No! I cannot give you my book to read. You'll throw it aside
impatiently; I would rather begin with one of *your* books.

"You know, gentlemen, many people think that our
world lacks many sciences. For example, someone said that
the West lacks a rather important science, 'how to stoke a
stove,' which is completely reasonable. You also know that
in our day the analytical method is in great vogue. I cannot
understand why no one has yet thought of applying to
history the same method of investigation, as, for instance,
is used by chemists when decomposing organic bodies. First
they arrive at its basic elements, such as acids, salts, and
so on, and finally at its remotest elements, such as the four
basic gases. The former differ in every organic body; the
latter are the same in all organic bodies.

"One could establish a wonderful science with some sort
of sonorous name, such as *Analytical Ethnography* for this
kind of historical investigation. This science would have the
same relation to history as chemical decomposition and
chemical combinations have to ordinary mechanical splitting
and mechanical fusion of bodies. But you know the difference between them: you split a stone; each particle of stone
remains a stone and doesn't disclose anything to you; conversely, you can collect all these particles and you'll have
only a heap of stone particles—nothing more. On the other
hand, you decompose a body chemically and you find that
it consists of elements which could not be suspected in it at
all from its external form; you combine the elements chemically, and again you obtain the decomposed body, the external form of which is unlike its elements. Who would have
thought by looking at fluid water that it consists of two airs
or gases! Who could guess by looking at gaseous oxygen and
hydrogen, without the help of chemistry, that their combination would form water? No wonder chemistry is in such
demand in our century!

"True, the spirit of our age raises technological rubbish
around it and makes it live in this stuffy atmosphere; but
perhaps, despite that, physical chemistry will little by little
approach its secret goal: to direct scientists to higher chemistry. Like various other branches of human activity, although
it is under the yoke of the dark spirit of time, just by its
nature it must deal with inner, secret elements of nature, and
therefore it involuntarily escapes the bridle of materialists
and *examines the depth.* How can we know?

"Perhaps historians will arrive at the results attained by chemists in the physical world by means of *analytic ethnography*; perhaps they will discover a mutual affinity of some elements, a mutual counteraction of others and means of destroying or reconciling this counteraction; perhaps they will inadvertently discover that wonderful chemical law by which elements of bodies combine in definite proportions and in progression of simple numbers as one and one, one and two, and so on; perhaps they will come across what chemists in despair called the catalytic power; that is, the transformation of one body into another in the presence of a third, without any visible chemical combination; perhaps they will reach the conviction that in historical industry one should use *pure rectifiers* without any admixture, for fear of being punished by false results; perhaps they will even approach the basic elements.

"The final ideal aim of analytical ethnography would be to *re-establish history*; that is, having analytically disclosed the basic elements of a nation, to construct its history systematically upon these elements. Then, perhaps, history would have gained some trustworthiness, some significance, would have gained some rights to be called a science; whereas until now it has been a rather boring novel filled with pitiful and unexpected catastrophes which remain without any solution, a novel where the author constantly keeps forgetting his hero, called man. Perhaps both in chemistry and ethnography it would be more convenient to proceed conversely, that is, to begin directly with the basic elements and to follow them through all their branches."

VICTOR: "What a dream! Where can you take these basic elements directly? Who will assure you that they are really the basic ones and not some others?"

FAUST: "One must assure oneself by means of an *experiment*."

VICTOR: "Victory, gentlemen, victory! Our idealist, without realizing it, has arrived at what he was against; he arrived at the necessity of an experiment, of empiricism. That's it, friend: whatever ways you walk around and about knowledge, you'll arrive at its single starting point, that is, the tangible experiment."

FAUST: "I never denied the necessity of experimenting in general, and the importance of tangible experiments. If man can become assured of truth by means of all those organs

given to him for that purpose by Providence—even by his
hand—then fine. The whole question is: Do we use all these
organs? People have long been saying that one bodily sense
serves to check another. Sight is checked by the sense of
touch, hearing, by sight; in schools they also say that impressions acquired by external senses are controlled by the soul—
but this statement usually remains inexplicable both for the
listeners and their professor. How does this second control
take place? Does it really take place? Do we take all precautions which we consider necessary to ensure the correct operation of our external senses? In order to examine an object,
we try first of all to remove all other objects which may stand
between it and our eyes; in order to hear a sound we try not
to hear any other sounds; we carefully cork up a fragrance so
that it should not get mixed with other smells. And despite
our numerous experiences of this kind, we can never guarantee that we have not perceived one object instead of some
other.

"Something similar must take place also in our psychic perception; a pure psychic opinion is just as difficult to achieve
as a pure sensual experience. In both cases we are too much
distracted by manifold perceptions, and it is almost impossible to isolate our attention. We must take great precautions
in order to think *our own* thought, in order to remove all
foreign, acquired, and inherited thoughts which may stand
between us and an object.

"I found only one description of an interesting experiment
of this sort. 'Do you want to examine how this machine op-
erates?' one quite remarkable writer asks. 'Go somewhere into
a dark corner so as not to see or hear anything, if possible;
try to get rid of your thoughts, or, better, keep trying to get
rid of them, because you can't do it easily and at once without a special willpower. You'll see what various and unexpected groups of thoughts will begin occurring to you;
quite unexpectedly you'll see some phantoms of a magic lan-
tern appearing before you. Then you'll learn how difficult it is
to digress from ideas. But don't hurry with this experiment,
do not quit it in five or ten minutes.'[39]

"There haven't been many experiments on the *sobering* of
thought made as yet; a few of them are described, and mostly
in books where no one usually looks for them, and these experiments are most interesting! The most inconvenient thing

[39] See *Confession, or a Collection of Reasonings by Doctor
Yastrebtsev*, SPb. (1841), pp. 232 and 233.

is that each person can make this kind of experiment and its conclusions only *in himself*. There is something childish in ordinary demands to show, to make felt an experiment, as, say, the magnetic power of a man. Here, the *instrument is the experimenter himself*—his degree of knowledge depends upon his habit of using his instrument. And, in general, one can affirm one's words only by referring to such experiments which the listener too performed. That is obvious. Consequently, until a person has not himself performed a psychological experiment which would convince him of the possibility of seeing beyond feelings, by a free and complete penetration of the spirit, he should neither deny this possibility, because this would be unjust, nor demand to be given this possibility, because such a transfer lacks the essence and conditions of the experiment.

"It should be remarked, however, that we come across certain hints at such experiences quite often, hints which should have made us more careful when denying the conclusions of this psychological experimentation. Thus, according to some hints we are assured that a certain feeling exists in organisms, although we cannot touch them. We notice, for instance, that food harmful to an organism frequently produces in it an aversion unexplainable by any observations. What is the meaning of an obscure inclination of taste in pregnant women, often very odd, and always correct? What is this involuntary shudder felt by a man walking across the field of a legal battle, or when seeing an inveterate criminal being punished? It is a great thing to understand one's own instinct and to feel one's mind! Therein, perhaps, lies the whole task of mankind.

"Until this task is solved for everyone, let us go seek the instructions given to us, absentminded, frivolous children, by some good teacher, that we might not take one word for another so readily. One such instruction people call creation, inspiration, poetry, if you like. With the help of these instructions, mankind though not very well versed in the basic principles, has learned many rather important things, as, for instance, the fact that a man and a human society are *living organisms*. It is surprising that people haven't got any further by means of this knowledge, which, not without a purpose, came out of the luminous world of poetry, and shone brightly in the dark world of science. Apparently it can explain at least a few individual problems, even as the swift passage of a planet before the sun can serve to determine its diameter.

"An organism is apparently usually understood as several basic things, or elements, operating with a definite purpose. Let us accept this definition, as we accepted the definition of the word 'metal,' although neither of them is correct. We are well aware of certain circumstances accompanying the existence of an organism. For instance, we know that very often the basic substances forming a particular organism would mean death for another; often a plant feeding on certain substances dies with an addition of others, and a plant dying under certain circumstances suddenly comes to life through new food. Finally, we also know that a plant often changes, reaches a higher level of its development when inoculated with the elements of another plant, or when it is planted next to or behind another plant. We know that diseases of the seed can penetrate the plants themselves, which in their turn will produce even more contaminated seeds; that, on the other hand, skillful care can gradually destroy this disease and improve the organization of a plant. We know that if a plant doesn't find means for reviving its basic elements, it withers and slowly perishes, and that consequently an organism needs a full development of its elements, it needs fullness of life. We know also that the food of an organism can be poisoned by mineral or vegetable poisons.

"Examining higher organisms, such as, for instance, the human organism, we become convinced that as it undergoes the inevitable laws of epochs, for example, aging, it nevertheless maintains its will to squander, to distort its vital powers, or to strengthen and to elevate them. Finally, we see that all these organisms have some sort of mysterious alarm clock which reminds them of the necessity to nourish their elements. That is why a plant turns with its blossom toward the sun, and with its roots avidly looks for moisture in the soil; hunger makes an animal realize the necessity of assimilating a certain amount of nitrogen—a rather complicated and important operation of which the animal often is not completely conscious, but only vaguely feels. As a corollary to all these observations, we notice that if a plant or an animal waited for Dumas, Boussingault, or Liebig to show him how nitrogen and carbon is obtained, or why they need one or another—both the plant and the animal would have died of starvation without having reached the pure and tangible experience. This, gentlemen, is all the novelty which I wanted to share with you. As you see, this novelty is not new at all, nor is it strange. You can find it in any textbook of chemistry, natural history, or physiology, because in the world, as in a good weaving factory, one wheel catches another—it's of Dr. Ure's own choosing to stand in front of a machine and not to see the meaning of this linking!

"I recommend to you, gentlemen, first to provide yourselves good, clean, achromatic glasses, which do not mar objects by earthy, cheerful, fantastic colors, and, second, to read two books: one of them is called *Nature*—it is well printed and its language is quite comprehensible; the other one is *Man*—a manuscript written in a little-known language and the more difficult because there is neither a dictionary nor a grammar compiled for it yet. These books are related to each other, and one explains the other. However, if you are unable to read the second book, do without the first one too, although the first one will help you to read the other one. For your entertainment you may read other books, supposedly written about the first two; but take care: don't read the lines, but rather between the lines; you'll find there much of interest if you use the glasses, upon which I insist. You'll find there that a man is really an organism, composed of elements that require space and time for their growth. If two people unite in friendship or love, a new organism is formed in which the elements of individual organisms are modified as acids are modified when combined with alkali. If the organism of matrimony is joined by a third organism, a new interaction between the constituting elements take place, and so forth, up to a whole society, which in turn is a new organism composed of other organisms. You'll find that each organism, whatever it be, has elements common to all organisms in varying degrees, and individual elements, originating from the first and belonging to one organism or another and forming a characteristic distinction of each.

"My work in chemistry led me to four basic elements, common to all human organisms; perhaps there are more or fewer; that depends on the art of a chemist. But I'm satisfied with them in the meantime, as atomic chemistry is satisfied with the sixty so-called simple elements. I think that these four elements have simple names: the need for truth, love, awe, and strength or power. These elements are common to all human beings. Their various combinations, predominance of one over another, stagnation of one or another, create all the various related elements. There must be a definite proportion between these elements, but it can be known only to a few alchemists. For practical purposes, however, an approximate calculation will suffice. Don't be surprised that these elements sometimes produce actions obviously contrary to their nature—it's an optical illusion! A well-known chemist, by the name of Bossuet, who did much work on organic decomposition, said: 'If we look carefully at what takes place within us, we will find that all our passions depend on love, which embraces and excites them all. The very hatred we feel toward one thing stems from our love for another; so, for instance, I feel an aversion to one thing only because it prevents me from possessing the thing which I love.'[40]

"Sometimes one element is developed at the expense of another, and, having escaped the fixed proportion, is not modified by other ones. Thus, for instance, it is very pleasant to inhale refreshing oxygen alone, but it kills in the same manner as asphyxiating nitrogen; in the air, however, they are united in such a proportion that the harmful property of each is modified by the other. In a human organism, for instance, the feeling of power can turn into complete carelessness and lightheartedness, or into seeking for a satisfaction in material desires. The need for complete truth may lead to a superficial encyclopedism or to an all-denying skepticism; the feeling of friendship may lead to extravagance, and so on. In all such cases the organism suffers, like a plant without water, or one watered excessively.

"Man is given the privilege of creating his own particular world, where he may combine the basic elements in whatever proportion he wishes, even in their real, natural equilibrium; this world is called art, poetry; it is an important world because in it man may find symbols of what takes place, or should take place, within and around him. But the architects of this world frequently bring into it also the disproportion between elements from which they suffer themselves, without noticing it. Other, more fortunate ones build this world just as unconsciously as the first ones, and unexpectedly their world reflects the harmony of which the soul of the architects themselves is full. In ancient times this remarkable human act was expressed by the name Amphion.

"Whatever the situation, the lack of equilibrium and harmony between the elements makes the organism suffer; and this law is so imbued with pedantry that nothing can save it from this suffering: neither the development of will nor creative talent nor supernatural knowledge, be it a country en-

[40] Bossuet, *Connaissance de Dieu et de soi-même*, Chap. I.

dowed with all the means for power, be it called Beethoven or Bach—the organism suffers, because it hasn't *fulfilled the fullness* of life. A luxurious cactus, surprised by frost, sometimes produces a fragrant blossom—but then it immediately perishes.

"Another remarkable phenomenon takes place here: an organism, isolated in its own elements, knows only them and cannot ever understand the possibility of another combination of elements. Frequently, the elements of one national organism are so remote from the elements of another that they cannot understand the life of the other, because each of them sees conditions of life only in the frame of his own elements. Thus, Western writers write a history of mankind, but they understand by this word only what surrounds them, sometimes forgetting the ninth part of the earth, and hundreds of millions of people; when they come to the world of Slavs, they are ready to prove that it doesn't exist, because it doesn't fit the form which is made of Western elements. If fish knew how to write, they would probably prove, and very clearly, that birds cannot possibly exist because they can't swim in water. The reverse could happen as well.

"A great natural scientist lived in this world, Peter the Great. He was given a marvelous organism, worthy of his spirit. The Great One gained a profound insight into the structure of this wonderful world. In it he found huge resources, gigantic powers, strong, tempered cogwheels, firm supports, fast-moving gears—but this huge system of power lacked a pendulum. This made the powerful elements of this world perform contrary to their nature. The feeling of power swung to utter carelessness, which had devoured Asiatic tribes; the versatility of spirit, expressed in wonderful receptivity to and affinity with truth, failed to find nourishment, and withered from lack of activity; a few more centuries of these moments in the life of the people, and the powerful world would exhaust itself by its own power.

"Knowing both nature and man, Peter the Great did not despair. In his people he saw the action of other elements almost lost among other nations: the feeling of love and unity, strengthened by centuries-long struggle with hostile powers; the feeling of awe and faith which had sanctified centuries-old sufferings; it remained only to curb excess and to rouse that which had fallen asleep. And the wise man inoculated his people with those secondary Western elements it lacked: he altered the feeling of dissipated courage by building; he strengthened national egoism, isolated in the sphere of its beliefs, by the sight of Western life; he nourished receptivity with science. The inoculation was potent; time passed, foreign elements were appropriated, modifying the original ones—and a new, hot blood began to stream in the broad veins of the giant; all his feelings turned into activity; huge muscles were strained; he remembered all the vague dreams of his childhood, all the suggestions of the highest power which he hadn't understood before. He discarded some, gave body to others, breathed the breath of life freely into them, turned his powerful head toward the West and sank into profound thought.

"The West, immersed in the world of its own elements carefully cultivated it, forgetful of the existence of other worlds. Its work was marvelous, and it created wonderful things. The West produced everything that his elements were capable of producing, but nothing more; in its restless, accelerated activity it developed one element, having stifled the others. Equilibrium was lost and the inner disease of the West found its reflection in discords of crowds and in the dark, pointless dissatisfaction of its higher intellects. The feeling of self-preservation reached the point of a punctilious egoism, and hostile suspicion of one's neighbors; the need for truth became distorted in the coarse demands of senses of touch and insignificant details. Preoccupied with material conditions of material life, the West invented laws without trying to find their roots in itself. The elements of the body, not the elements of soul, were transferred into the world of science and art; the feeling of love, of unity, even the feeling of power was lost, because hope for the future vanished. In its intoxication with materialism the West dances on the graveyards of its great thinkers' ideas, and tramples into the mud those who want to denounce its madness in powerful and sacred words.

"In order to reach the full, harmonious development of basic, common human elements, the West, in spite of all its greatness, lacks another Peter, who would inoculate it with fresh powerful juices of the Slavic East!

"Meanwhile, what was not done by human hand is being done by the course of time. Not in vain does man, obviously carried away by momentary gain, perfect the means of communications. Not in vain do people draw closer to one another, like animals, feeling the approach of danger. The West feels the approach of the Slavic spirit, and fears it as our

predecessors feared the West. A self-contained element as-
similates foreign elements unwillingly, although they would
mean the support of its existence; on the other hand, it feels
drawn toward them, despite itself, unconsciously, like a plant
toward the sun.

"Do not fear, brothers! There are no destructive elements
in the Slavic East. Study it and you will see. With us you'll
find partly your own forces, preserved and multiplied; you'll
find also our own forces, unknown to you, which will not
suffer by being shared. With us you'll find a new sight unfamiliar to you until now: you'll find historical life born not
in an internal war between the power and people, but developed freely, naturally, fostered by the feeling of love and
unity. You'll find laws invented not amidst turbulent passions
and not for the satisfaction of a momentary need, not introduced by foreigners, but slowly, over many centuries, nourished in the bowels of our native land.

"You'll find belief in the possibility of happiness not only
for the majority but happiness for *all* and *everyone*. Even in
our younger brothers you'll find the feeling of social unity,
for which you search in vain, raising the dust of ages and
inquiring symbols of the future. You'll understand why your
papism inclines toward Protestantism and protestantism toward papism, that is, each toward its own denial; and you'll
understand why your best minds, gaining insight into the
treasury of the human soul, unexpectedly carry away from it
those beliefs which for a long time have been casting light
over the history of Slavs and which were unknown to them.[41]

"You'll be amazed at the existence of a nation which began
its literary life with the end product of other nations, with
satire, that is, a strict judgment of themselves, refusing any
partiality toward national egoism. You'll be amazed to learn
that there is a nation whose poets have guessed history before
history by means of their poetic magic, and have found in
their souls the colors the West draws from slow, lengthy cul-
tivation of centuries of history.[42] You'll be amazed to learn

[41] Baader, Koening, Balanche, Schelling.

[42] The element of *universality*, or better, of the *all-embracing*,
created a remarkably characteristic line in our scholarly development: everywhere else scholarly investigations preceded the poetical view of history; with us, on the other hand, poetic *insight*
anticipated the real examination; Karamzin's *History* led us to the
idea of studying historical monuments, which still goes on; Pushkin
(in *Boris Godunov*) guessed the character of our Russian chronicle

that there exists a nation which understands musical harmony naturally, without a materialistic approach; you'll be amazed to learn that not all of the ways of melody have been exhausted, and that an artist, created by a Slavic spirit, one of the members of a triumvirate[43] which preserves the sanctity of art, corrupted, belittled, and abused in the West, found a new and original way. Finally, you'll become convinced of the existence of a nation with a natural tendency to the all-embracing versatility of the spirit, which you try to incite by artifiical means. You'll become convinced of the existence of a nation forced by ice and snow, which frighten you so much, to withdraw inside unconsciously, and to conquer nature from outside.

"You'll bend your knee before a man unkown to you, a man who was a poet, a chemist, a linguist, and a metallurgist, a man who brought lightning down to earth before Franklin, who wrote history, observed the course of the stars, created mosaics with glass of his own manufacturing, and who made each branch of science progress. You'll bend your knee before Lomonosov, this native representative of the versatile Slavic thought, when you find out that, along with Leibnitz, with Goethe, with Carus, in the depth of his spirit, he discovered the mysterious method which studies all aspects of nature as a whole, not its torn-off members, harmoniously absorbing all manifold knowledge into himself. Then you will believe your vague hope for the *fullness of life*; you'll believe the approach of the epoch when there will be *one science* and *one teacher*; and full of enthusiasm you'll utter words you hadn't noticed in an old book: 'A man is a harmonious prayer of the earth!' "

Faust became silent.

---

writer, although our chronicles have not passed through ages of historical criticism, and the chronicle writers themselves are still a sort of myth, historically. Khomiakov (in *The False Dimitrij*) deeply penetrated into an even more difficult character: the character of a Russian woman in ancient times—that of a mother. Lazhechnikov (in *The Moslem*) re-created a character more difficult than the last mentioned: that of a young Russian girl of old times; meanwhile, the significance of a woman in Russian society before Peter the Great remains a riddle in a *scholarly sense*. Now, if you follow up these characters in the historical monuments which are now being published, you will be surprised at the correctness of the phantoms called forth by the magical activity of our poets. One cannot help wondering how people given to ultra-Slavism have not noticed this phenomenon until now.

[43] Mendelssohn-Bartholdy, Berlioz, Glinka.

"That is all fine," said Victor, "but what do we do meanwhile?"

"Wait for the guests, and welcome them with all hospitality."

VYACHESLAV: "And then, put on a teacher's cap and ask your guests to take seats."

FAUST: "No, gentlemen, you're still in a state of agitation which is the result of inoculation; you must wait for the moment when all the elements forming you will achieve harmony, when, like Lomonosov, you'll be drawing from all cups without distinction, whether your own or another's. This moment is not too far away from us. Meanwhile, however, it wouldn't be a bad idea to get ready to welcome the honored guests—our old teachers. The room has to be tidied up and supplied with everything needed for life, so that nothing will be lacking; we must dress ourselves and take care of our younger brothers; for example, we could place science in their hands, at least, to keep them busy. It wouldn't be a bad idea to follow our predecessors and occasionally use the whip of satire to scare away the mice creeping into the house without the permission of its owner. In general, we should neither shun what is ours nor fear what is foreign, but, most important of all, we should clean our own glasses carefully and remember that the frame is not all and that even the best glass is useless when covered by mold."

VYACHESLAV: "All that I can say is, *C'est qu'il y a quelque chose à faire.*"

VICTOR: "I'll wait for a steam balloon, to take a look then at what has happened to the West."

ROSTISLAV: "The idea of the authors of that manuscript remains in my mind: 'The nineteenth century belongs to Russia!'"

AFTERWORD
by Neil Cornwell

Olga Koshansky-Olienikov and Ralph Matlaw based their 1965 translation of *Russian Nights,* reprinted here, on the 1913 Moscow edition (which itself, as a bibliographical rarity, was to be reprinted a little later, in 1967, by Wilhelm Fink in Munich). The 1913 edition, edited by S. A. Tsvetkov, was only the second publication ever of *Russian Nights,* and it incorporated the corrections and annotations Odoevsky had intended for the unrealized second edition of his *Collected Works* in 1862. This accounts for the unusual order of presentation: Odoevsky's later emendations preceding his original foreword to the first printing of 1844. We had to wait until 1975 for the fine "Literary Monuments" Leningrad academic edition, with its own additional scholarly apparatus, edited by B. F. Egorov (with material supplied by E. A. Maimin and M. I. Medovoi). The most recent edition to date is the first volume of the 1981 Moscow two-volume "works" (*Sochineniia*), edited by V. I. Sakharov.

There have been, therefore, a total of only four Russian editions of *Russian Nights* (five, if we count the German reprint). A German translation of the work appeared in 1970 and an Italian version in 1983. The original publication by Dutton in 1965 of this English translation can now be seen, therefore, as a bold stroke: all the more so as nothing had been written on Odoevsky in English up to that point, except for the briefest accounts in histories of Russian literature. Simon Karlinsky's pioneering article appeared only in 1966. Even now, when a number of substantial recent publications have appeared both in English and in Russian, it is still possible to argue that Odoevsky does not receive the critical attention he deserves.

Indeed, the claims made for Odoevsky by Matlaw in his still very serviceable (and, in its day, highly informative) introduction now seem, if anything, to err on the side of modesty. Even if posterity "rightfully has not sanctioned" the position Odoevsky occupied for a while in the 1830s when "he was among Russia's most popular writers, ranked in stature not very far below the two literary giants, Pushkin and Gogol" (p. 7), he is probably closer now to regaining such status than any time since he dropped from public view in the 1840s.

Certainly, few would now wish to argue, as even Matlaw suggests (p. 9), that his stories for children, still enormously popular as a few of them are, "may be the most lasting of his work." The revival of interest in Odoevsky that was fueled by the post-Stalin reconsideration of Russian romanticism, which arguably began with the publication of a volume of Odoevsky's tales and stories in 1959 (the first such edition for thirty years), has led to a major scholarly reappraisal. For that matter, romantic (and latterly Gothic) literature has undergone its own Western revival, too. However, a 1988 Moscow paperback edition of Odoevsky's stories (which includes several from *Russian Nights*) enjoyed a print run of no less than 2,700,000 copies. It would be little, if any, exaggeration to describe Odoevsky as a cult author in today's Russia. Marietta Tur'ian's biographical study of Odoevsky, published in 1991, is the first book-length work on him in Russian since 1913.

Why, in any case, has *Russian Nights* remained so little known? Partly because, as a quintessential work of high Russian romanticism, it was already perceived as out of date upon its very appearance. Therefore, it got less critical attention than it would have received had it been published ten years earlier (as the constantly overworked Odoevsky—ever a man of many parts and careers—would have wished). The book never quite recovered from this, despite minor revivals of interest in Odoevsky at the turn of the century and again in the 1950s. Published in full and under the title of *Russian Nights* only in 1844, this book represents the culmination of Russian romanticism and proved to be, to all serious intents and purposes, the valedictory work of Odoevsky's literary career: a fond retrospective, ranging over Russian—and indeed European—romanticism, which appeared a trifle late, at the dawn of the new psychological realism (as displayed by Lermontov's *A Hero of Our Time* [1841] and Dostoevsky's *Poor Folk* [1846]). Odoevsky's disappearance from the literary scene (the "nine years," from 1846–55, "swallowed up" by his philanthropic activities—see the author's foreword, p. 22) hastened his neglect. Although mildly praised by Belinsky, Odoevsky's fiction was of little interest to the ultra-utilitarian brand of literary criticism that came to dominate in Russia for the rest of the nineteenth century, and again under Stalinism.

The other difficulty involving *Russian Nights* throughout nineteenth- and twentieth-century Russian criticism has been its generic peculiarity, which has served to cut it adrift to a large extent from any acknowledged tradition of the emerging Russian novel, which nevertheless remains flexible enough to accomodate such formal eccentricities as Pushkin's "novel in verse" (*Eugene Onegin*), Gogol's incomplete episodic "poem" (*Dead Souls*), and the "novels" of Lermontov and Dostoevsky already alluded to (a cycle of stories and an epistolary saga, respectively). For its first genuine novels of any significance, in anything like a strict formal sense, Russian literature had to wait for the works of Goncharov and Turgenev.

As for Odoevsky's *Russian Nights*, this was an even greater formal curiosity: not only was it outmodedly and unashamedly romantic, but it mixed fiction with nonfiction in a manner only Tolstoy, among the Russian literary giants (and he in his own no-nonsense way), was ever remotely to follow. The stories comprising the fictional element were written over a period of nearly fifteen years, most of them having been published separately, and often successfully enough, along the way (which of course contributed to the déjà-vu factor in 1844). The better of them stand comparison, as individual short stories, with Odoevsky's best, and indeed with most of the romantic and society tales produced in the 1830s in Russia. Only obvious masterpieces, such as Pushkin's "The Queen of Spades" and Gogol's "The Overcoat," can claim clear superiority; "Sebastian Bach," for instance, is a minor masterpiece in its own right (and Tur'ian is now intriguingly able to link this work with Odoevsky's own "hidden" biography). Taken together, all the links and themes connecting the stories with their surrounding "frame" (the inadequacy of language; problems of musical and poetic expression; the quest for truth and communication; social responsibility; madness, the supernatural, and anti-Utopia) only struck the author with their full significance, it would seem, in hindsight. The original design, at least, for a cycle to be called "The House of Madmen," was changed in midstream; the whole, one continues to suspect, somewhat exceeds the sum of the parts.

Russian Nights is perhaps best described as a "philosophical frame tale"; it has sometimes been termed a philosophical novel. The short stories, of an assorted romantic nature and presented by means of a complex narrative structure, are embedded in a loosely dramatized philosophical discussion of many issues, but largely centering on romantic aesthetics and the prospects for Russia as a force for the reinvigoration of the "dying West." Odoevsky himself suggested the work represents a "higher synthesis" between the genres of drama and novel. It can equally be seen as a synthesis of the novella tradition, stemming from the Eastern tale (*The Thousand and One Nights*, for example), and the Western line descending from the Greek philosophical dialogue. As such, it is a work structurally unique in Russian literature and perhaps even in European literature. Generic comparisons have been made with the Platonic dialogues, *The Decameron*, Hoffman's *The Serapion Brothers*, and various other works from the German romantic period, and Joseph de Maistre's *Les soirées de Saint-Pétersbourg*, among other possible precursors. None of these is valid in isolation, although all may have been contributory influences. Undoubtedly, it is an illustration par excellence of the romantic principle, inspired by Schelling, Novalis, and others, of the mixing of genres. It derives from the poetics of romanticism, and the fullest range of the antecedents of romanticism, including the Gothic, alchemical, and esoteric traditions. *Russian Nights* has indeed been termed aptly, in the 1981 Soviet *History of Russian Literature,* "an encyclopedia of romanticism."

What sets it apart from other models is the almost equal treatment accorded the philosophical and the fictional elements. Whereas in most instances of such cycles or frame tales the "frame" is very perfunctory, in *Russian Nights* it occupies almost equal space with the fiction, includes the loquations of the apparently authorial protagonist named Faust (an intellectual quester, but no demonic bargainer), and constitutes the forum, in something of the fashion of a Greek chorus, for many of the main ideas of the work, especially in its weighty epilogue, which provides an overview of the main strands of Russian thought of the 1820s and 1830s: in sum, a kind of proto-Westernizer/Slavophile debate.

Traces from Odoevsky's stories and ideas are to be found from the 1830s onward in Russian literature, deriving both from *Russian Nights* and from elsewhere. There was a mutual influence between Odoevsky and his immediate artistic contemporaries, Pushkin and Gogol. Odoevsky proposed the poet as "the first judge of humanity" (hence perhaps the later commonplace of regarding writers as Russia's, or the Soviet Union's, "second government"). A number of Dostoevsky's ponderings and innovations can be traced to Odoevsky, not least the science fiction element in "The Dream of a Ridiculous Man" (which carried on in Western literature into the writings of William Hope Hodgson, David Lindsey, and Olaf Stapledon). Echoes of Odoevsky's treatment of the figure of the artist can be found in the early prose of Pasternak. Such fantasists as Bulgakov and Siniavsky must have known Odoevsky. Parallels may also be found in a number of Western writers (surprisingly, perhaps, George Eliot, to name but one). There is even one case of clear plagiarism. The Irish-American writer Fitz-James O'Brien, not content with imitating Odoevsky's *The Sylph,* via a French translation, in his *The Diamond Lens* (1858), translated almost word for word "The Improvvisatore" (from *Russian Nights,* see pp. 132–45), and published it in *Harper's New Monthly Magazine* (September 1857) under the title "Seeing the World."

Russian Nights, then, is a unique work of Russian literature and a key sourcebook for both Russian romanticism and Russian social and aesthetic thought of its epoch written, for the most part, in a high post-Pushkinian prose style, fully recognizable as modern literary

Russian. It is also a work of deep European erudition in the fullest sense, its references ranging from the Pythagoreans to the American slave trade. Like Coleridge, De Quincey, and other prominent European romantics, Odoevsky spotted the significance of Piranesi as an archetypal figure. His interest in Bruno and Boehme was to be taken up later by the Symbolists and James Joyce, among others. Most of his concerns still confront the modern world, many of them with a vengeance: the conflict between the environment and utilitarianism; the resurgent monetarism of Adam Smith; the morality of free-market economics. There is even a passage in the anti-Benthamite story "A City Without Name" that seems to anticipate Pol Pot: "And everyone whose hands were not used to the coarse work on land was driven out of the city" (p. 113). Now again, for the first time since 1917, Russians are looking back to nineteenth- and early twentieth-century discussions and blueprints for solutions to those old "accursed questions": the future, the role, and the direction of Russia.

It is also fitting that *Russian Nights*—the Russian book which is, perhaps above all Russian books, a book based on other (one is almost tempted to say on *all* previous) books—should appear again at a time when not only the West "is perishing." Books and culture seem under threat as never before—above all, from a media avalanche of instant trivia. A recent cultural debate in England has centered on the relative merits of Keats and Bob Dylan. Would that it were containable at that exalted level! Unfortunately, it seems more a matter of the Louvre versus Disneyland; Covent Garden against karaoke. Odoevsky, for all his "encyclopedic dilettantism" and occasionally excessive pedantry, is needed now more than ever.

Russian Nights may also appeal more to the "postmodern" age than to earlier epochs. Odoevsky's mysticism and his Gothicism may be, if anything, better displayed in certain of his other works (see *The Salamander and Other Gothic Tales*). However, *Russian Nights,* Odoevsky's single completed magnum opus, with its mixture of genres and styles, mingles fiction with nonfiction, romanticism with social reality, philosophical dialogue with historical reportage. It will perhaps be in the twenty-first century that Odoevsky's reputation will finally be made.

Further Reading: Works by Odoevsky in English

Odoevsky, Vladimir. *The Salamander and Other Gothic Tales*. Translated by Neil Cornwell. London: Bristol Classical Press; Evanston: Northwestern University Press, 1992.
The Ardis Anthology of Russian Romanticism. Edited by Christine Rydel. Ann Arbor: Ardis, 1984.
Pre-Revolutionary Russian Science Fiction: An Anthology. Edited and translated by Leland Fetzer. Ann Arbor: Ardis, 1982.
Russian 19th Century Gothic Tales. Edited by Valentin Korovin. Moscow: Raduga, 1984.
Russian Romantic Prose: An Anthology. Edited by Carl R. Proffer. Ann Arbor: Translation Press, 1979.
Russian Tales of the Fantastic. Translated by Marilyn Minto. London: Bristol Classical Press, 1994.

On Odoevsky

Brown, William Edward. *A History of Russian Literature of the Romantic Period*. Ann Arbor: Ardis, 1986.
Campbell, J. S. *V. F. Odoyevsky and the Formation of Russian Musical Taste in the Nineteenth Century*. New York: Garland, 1989.
Cornwell, Neil. "V. F. Odoyevsky's *Russian Nights*: Genre, Reception and Romantic Poetics," *Essays in Poetics* 8, no. 2 (1983): 19–55. Revised and reprinted in Cornwell, *Vladimir Odoevsky and Romantic Poetics*. Oxford and Providence, R.I.: Berghahn Books, 1997.
———. *V. F. Odoyevsky: His Life, Times and Mileu*. Foreword by Sir Isaiah Berlin. London: Athlone Press; Athens: Ohio University Press, 1986.
Karlinsky, Simon. "A Hollow Shape: The Philosophical Tales of Prince Vladimir Odoevsky," *Studies in Romanticism* 5, no. 3 (1966): 169–82.
Maimin, E. A. "Vladimir Odoevskii i ego 'Russkie nochi,'" *Russkie nochi*. Leningrad: Nauka, 1975. 247–76.
Mann, Iu. V. *Russkaia filosofskaia estetika (1820–30ye gody)*. Moscow, 1969.
Mersereau, John, Jr. *Russian Romantic Fiction*. Ann Arbor: Ardis, 1983.
Reid, Robert, ed. *Problems of Russian Romanticism*. Aldershot: Gower, 1986.
Tur'ian, M. A. *"Strannaia moia sud'ba. . .": O zhizni Vladimira Fedorovicha Odoevskogo*. Moscow: Kniga, 1991.

Errata

p. 21, n. 1: "The foreword was written in the early 1860s by the author for a second edition of his collected works, then in preparation, but never completed."
p. 42, n. 1: "Pordage and *le philosophe inconnu*" for "Pordetsch and *Philosophie inconnu*"
p. 45, n. 2: "*du philosophe inconnu*" for "*du Philosophie inconnu*"
p. 51, n. 3: "Lord Brougham" for "Lord Broom"
p. 135: "Graham" for "Grem"
p. 156: "Lavater" for "Lafater" .
p. 204: "Voltaire" for "Volaire"
p. 214: "VYACHESLAV" for "VICTOR"
p. 239: "Delille" for "De Lille"
p. 253, n. 41: "Koenig" for "Koening"